KAREN TEMPLETON

spent her twentysomething years in New York City, which provided some of the fodder for Ginger's experiences in *Loose Screws*. Before that, she grew up in Baltimore, then attended North Carolina School of the Arts as a theater major. The RITA® Award-nominated author of nearly twenty novels, she now lives with her husband, a pair of eccentric cats and four of their five sons in Albuquerque, where she spends an inordinate amount of time picking up stray socks and mourning the loss of long, aimless walks in the rain. Visit her Web site at www.karentempleton.com.

Loose
Screws

Karen Templeton

**RED
DRESS
INK**™

LOOSE SCREWS

A Red Dress Ink novel

ISBN 0-373-81081-4

www.RedDressInk.com

Printed in U.S.A.

This book is dedicated to all the crazy, courageous,
unsinkable, wonderful people who live in a city
that still feels like home even after many years away

and to a certain lovely, pushy editor
who insisted I had this book in me.

Thanks, Gail.

One

First off, let me just state for the record that I didn't fall for Greg Munson because he was successful, or handsome—even though I sure didn't mind the dirty how-did-*you*-get-*him?* glances whenever we went out—or even to piss my mother off. I swear, his being the son of a Republican congressman was pure serendipity.

No. I fell in love with the guy because he gave me every indication that he was *normal*. And, since the odds of finding such a creature in this town are roughly a quadrillion to one, when he proposed, I pounced. I may not be proud of that, but hey. We're talking survival of the species here.

And I have no doubt we might have had a very nice life together if he'd bothered to show up for the wedding.

Now, granted, it's only been four hours since I smushed twenty-five yards of tulle into a taxi and hauled my sorry self back to my apartment from the hotel, so it's not as if I've had a lot of time to figure any of this out. Not that I expect to.

For one thing, I'm not some infantile twit blinded by infatuation, a condition to which I've never been prone in any case. I'm thirty-one, have lived my entire life in Manhattan and endured a childhood that, trust me, taught me early on how to spot a jerk. Greg and I didn't even date until a good two months after I first schlepped carpet and wallpaper samples up to his new Scarsdale house, didn't sleep together for another couple months after that. I was careful. I didn't cling. Never brought up marriage. Never demanded any more of his time than he was willing to give. If anything, *he* was one who seemed hot to take things to The Final Plateau.

So, nope. No clues there. Not even a crumb.

We held up the ceremony as long as we could. But I knew it was all over when, like a pair of priests being called to give last rites, my mother and grandmother appeared in the hallway outside the hotel ballroom to hold vigil with me and my two bridesmaids: my cousin Shelby (Jewish, terminally married, bubbly) and best friend Terrie (black, twice divorced, cynical). Yet, ever optimistic, I persisted in covering Greg's butt. Not to mention my own.

"Traffic on the parkway must be horrendous this time of day," I said brightly, ten minutes past the point where the pair of ice swans, not to mention some of the more elderly guests, were beginning to melt in the late May heat that had managed to override the hotel's cooling system. When Terrie pointed out to me that Greg's cell phone was like a fifth—or in his case, sixth—appendage, I averred, with only the barest hint of hysteria in my voice, that his battery must have gone dead, of course, that had to be it, because, after all, he'd helped me pick out the lousy *flow-*

ers, for God's sake, not to mention the cake and the invitations, so why wouldn't he show up for his own *goddamn wedding?*

"Maybe he'sa dead?"

We all looked at my grandmother, calmly plucking at her underpants through the skirt of her new pink dress, who, being basically deaf as a post, had delivered this line loud enough to reach the Bronx.

I shot a don't-say-it look at my mother, resplendent in some schmata straight from *The Lion King.* Although, frankly, as the guests began to filter out in embarrassed silence, as the judge—flanked by Phyllis and Bob Munson, Greg's parents—mumbled his condolences, as I bleakly surveyed the lavishly decorated, now-empty ballroom, I have to admit *Kill the bastard* had shot to the top of my To Do list.

There's no need for your mother to pay for the wedding, Greg had said. *Between us, we can foot the expenses, right?*

Considering what we were doing when he laid that proposal on the table—which, come to think of it, pretty much describes our activity at the time—he could have probably suggested just about anything and I would have agreed. But even once again clothed and in my right mind, I still thought, well…sure. We both had solid careers—Greg had made partner in his midtown law firm before thirty, and my growing client base meant I hadn't had to furtively paw through a markdown rack in years. Although, since Greg thought we should go halfsies, it meant dipping into my savings. Okay, annihilating them. We weren't talking city hall and a reception at Schrafft's. But, hey, Greg Munson was the pot of gold I'd inadvertently tripped over at the end of the rainbow. It was worth it, right?

Do you have *any* idea how much a Vera Wang wedding dress costs?

Do you have any idea, Shelby had said, appalled, when I'd weakly insisted, my eyes locked on my enchanted reflection in the dressing room mirror, I'd be just as happy with the ivory silk shantung Ellen Tracy suit I'd tried on three days ago in Bergdorf's, *how much you'd regret blowing this once-in-a-lifetime opportunity to look like a princess?*

Do you have any idea, my mother had said, equally appalled, when I dragged her and Nonna into the Madison Avenue showroom to model the gown (Shelby's princess comment having effectively annihilated my sticker shock), *how many homeless people you could feed for what you just threw away on a dress you're only going to wear once?*

Damn, girl, Terrie had said, hands parked on rounded hips that have seen action in two marriages and any number of skirmishes, *you actually look like you've got tits in that dress.*

Could somebody hand me a tissue?

My mother tried to convince me to ride back uptown with her and my grandmother, spend the night with them in my mother's Columbia University-owned apartment. Since I'd basically rather put out my own eye, I declined. Which may seem extremely disrespectful to those of you who have someone other than Nedra Cohen Petrocelli as your mother.

Okay, I suppose I'm being just the teensiest bit unfair. Nedra means well, she really does. It's just that she tends to suck the life force out of anyone unfortunate enough to find himself or herself within a city block of her.

Sometimes, when I look at a photo of my mother when she was younger and skinnier, I swear to God it's like looking into a mirror. The same black springy hair, dark eyes, high cheekbones, long limbs, a wide mouth that often gets us into trouble. Personality-wise, though…well, let's just say genetics took a dive into the deep end of the pool there. While Nedra literally goes limp if she's deprived of human company for longer than two hours, I need solitude in order to recharge. Her reaction to tragedy or stress is to invite a dozen chums over for dinner. Mine is to clutch my mortification—and in this case, a bottle of very expensive champagne—to my flat little chest (genetics played a nasty little trick on me there, too) and retreat to my lair.

A lair that, though miniscule and un-air-conditioned, I am now exceedingly glad I did not give up, even though I'd moved most of my clothes and stuff to the Scarsdale house last week (note to self: new clothes?). So. Here I sit, in a frothy heap in the center of the pseudo-Turkish rug I bought three years ago at one of those Fifth Avenue emporiums that's been going out of business since 1973, swigging the bubbly like it's diet Coke and entertaining myself by counting how many times my answering machine has beeped. Since I'm sure at least half the calls are from my (disgustingly stereotypical) mother, I have no interest in hearing who they're from. Not even if one of them's from Greg.

Especially if one of them's from Greg.

I should really get out of the dress. It itches like hell, for one thing. But I can't. Not yet. I know, it's stupid. And it's not as if I think that Greg's suddenly going to show up, all smiles and profuse apologies, and we'll just zip right back to the hotel and get married as if none of this ever happened. Which we couldn't do anyway because the guests are long gone and the caterers already took away all the food and the judge had another wedding later this afternoon and I'll never get my hair back the way Alphonse had it—

You know what really fries my clams? (I stare at the bottle as I think about this, finding a certain comfort in the predictability of the oscillating table fan's intermittent, albeit ineffectual breeze.) Before I met Greg, I was perfectly happy. Didn't feel like anything was missing from my life, you know? Oh, sure, I suppose I assumed I'd get married one day, since most people do, especially if they want kids. Which I do. I mean, hell, even my mother had gotten married—to my father, conveniently enough—and this is a woman who redefines the term "free radical." But I hadn't been stumbling around, desperately searching for my other "half" and crying in my latte because I'd reached the ripe old age of thirty without finding him. Dating has never been goal-oriented for me. No, I swear. I went out on the odd occasion, had sex on even odder ones, but you know, there's something to be said for being able to rent any damn video you want, watching it when you want, wearing whatever you want, eating whatever you want without getting grief from whoever else is in the room with you. And if I've never exactly been the type to make men salivate…so what? I have a flourishing career, this fabulous East Side studio I've been illegally subletting for five years, and a hairdresser who hadn't gasped in horror when I'd removed my hat that first time.

So things were fine. Before Greg, I mean. Then he goes and does this, leaving me with that fresh roadkill feeling.

But why should I feel this way? Am I any less whole than I was before four o'clock this afternoon? Is my sense of self-worth any less diminished because some idiot has seen fit to screw up my life for the foreseeable future? Is my hair kinkier, my nose bigger, my chest smaller?

I look down to check; reassured, I take another swig of champagne, right from the bottle. No muss, no fuss, no bubbles in the nose.

Hmm. I seem to have lost all feeling below my knees.

Oh, hell…there must be a hole in the screen, 'cause there's a pissed off mosquito in here somewhere…no, wait.

That's my intercom buzzer. Which means either I ordered Chinese and don't remember, which is very possible, or somebody—most likely my mother, which is a depressing thought—has come to bear witness to my degradation.

I hoist myself upright, willing sensation back into my feet, after which the dress and I float over to the intercom. After only three or four tries, I manage to poke the little button and grunt, "Go 'way."

But wait. The buzzer is still buzzing. I finish off the champagne—I feel the need to interject at this point that I am *not* a drinker, that in fact this is the first serious alcohol to pass my lips since my cousin Shelby's wedding in 1996, which is probably why I am seeing multiples of everything right now—on the off chance that it will clear my head. I was wrong. I also realize that the pissed-off mosquito is not trapped inside my intercom but is, in point of fact, hovering outside the front door to my apartment.

I burp delicately, gather up as much of the dress as I can catch, and embark on a zigzag course toward where I last saw the door. I possess just enough…something to peer through the keyhole. "Whoozit?"

"Ginger Petrocelli?"

I steal a moment to wonder, as I do from time to time, what on earth possessed my parents to name me Ginger, before clunking my forehead against the door and peering through the peephole, which affords me a distorted glimpse of a vaguely familiar clefted chin, hooded blue eyes and a very male hand with neatly trimmed nails clutching an official-looking ID. The guy says his own name, I think, but a fire truck chooses that moment to blast its horn eight stories below my open window, so I don't hear it. I also almost wet my pants, which, considering the amount of champagne I have consumed, could have been disastrous.

So, I try to read the ID. Only there is no way I can focus

enough to see the name, let alone the face beyond it. But I sure as hell catch the N.Y.P.D. part.

My stomach lurches. Until, always one to see the bright side to things, I console myself with the thought that at least it's not my mother.

Ohmigod. My mother.

Images of a taxi door slamming shut on my mother's *Lion King* tent and dragging her for ten blocks through midtown traffic spur me to fumble with the first of the three locks I'd bothered with when I came in—

*Waaaait*aminnit.

"How do I know…" I brace one hand against the wall. When the dizziness passes, I say, "How do I know you're really the police?"

Through the three-inch-thick door, I hear what sounds like a very patient sigh. "Dammit, Ginger—did you bother *looking* through the peephole? It's Nick Wojowodski. Open up."

With a gasp, I undo the rest of the locks and swing open the door. A hand darts out to catch me as I stumble out into the hallway, tripping over a foil-covered something on the floor and straight back to June 16, 1992. "Holy crap," I breathe, snared in a pair of eyes the color of the New York sky that one day in October it's actually blue.

Nicky tries valiantly not to wince from the fumes while I, equally valiantly, try not to wince from the memories.

My father's cousin's daughter Paula's wedding to Nicky's older brother Frank. I was one of twelve brides-maids. The gowns were hideous and I was in serious venge-ful mode. And old Nicky here was the best man.

Well, he sure as hell was the best man *I'd* ever had, up to that point. I didn't stand a chance, not against those lethal eyes and all the champagne I'd lairped up (do we see a pattern here?) and a hundred-eighty pounds of solid, uncomplicated maleness with an equally solid, uncomplicated erection the size of Cincinnati plastered against me when we danced. Especially in light of the fact that my boyfriend…Jesus, what was his name? Doesn't matter, I forget now, but he'd just ditched me in favor of some female Visigoth from Hunter College with serious bazongas and even more serious mutilation issues, and I was feeling lonely and horny and boring and Nicky was all too willing to do what he could to bolster my sagging self-esteem. Not to mention relieving me of my virginity, which was beginning to get a little frayed around the edges anyway.

Which he did, all righty, in a storage room about twenty paces behind the altar.

"I'll call you," he'd said. Only he hadn't.

I don't think I've seen Paula more than two or three times since then. We were never really close, anyway; she just asked me to be a bridesmaid to make an even dozen. Besides, she lives in Brooklyn. We do, however, touch base from time to time whenever there's a family crisis or something, since her grandfather and my grandfather were brothers. So I know Nicky lives on the third floor of the Greenpoint house Frank's and his grandmother left to the guys a couple years ago, that he went through the police academy, eventually became a detective. What I didn't know was that he was assigned to the 19th Precinct. Which would be mine.

Trying to work up a good head of anger, I watch as Nicky squats down to pick up the foil-wrapped whatever, which I'm gathering is something homebaked from Ted and Randall across the hall. There's a black satin ribbon tied around it.

Nicky straightens, frowning at the ribbon for a second before he hands me the package. I shift the empty bottle, which I can't seem to let go of, to take it. A comforting, lemony smell drifts upward. Wow. Ted must've gone straight into the kitchen the minute he got home from the wedding.

"Hey, Ginger," Nick says in this gruff-gentle voice, and the anger just goes *poof* along with the fear that my mother's body parts are scattered all over 57th Street. I mean, really, like I've got the energy to be ticked about something that happened ten years ago when I've got a much juicier, more recent affront to my pride to deal with.

My eyes narrow. "Why are you here, Nicky?"

Nicky plants his hands on his hips—ever notice the interesting places men's jeans tend to fade?—his eyes like blue flames under thick, dark blond hair, his mouth turned slightly down at the corners, and I think, is it me, or is this weird? That I'm standing here in a wedding dress my husband will *not* be tearing off my body tonight, holding consolatory, still-warm baked goods from my gay neighbors, whilst strolling down memory lane about a quickie in a church closet?

That I'm staring up at the iron jaw of the man who ten years ago annihilated a pair of brand-new, twenty-dollar Dior bikinis and who, it pains me to admit, I would probably allow the same privilege today? That is, if I were not of the current opinion that all men should be shot.

"Look," the Virginator says, "this is sort of...unofficial. I'm not even on duty, in fact, but..." He grimaces. "Mind if I come in?"

I wobble out of the way, let him pass.

All available air in the apartment has just been effectively displaced. Nicky doesn't seem to notice, probably because he's too busy taking in my crushed-moth look, my frizzled hair, the fact that I am slightly swaying, as though to music only I can hear. He then crosses his arms and dons a troubled expression, which I decide he practices in front of his mirror at night. I also decide we are both going to pretend ten years ago didn't happen.

"I'm really sorry," he says, "but I gotta ask you this… the guy you were gonna marry, Greg Munson? When'd you last see him?"

I hug the bottle, tears cresting on my lower lashes. Oh, God, no. Please don't tell me I'm a maudlin drunk. "Th-Thursday night."

"You sure about that?"

"I'm d-drunk," I say, indignantly, still swaying, still clutching the empty bottle to my stomach. "Not lobotomized. Of course I'm sure about that."

Nicky gently removes the bottle from my grasp, as if it's a loaded gun, and glowers at it. "Christ. You drink this whole thing by yourself?"

"Every stinkin' d-drop." He suddenly tilts off to one side, just before I feel him clasp my shoulders and turn me around, steering me toward my sofa.

"Sit," he says when we get there.

Not that he has to ask. I drop like a stone, the dress *whooshing* up around me. I also feel like giggling, which, since a policeman is questioning me about my fiancé's whereabouts, is probably an inappropriate reaction. I look up to see Nicky and his twin doing that glowering thing again, his—their—arms crossed. I will a sober expression—as it were—to my face.

"Seems nobody else has seen Munson since then, either," he says. "His parents just filed a missing persons report. Tried to, anyway."

I feel my eyebrows try to take flight. "Already?"

"I know, it's premature. And probably a huge waste of time, since instinct tells me—excuse me for saying this—nothin's happened to this guy except he got cold feet. But people like Bob Munson are very good at making waves."

Nicky glances around the studio apartment, which takes maybe three seconds. "So how come, if you were gettin' married, all your stuff's still here?" He looks back at me, eyes narrowed. "You don't expect me to believe your husband was gonna move into this hamster cage with you?"

I ignore the derision in Nicky's voice. Okay, so between all my books, my plants, the full-size drafting table, the computer and all its attendant crap, the TV and stereo, a sofa bed, two chairs, my exercise bike, a coffee table, a bistro set, and five pieces of matching, packed Lands' End luggage, things might seem, to the uneducated eye, a little cramped.

"I decided to hang on to it, in case I needed to stay over in the city from time to time. Most of my clothes are out at our new house, howev—" My jaw drops. "You mean they think *I* have something to do with Greg's disappearance?"

I'm usually a little quicker on the draw. I swear.

At that, Nicky perches on the edge of my Pier One coffee table (and if you breathe a word to my clients that my apartment is done in mass-market kitsch, you're dead meat) and looks me straight in the eye. "What I think doesn't matter here. God knows, it wasn't me that came up with this asinine theory. And that's all it is, believe me. In any case—" he digs around in his coat pocket for a scrawny little notepad and a Bic pen "—nobody's accusin' you of anything, okay? It's just that, well, seeing's as he stood you up, you do have a motive. I mean, should…"

He stops.

I grip the edge of my sofa bed (Pottery Barn, cranberry velvet, three years old) and make myself focus on Nicky until there's only one of him. "Hey. I went ballistic back there," I say, swatting in the general direction of midtown. "That wasn't faked. I can't fake anything," I add, which gets a quick hitch of the pair of eyebrows across from me. "Besides, even I know you can't have a murder without a bo—" I burp "—dy."

Tell me that didn't sound as blasé as I think it did.

Nicky is looking at me as if he's not sure. But then he says, "Nobody's sayin' anything about murder, Ginger. I'm just tryin' to fit the pieces together. All anybody wants is to find this guy and get his frickin' father off our case."

"Well, why point a finger at *me?*" Sober, I can do high dudgeon with the best of 'em. However, considering the definite possibility that my speech is slurred, I'm probably not pulling it off as well as I might have hoped. Nicky's long, dark, silky eyelashes sidetrack me for a second, then I say, "Sure…*now,* I have a motive. *After* he stands me up. I didn't *before* this afternoon. I mean, come *on*…why would I want to do in the man who gave me my first multiple orgasm?"

I try clamping my hand over my mouth, only I miss and smack myself in the chin.

Nicky puts his pad and pen away. And in those crystalline eyes, I see…awe. Respect. A pinch of what I'm afraid to identify as challenge. And I find myself thinking, damn, there's all this hot, sizzling testosterone in the room, and I'm feeling really sorry for myself, which is closely followed by my wondering what might have happened if he *had* called me, all those years ago. Only then I remember that Nicky is a cop, for one thing, and that his family is even crazier than mine—which is going some—and that I have already had all the craziness I can stand for one lifetime. Oh, and that, according to Paula, her brother-in-law apparently has a penchant for giggly, jiggly twenty-year-olds.

And that, had events unfolded as planned, I'd be—I

glance at the clock over my stove—less than fifteen hours away from my initiation into the Mile High Club.

I'd been really, really looking forward to that.

Venice, too.

"So," Nicky says, all back-to-business. "You got an alibi for after when you last saw Munson?"

I think, a task that doesn't usually strain me this much. "I was here, alone, most of that time. Packing and stuff."

"Anybody see you coming in or going out?"

Again, I think. Again, I draw a blank. "I don't think so. Sorry."

Then the thought jumps up in my face and screams, *What if Greg is dead?*

I look at Nicky, feel my skin go clammy. My stomach rebels. I guess I turn green or something, because with one swift move, he grabs me and pushes me into my bathroom, where I puke out the champagne into the toilet. Which seems aptly symbolic, somehow. Afterward, Nicky hands me a cup of water to rinse my mouth, a damp cloth for my face.

I sip, mop, feel a single tear track down my cheek, undoubtedly dragging mascara behind it. Silently, Nicky steers me back out into the living room. I look at all the packed luggage and heave a great, sour-tasting sigh.

"Here," he says behind me.

I turn, take the business card imprinted with the precinct address and phone number. "Be sure to let us know if he contacts you. Otherwise, well…just…stick around, okay?"

I languidly rustle to the door in his wake, sniffing occasionally, feeling pretty much like something freshly regurgitated myself. One slightly dented, recycled single woman, vomited back into the system to start over again. Once in the hall, Nicky turns, his heavy eyebrows knotted.

"What?" I say when the silence drags on too long.

"You gonna be okay? I mean, here by yourself?" he says, and I think, *Aw…how sweet,* only then he adds, "Maybe you should get your mother to come spend the night or something—"

I frown.

"—or not."

The woman is legendary. Even after more than thirty years, my father's family, according to Paula, still talks about my mother in hushed tones.

"My wife walked out on me three years ago," he now says. "It sucks."

Wife? What wife? Paula never said anything about a wife.

"Why?" I ask, because I really want to know.

Still not facing me, he shrugs, like it doesn't matter anymore. Only his jaw is clenched. "She couldn't deal with me bein' a cop. Said it scared her too much. We split after less than six months."

"Oh. I'm sorry."

He nods, then says, "She's okay, though. Got married again last year. To an accountant." He finally turns back, for a couple seconds looking at me the way a man does when he wants to touch you but knows to do so would shorten his life expectancy. Then he says, very quietly, "I should've called you. After Paula's wedding, I mean."

Then he turns and walks down the hall. I watch him for a minute, until he gets on the elevator, after which I go back into my apartment and lean against the closed door, suddenly possessed with an inexplicable urge to sing "Don't Cry for Me, Argentina."

Two

"**Y**ou shouldn't trek up there by yourself," Nedra says on the other end of the line, a scant week after my aborted nuptials. "I'm going with you."

"Up there" is Scarsdale, where I'm about to go to pick up at least some of my clothes, as per Greg's—who is very much alive, by the way; more on that in a minute—suggestion. Although Nedra and I have talked on the phone several times since Sunday, I haven't yet seen her live and in person. A state of affairs that I intend to continue as long as I possibly can. Hey—I'm having enough trouble finding my own snatches of air to breathe; competing with my mother for them could be fatal. Still, for a moment, I am tempted to give in to the suggestion that I do not have the strength or enthusiasm requisite to argue. Especially since it's my own dumb fault for telling her my plans.

Then my survival instinct saves the day with, "Over my dead body."

This declaration, however, does not bother a woman whose idea of a hot date was being bodily dragged from the scene of a political protest. If anything, I can feel her cranking up to the challenge. I cut her off at the pass.

"This is something I have to do myself," I say, thinking, *Hmm…not bad.* I pour myself a glass of orange juice, take my Pill even though I obviously don't—and won't—need birth control for the forseeable future. But the thought of dealing with heavy periods and cramps again, after ten years without, gives me the willies. After I swallow I say, "I'm all grown up now. Don't need my mommy to hold my hand."

"Did I say that? But how are you planning on lugging everything back on the train by yourself?"

So I hadn't thought that part through. But there are times when self-preservation outweighs logic.

"I'll manage."

"You shouldn't have to face That Woman alone."

Why Nedra detests Phyllis Munson so much, I have no idea. Greg's mother has always been gracious to mine, the few times they've met. But then, Phyllis is gracious to everybody. While my mother was burning bras and flags in the sixties, Greg's mother was kissing up to pageant judges. She even made it to Atlantic City as Miss New York one year, I forget which. Something tells me she's never gotten over not making the top ten. But my point is, I don't think Phyllis knows how *not* to smile. Although you do have to wonder if all those years of just being so gosh-darn *nice* don't take their toll.

In any case, things are liable to be just a bit on the tense side between Phyllis and me, since her son skipped out on our wedding and we're both going to feel weird and not know what to say and all. Adding my mother to the mix would be like pouring hot sauce over Szechuan chicken. Besides, the last thing I need is for my mother to see how terrified I am of venturing out into the real world.

So I muster every scrap of conviction I can and say, "I'm going alone, and that's that," and my mother gives one of those long-suffering sighs that daughters the world over dread, then says, "Okay, fine, fine…" which of course means it isn't fine, but she'll deal with it. For a moment I savor the small, exquisitely precious victory. Only then she says, "You know, it's not as if I'm going to embarrass you or anything."

If I had the energy, I'd laugh.

"So," she says, as if my not refuting her comment doesn't matter, "when are you leaving?"

I hedge. "Elevenish." My heart starts thundering in my chest. I open the freezer, find three Healthy Choice dinners, a half-filled ice cube tray, and one lone Häagen-Dazs bar. With nuts. "Maybe." I rip off the paper, sighing at the sensation of creamy chocolate exploding in my mouth. Yes, I know it's barely 9:00 a.m. So? "I'm not sure." Which of course is a bold-faced lie, since if Phyllis is meeting me, obviously I can't just mosey on up there whenever the mood strikes.

"Call me when you get back," Nedra says, and I say "Sure," although we both know I won't.

I hang up and sigh, relieved to have my thoughts to my-self again, hating having my thoughts to myself again. God, this is so creepy, this walking-a-tightrope-over-Niagara-Falls-in-a-dense-fog feeling. I keep thinking, if I just keep still, don't rush things, the real Ginger will come back to play. The real Ginger will come back to *life*.

I've turned into an absolute slug. I've spent most of the past week on the sofa in my pj's, scarfing down Chee●tos and Häagen-Dazs and cherry Cokes whilst staring zombie-fashion at the soaps. And then there's Sally Jesse, and Oprah, and all those morbidly fascinating court TV shows. Criminy, where do they get these people? From a cold storage locker in Area 51?

Munching away on the ice cream bar, I gaze at the wedding dress, still lolling in the middle of the floor like a wilted magnolia. I have no idea what to do with it. I can't exactly throw it out, I certainly can't see packing it away as a keepsake, or giving something with this much bad karma to someone else. So there it sits. With any luck the silk will eventually biodegrade, leaving behind a small, neat pile of satin-covered buttons I can just bury or something.

The tulle snags on my leg stubble as I shuffle through the dress on my way to the sofa. Guess I should shave.

Guess I should *bathe*.

I sink onto the sofa—my only concession to "cleaning" has been to push the bed back into the sofa sometime during the day—my mouth full of melting chocolate and ice cream. I am one miserable chick, lemme tell ya. What's weird though, is that I actually felt better a few days ago than I do now. There was a period there—

Okay, wait. Let's back up and I'll fill you in.

The day after the wedding is a total loss. Whoever said champagne doesn't give you a hangover lied. By the following day, however, I had recovered enough to face my kitchen, as well as my phone, which, when I finally got up the nerve to check, was up to twenty-five messages. A new world's record. (I'd turned my cell ringer off, too. I figured the world could do without me for a couple days.) Gathering the tatters of my courage—and Ted's fabulous lemon poppyseed bundt cake—I plopped my fanny up on my bar stool and pressed the play button.

The first thirteen messages, as I'd suspected, were all

basically variations on the "Are you okay? Call me" theme from my mother. Then:

"Hey, Ginger, it's Nick. Just checkin' in, see if you heard anything. Let me know."

"Nick." Not "Nicky." Got it. I also got something else, a genuine concern that wasn't at all sexual in nature. No, really. He was family, after all, in a peripheral kind of way. And once sober, I realized my reaction to him had been due to nothing more than booze and shock. Besides, the last time I talked to Paula, she told me Nicky—Nick—had a new girlfriend, she'd met her once, she was okay but for God's sake this was like the sixth one this year and God knew she thought the world of her brother-in-law, but when the hell was he planning on growing up, already?

Another three messages from my mother, then:

"Girl, pick up the damn phone!" Terrie. *"Come on, come on…damn. I know you're in there, probably cryin' your eyes out, which is a shame 'cause the sorry skank ain't worth it…."*

One thing I'll say for Terrie—there won't be any "there are other fish in the sea" pep talks from that quarter, since as far as she's concerned, the only thing that happens when you take fish out of the water is they start to stink.

"Okay, I guess this means you're either sittin' there not answering or you've turned off your ringer. I don't suppose I blame you. But you just remember, if you hear this anytime in the next decade, that this is NOT your fault. Okay, baby—you give me a call when you return to the land of the living, we'll go out and par-tay."

Uh-huh. At that moment I'd been feeling a strong affinity with Mrs. Krupcek in 5-B who, legend has it, got stuck in the elevator for two hours one day back in the eighties when the building lost electricity and consequently peed all over herself. Nobody's seen her leave the building since.

I haven't called her back yet. Terrie, I mean, not Mrs. Krupcek. But Terrie will understand. I hope.

"Uh, yeah?" the next message started. *"It's Tony from Blockbuster?"* At the time, I wondered which he wasn't sure about, that his name was Tony or that he was from Blockbuster. *"I'm just calling to let you know that* Death in Venice *is five days overdue? Okay, 'bye."*

First thought: Who the hell rented *Death in Venice*?

Second thought: There's a video in here somewhere?

"Hi, honey, it's Shelby. Are you there? Okay, I guess not. Anyway, Mark and I thought maybe you might like to come over for dinner one night this week? The kids have been asking about you. Well, okay. Love you. 'Bye."

To answer your question, no, I didn't accept her invitation. Although I did eventually call her back and thank her. But God knows the last thing I need right now is to spend an evening with Ozzie and Harriet Bernstein. Maybe next month. Or something.

I shoveled another bite of cake into my mouth, then:

"Hey, Ginge—"

The fork went flying as I grabbed for the phone at the sound of Greg's voice, totally forgetting it was a message, stupid.

"…I heard via the grapevine that my father went off the deep end and called in the authorities, so I figured I'd better let everybody know I'm okay. I just couldn't…" I heard him sigh. *"Damn, there's no easy way to do this…"*

Now you have to remember that, up to this point, I had convinced myself the guy was either dead, kidnapped, or had an otherwise perfectly reasonable explanation for his vanishing act. When it was immediately obvious the first option was moot, and the second was highly doubtful—this was not someone who sounded as if a gun was being held to his head—that left me with Door Number Three. Which wasn't looking promising, either.

"...I know you're probably angry—okay, extremely angry."

Yeah, okay, I'd been that a time or two in the past forty-eight hours.

"...and you have every right to be. What I did was unforgivable, and if I live to be a hundred, I'll never completely understand why I bolted like that. No, no...that's not entirely true. I guess I...um...panicked. About us, about getting married, about the way you'd set me up on some sort of pedestal—"

I choke on my cake.

"—and I realized I hadn't taken the time I needed to think this through..."

By that point, my ire was beginning to perk quite nicely. I mean, hey—there was some reason why he couldn't have arrived at this conclusion *before* I spent my entire life's savings on food that nobody ever got to eat?

And what is this *I set him up on some sort of pedestal* crap?

"...I mean, I really didn't see this coming, so I don't want you to think this was all a game or anything like that. But...God, Ginge, I'm slime."

No argument there.

"...my main regret is that I didn't realize how I felt until I was getting ready to leave the house on Saturday. I guess I'd just gotten so caught up in...everything, I didn't take five minutes to ask myself if I was really ready for this..."

The man is thirty-five frickin' years old, for God's sake. When did he think he *would* be ready?

"...I mean, the sex was great, wasn't it?"

I looked over at my coffee table and sighed.

"...and who knew my parents would file a missing per-

*son's report, for chrissake? I mean, I hope that didn't cause
you any more distress…''*

Oh, no. Not at all.

*''…and I hope maybe one day, we can be friends again,
although I'll completely understand if you hate my guts.''*

You think?

*''…anyway, I'll settle up with Blockbuster sometime this
week—''*

Which answered that question. Still haven't found that
sucker, by the way.

*''—if you wouldn't mind dropping off the flick when
you're out? And I guess maybe we should arrange for you
to get your things, whenever it's convenient? Maybe you
could call Mom. I mean, that would probably be easier,
don't you think?''*

Hence the Scarsdale pilgrimage.

''Oh, and listen…'' I heard what could pass for a heartfelt sigh. *''I didn't mean for you to get saddled with all the
bills, I swear. Please, send them on to the office, okay? I
promise I'll take care of them. Well.''* Throat clearing
sounds. *''I guess…well. 'Bye. And, Ginge?''*

''What?'' I snapped at the hapless machine.

*''This has nothing to do with you, okay? I mean it.
You're really terrific. God, I'm sorry.''*

You got that right.

After fast forwarding through the rest of the messages,
all from my mother, I glanced down at the cake to discover
I'd somehow eaten half of it. Not that this was really any
big deal since—don't hate me—I can eat anything I want
and never gain weight (although I have a sneaking suspicion all those calories are lying around my body like a
bunch of microscopic air mattresses set to inflate on my
fortieth birthday). But it was all sitting at the base of my
throat when I started to cry—a sobbing-so-hard-I-can't-

catch-my-breath jag that, combined with the cake residue in my mouth, made me choke so badly I thought my brain was going to explode.

Five minutes later, reduced to a limp, shuddering, sweating rag, I came to the disheartening conclusion that although eviceration with a dull knife would have been preferable to what I was feeling at that moment, I still loved the scumbag. Nearly a week later, I still feel that way. I mean, why else would I have put away a dozen bags of Chee●tos? I should hate him, I know that, but I've never been in love before, not really, and I find it's not something I can just turn off like a faucet. Which either makes me very loyal or very stupid. Yes, I'm hurt and furious and want to inflict serious bodily damage, but when I played back the message (oh, and like you wouldn't?), he just sounded so upset....

Well. Anyway. I sat, still shoveling in cake and letting my emotions buffet me when the phone rang, making me jump out of my skin because I'd pushed the ringer too high. Too stunned to remember I wasn't supposed to be answering, I picked up.

"Hey, Ginger? It's Nick."

Bet you saw that coming, didn't you?

I, however, didn't. And I thought, oh, yeah, like this is really going to make me feel better. I rammed my hand through my hair, only my engagement ring got caught in a snarl, which made me wince, which launched me into another coughing fit.

Nick asked if I was okay, but of course I couldn't reply because I was choking to death. "Hang on," I croaked into the phone, then lurched toward the sink, gulped down a half glass of tepid water since I'd run out of bottled. Yech.

A minute later, I picked up the phone and got out, "Guess who I just heard from?"

"I know," Nick said. "I just got word. Munson's fine."

He almost sounded disappointed.

Bet Nick wouldn't just walk away like that, I thought, only to remember that's exactly what he'd done.

My gaze drifted to my left hand and the engagement ring the size of Queens I'd worn proudly since Valentine's Day. Two carats, emerald cut, platinum setting. Hell, for this puppy, I'd even let my nails grow out.

I haven't decided what to do with that, either.

But back to the phone call.

"Yeah," I said. "Great news, huh?"

"Damn," Nick said softly. Like it wasn't a swear word, somehow. "What happened?"

Much to my chagrin, tears again stung my eyes. "He left a message on my answering machine. My *answering machine.*"

"You're kidding me? Man, that is so lame," Nick said, and anger tried to suck me back in. And it would have felt good, I suppose, to have just gone with the flow for a minute. But then I reminded myself of the conscious choice I made as a child, not to let my emotions control *me,* to make decisions based on reason and logic, not on passion and impulse.

That I am not my mother.

And at that moment tranquility rippled through me. Or it might have been a breeze from the open kitchen window. But for just a few seconds there, I felt that everything was going to be okay, that maybe the storm had tipped my boat, but it was completely within my power to right it again.

I stretched, popping the knotted-up muscles at the base of my neck. "He was very apologetic, though." My voice seemed eerily level, even to my own ears. "I mean, he's not sticking me with the rest of the bills or anything."

"Jesus."

"What?"

"You're scaring me."

"Scaring you? Why?"

"Aren't you supposed to be incoherent and breaking things right about now?"

I wasn't sure whether to be dumbfounded or indignant. "That would be like me saying all men sit around every Sunday afternoon, watching sports and stuffing their faces with nachos and pork rinds."

"Yeah. So?"

I huffed a little sigh. "Greg didn't."

"No, all he did was go AWOL on your wedding day."

I frowned. Just a tiny one, though. "But he said—"

"I don't give a shit what he said. Guy doesn't even have the balls to tell you in person. He treated you like dirt, Ginger. Like I should've called you after...you know. Paula's wedding. But I didn't. And even though I was only twenty-one and still functioning on half a brain, that still makes me scum, which I can live with. But what that guy did to you...dammit! Why aren't you more pissed?"

"Because anger is counterproductive—"

"That's bull. And holding it in isn't healthy."

"Then you must not be paying attention in those anger management classes they make you take," I said, feeling my face redden. What the hell was this guy trying to do to me?

"Managing it isn't the same as stifling it."

"Speaking of stifling it—"

"I bet you're even still wearing his ring."

"That's none of your bus—"

"Take it off, Ginger. Now."

That's when, in the process of swiping my hand across the face, I scraped my nose with one of the prongs (something I'd managed to do at least once a day since I put the damn thing on, if you want to know the truth), which was just enough to send me over the edge. So I yanked off the ring and hurled it against the counter backsplash. The clatter was surprisingly loud. And satisfying.

"Is it off?" Nick said.

"I hope you're alone," I said, suppressing the urge to paw through my cookbooks before the roaches carted it off (yeah, we got 'em on the East Side, but they've got little Louis Vuitton gold initials all over them), "because do you have any idea how your end of the conversation sounds—"

"Is...it...off?"

"You know, you've got a real problem with patience—"

"Goddammit, Ginger—"

"Yes, Nick. The ring is off. Happy?"

"Delirious. Did you throw it?"

I shoved my hair out of my face. "Yeah. As a matter of fact, I did—"

"Hard?"

With a weighty sigh, I hauled myself off the stool, leaned over to squint at the backsplash. Sure enough, there was a tiny scratch. Which I will swear was there when I moved in. Since I was in already in the neighborhood, I picked up the ring, then I sat back down with a grunt, twiddling the bauble between my thumb and index finger. "Hard enough."

"Good," Nick said, with a note of my-work-here-is-done accomplishment in his voice. "Anyway. Just wanted to touch base. Let you officially know you're in the clear."

"Oh. Yeah. Thanks."

Silence strained across the line.

"So. You take care, okay? And, Ginger?"

"Yeah?"

"Don't put the ring back on."

After he hung up, I sat and listened to the dial tone for several seconds, my body humming like I'd just had insta-sex.

So now that you've been treated to Day 3 of How Ginger Spent Her Honeymoon, we can skip ahead to the equally fun-filled present, where I'm doing the catatonic number in front of the tube. Nick hasn't called since. Not that there's any reason he should.

And the ring is safely snoozing in its little Tiffany box, tucked underneath my undies.

And, as you may have guessed, the I'm-gonna-right-this-boat feeling passed. I might have ridden the crest for a moment or two, but then the wave took me under again. I hadn't fully realized how much I'd loathed dating until I no longer had to. The gruesome prospect of having to start over is more than I can bear thinking about.

Credits roll on the screen in front of me, which means it's later than I thought, which means I have to face the music, or in this case the shower, and fix myself up at least enough so I don't frighten little children when I step outside. Last time I caught my reflection, I looked like an electrocuted poodle. And I really should take the cake plate back to Ted and Randall. Maybe I'll look sad enough that they will take pity on me and fill it up again. I'm thinking maybe chocolate-chip-macadamia-oatmeal cookies. Or brownies would be good, too…

My phone rings again. I hesitate, then answer.

"Cara?"

My heart stops. It's my grandmother.

Who never, ever, ever makes phone calls.

"Nonna, what's—?"

"Your mother, she is onna her way to your place. Inna taxi. But you never heard it from me."

* * *

For about ten seconds after Nonna hangs up, I contemplate the fortuity of Greg's not being dead and my consequent removal from the N.Y.P.D.'s suspect list because now it will take them longer to connect me to my mother's murder. Of course, if and when they finally did, maybe Nick would have to come back and question me again—which held a definite appeal, over and above being rid of my mother—only I don't think I could stand the look of disappointment in his eyes when he found out I dunnit. So I guess I'll let my mother live.

And please don't take my ramblings seriously. I can't even set a mouse trap.

In any case, while I've been standing here plotting my mother's demise, the clock has been quietly ticking away. Now I quickly calculate how long it will take a taxi to get here from Riverside Drive and 116th Street and realize I can either clean me or clean the apartment, but not both, which provokes a spate of agitated swearing. Not that my mother's a neat freak, believe me—until Nonna came to live with us after my grandfather died when I was ten, I didn't even know you *could* make a bed—but one look at this place, and she's going to know I'm not exactly in control.

Not an option.

Naturally, every single muscle immediately seizes, a condition in which I might have remained indefinitely had not the doorbell rung. I let out a single, one-size-fits-all expletive and force myself to the door. Tell me Nedra got the one cabbie in all of Manhattan who actually knew where he was going.

I peer through the keyhole, practically letting out a whoop of joy. When I yank open the door, Verdi engulfs me from the open door across the hall as Alyssa, my neighbor Ted's twelve-year-old daughter, grins up at me, all legs and braces and silky honey-colored hair and big green eyes. I am so grateful it's not my mother that I don't even care about my fried poodle head or that the melted chocolate splotch on my jammies right between my booblets calls attention to the fact that I'm not wearing a bra. Not that Ted would care, although I'm not sure I'm setting a good example for Alyssa.

In spite of my panic, I grin back, although I can feel it tremble around the edges. Alyssa's my buddy; I've sat for her more times than I can count since Ted won custody of her four years ago, no mean feat for a gay man, even today. In the last year, she's begun to notice boys, which I gather is about the same time her father did. But you know how it is, always easier to talk to someone outside the family about these things....

I notice her hands are clamped around a plate of cookies. Oh, yeah—things are definitely looking up.

"We got concerned when we didn't hear you leave the apartment," her father now says, looming behind his daughter. I get a glimpse of a faded navy T stretched across a solid torso, and bare, hairy legs protruding from the bottoms of worn drawstring shorts—the freelance writer's summer chained-to-the-computer ensemble. Underneath silver-splintered, dark brown hair as curly as mine, worry lurks in hazel eyes as he takes in my less-than-reputable appearance. "I hope you didn't spend longer than ten minutes to get that look, honey, because, trust me, it isn't you."

My attention really, really wants to drift back to the cookies, but I suddenly remember the peril I'm in. "Oh, God. My mother's on her way. In a *taxi.*"

Ted looks at me, glances over my shoulder into my apartment. I swear he blanches. He, too, has met my mother. "Got it. We'll be right there."

"Oh, no, you don't have to—"

Ted throws me a glance that brooks no argument, then says, "Al, go back inside and get the box of trash bags. And grab Randall while you're at it."

Knowing the cavalry is coming shakes me from my stupor enough to send me back into my apartment, where I once again freak out. Where did all this crap *come* from? Do I really subscribe to this many magazines? Why do I have so many dishes? And where am I going to stash it all?

I grab the wedding dress, then stand there doing this bizarre, twitching dance with the thing—there's no way this puppy is gonna fit in any of my closets and the only door behind which I could conceivably hide it leads to the bathroom. Where I need to be right now—

Randall, Ted's lover, slips his bold, buff, black, bald self in through the open door, lets out a deep bark of laughter. He's in High-Wasp casual mode—Dockers, blue Oxford, striped tie, penny loafers. And a diamond earring. "Lord, woman—you have a consolation orgy in here or what?"

Out of the corner of my eye, I see Ted and Alyssa return. To my immense relief, she still has the cookies, which she sets on the counter. A synapse or two misfires.

"I don't know," I say. "I mean, no. I mean, I don't know how it got this way. Are those for me?" I finish with a bright smile for Alyssa.

"Uh-huh," the kid says. "Dad taught me how to make them this morning." She peels back the Saran and carries the plate over to me. Randall pries the crushed dress from my hands before I salivate all over it. I take a cookie, watching him stride out the door. It is a bittersweet moment.

"The place got this way, honey," Ted says, deftly picking up the thread of the conversation, "because you're a pack rat living in a shoebox. Okay, Al," he says to his daughter, attacking the corner where the desk used to be, "the object is not to clean, but to make it *look* clean."

"You mean, like when Mom comes over?"

"You got it."

I stand there munching as the child calmly opens a closet, begins shoving things inside like a pro, while her father straightens and stacks and fluffs. "You know," he says, "a cousin of mine just got a three bedroom in Hoboken for probably half what you're paying for this dump."

That's enough to make me stop chewing. "But it's in *Jersey.*"

Ted considers this for a moment. "Good point."

Randall returns, sans dress.

"What did you do with it?" I ask.

"Do you really care?"

"I—no, actually."

It might be my imagination, but I think I see something akin to relief in his dark eyes. I don't think either Ted or Randall cared much for Greg, although they never said anything. Then a grin stretches across Randall's molasses-colored face, popping out a set of truly adorable dimples, before he says something about hiding a wedding dress being a damn sight easier than hiding Ted when Randall's mother pops in for a visit. So I grab another cookie, since they're sitting right there on the coffee table, and start in about how, since Randall's well into his thirties and not married, his parents might have a few suspicions, when Ted straightens and says, "Hello, Miss Chatterbox? I'm busting my butt here while you're standing here dispensing advice about honesty issues?"

When I jump and head toward the kitchen, he snags me

with one long arm, whipping me around and flinging me toward the bathroom door. "We do this. You do you. And burn that…thing you're wearing."

Seconds later I step into the shower and imagine I hear Shelby's perky little voice saying, "Now, think positive, honey. Things really will turn out for the best," followed immediately by Terrie's, "You don't need that sorry piece of dog doo in your life, girl, and you know it." And between that and the sugar high, I think, You know, they're right. I have terrific friends and hot water when I actually need it and a new client to see on Monday and a brand-new bottle of shampoo to try out and my period isn't due for two more weeks. So I was supposed to be on my honeymoon right now. So my heart is broken. I will heal, life will go on, because I am woman and I am invincible and no man is gonna get me down when I live in a city where I can get Kung-Pao chicken delivered to my door twenty-four/seven.

Now if I could just convince this permanent lump in the center of my chest to go away, I'd be cookin' with gas.

When I emerge, ten minutes and one hairless body later—my mother equates shaving with kowtowing to male standards of beauty; my take on it is I prefer not to look as though I've missed several rungs on the evolutionary ladder—my apartment once again looks like someone reasonably civilized lives here and Ted and Randall and Alyssa are nowhere in sight. The Blockbuster box, however, is. Which means, yes, the movie's now so late, I'm surprised they haven't sent their goons after me. On that cheery note, I grab another cookie (huh—looks like they took a few back with them) and I think how much I love this silly little place, with its Barbie kitchen and high ceiling and two big windows looking east across Second Avenue to the apartment directly across from mine.

Five years ago, I sublet it from a costume designer named Annie Murphy for six months while she went out to L.A. to do a movie. Only, she kept getting work out there and never came back. And over the years, her sister from Hoboken would come to cart off Annie's furniture—with Annie's blessings—and I'd replace it. The place was truly mine now, in every sense but the lease.

But I would have been happy in suburbia, too. I was going to get a dog. A big dog. Something that slobbered.

Oh, well.

Anyway, while I'm musing about all this, my mouth clamped around half a cookie, I make myself open one of the bags I'd packed for the honeymoon, where whatever clothes I do have reside. All sorts of slippery, shiny, weightless things—some new, some old favorites—wink at me when I flip back the top. I spend my working day in simple, neutral outfits: black, beige, gray, cream. Nothing that would distract my clients—I want them to see my designs, not the designer. On my off hours, I go wild. Salsa colors. Bold prints. Stuff that makes me happy.

Licking crumbs from my lips and telling myself I do *not* need another cookie, especially on top of the Häagen-Dazs bar, I slip into a pair of brand-new, fire-engine-red bikinis and matching lace bra that are more concept than substance, a short purple skirt, a silk turquoise tank top. I may have pitiful tits but my legs are good, if I do say so myself, especially in this pair of gold leather-and-acrylic mules that make me nearly six feet tall. On my Favorite Things list, shoes rank right behind food and sex. Although sometimes, on days like today, sex gets bumped to third. I turn, admiring my feet. God, these are so *hot*.

A pair of combs to hold back my hair, a spritz of perfume, a slick of lip gloss—

I look at my reflection and think, *God, Greg. Look what you're missing.* Then the intercom buzzes.

And I just think, *God.*

Three

The tile floor in the bathroom in my first apartment, a fifth-floor walkup way downtown off First Avenue, was so caked with crud that everyday cleaning agents were worthless. So one day I hauled my butt to the little hardware store around the corner and explained my plight to the stumpy old man on the other side of the counter who'd probably been there since LaGuardia's heyday. From behind smudged bifocals, he seemed to carefully consider me for a moment, nodded, then vanished into the bowels of the incredibly crammed store. A moment later he returned bearing a jug of something that he reverently placed on the counter, still eyeing me cautiously, as if we were about to conduct our first drug deal together.

"This'll cut through anythin', guaranteed," he said.

Muriatic Acid the label proclaimed in ominous black letters. The skull and crossbones was a nice touch, too.

"Just be sure to keep windows open," Stumpy said, "wear two pairs of gloves, and try not to breathe in the fumes, cause', y'know, it's poison an' all."

Undaunted, I trekked back to my hovel, suited up, pried open the bathroom window with a crowbar I bought at the same time as the acid, and poured about a tablespoon's worth of the acid on a really bad spot by the bathtub. The sizzling was so violent I fully expected to see a horde of tiny devils rise up from the mist. For a moment, I panicked, wondering if the acid would stop at devouring roughly a century's worth of dirt and grime, but would also take out the tiles, subflooring, and plasterboard of my downstairs neighbor's ceiling, as well. After a few mildly harrowing seconds, however, the fizzing and foaming stopped, and I was left with what had to be the cleanest three square inches of tile in all of lower Manhattan.

And that, boys and girls, pretty much describes what happens when my mother and I get together.

The instant Nedra enters my space, or I hers, I can feel whatever self-confidence and independence I'd managed to accrue over the past decade fizz away, leaving me feeling, temporarily at least, tender and raw and exposed. Which is why I avoid the woman. Hey, I'm not into bikini waxes, either.

It's not that she means to be critical, or at least not with malicious intent. It's just that, unlike the vast majority of her peers, Nedra hasn't yet lost her sixties idealistic fervor. If anything, age—and a few years as a poli-sci prof at Columbia—has only fine-honed it. I, on the other hand, am a definite product of the Me generation. I like making money, I like spending it, preferably on great-looking clothes, theater tickets and trendy restaurants. The way I figure it, I'm doing my part to keep the economy from collapsing. Not to mention supporting entrepreneurship and the arts. Nedra, however, cannot for the life of her understand how her womb spawned such a feckless child. Nor has she yet been able to accept the hopelessness of converting me.

The good news is that the stinging usually doesn't last for long. Underneath the insecurities, I'm not the piece of fluff I appear. I can survive a Nedra attack, much as I'd probably survive a tornado. And while that doesn't mean I have the slightest desire to move to Kansas, I have also learned how to play the game.

Take now, for instance. I open my door, glower at her. Take the offensive for the few seconds she'll let me have it. After all, she doesn't know I've been tipped off.

"Nedra! What the hell are you doing here?"

"Oh, would you just get over it and let me be a mother, already?"

"That's what I'm afraid of."

She barges in, a grocery bag banging against her leg.

"I thought I told you I didn't want company?"

"You're distraught," she says. "You have no idea what you want. Or need. And right now, you need a mother's support."

Except then she scans my outfit, disapproval radiating from her expression. Not because of the way I'm dressed, but because she knows I spent big bucks on it. She, on the other hand, is in full aging-hippie regalia—print broomstick skirt, white T-shirt underneath a loose embroidered blouse (no bra), Dr. Scholl's wooden sandals.

I cross my arms. Glower some more. "Don't worry. They're all made in America." Never mind that my avowal is full of bunk, and we both know it—the shoes, especially, positively scream Italian—but even at her lowest, Nedra isn't likely to yank out a tag and check. Instead, she gives in to five thousand years of genetic conditioning and goes all Jewish Mother Affronted on me.

"Did I say anything?"

"You didn't have to. And how old *is* that skirt, anyway?"

She waves away my objection and clomps toward my kitchen, and I once again—much to my chagrin—stand in awe of my mother's commanding presence.

On a good day Nedra reminds me a lot of Anne Bancroft. Today, however, the effect is more that of a drag queen doing an *impression* of Anne Bancroft. Rivers of gray surge through her dark, shoulder-length hair, as thick and unruly as mine. The bones in her face jut; her brows are dark slashes over heavy-lidded, nearly black eyes; her mouth, never enhanced with lipstick, is full, the lips sharply defined. Although she has never smoked—at least not cigarettes, and never in my presence—her voice is low and roughened from one too many demonstrations; her boobs sag and sway over a rounded stomach and broad hips; her hands are large and strong, the nails blunt.

And yet there is no denying how magnetically attractive she is. She moves with the confidence of a woman totally comfortable with her body, her womanhood. All my life, I have noticed the way men become mesmerized in her presence. Struck dumb, many of them, I'm sure, but I early on learned to recognize the haze of respectful lust. Not that I've ever been the recipient of such a thing—not in that combination, at least. A shame, almost, that she's refused to date since my father died. She insists love and marriage and men are part of her history; now she's free to devote her life to her work, her causes, and, when I don't duck quickly enough, to me. Yes, she is a formidable woman, someone you instinctively want on your side—or as far away from your side as possible—but her sexuality is so potent, so uncontrived and primal, she could easily serve as a model for some pagan fertility goddess.

The clothing disagreement has been laid to rest for the moment in favor of—I see her scan the apartment—reviving the Living Space Dispute.

My fists clench.

"I still don't see," she says, plunking down the grocery bag filled with something intriguingly solid onto my counter, "why you feel you have to line a greedy landlord's pockets for a space this small. Honestly, honey—you could drown in your own sneeze in here."

"The place is rent-stabilized," I say. "Which you know. And it's mine." Well, for all intents and purposes. "And it's a damn good thing I didn't let it go, considering… things." I clear my throat. "What's in the bag?"

"Ravioli. Nonna made it this morning. And you could live with Nonna and me, you know. Especially now that I've moved all my stuff up front to the dining room, since we don't really need it anymore, so there's an extra room besides the third bedroom, you could use it for an office or studio or something. I mean, c'mon, think about it—even if you split the rent with me, think how much money you'd save, and have twice the space besides."

Twice the space, but half the sanity. I cross to the kitchen, remove the plastic container from the bag. "Right. You wanna take bets on who would kill whom first? Besides, you actually expect me to believe those rooms are *vacant?*"

My childhood memories are littered with images of tripping over the constant stream of strays my parents took in, friends of friends of friends who needed someplace to crash until they found a place of their own, or the grant money came through, or whatever the excuse *du jour* was for their vagrancy. I never got used to it. In fact, every time I got up in the middle of the night and ran into a stranger on my way to the bathroom, I felt even more violated, more ticked, that my space had been invaded. Which is why, I suppose, despite the pain of paying rent on my own, I've never been able to stomach the idea of a roommate. Not one I wasn't sleeping with, at least.

And Nedra is well aware of my feelings on the subject, that much more than the normal grown child's need for independence propelled me from her seven-room, rent-controlled nest. Unfortunately, what I call self-preservation, she has always perceived as selfishness.

"I don't do that anymore," she says quietly. "Not as much, anyway." I snort, shaking my head. "Look, I'm not going to turn away someone who genuinely needs my help," she says, almost angrily. "And, anyway, Miss High and Mighty, since when is it a crime to help people out?"

I look at her, feeling old resentments claw to the surface. But I say nothing. I'm feeling fragile enough as it is; I have no desire to get into this with her right now. Which is, duh, why I didn't want to be around her to begin with.

Then she sighs. "But I am more cautious than I used to be. I don't take in total strangers the way Daddy and I used to. Not unless I have some way of checking them out." She rams her hand through her hair, frowning. "It upsets your grandmother, for one thing."

Well, good. At least her mother-in-law's getting some consideration, even if her daughter didn't. I notice, however, she doesn't contradict me about the killing-each-other part of my observation.

I return my attention to the plastic container of pasta in my hands. Defying their imprisonment, the scents of garlic and tomato sauce drift up. Traditional, artery-clogging ravioli, stuffed with plain old meat sauce, the pasta made with actual eggs. My knees go weak. I put the container in my empty fridge, make a mental note to call Nonna when I get back to thank her—

"I'm sorry, sweetheart," Nedra says softly. So softly, in fact, I look up in surprise.

"About?" I ask, since I don't think we're talking about the Hotel Petrocelli anymore.

"What do you think?"

Ah. I almost smile. "Oh, right. You hated Greg, you detest his family and everything they stand for. I somehow don't think you're real torn up that it didn't work out."

"Well, no, I'm not, I suppose. I couldn't stand the thought of your marrying into that bunch of phonies."

An exquisite pain darts through my left temple. "Just because they don't live the way you do, don't think the way you do, that doesn't make them phonies."

She gives me that okay-if-that's-what-you-want-to-believe look, then says, "Whatever. But what I feel about them doesn't matter. Not right now. I can still feel badly for you. I know you loved him."

And I can tell it nearly kills her to admit that. But before I can say anything else, she goes on.

"And it kills me to know you're hurting. I remember what it feels like, suddenly being single again. And it's the pits."

I'm staring at her, unblinking. Is this a "Twilight Zone" moment or what? Empathy? From Nedra? On a personal level?

I think I feel dizzy.

"And I also know what it feels like," she continues, her dark eyes riveted to mine, "the first time you go out into the world after something like this. That you look at everyone around you and wonder how they can just go on, living their normal lives, when your own has fallen apart."

For the first time, I notice the dark circles under her eyes, that she looks tired. Worried, even.

I have seen my mother outraged, exhilarated, devastated.

But not once that I can remember have I ever seen the look in her eyes I see now. And I realize she's really not here to torture me, at least not intentionally, but because she needs me to need her. As a mother, as a friend, as anything I'll let her be.

Oh, dear God. She wants to *bond?* To do the whole we-are-sisters-in-tribulation thing?

My eyes are stinging as I turn away to toss my sunglasses and a book into a straw tote. The criticism, the clashing of opinions…I know how to brace myself against those, how to grit my teeth against the sting. This…this compassion, this whatever it is…

I have no idea what to do with that.

"We better get going," I say, snatching the stupid video off the coffee table before tramping through the door.

An hour and a half later things have returned to normal. Or what passes for normal between my mother and me. We got into a political fracas before I even hailed the taxi, an argument that wasn't fully cold in its grave when we arrived at Grand Central and she launched into an unprovoked attack on several hapless passersby for ignoring a homeless man on the sidewalk, to whom she gave a ten dollar bill.

It was ever thus. I know my parents sure didn't earn the big bucks as instructors at Columbia, especially not in those early years, but they were profoundly aware of those who had less, to the point where their socialistic consciousnesses weren't at peace unless they'd given away so much of their earnings to this or that cause, we were barely better off than the poor wretches they supported. Generosity is all well and good—don't look at me like that, I give to charity, jeez—but weeks of living off lentils and boxed macaroni and cheese night after night because we couldn't afford anything else got old *real* fast.

I suppose they thought, or at least hoped, their altruistic example would instill a like-minded spirit of sacrifice for the common good in their daughter. Instead, a childhood of forced culinary deprivation has only fostered an insatiable craving for prime rib and ridiculously expensive, ugly little fruits that are only in season like two days a year.

So. I pretended I'd never seen her before in my life as I sauntered into Grand Central as gracefully as one can with a trio of soft-sided canvas bags in assorted sizes hanging about one's person. I was also profoundly grateful it was ninety degrees and therefore highly unlikely we'd pass somebody wearing a fur. Don't even think about walking down Fifth Avenue with Nedra anytime between October and April. Dead things as fashion statement send her totally postal.

Which is why she must never know about the Blackglama jacket hanging in my closet, an indulgence I succumbed to, oh, four years ago, I think, when I got my First Big Client, a dot.com entrepreneur who basically waved a hand at the SoHo loft he was thrilled to have "only" paid a million five for and said, "Just do it."

At least I've got a mink jacket to show for it. The client, sad to say, is probably lucky to still have his shirt.

But I digress. Once I got Nedra past all the potential land mines and onto the train, I realized having my mother with me did have certain advantages. For one thing, I couldn't bicker with my mother and moon over Greg at the same time. For another, men were far less likely to hit on me with my mother gesticulating wildly beside me, which was a good thing because I was seriously uninterested in fending off the deluded. Although one or two intrepid souls tried to hit on *her*. For the most part, however, I could count on my fellow New Yorkers to stay true to type and basically ignore the dutiful daughter escorting the crazy woman back to Happy Acres after her little field trip to the city. And while I still cringed at the thought of Phyllis in the face of my mother's Open Mouth Policy, at least there wouldn't be any long stretches of awkward silence. Although there would undoubtedly be a legion of short ones.

Although, really, I have no idea what I'm so nervous about. Phyllis and I have always gotten on together just fine. And after all, I'm the dumpee. If anything, she should feel embarrassed about seeing *me*, not the other way around.

And while I'm mulling over all this, I notice my mother's been oddly subdued for the past half hour or so. Of course, applying that word to Nedra is like saying the hurricane's been downgraded to a tropical storm. But it's true: she's actually been reading quietly, the silence between us punctuated by nothing more than an occasional snort of indignation. I glance over from the racy novel I'm reading, something with heaving bosoms and flowing tresses adorning the cover. The heroine's not too shabby, either.

"Whatcha reading?" I say, noting that the tome on my mother's lap weighs considerably more than I do.

"Hmm?" She frowns at me over the tops of her reading glasses, then tilts the book so I can see the cover. Ah. Some feminista treatise on menopause, which is definitely the topic of the hour these days, since Nedra apparently stopped having periods about six months ago. When she passes the first year without, she says, she's going to have a party to celebrate her official entrée into cronehood.

She refocuses on the book, the corners of her mouth turned down. "You have no idea," she says in a voice that would carry, unmiked, to the back row of Yankee Stadium, "the insidious ways the medical establishment tries to foist off the idea that every natural function of the female body should be regarded as a disability. It's absolutely *outrageous*.''

At least four passengers across the aisle give us disapproving looks. Except for one middle-age woman who nods.

I ''hmm'' in reply and look back at my book, suppressing a long-suffering sigh. The odd thing is, it's not that I don't agree with her about a lot of what she gets so fired up about—I'll probably read that book myself—it's just there are quieter, more dignified ways to make one's point. After all these years, Nedra still has the power to embarrass the hell out of me. You would've thought I'd become inured to her outbursts by now. I haven't.

Many's the time as a child I was tempted to call Social Services, get a feel for what the adoption market was for skinny, Jewish-Italian mutt girl-children of above-average intelligence. Of course, I do understand that parents' embarrassing their kids goes with the territory. But there are limits. Nedra, however, never seemed to learn what those were.

Since we've already discussed the fact that I'm not going to kill my mother, I do the next best thing: I pretend we're not related.

When the train pulls into our station, my stomach lurches into my throat and stays there. I wrestle out from underneath my seat the three bags into which I intend to pack the essentials, although the plan is to ask Phyllis to stop by the local Mailboxes, Etc., on our way for some boxes so I can pack up and send the rest back to Manhattan via UPS. And yes, it would make more sense to simply rent a car and drive everything back. But neither Nedra nor I drive, since both of us were raised in Manhattan, where cars are a liability, not a convenience.

Of course, Greg insisted I'd have to learn how to drive once I moved out to the suburbs, and because I was blinded by love and basically not in possession of all my faculties, I plastered a game smile to my face and said, "Why, sure, honey." He even tried to teach me. Once. Let's just say, the roads are safer with me not on them. I do not, apparently, possess any natural aptitude for steering two tons of potentially lethal metal with any degree of precision.

We and the cases spill out onto the platform, where we both remark how nice it is to breathe without the sensation of trying to suck air through a soggy, moldy washcloth.

The train pulls away. We are conspicuously alone on the platform, with nothing but a soot-free breeze and birdsong to keep us company.

"You did tell her you were coming up on the 11:04?" my mother says.

I refuse to dignify that with an answer.

"Her hair appointment must have run over."

"Don't start," I say on a long-suffering sigh, but she either doesn't hear me or chooses not to respond. Instead she treads over to a bench, sinks down onto it, drags her book back out of her tote bag and calmly resumes her reading. Not ten seconds later, however, I nearly jump out of my skin at the sound of a male voice calling my name from the other end of the platform. I whip around, shielding my eyes from the glare of the sunlight bouncing off the tracks, nearly losing my cookies—literally—at the sight of the tall man in khaki shorts and a polo shirt loping down the platform toward us.

I swear under my breath, thinking it's Greg, suddenly giving serious consideration to the idea of swooning onto the tracks in the path of an oncoming train. Except the next train isn't due for at least an hour and as the man gets closer, I realize the man's hair is too long and dark, his shoulders too broad, to be Greg. Instead, it's Bill, his younger-by-ten-months brother.

Persona non grata in the Munson clan. In other words, a Democrat.

He is also apparently a leg man, given the way his gaze is slithering over the area south of my hemline.

When Greg and I were together, Bill simply never came up in the conversation. In fact, I nearly gagged on my white wine when, at our engagement party, Greg grudgingly produced this handsome, charming, six-foot-something sibling of whom I had no previous knowledge. He seemed like a nice enough guy to me, but Greg's family acted as if the man ran drugs in his spare time.

If only.

From what I was able to glean from pumping Greg's friends, seems Little Bill backed Big Bob's opponent's campaign in the last election.

Ouch.

However, now that I owe Greg basically no loyalty whatsoever, I decide to like his brother, just for spite. After all, I don't even live in that congressional district—what the hell do I care who represents it? Besides, don't look now, but my po' little ol' trounced Ego is just batting her eyes and sighing over the way the man's grinning at me.

Not that I'm ever going to have anything to do with another man, ever again, you understand. A fact that Prudence and Sanity, in their prim little lace-collared dresses and white gloves, remind that hussy as they snatch her back from the brink of disaster, shrieking something about frying pans and fire and let's not go there, dear.

Of course, even if they hadn't stepped in, my mother did. I may have legs, but she has that whole Earth Mother/Goddess thing going on, and once Bill catches sight of her,

I might as well go ahead and leap onto the tracks, nobody would miss me.

I watch her—or more important, I watch his reaction to her—and I think, Jeez-o-man...a body could get knocked down by the waves of sexual awareness pulsing from this man. Except then he turns back to me, and his smile widens, and the tide heads for my beach, and I think, whoa. Okay, so maybe Billy Boy is just one of those men who gets turned on by every stray X chromosome that crosses his path. Either that, or just when I finally give up trying to figure out what It is that provokes the kind of male response Nedra has effortlessly provoked her entire life, It lands in my lap.

Talk about your lousy timing.

"I happened to stop by the house today," Bill was saying with a whiter-than-white smile aimed at first my mother and then me, "and Mother said Ginger was coming up to pack up some things from Greg's?"

So Billy Boy talks to Mama, huh? Interesting.

"Yep. That's the plan," I say, firmly telling my hormones to stop whining. "So I need to stop by someplace to get some boxes...."

"Don't worry about it." He takes the bags from me. Winks. Starts walking away, which I presume is our cue to follow. Although the wink was kinda irritating, I can't help but notice he has a cute tush. When I glance at my mother, I have a sneaking suspicion she's thinking the same thing. Between my clacking mules and my mother's clomping Dr. Scholl's, we are making a helluva racket heading for the stairs, so much so I almost miss Bill's saying over his shoulder, "We can load up everything in the Suburban, if you like, and I can drive you back to the city."

There is a God.

Thanking my almost-brother-in-law profusely, we tromp

down the stairs and over to the car, which is only marginally smaller than the *QE II*. Excited barking emanates from what I can just make out to be a hyperactive golden retriever in the back seat.

"Damn." Bill frowns at my outfit. "I hope my bringing Mike isn't a problem?"

I give a wan smile, shake my head, trying to dodge the effusive beast as he rockets out of the car when the door's opened, frantic in his indecision who to kiss first. We settle in for the ride to the Munson home—Mother has luncheon prepared for us, Bill says—my mother and I briefly skirmishing over who would sit in front. She wins.

No matter. I'd much rather have the dog than the man, anyway. Mike plops his entire front half on my lap once we've scrambled in, happy as, well, a dog with a human to use as a cushion. I sigh.

We start off. As always, it takes my head a while to adjust to the disproportionate ratio of cement to trees out here. But then, wiping dog pant condensation off my arm, something occurs to me.

"Oh, God. Greg's not there, is he?"

I see Bill shake his head, his nearly black waves long enough to actually graze his linebacker shoulders. I believe the appropriate adjective to describe him is *studly*. His cologne is a little too strong for my taste, his attitude a bit too self-assured. And overtly supporting the enemy camp is a little ballsy, even for me. But, hey, the man has a car and is willing to cart me and all my crap back to town. He could sprout fangs and fur at the full moon for all I care.

"All I know is he's *in seclusion* for a couple weeks. Nobody knows where." Gray eyes glance at me in the rearview mirror. "Tough break about the wedding," he says, sounding sincere enough.

Bill had been invited—I insisted—but he hadn't shown.

For far more obvious reasons than his brother's MIA number, I suppose. I shrug. "It happens."

I see his grin in the mirror, one a lesser mortal might well fear. Did I mention that Billy here has been divorced? Twice?

"All for the best?" he says.

"You can say that again," I think I hear my mother mutter as I, who have been around the block more times than I care to admit, say, "Ah."

In the mirror, I see brows lift. "Ah?"

"You're flirting."

Bill laughs, uncontrite. It's a pretty nice laugh, I have to admit. "And here I was doing my damnedest to sound sympathetic."

Okay, so the guy may be cocky as all get-out, but his honesty is refreshing. Well, it is. And it's not as if I don't understand the compulsion to get one's parents' goats, even if his methods are a bit extreme. So little Miss Ego, who's been sulking in a corner of my brain since being banished there by her well-meaning, but self-serving, stepsisters, looks up hopefully. Not that it will do her any good. I've got other fish to fry.

"So…you and your mother do communicate?"

Bill shrugs. "From time to time. One of those maternal things, I suppose. She can't find it in her heart to write me off entirely. And my father simply pretends I don't exist."

"Can you blame him?" I say.

That gets a laugh. "No, I don't suppose I can."

Which somehow prompts a conversation between Bill and my mother I have no wish to participate in. So instead I find myself mulling over Bill's news about Greg's "hiding out." What does this mean, exactly, especially in regard to all those invoices I've sent to his office? And don't I sound crass and insensitive, thinking about money barely a week after having my heart ripped to shreds?

Thank God I've got a nice chunk of change coming in from last month's billings. It won't be enough to get me caught up, but at least I'll be able to stay afloat.

I lapse into semi-morose silence while my mother and Bill keep chatting away about who looks good for the Dems in the next national election. Which leads to my pondering one of life's great mysteries: Why, oh why, if God is so all-fired omnipotent, does He regularly bite the big one when it comes to sticking the right kids with the right parents?

The Munson manse is stately as hell. You know—gray stone, pristine-white trim, lots of windows, a few columns thrown in for good measure. Very traditional, very classy, probably built somewhere in the fifties. Bill pulls the Suburban just past the front entrance, parking it underneath a dignified maple hovering over the far end of the circular drive. Before either my mother or I can get it together, he's out of the car and around to our sides, opening first my mother's, then my door.

"I've got some errands to run," he says as Mike bounds off my lap, leaving a shallow gouge in my right thigh in the process. Bill lunges for the excited dog, grabbing him by the collar and shoving him back in the car. "So I'll pick you up to go to the other house say in—" he checks his watch "—an hour?"

My mother and I exchange a glance. "You're not having lunch with us?"

He laughs. "Uh, no. Dad's in the neighborhood today, doing his relating-to-the-constituency thing. I don't dare hang around."

He walks back around to the driver's side, says "See ya," and is gone.

"I told you this was a weird family," my mother mutters as we tromp up to the front door.

I bite my tongue.

Concetta, the Munsons' Salvadoran housekeeper, opens the door before we ring the bell, although Phyllis is right behind her, that smile as carefully applied as her twenty-dollar lipstick.

"Oooh, you're just in time," Phyllis says as the maid rustles out of sight. Her eyes dart to my mother, right behind me; if Nedra's unexpected presence has thrown her, she doesn't show it. Instead, she clasps my mother's hand in both of hers, welcoming her, after which she flings out her arms and engulfs me in a perfumed hug, which I hesitantly return. She is nearly as tall as I am, but she feels frail somehow, more illusion than reality. Sensing my discomfort, Phyllis pulls back, her hands gently clamped on my arms, sympathy mixed with something else I can't quite define swimming in her pale blue eyes. I tense, panicked she's going to say something for which I'll have no intelligent reply. I'm a little in awe of this woman, to tell you the truth, even though she's never done a single thing to engender that reaction. Well, except be perfect. To my immense relief, all she does is smile more broadly, taking in my outfit.

"Don't you look absolutely *adorable!*" she says, glancing at my mother as if expecting her to agree. Quickly surmising she'll get little support from that quarter, she returns her gaze to me, shaking her head so that her perfectly cut, wheat-colored pageboy softly skims the shoulders of her light rose silk shell. "What I wouldn't give to be young enough to get away with those colors! And those *legs!*"

She laughs. "I had legs like that, about a million years ago!"

Underneath those white linen slacks, I imagine she still does. *Faces may fall and bosoms may sag, but good legs go with you to the grave,* Grandma Bernice, Nedra's mother, used to say.

"But come on back," Phyllis says with a light laugh. "Concetta has set lunch out on the patio, but it's no trouble at all to add another place."

As always, Phyllis Munson's graciousness blows me away. Chattering about the weather or something, she leads us through the thickly carpeted, traditionally furnished Colonial Revival, one befitting a Westchester congressman and his lovely anorexic wife.

Although the decor is a little bland for my taste—the neutral palette seems almost afraid to offend—there's something about this house that's always put me at peace the moment I set foot inside. The orderly, predictable arrangement of the furniture; the way the lush pile carpeting feels underfoot; the almost churchlike hush that caresses us as we make our way through the house to the back. What it says is, sane people live here.

Which is not to say that the house doesn't tell Designer Ginger things about the owners they'd probably just as well the world not know. While the blandness isn't offensive, the paint-by-number decor doesn't reveal a whole lot about the owners' personalities, either. There are no antiques, no quirky family heirlooms, to break the monotony of the coordinating upholstery and draperies, the relentlessly matching reproduction furniture. Oh, the quality is as good as it gets for mass production—Henredon rather than Thomasville—but it is a bit like walking into a posh hotel suite. Not that that's necessarily a bad thing. I've always fantasized about staying in the Plaza, too.

But there's something more, something I discerned within minutes of my first visit, six or so months ago: that the house's self-conscious perfection stems in large part from the Munsons' eagerness to cover up that neither of them hail from either old money or prize stock.

Unfortunately, it's all too easy to spot the newly, or at least recently, arrived. They're the ones petrified of making a mistake, the ones who constantly ask me if I'm sure this fabric or that piece of furniture is "right," far more concerned about what their guests will think than they are their own preferences. The moneyed, the monikered, don't give a damn. And now, as Phyllis leads us out onto the patio, her back ramrod straight, her voice carefully modulated and devoid of even a trace of a New York accent, I realize that describes my ex-almost-mother-in-law, as well. As gracious and naturally friendly as she is, her fear of being exposed as a poseur—White Plains masquerading as Scarsdale—is almost palpable.

Her insecurities do not bother me. If anything, they make her more human. More accessible. In her place, I imagine I would feel much the same way. I mean, wouldn't you? Unfortunately, it's Phyllis's very insecurities about her background that brand the Munsons as phonies in my mother's eyes.

Phyllis touches the uniformed maid lightly on the arm, whispers something to her. The woman nods, disappears through a second set of French doors leading, if I remember correctly, to the kitchen. The terrace is open-air, although deeply shaded at this time of day. I've never been out here before, I realize, I suppose because it was either nighttime or too cold, the other times I was here. Now I glance out across the "yard": if there are other houses beyond the dense growth bordering the property on all three sides, they are undetectable. A pool, flanked by dozens of urns and pots overflowing with brilliantly colored annuals, shimmers below us. I somehow doubt it's ever used.

Oh, yes, I'm well aware I'm having lunch in The Land of Make Believe. I don't care. That doesn't make it less peaceful, or tranquil. Besides, after two hours in my mother's company, I'm desperate.

We sit. Concetta bustles about, setting the extra place, deftly serving the first course, fresh fruit segments in a serrated cantaloupe half, followed by deli sandwiches on fresh rye. Nothing fancy or pretentious. We make excruciatingly brittle small talk, for a while, until Phyllis unwittingly gives my mother the opening she's been waiting for.

"It must be very comforting, Ginger, having your mother around at a time like this."

I can sense my mother's coiling for the attack, but unfortunately I can't get hold of a rock quickly enough to stop her before she strikes. I try glaring, for all the good it does.

"And maybe," Nedra says, "if you'd taught your son that social prominence is no excuse for cowardice, there wouldn't be a 'time like this.'"

"Nedra—"

"No, Ginger, it's all right," Phyllis says quietly, even though her face is now a good three shades darker than her blouse. Her left hand, braced on the table in front of me, is trembling slightly; I notice her diamond wedding set is askew, too large for her sticklike finger. I feel sorry for her—I'm at least used to my mother. She isn't.

"Gregory has embarrassed all of us, Mrs. Petrocelli. I assure you, he wasn't raised to be inconsiderate, or to act like a coward. The last thing I would do is insult your intelligence by trying to make excuses for him. Both his father and I are deeply ashamed of our son's actions—" she looks at me, reaches for my hand "—and cannot begin to convey how badly we feel for your daughter. Both Bob and I truly love her, and are heartbroken at the idea of not having her as our daughter-in-law.''

Wow. I knew they liked me, but...

Wow.

My mother seems equally stunned. Which is a rare phenomenon, believe me. Although I'd like to think my glaring at her had something to do with it, as well. You know the look—*if you ever want to see your grandchildren again, you will apologize?* Okay, so there aren't any grandchildren. Yet. But I believe in planning ahead.

Then I noticed something else in her expression, a slight pursing of the lips, the merest narrowing of the eyes. An expression that says, clear as day, *"Bullshit."*

My face warms at the implications of that expression, even as anger incinerates the remains of sandwich and fruit in my stomach. *What?* I want to scream. *You got a problem with believing that maybe, just maybe, they really do like me?*

And while I'm sitting here, trying to get my breathing under control, I hear Nedra take a deep breath, then say, "I'm sorry. That was uncalled for. After all, I don't suppose it's fair—'' she looks pointedly at me "—to hold the parents accountable for their children's irrational behavior.''

I tear off a bite of roast beef sandwich and masticate for all I'm worth. Hey—there was nothing *irrational* about agreeing to marrying Greg. I've had one irrational moment in my entire life, and that took place ten years ago, in a cluttered supply closet smelling of musty mops and Lysol and Aramis. I catch on quick, as they say, and *that* lapse of judgment has not been, nor will it be, repeated. Obviously, considering the events of recent days, I cannot always prevent my being made a fool of, but I can at least control my contribution to my own downfall.

In the meantime, Phyllis is waving away my mother's half-assed apology with another smile and some murmured reassurances about her understanding. But the damage has been done. True, after this afternoon, I probably will never see Phyllis Munson again. But I wouldn't have minded leaving things on at least something of an up note, for crying out loud. But noooo, my mother has to open her big mouth and screw everything up. As usual.

This is exactly what I was afraid would happen, because it always does. It simply never occurs to Nedra that she doesn't have to voice every thought that goes tromping through her brain. I really don't give a damn if she hates Greg's guts—I'm not exactly in a forgiving mood myself—but why take it out on the man's mother?

Not to mention her own daughter?

I'm so upset, I can barely get down more than ten or twelve bites of the chocolate mousse Concetta has brought out.

Suddenly I realize Phyllis is saying, her voice tinged with sadness, "You have a wonderful daughter, Mrs. Petrocelli, which I hope you realize," and I nearly choke on what I now realize is the last spoonful of mousse.

Fortuitously, Concetta picks that moment to appear with the extremely welcome news that Bill is waiting for us out front. My mother and I both spring up from our chairs as if goosed, although for very different reasons, thanking our hostess for the lovely lunch as we angle ourselves in the direction of the doors.

"No, please," Phyllis says, rising to her feet. She's around the table in an instant, her hand grasping mine. "Would you mind," she says with a fixed smile for my mother, "letting Bill show you around the house and grounds? And you can assure him his father won't be here, that he called and said he wouldn't be home before dinnertime.'' Then the smile zings to me. "I'd like a minute alone with Ginger.''

Four

"And then what happened?"

It's the next afternoon. Sunday. Terrie is looking at me with huge black eyes across Shelby's Danish contemporary dining table in the three-bedroom West End Avenue apartment Shelby's in-laws bought for some ridiculously low ground-floor price when the building went co-op in the early eighties, then "sold" to Shelby and Mark for an even more ridiculously low price when they decided life was better in Boca. My cousin, a pair of tortoiseshell barrettes holding back her perky little blond bob, sits on the other side of the table, a forkful of Nonna's ravioli poised exactly halfway between her plate and her mouth. Her expression is equally poleaxed.

I'm still shaking from yesterday. After Bill dropped me and all my junk off about four, then took Nedra (note to self: research feasibility of having some old gnarled Italian female relative put evil eye on own mother) on to her place, I played about a million games of FreeCell on the laptop, went to bed, got up, played another million games of FreeCell, finally deciding this definitely called for an emergency Bitch Session.

Shelby, Terrie and I have been calling these with sporadic regularity for probably twenty years, or approximately for as long as we've known that meaning for the word. Bitch, not years. Rules are simple: anyone can call one at any time, no low-fat food items allowed, and whoever calls the session gets the floor first. In the past ten years, I think I've called maybe a half dozen, Shelby none, and Terrie approximately five hundred.

And yes, I know what I said, about preferring to handle crises from the comfort of solitude, but these are extenuating circumstances. First off, it's a known fact that too much FreeCell causes brain rot. And second, these two women are like extensions of my psyche. They'd only nag the hell out of me until I spilled my guts anyway. A favor that, in the past, I have regularly returned.

It's definitely weird, the way we're so close, since we're all so different. But we go way back—Shelby and I to birth, practically, since we're first cousins and only three months apart in age, with Terrie joining us in kindergarten. I suppose we initially glommed onto Terrie because she'd regularly beat up the other kids who'd hassle Shelby—who was eminently hassleable in elementary school—thus taking the pressure off me to do something for which I have no natural proclivity, namely, shedding blood. Especially my own. As for why Terrie, with her sass and street smarts, hitched up to a pair of white wusses…well, that's a no brainer. We kept her supplied in Twinkies and Cokes for at least six years.

In any case, even after we grew out of needing her protection—Shelby grew into a Cute Little Thing and wormed her way in with the popular crowd, while I went on to cultivate the fine art of the Cutting Remark—we remained friends. The kind of friends who can say anything to each other, and do, which means we regularly tick each other off but we always get over it. All through adolescence, Shelby and I looked to Terrie to pave the way for us, a role Terrie was more than willing to accept. Not to mention reporting back to the troops, who'd listen in silent, envious awe. Or disgust. (Took poor Shelby six months to recover after Terrie described, in minute detail, her first French kiss. Of course, we were only twelve: at that point, we couldn't even imagine a boy's *lips* touching ours, let alone his *tongue*. We got over it.) In any case…Terrie got her period first, got kissed first, got felt up first, got laid first, got married first, got divorced first. Twice. Shelby bested us both only in one category—getting pregnant. Other than death or an IRS audit, I don't suppose there are many firsts left.

So these days we content ourselves with muddling through our lives, dealing with our womanhood and all the crap attendant thereto. Shelby, of course, has been the Resident Married Lady since she was twenty-five; I have, for lo these many years, borne the standard as the singleton; and Terrie has been the switch-hitter, considering herself an expert on both sides.

The Bitch Sessions, and a passion for all things edible, unite us. But these sessions serve more of a purpose than simply outlets for venting and binging, at least for me: I know I can count on Shelby to be sweet, on Terrie to be snide, thus giving me two views of any given situation I may not be able to see myself, even as I know they both only want the best for me, as I for them. Husbands, boy-

friends, jobs, may come and go, but these are my friends
forever.

Friends who, at the moment, are hanging breathlessly on
my every word as I relate the conversation between Phyllis
and myself. I've already dumped on them about my mother,
Greg's phone call, and Bill's flirting—every Bitch Session
needs a little comic relief—although I decided to forgo the
Nick business for now. See, Nick was the main course at
a particularly hot Bitchfest some ten years ago. Dragging
his sorry butt into a conversation now would only raise too
many eyebrows—not to mention rampant speculation—for
my comfort.

Anyway. Terrie, sporting about a thousand sleek little
braids that hit her just below the collarbone, is giving me
her get-on-with-it look. Not one to be rushed, I drag over
the cheesecake. It's presliced. I pick up a slice as if it's a
piece of fruit and bite into it. Much as I adore Nonna's
ravioli, today I go straight for the hard stuff.

"So," I finally say, "after my mother leaves with Concetta, Phyllis leads me into her study. So I figure my best
bet is to apologize for my mother before Phyllis can say
anything."

Shelby pops the fork out of her rosebud mouth. "What'd
she say?"

"Well, she laughed, which was the last thing I expected.
Then she went on about it was just a motherhood thing,
you know. Nedra protecting her pup. Then she says something about knowing all about women like Nedra."

That got a grunt from Terrie, whose beaded braids were
beginning to remind me of a Gypsy fortune-teller's plastic
bead curtain. But don't you dare tell her I said that. "There
are no women like your mother."

"That's what I would have said. But then she
said…what was it? Oh, right—" I take another bite of

cheesecake "—about how when she was in college, she had to deal with all these liberal, feminist types who were convinced she was whoring herself because she did beauty pageants...."

I fade out for a moment, chewing and thinking about Phyllis's pale blue eyes as she spoke, like a pair of small, cautious creatures peering out from behind a thicket of heavily mascara'd lashes.

Oh, they made a lot of noise, and raised a lot of hell, all those women whose families could afford to pay for their education, about women's rights and how people like me were setting the women's movement back by at least three centuries. None of them ever bothered asking me what I really thought, or bothered to consider that perhaps there were worse things in the world than a woman using her looks to get ahead.

I'd caught a whiff of desperation then, which I'd never noticed before, in her voice, her expression, the way her makeup was a little too carefully applied....

Terrie smacks my arm, making me jump. "Hey. Back to earth."

I blink, fill them in, at least about Phyllis's comments. Terrie opens her mouth as if she has something to say, only to close it again. Frowning, Shelby reaches for the cheesecake while there's still some left. As I repeat the conversation as best I can remember it, I realize rehashing it is stirring something inside me, way below the surface, too far down to identify.

"Then she said something about how we all make choices, and that it doesn't really matter what they are, as long as we're happy with them—"

"Well, I think that's very true," Shelby says.

"—that so many women today seem to forget, or perhaps they don't want to acknowledge, that sometimes we

have to take what seems to be a step or two back in order
to get enough momentum to propel ourselves through the
barriers men have been erecting in front of them since time
began.''

''Huh.'' Terrie grabs her own piece of cheesecake, opting as well for the direct-from-box-to-mouth approach.
''Spoken like a white woman who *had* choices.''

''Not as many as you might think,'' I say. ''She didn't
come from money, remember. Which is why she got into
the beauty pageant stuff to begin with. But, anyway, that's
just a sidetrack issue, because *then* she says, out of nowhere, that she just wanted me to know Greg didn't back
out because of anybody else.''

Two sets of eyebrows dip simultaneously.

''I know,'' I say. ''So of course the minute she says that,
I'm like, oh, crap—is she covering up something?''

But Shelby shakes her head. ''No,'' she says, then swallows. ''I don't think that's why he dumped you, either.''

Terrie and I just look at her. Shelby continues eating,
oblivious.

Then Terrie squints at me. ''But you *are* ready to rip his
entrails out, right?''

Shelby glances up for this. I sigh. ''I don't know. I
should be. I mean, I am, but…'' I look from one to the
other. ''I think mostly I'm just confused. And hurt.''

Terrie humphs. Shelby nods, even though I can tell the
whole thing's going over her head. She clearly can't imagine her and Mark ever going through anything like this.

''So,'' Terrie says. ''She know where the jerk is?''

''No. Or so she swears. But then…she said I should forgive him, give him a second chance.''

''Like hell,'' Terrie says. ''Besides, it's kinda hard to
forgive somebody whose sorry ass isn't around for you *to*
forgive.''

I open my mouth to say something, but nothing comes out. I feel Shelby's hand light on my wrist. A light breeze from the air conditioner stirs her hair. "You still love him, don't you?" she asks, a note of hope hovering in her wispy voice. Shelby cannot stand an unhappy ending. I don't think she's ever quite forgiven Shakespeare for *Romeo and Juliet.*

"The man stood her up," Terrie interjects. "What do you think?"

"What's that got to do with how she feels?" My cousin may be the most gentle soul in the world, but that doesn't mean she can't stick up for her convictions. And right now, she's glaring at Terrie like a Yorkie whose chew toy is being threatened. "I mean, Mark once forgot my birthday, and I was so hurt I could have spit. But that didn't mean I didn't still love him, did it?"

I can tell Terrie is fighting the urge to bang her head on the table. Shelby is no dummy, believe me—she'd been a crack editor for a major magazine prior to her deciding to stay home with her first baby—but her eternally optimistic nature has definitely corroded her brain when it comes to matters of the heart.

In any case, I wrest back the conversation, since I called the meeting. "*Anyway,* what I said was, I didn't know what I was feeling."

They're both frowning at me again.

Exasperated, I throw both hands into the air. "Whaddya want me to say? Okay, no, it's not like I expect this to get patched up—sorry, Shel—but I'm not like you, either, Terrie. I haven't had the practice you've had at getting over men."

"Gee, thanks."

"Okay, so that didn't exactly come out right, but you know what I mean." I reach for the cheesecake; Terrie slaps my hand. So I guess I'm stuck with the ravioli. I get up to stick the plastic tub in Shelby's microwave. "In any case, while a good part of me says I should write him off, there's another part of me that isn't sure. I mean, if he should come back."

Terrie is clearly appalled. "You have got to be kidding. You'd crawl back to the skunk?"

"Did I say that?" The microwave beeps at me; I take out the ravioli, sink back into the chair at the table with a disgusted sigh, although I'm not sure what I'm disgusted at. Or with. Or about. My own ambivalence, maybe. Or that Greg's actions have put me into this untenable position. "Of course I'm not about to crawl back to *him.*" I look up, fighting the tears prickling my eyelids. "He humiliated me. If, by some chance, he wants me back, he'd have some major groveling to do. But…"

"Oh, Lord. Here we go." Terrie lets out an annoyed sigh. Shelby shushes her.

"But what, honey?"

"You weren't there," I say. "You didn't see Phyllis's face when she told me that I was the best thing that ever happened to Greg. That I would have been more of an asset to him than he could possibly have understood. That…" I take a deep breath, setting up the punch line. "That women are always the ones who have to *fix* things, that pride is a commodity we can't afford."

"That's true," I hear Shelby whisper beside me, although Terrie lets out an outraged, "Oh, give me a freaking *break.*" Her eyes are flashing now, boy, as she leans across the table and buries herself in my gaze.

"Girl, men have been able to get away with the crap they have for thousands of years because women like Phyllis Munson feel they have some sort of duty to perpetuate that myth. God—it makes me so mad, I could spit." At this, she gets up, grabs her handbag from the buffet along one wall, rummaging inside it without thinking for the cigarettes that aren't there, since she quit smoking a year ago. So she slams the bag back down onto the buffet and turns back to me, one hand parked on her hip.

"What that man did to you isn't forgivable. Or fixable. I mean, come on—he calls you up and apologizes on the *phone?*"

Shelby actually laughs. Terrie and I both turn to her. "Well, of course he did," she says. "He's a man."

"No kind of man I'd want hanging around me, that's for damn sure. Besides, none of us is ever gonna break these chains of male domination and oppression if we don't change the way we think about who's gotta do what—"

"Oh, get off your high horse, Terrie," Shelby says, a neat little crease between her brows. "Women are the peacemakers, honey. We always have been. That's a sociological, not to mention biological, fact."

"And I suppose you think that means we have to kowtow to them on every single issue?"

"No, of course not. But what good does it do for us to back them into a corner, either?"

"Making them accountable isn't backing them into a corner."

Shelby goes very still, then says quietly, "Says the woman who's had two marriages crumble out from under her."

Uh-oh.

I stand up, my hands raised. "Hey, guys? This is supposed to be all about me, you know—"

"Shut up, Ginger," they both say, then Terrie says to Shelby, "And what's that supposed to mean?"

Twin dots of color stain my cousin's cheeks, but I can tell she's not going to back down. "That I've watched you with your boyfriends, your husbands, how every relationship you've ever had has degenerated into a mental wrestling match. How your obsession with never letting a man...control you, or whatever it is you're so afraid a man's going to do to you, has always been more important to you than the relationship itself. No wonder you can't keep a man, Terrie—you castrate every male who comes close.''

Terrie actually flinches, as if she's been slapped. A second later, though, she comes back with, ''You are so full of it.''

''Am I?'' is Shelby's calm reply. ''Then how come I'm the only one in the room who knows who she's going to bed with tonight?''

Holy jeez.

Terrie glares at my cousin for several seconds, then snatches her purse off the chair and heads for the door, throwing ''If you need to talk, Ginge, call me'' over her shoulder before she yanks open the front door, slams it shut behind her.

For a full minute after her exit, the room reverberates with her anger. I'm not exactly thrilled to still be there, either, to tell you the truth, but I can't quite figure out what to do. Let alone what to say.

Shelby gets up, starts clearing the table, her mouth turned way down at the corners. ''I guess things got a little out of hand.''

I lick my lips, get to my feet to help her clean. ''I thought the point of these was to get mad at other people. Not each other.''

On a sigh, Shelby carts stuff into the kitchen. ''I know. But honestly, Ginge...Terrie's attitude toward men sucks. And don't give me that face, you know I'm right.''

I grunt.

Shelby turns on the water, starts to rinse off our few dishes prior to sticking them into the dishwasher. This kitchen does not look like a typical prewar Manhattan kitchen. This kitchen, with its granite countertops and aluminum-faced appliances, looks positively futuristic. I half expect Rosie, the robot from *The Jetsons,* to come scooting in at any moment.

I cross my arms, lean back against the countertop. "She's entitled to her opinion, honey."

"And if that opinion made her happy," Shelby replies, "I wouldn't say a word." She slams shut the dishwasher, looks at me. "But she's not. She wants the world to mold to her view of the way things should be, and since that's not going to happen, she's turning more bitter and cynical by the day."

I humph. "Terrie was born cynical."

A bit of a smile flits across Shelby's mouth. "But not bitter." Then she reaches over, grabs my hand. "The thing is, Greg's mother is right. We are the ones who have to fix things. Forgiveness doesn't make us weak, no matter what Terrie thinks. If anything, it only proves we're the stronger sex." Then the smile broadens. "Besides, if men were left to their own devices, we'd all be extinct by now." She reaches up, brushes my hair back from my face. "You just have to ask yourself if you'd be happier with Greg, or without him."

I knuckle the space between my brows, then sigh. "Well, I sure don't like the way I'm feeling right now. As if somebody ripped off a major appendage."

"Then maybe you should work with that."

"So you're saying you think I should give Greg a second chance, should the opportunity present itself?"

"I'm saying, just because a man is clueless, that doesn't

mean he's hopeless. Here—'' She hands me the ravioli container, now sparkling clean. "Don't forget this."

I take it from her, managing a wan smile.

The instant I step outside, the heat crushes me like groupies a rock star. Taking the smallest breaths possible so my lungs don't incinerate, I troop toward 96th Street and the crosstown bus. After that little scene in Shelby's apartment, I'm more confused than ever. But I refuse to believe my world is falling apart, despite the evidence to the contrary.

Who am I kidding? That was totally weird. Not to mention downright scary. Oh, sure, we've had about a million squabbles over the years, but nothing like that. And you know what? It ticks me off, in a way. I'm supposed to be able to count on Terrie and Shelby to restore my equilibrium when things get a little strange, as they count on me. They're supposed to help me see things more clearly, not scramble my brains.

Well, forget it. Just forget it. I simply cannot wrap my head around this, not today. I am too hot and enmeshed in my own tribulations to care. Tomorrow, maybe, I'll work up to trying to figure out how to smooth things over between them, but not now.

Now, I just want to go home, maybe have a good cry, finish the book I'm reading, even though it's a romance which means it ends happily ever after, which is just going to depress the life out of me. It's hotter than hell in my apartment, but I can strip to my panties if I want to, which, at the moment, is eminently appealing.

I turn east on 96th Street, trek up the hill toward Broadway. A hot breeze off the river slaps me in the back like a nasty little kid pushing me in line. I pass several people lurching downhill toward Riverside Park: a young couple with a toddler in a stroller, a pair of joggers, a middle-aged man with a Russell terrier. Well-dressed, affluent, secure. A far cry from the people who used to inhabit most of these buildings when I was a kid, until gentrification in the early eighties purged the legion of seedy SRO—single room occupancy—hotels on the Upper West Side of their decidedly unaffluent inhabitants.

As I pass the recently sandblasted buildings with their newly installed glass doors, their fatherly doormen, I remember my parents' horror as, one by one, the helpless, hopeless occupants of these buildings were simply turned out onto the streets like thousands of roaches after extermination. Joining the already burgeoning ranks of the homeless, many of them were left with no recourse but to panhandle from the very people who now lived in what had once been their homes.

Over the past decade, the homeless aren't in as much evidence as they were. I'm not sure where most of them went, since God knows there are even less places in Manhattan for the poor to live than there ever were. Even apartments in so-called "dangerous" neighborhoods now command rents far out of the reach of the middle class, let alone those struggling by on poverty level wages. But the dedicated homeless are still around, a life-form unto themselves, with their encrusted, shredded clothing and shopping carts and bags piled with whatever they can glean from garbage cans and Dumpsters, hauling their meager possessions about with them like a turtle its shell.

And yes, they make me uncomfortable, as they do most New Yorkers fortunate enough to not count themselves among their number, mainly because I'm not sure how to react to their plight. I'm as guilty as anyone of ignoring them, of looking the other way, as if, if I don't see them, their problem isn't real. At least, not real to me.

I know the vast majority of these poeple are not responsible for their present condition. Who the hell would *choose* to live on the street, after all? Many are mentally ill, incapable of achieving any success in a city in which that concept is measured in terms most of them couldn't even begin to comprehend, let alone aspire to. Others have been beaten down so often, and so far, over so many years, that I doubt they have the slightest notion of how to even begin digging themselves out. So I do feel compassion. Just not enough to override my inertia. Or my guilt.

I used to think winter was the worst time to be without someplace to go. The wind that whips crosstown between the rivers can be brutal, icing a person's veins instantly. But today, as heat pulses off the cement, as the humidity threatens to suffocate me, I'm not sure summer is much better.

And I suppose I'm thinking about all this because, as I'm standing under the Plexiglas shelter at 96th and Broadway, in a clump of six or seven other people waiting for the bus, one of these men approaches us. I watch as, as discreetly as possible, everyone else casually removes themselves from his path, turning from him, deep in their cell phone conversations, their newspaper articles, their own clean, neat lives.

The urge to follow their lead is so strong I nearly scream with it, even as I'm disgusted at my own reaction. But the man reeks, making it nearly impossible for me not to recoil. As I have most of my life, I wear my shoulder bag with the strap angling my chest to deter would-be purse-snatchers; however, my hand instinctively clutches the strap, hugging the bag to me.

Mine, the gesture says, and I am sorry for it.

I am now the only person still under the shelter, although dozens of people swarm the intersection like lethargic ants. The other bus waiters, undoubtedly relieved that I've been singled out and they can breathe more easily—literally—hug the curb and storefronts a few feet away, still close enough to easily catch the bus when it comes.

The man creeps closer, forcing me to look at him. He is filthy and unshaven, his posture stooped. Nearly black toes peer out from rips in athletic shoes only a shade lighter, a good two sizes too large. I cannot tell his age, but behind his moth-eaten beard, I can see how thin he is.

He holds out his hand. It is shaking. From the heat, hunger, the DT's…? I have no way of knowing. I do, however, feel his embarrassment.

Nedra would have emptied her wallet into that hand, I know that, without a moment's hesitation. But then, my mother's crazy.

I glance away, my mouth dry, then back.

"Are you hungry?" I ask, the words scraping my throat. I notice a well-dressed Asian woman a few feet away turn slightly in our direction. But I only half see her frown, her head shake, because my gaze is hooked in the gray one in front of me, buried under folds of eyelids. Hope blooms in those eyes, along with a smile. He nods.

The rational part of me thinks, I should take him to a cheap restaurant, feed him myself. If I just give him money, what will he spend it on?

And then I think, who am I to judge?

But before I can make up my mind, a cop comes along and hustles the protesting man away, at the same time my bus squeals up to the stop. I board, behind the disapproving Asian lady, who asks me, as we take seats across the aisle from each other, if I was afraid. I say no.

The bus is air-conditioned and nearly empty, and I feel some of the tension that's wormed its way into my head over the past few days slink away. We pull away from the stop; outside the man shuffles off toward Amsterdam Avenue, and my insides cramp.

As unsettled as I feel, as unhappy as I am, I still have a job. I still have a home. I still have my friends and my shoe collection and even, I have to acknowledge, my family. Life might be a little bizarre at the moment, but it's far from horrible.

I pull out my novel, try to reimmerse myself in Gunther and Abigayle's trials and tribulations, which has the unfortunate effect of only yanking my thoughts back to the men-and-women discussion of earlier. At the moment, I have to admit I'm inclined to side with Terrie on one thing: men are expendable. Their sperm might not be, but they are. I personally don't need one to survive, or even flourish. I guess, if push came to shove, I could even go without sex. Nuns do. And it's not as if I haven't had my share of dry spells. And then there's my mother, who's gone without for, gee, how long is it now? Fifteen years?

I mean, really—*are* they worth the aggravation? Because, much as I'm inclined to agree with Terrie's theory about how things *should* be between men and women, I think Shelby's the realist. Oh, maybe there are true equalitarian male-female relationships out there, but by and large, women do have to defer to the men in their lives in order to keep harmony, don't they? At the moment, I'm not sure if this is a good thing or a bad thing, it just *is*. And right now, I don't have the energy to be a feminist. I'm having enough trouble dealing with being a woman.

I give up on the book, stick it back in my purse. The Asian woman gets off at Central Park West; I settle in for the short ride through the Park, as I mentally settle in for the next phase of my life. Tomorrow, I go back to work. Tomorrow, I resume my normal, predictable, pre-Greg life. Selecting wall colors, I can handle. Sketching window treatments, I can handle. Charming the pants off a new client, I can handle. Granted, I'm not exactly eagerly anticipating the idea of facing Brice Fanning—my egomaniacal boss of the past seven years—and his inevitable snideties, but at least my work is one area of my life I can count on. I bring in a helluva lot of business, so we both know I'm not going to leave, and he's not going to get rid of me. So. My plan is to reimmerse myself in my work, which, if not exactly exciting, is at least fulfilling and stimulating. Or at least it was.

And will be again, I vow as another layer of tension shucks off. After all, what's the point of missing what I've never had, right? What do I know about being married anyway? Let alone about living in Westchester? I'm not only used to being single, I think I'm pretty damn good at it.

As of this moment (she says without the slightest shame whatsoever) I'm burrowing so far into my comfort zone, nothing on God's earth is going to blast me out of it.

Not even the memory of a brief, hopeful smile beneath discouraged eyes.

Five

So here I am the next morning, clicking smartly down 78th Street in my tobacco-colored linen sheath (short enough to be chic but not slutty) and my new Anne Klein pumps, my fave Hermes scarf billowing softly in the breeze, when I notice a small herd of police cars clogging the street about a half block away. Which would, coincidentally, place them just outside the building where the offices for Fanning Interiors, Ltd., reside. It is not, however, until I notice the trembling band of yellow police tape stretched from one side of the entrance, around the No Parking sign out by the curb, on around the Clean Up After Your Dog sign, then back to the other side of the steps that I get that awful, knotty feeling in the pit of the my stomach that this does not bode well for my immediate future.

Still, I'm doing okay until I see the chalk outline on the

sidewalk. Somebody screams—me, as it turns out—which garners the attention of at least three of the cops and one sanitation engineer across the street. Okay, so maybe my reaction is a bit over the top, but just because I live in Manhattan doesn't mean I stumble across body outlines on anything resembling a regular basis. Besides, I haven't had my latte yet. Not to mention that it's barely eight-thirty and the temperature/humidity index is roughly equivalent to that on Mars. And I was already in a bad mood because my hair looks like Great-Aunt Teresa's wig, which, trust me, is not a good thing.

"Jesus, Ginger," I hear a foot away, which makes me scream again. I pivot, my purse smacking into some gawker who is dumb enough to come up behind a hysterical woman, to see Nick Wojowodski frowning at me. "What the hell are you doing here?"

His rough voice, the creases pinching his mouth, give me a pretty good idea he's not having a wonderful morning, either. My shaking hand clamped around my still-lidded latte, I stare at him, but all I can think of is that outline. And the dark red stain I saw ooching out from it. I shudder, then say, "I work over there."

"Oh," he says, a world of meaning crammed into two letters. By now, onlookers are beginning to clot around us, including a couple of the other designers, the receptionist, the lady who does most of our window treatments.

"Would everybody who works here please go check in with Officer Ruiz?" Nick says, his baritone piercing the burr of voices beginning to make the hairs on the back of my neck stand at attention. I hear a gasp or two, but more out of surprise than actual shock. Or dismay. I don't hear what Nick says next, or what anybody else says, either, because my stomach has just dropped into my crotch and I'm thinking that shape of the outline was suspiciously…familiar. Like it might have belonged to a short-ish, balding gay man of about sixty or so who took great pleasure in regularly making my life a living hell. Next thing I know, Nick is hauling me off to one side, encouraging me to take a sip of the latte. I nearly gag on it, but I manage. It's at this point that I notice the guy who owns the brownstone next door talking to one of the cops. He doesn't look so good.

Nick follows my gaze, turns back to me. "You know that guy?"

"Nathan Caruso. Lives next door."

"He positively ID'd the body," Nick says softly. My eyes shoot to his, dread making my stomach burn.

"Who—?"

"Brice Fanning. Your boss, I take it?"

"*Shit!*"

Nick's expression goes a little funny, which I guess isn't too surprising, considering my reaction.

Oh, God. I am a horrible, horrible person. A man is dead, most likely not from natural causes, and all I can think is, *"This is so freaking unfair!"* Okay, so Brice was a mean, petty little man and I couldn't stand being in the same room with him for more than five minutes—which made weekly meetings a bit problematic—but he was still a human being and thus deserves some respect, at least, if not an indication of sorrow.

I hold my breath for a second or two…nope, sorry, not gonna happen. Didn't like the guy when he was alive, don't much care that he's dead.

If you want to leave now, I'll completely understand.

But, God. Brice *was* Fanning Interiors. I was just a min-ion among many, one of the small army of designers Brice's prestige and reputation were able to keep busy. I'd recently begun to get a serious leg up on establishing my own rep apart from Fanning's, but there is not a doubt in my mind that I wouldn't be living the lifestyle I was today had it not been for Brice's taking me on seven years ago. In many ways, I was indebted to the man.

And now he's nothing but a schmear on an East Side sidewalk. Oy. That poor guy who found him…

"How did he die?" I ask over the constant squawking of the police radio nearby.

Nick's face undergoes this whole impersonal-police-mask thing, but his jaw is stubbled, as if he hasn't had time to shave, and there are bags under his eyes. "I'm not at liberty to say."

For some reason, this irks me. So I tuck one of the many curls that will spring forth like snakes from my French braid over the next fourteen hours and say, "I saw the blood, Nick. Somehow I doubt he was pecked to death by a rabid pigeon."

Nick gives me this look. "Pigeons don't carry rabies. And besides, you're just assuming that was blood."

I give him a look back. Then he sighs and says, "He was shot."

I visibly shudder. I don't much care for guns. Especially when they've been used on people I know. I take another sip of latte. "When?" I whisper.

"Real early this morning."

I look up. "Any witnesses?"

"No."

"The man was shot in the middle of 78th Street and there were no *witnesses*?"

"Another assumption. We *found* him in the middle of 78th Street. Doesn't necessarily mean that's where he was shot."

"Oh," I say, then frown in concentration, which earns me another heavy sigh.

My brows lift. "What?"

"Please don't tell me you dream about being an amateur detective."

"Not to worry," I say. "I don't even like to *read* murder mysteries." He looks relieved, at least until I ask, "I don't suppose you know who?"

Nick shakes his head, rubbing the back of his neck. "Nope. Which means we've got a lot of questioning to do. Starting with everybody who worked for him."

"Today?"

"Yeah, today. What did you think?"

I shake my head. "Sorry, but I've got a ten o'clock, then appointments straight through the day—"

"Ginger," Nick says, patiently. "Your boss is dead. Trust me, none of you are going to be doing any decorating—"

I bristle. *"Designing."*

"—whatever, today…"

But before we can pursue this conversational track, another cop calls Nick over and I'm left entertaining a sickening sense of foreboding.

People are milling about, looking more put out than concerned. I let out a heavy sigh of my own, then take a tissue out of my purse, spread it on the step of the town house next door, and plunk down my linen-covered tush. Perspiration races down my back.

My poor little brain goes positively berserk. Dead people tend to do that to me. Especially dead people who had help getting that way, even if I couldn't stand them. Brice Fanning might have been a brilliant designer, but he drove his employees *nuts.* I have never met anyone whinier, or pickier, or less inclined to give the people who worked for him the respect or recognition they deserved. The only reason most of us put up with him was for the money, as well as that reputation thing. But I think it's safe to say once the shock wears off, he won't be missed.

Except then, because my brain is already on overload and I tend to have an overly active imagination anyway, I think, gee, what if Brice didn't bite the big one because somebody simply hated his guts? What if there's some crazed person running around who has it in for interior designers? A client displeased with her faux painting job? A homophobe? An architect?

Or maybe his murder is even more random that that. Maybe somebody just did him in for his Rolex or something?

Carole Dennison, Brice's top designer, joins me, although she doesn't sit, out of deference to her vintage Chanel suit, I imagine. How can she not be dying in that jacket? She digs in her LV purse for a cigarette, lights up.

"Great way to start the week, huh?"

"Might rain later, though," I say. "Maybe cool it off a little."

She laughs, a raspy, braying sound that always makes me feel better. Carole has worked for Brice for about a hundred years, although, if the lighting is subdued and her makeup is thick, she only looks sixty. Ish. I like Carole a lot. She's a tough, ballsy broad who doesn't take anything off anyone, while instilling the unshakable conviction in her clients that nothing is impossible, given enough money. I started out at Fanning's as her assistant, in fact, and learned more from her in one month than I'd learned in all my years of design school. We're fairly close, enough that I'd even invited her to my wedding. So I've known for a long time that one of her major gripes was that, even though she brought in more business than any three of us put together, Brice refused to make her a partner. She'd also confided in me that she didn't dare go out on her own, that Brice threatened to make her life a living hell if she did.

She crosses her arms, squints over at the herd of police cars. "If you ask me, I think it was that last lover of his."

I'm not sure what to say to that, so I leave it at, "Oh?"

"Yeah. Bet you anything. Jealousy, pure and simple, since Brice took up with someone new about a month ago." She looks at me. "Did you know?"

I shake my head. If I didn't care about the man, I sure as hell wasn't interested in his love life. Then, for a couple minutes, we make appropriate noises about how shocked we are, how stunned, how grossed out, both of us avoiding the one question hovering at the forefront of our thought:

What does this mean, job-wise?

Finally, because I can't stand it anymore, I say, "So. Do you have any idea how the business is set up? I mean, in the eventuality of, um…" I gesture lamely toward the chalk mark.

Carol thoughtfully pulverizes the cigarette stub beneath her twenty-year-old black-and-beige Chanel slingback. To my shock, a tear streaks down her carefully foundationed cheek.

Uh-oh.

One acrylic nail—a subdued cinnamon color, square-tipped—flicks away the errant tear before it leaves a visible track in her foundation. She struggles for obvious control for a minute, then says, "Max told me—"

(Max Sheffield, Brice's accountant. And I think Carole's lover at one time, although I can't confirm that.)

"—that he'd tried for years to get Brice to make provisions for the business to continue in the event of his death or incapacitation, especially after it took off the way it did in the late eighties. He suggested making the business a partnership with his senior designers, if not a corporation, or at least leaving it to someone in his will. A friend or family member, anybody.''

She lights up another cig and shakes her head, her Raquel Welch auburn hair shimmering in the hazy sunlight filtering through the buildings. "He refused. Said when he died, the business died with him."

My immediate future flashes before my eyes, and it is bleak. "Which means?"

"Which means, as far as I understand it, we'll all get whatever is currently due us and that's it. Whatever's left goes to pay outstanding bills, and if there's anything left after that, the money goes to some obscure charity."

My blood runs cold. "But what about our clients?"

Pale, glossed lips quirk up in a humorless smile. "They're outta luck. And so are we, unless we all manage to find jobs with other firms." She shrugs. "Get out your cell, honey, and start making calls."

A great tiredness comes over me, followed almost immediately by a lightbulb flashing on in my head. "Hey— why don't you start your own firm?"

Carole huffs out a stream of smoke that mercifully blows away from me. "Even ten years ago, I might have. But I'm going to be sixty-five in November. Way too old to start a business now. But why don't you go into business on *your* own, designing accessories or something? The Jorgensons are still talking about that set of iron and marble tables you designed for them, Jesus—how long ago was that? Four years? You know your talent is wasted picking out wall colors."

I smile wanly. "Hell, I haven't designed anything in probably two years."

"Well, you should." She hisses out her smoke, tosses the second butt out past the curb. "You want to work for someone else the rest of your life?"

"Forget it, Carole. This gal doesn't do Struggling Artist."

"Chicken," she says.

"But a chicken who eats."

Of course, after today, that may not be true, which is why I suppose we both go silent for a little bit. Then Carole says quietly, "This hasn't been a very good week for you."

There's an understatement.

"Although—" she looks in the direction of the outline, her mouth pulled into a grimace "—I suppose Brice's week has been worse."

I grunt.

For reasons I can't begin to decipher, Nick decides to question me last. Since it has been decided that the entire building needs to be considered the crime scene—the firm's offices took up the bottom two floors and the basement, while Brice lived in a very posh apartment on the third floor—we all had to schlep to the substation for questioning. I've never been inside a police station before, hope to hell I never have the privilege again. As far as the decor goes, suffice it to say it looks like every colorless, utilitarian police station you've ever seen on TV. In other words, not worth describing.

It's now nearly noon. I've made my dreaded calls to cancel my appointments, sidestepping the real reason for standing up my clients—as per Nick's instructions—by alluding to a personal emergency. Which wasn't exactly a lie, since, although the situation clearly had more of an impact on Brice than it did me, I was definitely facing a real emergency.

My stomach growls—the latte is long gone, and I hadn't eaten breakfast. Carole's in with Nick now; I decide the world won't collapse if I run down to the restaurant on the corner and snag a sandwich to bring back with me. The sergeant at the desk has other ideas.

"Uh, no, Lt. Wojowodski says you're to stay put until he's done with you."

I sigh. "Can I order in?"

His face screws up for a second, then says, "Yeah, I s'pose so." He pushes a couple of mangled photocopied menus in my direction. "Here. Live."

I pick a deli a couple blocks away, order a roast beef on rye with mustard and a cherry Coke, then decide to order another sandwich and a coffee for Nick. Why, I have no idea. Just one of those seize-the-moment kind of things. And, natch, I no sooner hang up the phone when Carole emerges from the interview room and Nick gestures me inside.

"I'll call you when your food comes," the sergeant says, and I nod.

"Have a seat," Nick says as I enter, so I do. Again, we're talking boringly typical, here. Table, couple of chairs, a two-way mirror. At least the air-conditioning is decent, for which I'm very grateful.

Nick sits down on the other side of the table, flipping over a page in his notepad. I frown.

"You look beat," I say, and his head snaps up. Then he drags one hand down his face, muffling a wry laugh.

"They called me in at five-thirty. I wasn't supposed to be on duty until eight, but with summer vacations and everything, they're short-handed. I'd just gotten to sleep around three-thirty, four."

"Up because of another case?"

After a far-too-lengthy pause, he says, "No."

Heat stings my cheeks. "Oh," I say, completely unable to stop the images that flash through my head. So I clear my throat and say, "Am I under suspicion for real this time?"

Nick's expression turns just this side of blank. "No more than anybody else who worked for Fanning. This is just a preliminary investigation. Information gathering, y'know?" He straightens. "Although I can't prevent you from having an attorney sit in on this with you, if you want."

I laugh. "Let's see…do I own a gun? No. Do I even know how to fire a gun? No. Was I anywhere around 78th Street at the time of the murder? No, again."

A half smile tilts one side of Nick's mouth. "This guy have any family that you know of?"

Something—his lack of enthusiasm, maybe—tells me Nick's asked these questions a dozen times already. "Never heard him mention anyone, although I don't suppose that means anything."

"No."

"There were lovers, I know, but nothing long-term." I hesitate. "I suppose you know he was gay?"

"Yeah, kinda figured that out from the earlier interviews. You know any of these lovers' names or their whereabouts?"

"Haven't a clue. Brice never…entertained during work hours. He didn't keep his homosexuality a secret, but he didn't make an issue of it, either. I guess he figured it wasn't anybody's business but his own."

More notes. Then, "You know anybody who might have it in for him?"

"As in, an enemy?"

"That'll do."

"Well, nobody liked him much, if that's what you're asking."

He writes that down. "Did you?"

"Hell, no. He was a total jerk."

His gaze meets mine. "That could be incriminating, you know."

"Like I'm worried. Look, he treated his clients like gold and his employees like dirt, and everyone in the industry knew it. Maybe he didn't have any actual enemies, but he sure as hell didn't have many friends, either."

He nods, as if he's heard this before. "How long have you worked for him?"

"Seven years."

Nick narrows his eyes at me. "You worked seven years for a man you didn't like? Why?"

I shrug. "The money. The prestige. A healthy survival instinct."

A knock on the door interrupts us; it's the sergeant, saying my food's here. I go out, pay the delivery man, bring the bag back inside.

"I got you a roast beef on rye," I say, emptying the contents of bag onto the table, "and a coffee. Hope that's okay." The resulting silence makes me lift my head. "What?" I say to the obviously dumbfounded male in front of me.

"You got me lunch?"

"Yeah. So?"

"Why?"

"Because it's lunchtime and I figured you were probably hungry?"

He continues to stare at me, then cracks a grin. "You tryin' to influence an officer of the law?"

"No. Trying to feed one." I push the wrapped sandwich toward him. "There's a pickle, too. Which I'll take if you don't want it—"

"No, no, I like pickles." He stares at the sandwich, much like Adam must have the apple.

"Hey." I lean over, nudge the sandwich an inch closer. "I'm Jewish *and* Italian. You don't stand a chance."

After a moment, another slow grin slides across his face. Chuckling, Nick unwraps the sandwich, takes a huge bite. "You know—" he manages to say with his mouth full "—if you turn out to be the perp, I'm gonna be real ticked at you."

The interview lasts another ten minutes, maybe. I tell Nick what I know about Brice and his life, which isn't much. Slouched back in his chair, silently chewing, he watches me—for telltale body language would be my guess—occasionally jotting down something I say. Something tells me he's good at what he does. Dedicated. Focused. I sure as shootin' wouldn't want to do it, but I have to admire his selflessness.

Suddenly he leans back in his chair with his arms crossed over his chest. "Okay, that's it."

"We're done?"

"For now."

I reach behind me to unhook my purse from the back of the chair. "Hey," Nick says softly. "You okay?"

His expression, when I turn back around, is thoughtful. "More or less," I say. "I still think I'm maybe a little in shock, that it hasn't sunk in yet."

"I'm not talkin' about this. I'm talking about the other."

"Oh…that." My hand drifts up to fiddle with my hair, then I shrug. "I'm coping. Or at least I was until a few hours ago. But, hey—" I spread my hands "—life goes on, right?"

He grunts.

"What about you?" I try a smile. "I guess you're doing okay in the romance department, huh?"

"C'mon," he says, getting to his feet. "I'll see you out.

You at the same place, if we need to get in touch with you again?''

"Oh. Um, sure." For some reason, his dismissal throws me off balance, although I recover enough to give him my cell phone number, which he scribbles on the next blank page along with my name.

We walk down the short hallway to the front desk in silence, in front of which a uniform is struggling mightily to hang on to a wriggling, snarling, furry sausage with twin radar screens on its head.

"Hey, Lieutenant—be *still,* you stupid mutt!—we found this in Fanning's apartment. Scared to death, damn thing nearly took off my hand when I tried to catch him."

"Ohmigod!" I say on a gasp. "It's Geoffrey! Brice's corgi!"

Relieved brown doggy eyes meet mine. But with a slight edge. Sort of a cross between *Thank God* and *It's about damn time.*

"You know this dog, lady?"

"Of course I do." I reach for the dog, whose enormous ears immediately tuck against his skull like a pair of dragon wings. Nick grabs my wrist, yanks back my hand a second before Geoff's tongue makes contact.

"Jesus, Ginger—you wanna lose a finger?"

"Honestly, you'd think *you'd* know a submissive pose when you saw it," I say, twisting my hand from Nick's grasp. I go for the dog again, who has turned into a shuddering blur in anticipation of sympathetic human contact. "I'd forgotten all about him!" I turn to Nick. "Brice used to bring him down to work with him sometimes." I look back at the poor orphaned creature, who is slathering my hand with hot dog spit and giving me one of those I'll-do-anything-you-say-just-don't-send-me-to-the-pokey looks.

Uh-oh.

"He looks like an irradiated rat," Nick observes. Geoff growls. Took the words right out of my mouth.

"You got any idea what we should do with him?" Since the officer is looking straight at Nick when he asks this, there is no reason for me to feel that the question is somehow directed at me. "Y'know, until we find out if the victim had indicated any preference as to the dog's disposition?"

I just keep scratching Geoff behind the ears, refusing to look at anybody else.

"I suppose the best thing would be to just keep him at the pound until we find out," Nick says.

The officer looks at me. Nick looks at me. The two vagrants seated on the bench five feet away look at me.

And don't even ask me what the dog is doing.

"Stop staring at me like that!" I snap, at the dog mostly, but I make sure everybody else gets their fair share of my annoyance, as well. "Hey," I said to Geoff, "the pound is great, you know? You'll get fed every day and there's all those delicious doggy smells and everything. And it won't be forever. Just until they find out who Brice wanted to get you…."

I feel myself falling into those limpid, pleading brown eyes. And I can hear the questions: What if the keeper is mean? What if the food sucks? What if nobody cleans my pen and I have to sleep with my own poop?

"It's going to be fine," I say, because I think I really need to hear those words right now and nobody else seems to be forthcoming. "After all, this is a New York City agency, right? What could possibly go wrong?"

Out of my sightline, somebody laughs. And Geoff slowly lowers his little chin onto the cop's arm and just…stares.

No. *No.* Okay, so maybe I always wanted a dog, but God

knows I do not need one now, not even temporarily. My life is a shambles, I just lost my job, I like the option of being able to sleep past 7:00 a.m. if I want to....

And will you be able to sleep at all knowing that if somebody slips up, somewhere along the line, Geoff could accidentally get sent to pooch heaven?

The dog gives a heartfelt sigh. Almost as heartfelt as the one I give immediately afterward.

"You guys got a piece of rope or something I could use for a leash?"

Three people take off like a shot to do my bidding. A minute later someone thrusts an actual leash into my hands, although one clearly designed for an elephant.

I hook the lead to the dog's collar; we walk outside, the leash dragging between us like the chains on Marley's ghost. Geoff doesn't seem to mind. In fact, now that his immediate needs have been met, he doesn't seem too torn up over Brice's death, either.

Nick frowns down at the dog. "Are his ears supposed to be that big?"

The dog looks up at me. "Ignore the clueless man," I say, then squint at the clueless man. "Well, I guess we'll be moseying along...."

"Hey, listen...would you like to maybe go get a cup of coffee or something sometime?"

My brows go up. "As in, a date?"

"As in, a cup of coffee."

Nick's eyes are even bluer in the daylight. With that beard shadow, he looks positively dangerous.

I glance away, the heat and sun stinging my eyes. Geoff tugs on the leash. "Just a second," I say irritably, and the dog heaves a sigh, flopping down in the scrap of shadow at Nick's feet.

"It's about whoever kept you up—" I blush "—until 4:00 a.m.?"

"Dammit," he mutters under his breath. "What is it with women that they assume if a man asks them to have a cup of coffee with him, it means he's coming on to them?"

"Oh, I don't know…experience?"

That gets an exasperated sigh. "Okay. You just bought me lunch. Did that mean you were making a play for *me?*"

"Of course not! That was just a…a friendly gesture."

"So how is this any different?"

"Because it just…is." I cannot believe he doesn't get this. "Hey, I didn't make up the rules. But I do know what they are."

He crosses his arms. "And some rules don't make any sense."

"You really expect me to believe you just—*just*—want to be my friend?"

"Yeah. What's so strange about that?"

I manage not to roll my eyes. "Uh-huh," I say. "You can really look at me and not think of sex."

"I really can," he says, too quickly, which somehow doesn't reassure me the way I think it should.

"I see."

"Oh, for chrissakes…"

"What?"

"You should see the look on your face, like I just insulted you." His mouth gets all twisted up. "A guy cannot win, you know that? If he lets a woman know he thinks she's hot, she goes off on one of those 'men just want one thing' tirades. If he says he's *not* attracted to her, she gets all depressed and wonders what's wrong with her. No matter what we do, we're screwed."

Had to admit, he had me on that one. "So…what *does* it mean, if a man says he's not attracted to a woman?" I mean, God knows, I've heard that enough in my life. Figured, seeing's as Nick seems to have pondered the subject in some depth, I might as well get some insight.

"It means *he's* not attracted to *her.* You know, because maybe the timing's not right, or he's got somebody else…whatever. Doesn't mean she's not attractive." Although this is accompanied by a sheepish grin and a half shrug. "Necessarily."

"But not in this case?"

God, I am so pathetic.

"You're fishing," Nick says.

"After the week I've had, you better believe it."

He chuckles. "No, Ginger, not in this case. In your case, I'd have to say on a scale of one to ten, you're maybe…an eight?"

Hey, I'll take it. Catherine Zeta Jones, I ain't.

Then he says, "So what about you? You think of sex when you look at me?"

What I'm thinking is, my goodness, it's warm out here.

"No," I say, because I really want that to be the truth. "After what I've been through, I might not think about sex ever again."

He raises a "yeah, right" brow but says, "So what's the problem?"

The problem is, I'm sure there's a catch here somewhere. And it's driving me nuts that I can't see it. "Gee, I don't know…I mean, I've never had a guy friend before. Not a straight one, anyway."

"So maybe now's your golden opportunity. Look, Ginger, I don't cheat on my girlfriends—"

Which naturally leads me to wonder just how many of those there have been over the past ten years.

"—ever. I *like* you. We're *family,* for God's sake. And yeah, to answer the question lurking in that female brain of yours, I'd tell Amy if we...had that cup of coffee. Or whatever.''

Now, see, it's that *whatever* that makes me nervous, because I do not want to want *whatever*. Ever. Because I know what Nick Wojowodski's *whatever* is like...

And I need to seriously get over myself because the man has someone with whom he shares *whatever* on probably a very regular basis and what the hell is going to happen over a lousy cup of coffee in a crowded diner?

"I gotta go," I say, fully aware that I haven't answered Nick's question.

"Sure," he says after a moment, his hands in his pockets. "You take care, okay?"

Tell me I did the right thing.

Geoff makes a beeline for my couch the instant I open the door to my apartment. Defying every law of physics heretofore discovered, he hauls his legless body up onto the couch, where he collapses, panting so hard I'm afraid his lungs are going to burst. Camel-colored dog hair and dog drool on red velvet. Oh, yeah. That'll work.

Too tired and hot and frazzled to care—it's just for a few days, and I vaguely remember how to operate a vacuum cleaner—I dump my purse on the counter, notice I have a message on the machine. Tough. It can wait. Right now, my priorities are water, rip panty hose off body, and pee, in that order.

My turning on the kitchen faucet brings Geoff off the sofa and into the kitchen like a flash. I find a plastic bowl, fill it for him, put it on the floor, grab the largest tumbler I own, fill it for me, put it to my lips. The next minute is filled with the sounds of off-sync gulping. If I get a stomach cramp from drinking too much too fast, I really don't give a damn.

Water sloshes in my stomach as I walk over and switch on the fan. After carefully aiming it toward my crotch, I hike up my skirt and divest myself of the nylon torture devices, then zip barefoot into the bathroom. Apparently my activity has prompted a similar urge in my new roommate, because he's now whining at the door.

"Forget it," I say, shucking off my soaking-wet dress and slip. "You piddled like three hundred times between the police station and here." (Yes, we walked. Don't ask.) I am now standing in my underwear in front of the fan, willing the sweat to evaporate. The dog, who had resumed his frantic panting, now sucks in his tongue, looks at my breasts and cocks his head, perplexed.

"Take my word for it. They're there."

Geoff does the canine equivalent of a shrug—*Sure, honey, if you say so*—then heaves himself back up onto the sofa.

Men.

Marginally cooler than I was five minutes before, I yank on a short sundress, grab a cherry Coke from the fridge, and plop down beside the dog, deciding I need to take stock of my situation *á la* Bridget Jones.

Okay. Lost: Fiancé, one. Job, one.

Gained: Dog, one. Possible male friend, one. But only if I get brave enough to test those waters, which isn't likely. So maybe I should scratch that off the list.

Holding steady: Apartment, one. Mother, one (big sigh here). Grandmother, one. Friends who aren't speaking to each other, two. Other friends, enough. Money in bank—I get up, dig my checkbook out of my purse, go back to sofa—enough to tide me over for a month, maybe. With whatever I get from Fanning, another month, maybe a bit more.

So, all in all, things could be worse—

I hear the neighbor's phone ring. No, wait, that's mine.

I hunt down the cordless, find it stuffed behind the sofa cushion with the remote and three Häagen-Dazs wrappers. I answer just before the machine picks up.

"Ginger, hi! It's Annie Murphy!"

Uh-oh. This is the woman I sublet the apartment from, remember? In five years, she's never called me once.

"Annie!" I say brightly. "Hi...um, did you get my last check okay?"

"What? Oh, yeah. That's not why I'm calling. I left a message on your machine, but figured I'd try again, since this is important..." Geoff plops his furry chin on my bare leg. Ick, ick, ick. I push him away, just as I hear Annie say, "God, I really hate to do this to you...."

Six

"I cannot believe she only gave you two weeks."

A too large University of Michigan T-shirt flopping around his hips as he works, Ted shovels far too many sliced carrots into the sizzling wok. When I presented my little terror-stricken self at his door a half hour ago, dog in tow, Ted ushered us both inside, gave me a Dasani and Geoff a pat on the head and insisted we both stay for dinner. "What *did* she expect you to do? And she does understand that all the furniture is yours, right?"

On top of everything else, this latest blip on my radar screen has basically fried my brain. I'm too stunned to even sigh, even though it's been several hours since Annie's call. Who would've guessed that, after five years of designing costumes for movies out on the West coast, she'd get a sudden offer to oversee the wardrobe for one of the soaps

taped here in New York? Since her mother had been ill fo
some time, Annie grabbed the opportunity to be closer to
her family again. And naturally, she wanted her apartmen
back.

What could I say? *It's mine now, you can't have it?* This
isn't like finding a ball on the playground. Or somebody
else's boyfriend. For one thing, the place is hers technically
anyway, since her name's on the lease. And my staying
there as long as I had was a fluke. Neither of us foresaw
that six months would stretch to five years, but it did and
now she's coming back and I can add homeless to jobless
and loveless on my list of indignities.

I fiddle with my cute little Nokia phone, lying in front
of me on the bar. I had to bring it, you know, in case Nick
might call. About Brice or the dog or something. And I'd
told him I'd be available. "Yes, she knows the furniture is
mine. Says she can pick up a few pieces once she gets
here."

Peppers and broccoli join the sacrificed carrots. "God,
that just bites." No argument there. Ted glances over his
shoulder at me. "You sure you don't want something
stronger?"

I shake my head. I'm still not sure I've worked all the
champagne out of my system yet.

Ted's cargo shorts ring. He hauls his cell out of one of
the pockets, answers it, never missing a beat with his stirring. From the living room, I hear Alyssa giggle, Geoff yip.
Maybe, if nobody claims Geoff, I can talk Ted into taking
him. Of course, their twin Siamese cats—who have been
sitting up on the highest shelf of the glass étagère and willing the dog to die ever since we got here—might not think
that's such a hot idea.

Randall drifts into the kitchen, his cell phone glued to
his ear, sighing a lot. Talking to his mother, I gather. Some-

thing about his younger brother Davis moving to the city, her wanting him to stay with Randall until he finds his own place. Needless to say, Mr. Still-in-the-Closet is trying to talk her out of it. My hunch is he's not winning. He plants his fine jeans-clad butt on the stool next to mine, pinching the space between his brows.

Ted finishes his conversation and comes over to the counter, setting his phone down to pick up a ceramic serving bowl. "Hey, honey—cheer up. We'll fix it, I promise."

That brings a smile to my lips, albeit a very small one. "That's very sweet, Ted. But right now, I don't even think I can find the pieces of my life, let alone put them back together—"

With a heavy sigh, Randall plunks down his phone on the counter. Those Nokia folks are really raking it in, boy.

"Let me guess," Ted says, shoveling sauteed stuff into the bowl. "We're having company next week."

"I tried to talk her out of it," Randall says to Ted. "I really did."

Ted carries the bowl out to the dining table at one end of the living room. "Hey, you're the one with issues about this. *I* don't have any problem with your brother staying with us. But then, *I* don't have any trouble admitting I'm gay."

"That's because *your* mother is dead."

Unperturbed, Ted returns to the kitchen, gently smacking Randall on the shoulder as he passes. "And telling your mother won't kill her, Rand."

"Like hell it won't."

Oh, goody. A distraction.

"Oh, come on," I say, reaching over to snitch a piece of mushroom Ted somehow missed. "Shocking our parents is part of our job description." The mushroom disappears into the great void under my rib cage. With everything I've been through, I shouldn't be hungry. Yeah, well, tell my stomach that. "Davis fulfilled his quota by being the first kid in three generations on either side to get a divorce, right? And what have you done? Diddly squat. So the way I see it, you're way overdue."

Randall sighs. "You've got a serious screw loose, you know that?"

"Hey, I'm not the one pretending to be someone I'm not."

I catch the glance that flutters between the two men at that, but before I can pin them on it, Alyssa and Geoff wander in to see what's holding up dinner.

"All I've got is veggies," Ted says to the dog, then looks at me.

"Don't ask me. I have no idea what he eats."

Ted reaches into the bag of carrots sitting on the counter, hands one to the dog. Geoff sniffs it, slides his gaze over to me.

"That's it for the moment. We'll get you the real stuff later, okay?"

The dog sighs, then gingerly takes the carrot. He stands there for a moment, the thing dangling from his mouth like a cigar, before dejectedly hauling it over to plop down on the Berber carpet underneath the coffee table. After staring at it for a good minute, he finally, with a huge sigh, braces it between his paws and starts chewing, but his expression clearly says, "You have got some *serious* making up to do."

"I can't believe you won't be living across the hall anymore," Alyssa says, sidling up next to me. Her mouth is all twisted up. "That so totally sucks."

I sling one arm around her slender waist, pull her to me. "I know. But we can still get together, you know. Wherever I live."

She eyes me speculatively. "You mean that?"

"Of course I do."

She wanders back out into the living room; I give the guys a what-was-that-all-about look. Ted sighs.

"Her mom's got a real bug up her butt about something recently. New boyfriend or something, never seems to have time for her own daughter. And Lyssa's at that age when she's beginning to have all these what's-going-on-in-my-body questions, and worrying about boys, and I can tell she doesn't think I could possibly know anything about boy-girl relationships."

I smile. "Well, do you?"

"More than I'd like to, honey, believe me. But anyway, back to you, since Mr. Randall here seems to think that denial is healthy—"

"Screw you," Randall mouths. Ted ignores him.

"—I can't do anything about the job, that's true. And God knows, I wouldn't begin to try to sort out your love life. But let's put our heads together about the apartment situation—oh, God!" He smacks his palm against his forehead. "I am so slow today! Jerzy told me Mrs. Krupcek's place will be ready to show tomorrow or Wednesday, if I knew anyone who was interested. And I bet he could swing it so you wouldn't even have to put down a deposit."

For a couple hundred bucks' finder's fee, our super has been known to give the head's up when one of the apartments becomes available. This suits everyone, since his little service saves the brokers the trouble of listing—

Realization dawns.

"Whoa, hold on—what happened to Mrs. Krupcek?"

Ted looks up, frowning. "You didn't hear? She died. A week ago, something like that."

Tears pop out of my eyes. "She *died*? Mrs. Krupcek *died*?"

This is far too many dead people in one day.

"She was ninety-eight, honey," Ted says gently. "She went in her sleep."

"Ninety-eight?"

"Yep. And healthy as a damn horse up until the very end."

"Oh." I let out a shuddering sigh. Well, that's not so bad. Besides, I don't think I exchanged ten words with the woman since I moved in, so it's not as if this is a personal loss. But still. "Who...who found her?"

"Her granddaughter. When she came to check on her that morning. Anyway, it's a one-bedroom, which would be nice, but since it's in the back, it probably won't cost you any more than what you're paying now. So you should go ask Jerzy. Tonight, preferably. Okay, let's eat."

See? Without even trying, things were beginning to get back to normal.

"Did you just say three *thousand* a month?"

"And it is steal at that, you should grab it, I already have five other people asking me about it." Jerzy grins, showing me his gold tooth. I have no idea how old this man is. Forty? Sixty? Hard to tell with the dyed hair. "But I give you first crack because I like you."

I ignore that. Jerzy leers at anything with boobs. Or reasonable facsimiles thereof.

"Let me get this straight—you're telling me three thousand bucks a month for an apartment that gets approximately five minutes of sunlight a day?"

"Hey, you want sunlight, move to New Mexico."

Everybody's a smartass, sheesh.

"Two thousand," I say.

He laughs.

I bite my lip. I have no job. I have no idea if, when, or

where I'll find one. But I've looked at the ads—got a paper when I went to the store to buy five different kinds of dog food in the hopes that Geoff would eat at least one of them—and I know what rentals are like. I also know there are plenty of idiots who'd sell their souls to the devil for the privilege of having a bedroom door.

"Twenty-five hundred."

"Miss Petrocelli, please do not embarrass yourself like this. I do not set the rents. I only pass along information I am given by manager. T'ree t'ousand, take it or leave it. Although, for you, because you are so nice—" another gold-plated leer "—I reduce my fee from t'ree hundred to two seventy-five."

"It's too dark, anyway," I say, and walk away.

Geoff is waiting for me when I get back to the apartment, ears pricked hopefully. I toss my keys onto the counter and sink onto the sofa beside him. "I didn't get it," I say, and he lays his chin on my knee with a little whine of sympathy.

This is going to be tricky. I have two weeks to find both a job and an apartment. And without a job, it's going to be damn tricky to land an apartment. But I am a plucky little thing, if I do say so myself, and I'm not going down without a fight.

So I call Terrie, figuring I'd fill her in on the events of my day as quickly as possible, since God knows I do not wish to rehash them any more than necessary. Only I no sooner get started than she goes, "You know, just once it might be nice if you ask how somebody else is doing before you go layin' your whole sorry life on a person's head, you know?"

Then she hangs up.

And that really freaks me out, because she's never done anything like that before. I almost call her back, except I realize I am on serious crisis overload right now and am in no fit shape to help anybody deal with theirs.

So then I call Shelby, only Mark answers and says, in what sounds like a tight voice only I can't quite tell because one of the kids is screaming in the background, that she's gone for a walk—at 8:00 p.m.—as if that's a perfectly normal thing for Shelby to do. He'll have her call me back, he says, clearly not interested in my plight—even though I haven't had a chance to tell him I *have* a plight—then *he* hangs up.

Then Terrie calls back, all apologetic, saying she had a really awful day at work (she's a financial adviser and when you hear the headline, ''Stocks fell today in the aftermath of...'' you would do well to give her a wide berth) and she's still all messed up about what happened between her and Shelby, but if I feel like talking, she's there. Now, my options are, saying, no, no, it's okay, we can talk another time, or taking advantage of her feeling guilty for blowing me off before.

I am so bad. But I am also sure she will provide me with ample opportunity to make it up to her in the future.

I cut to the chase.

''Brice was found murdered this morning in front of the offices so I don't have a job and Annie's moving back to New York so I have to be out of the apartment in two weeks, and I think Nick's trying to hit on me only he has a girlfriend and I don't really want to get involved with anybody else, not right now anyway, and especially not Nick.''

I swear I had *no* idea that last part was even lurking in my brain, let alone poised to fly out of my mouth. Good God.

''Nick? Nick who?''

"Wojowodski. You know, from my cousin Paula's wedding?"

"*Broom* closet Nick?"

"Yep."

After a lengthy pause Terrie says, "Kinda took him a while to get around to calling you, didn't it?"

So I bring her up to date.

"Oh," she says, only then there's another really long pause. Then I hear, "You know what really burns my butt? Here I'm thinking I'm fully and completely justified in feeling like shit, but then you come along and shoot that notion all to hell." She sighs. "Jesus have mercy, girl—what else can happen to you?"

"Oh, I forgot. I got a dog."

I hear her laugh. It's not a joyful sound, though. "And how did you manage that?"

So I tell her, ending with, "And I've always been a sucker for brown eyes."

"Uh-huh. And what color are Nick's eyes?"

Didja notice which item on my list she honed right in on?

"Blue."

"Well, I suppose that's something."

"Yeah, well, unfortunately, I've always been a sucker for blue eyes, too."

I hear a loud sigh, then a scraping sound, like a chair being dragged across the floor or something. "Okay, let's take this one item at a time. So, since we're on the Nick subject, we'll start there. Now you say he was hitting on you?"

"Well..." Now I'm embarrassed. "I don't suppose he was really *hitting* on me..."

"Honey, if you can't tell, you really are out of the loop."

"Terrie, I've never been *in* the loop."

"This is true. Okay, so what'd he do or say to make you think he was?"

"He, um..."

"Yeeesssss?"

"He asked me if I'd like to get a cup of coffee or something sometime."

Silence.

"So," I say, feeling the need to get things moving since I'm about to self-destruct, "what do you think that means?"

"That he needed a caffeine jolt?"

"Oh, come on...you don't honestly believe that?"

"No, I suppose not. And you say he has a girlfriend?"

"The kind that keeps him u-um, that keeps him awake until 4:00 a.m."

"In that case, I'd definitely nix the coffee. Except..."

"What?"

"Well, if the only reason—besides the girlfriend, I mean—you're not going out with him is because you're waiting around for Greg to come back—"

"I wouldn't be going *out* with him. *Out* is a movie or dinner or clubbing or something. I may not be clear on whether or not a cup of coffee qualifies as a sexual overture, but I sure as hell know it isn't *out*. I do have that much figured out."

"You do, huh?"

"Yes, I do," I aver with a faux confidence I've fine-honed over the years. "And this has nothing to do with Greg."

"You sure of that?"

"Sure I'm sure."

"Girl, you lie like a rug."

I remind myself that I walked right into this one. "For crying out loud, Terrie—it's only been ten days since the wedding! Besides, what kind of man tries to pick up a woman after questioning her as part of a murder investigation?"

"A horny one?"

"Remember the girlfriend?"

"And maybe he's just telling you that to throw you off the scent. You ever see this so-called girlfriend?"

"Well, no, but…"

"You know," she says as if I do when she knows damn well I don't know bupkiss, "some men do that. Pretend to have a girlfriend so they can sneak past your barriers without you even knowing it."

I frown. "I don't think Nick would do that."

"Why not?"

"I don't know, I just don't. Because he's family. And who the hell's side are you on, anyway?"

"My own. So what was this about Brice getting murdered?"

I'm used to abrupt subject changes with Terrie, but even I find this one a bit jarring.

"Are we finished talking about Nick?"

"Yes. So…?"

So I tell her what I knew about that, too. Which wasn't much. Although I linger a bit on the not-having-a-job part.

"I could get you on here," she says.

"Where, here? In your financial consulting dealie?" I laugh. "Doing what?"

"You type, don't you?"

"You are kidding, right?"

"Yes, baby, I'm kidding. So. You have any idea what you're going to do?"

"Wait to hear from the accountant, go down to unemployment, go look for a job."

"Well, at least you've got a plan."

"You betcha."

"You start looking for a new place yet?"

Considering I just found out this afternoon, this question might seem weird to anyone who doesn't live in New York. Apartment hunting in Manhattan is an activity that consumes the hunter's every waking moment until the new lease is signed.

"Yes, as a matter of fact." I tell her about Mrs. Krupchek. Terrie lets out a low whistle, then says, "Well, you sure as hell can't come live with me. I've just got the one bedroom…"

"I don't want to live with you. I don't want to live with anybody. I like living by myself."

I can hear the sigh of relief on the other end of the line. Then Terrie says, "Look…there's a guy at work who swears by this broker who found him this fabulous place in Inwood Park for like next to nothing."

"Inwood Park?" The northernmost tip of Manhattan. Any further north and you're in the Bronx. And "next to nothing" is a relative concept in Manhattan.

"There are still some great deals up there," Terrie says. But then, she lives in Washington Heights, which is just below Inwood Park. I get nosebleeds when I go up there to visit her. The thought of living even farther away from Bloomie's makes my ears ring.

"Inwood Park, huh?"

"And the Heights. I think he goes up as far as Riverdale, too."

"Bully for him."

After a moment of what I take for annoyed silence, Terrie says, "How much money you got in the bank?"

I tell her.

"Uh-huh. And just how far do you think that's gonna stretch when it comes time to shell out for deposit and first and last month's rent and broker's fees and new bathroom rugs and shit? And you with no job, to boot. So it seems to me you can't afford—literally—to be too fussy." She pauses. "Unless you want to move back in with your mother."

My heart jolts. "Oh, that's low, Terrie. Even for you."

"Woke you up, though, didn't it?"

True. I would live in hell before moving back in with my mother. Which would be the same thing, now that I think about it.

"*Anyway,* Julio swears by this broker. I'll get his name for you."

After we hang up, I realize there is no air in the apartment, even with both the windows open and the fan going. Geoff has abandoned the couch for the middle of the tiled kitchen floor, where he lies, panting and looking at me as if to say, "Maybe this wasn't such a good idea after all."

"Yeah, well, you could be lying next to your poop, you know."

With a little groan, he lays his head between his paws.

Day 3 of the Great Apartment Quest. The broker has sent me out to look at four places. Two had been rented before I got there, one looked like a set for the film *Independence Day* after the alien invasion, and the fourth one, which I actually kind of liked, was five hundred more a month than he'd said.

And, having finally reached Max Sheffield, Brice's accountant, after two days of trying, I have been halfheartedly job hunting as well, since, yes, Max confirmed Brice's will specifically ordered the business to be dissolved after his death. He couldn't tell me much more than that, other than he and the lawyer were working as quickly as they could to sort it all out, that they'd get whatever money was coming to us just as soon as they could.

Ever since, I've been trying to convince myself that I hadn't heard a smidgen of worry in Max's voice, but I haven't been terribly successful. I did, however, inform Max that I had Geoff, so the lawyer could get in touch with me to arrange handing over the dog to whoever Brice wanted to have him.

No news on that front, either.

Nor has there apparently been any further progress with the murder investigation itself. Last I heard, which was the five o'clock news, the police were still asking for anyone with information to come forward, but thus far, all the leads they'd had had fizzled out. I can't help imagining how annoyed and frustrated Nick must be. I mean, I know most murder investigations are time-consuming and frustrating, but I never had a personal stake in one before. Well, *stake* is too strong a word, I suppose. *Interest,* then. I keep thinking I want to help, somehow, which is totally insane, mainly because I'm the least analytical person I know. It used to really get my goat, when Greg and I would watch a movie and he'd figure out the mystery within the first half hour, while I'd still have trouble understanding what had happened after it was all over.

Speaking of Greg and mysteries, still nothing. Phyllis called to chat yesterday, just to find out how I was holding up after she heard about Brice's murder. I hemmed and hawed, did the "everything's fine" routine, even though the woman isn't stupid. How could I possibly be fine, after losing a fiancé and a job in less than two weeks? I didn't tell her about the apartment, though. There didn't seem to be much point. In any case, if she knew anything about Greg's whereabouts, she didn't volunteer, and I didn't ask.

After she hung up, she probably wondered why she'd bothered calling.

Of course, my mother called, too, the first time on Monday night, after the news broke. The first minute of the conversation was spent listening to her berate me for not calling her right away. I did more hemming and hawing, alluding to my being busy. And no, there is no way I'm telling her I'm looking for a new place. I'll call her from the new apartment after I've moved in. Otherwise, she'll not only insist on tramping all over Manhattan helping me look, but will, the entire time, make noises about wasting money, yadayadayada, when I could be living with her.

What else? Oh, I think Terrie and Shelby have somewhat reconciled, or at least so Shelby said when she finally called me back on Tuesday evening. She didn't sound too happy about it, however. Like she was too tired to care. Think the kids are beginning to wear her down.

So, that pretty much catches us up. Other than I'm sick of hearing chipper weather people tossing out phrases like "record-breaking heat wave" and "no rain for the forseeable future." Which, loosely translated, means eight million cranky, gritty bodies trying desperately not to make contact as they mill about through a snot-colored haze during the day and across sidewalks still griddle-hot at midnight. I nearly lost a good shoe yesterday when the asphalt at Lex and 83rd swallowed my heel. And lemme tell ya, you haven't lived until you've had taxi drivers swear at you in a dozen languages.

So basically, my life is still a mess, but I'm plugging along, alternating between abject misery and irritatingly cheerful optimism.

Which I'm guessing is kind of how my furry companion is feeling. At the moment, he's not looking any too cheerful. Which might have something to do with the fact that

he hates everything I've tried to feed him, with the not
surprising exception of steak and chicken. I thought dogs
had appallingly indiscriminating palates, joyfully scarfing
down anything even remotely resembling food. Not Geoff.
To date, I have tried out no less than a dozen different
brands of dog food—dry, canned, and pouched—and all
I've gotten for my efforts is a sniff, a pathetic whimper and
The Doleful Expression.

There might be a solution, but it's one I'd hoped to
avoid. However, I've run out of options, other than either
buying T-bones for this mutt or watching him waste away.
So I drag out my Day-timer, look up the precinct business
card Nick gave me, and dial.

The desk sergeant answers. Guy sounds about as thrilled
as a walrus with hemorrhoids.

"Oh, hi," I say. "This is Ginger Petrocelli, and, um,
see, I'm taking care of Brice Fanning's dog—he's the guy
who was, um—"

"Hold on."

A couple seconds later I hear "Wojowodski" grunted
into my ear.

Damn. Precisely what I was hoping to avoid.

"Nick, hi! It's Ginger."

Silence. "Yeah?"

Never has one four-letter word conveyed so much.

"I'm sorry, I didn't ask to be put through to you, I'm
sure this is something someone else might be able to handle…"

"What?"

Oh, God. I can visualize his whole body going on alert.
He thinks I've got a lead or something. Talk about feeling
stupid.

"See, it's like this…I can't get Geoff to eat—"

"Geoff?"

"Brice's dog?"

"Oh. Right." His voice deflates. "So, what's this got to do with me?"

"Well, nothing, really. Which is why I was just going to ask the desk guy if maybe someone could go over to the apartment, see if there's any dog food. You know, since nobody else except you guys can get in. Because I've tried just about every brand of food I can find, and he's not eating any of it."

"I'll have it taken care of."

Click.

I should be relieved he's not feeling chatty, right?

Forty-five minutes later, my doorbell rings. Geoff lifts his chin off his paws, his ears all aquiver. But it's clearly an effort. Because he's starving to death and all.

"Shall we see who that is? Huh? Shall we?"

Judging from Geoff's expression, I'm guessing he thinks I really need to get a life.

I call down through the intercom, but apparently some trusting soul has already let the person in. I suddenly realize I'm wearing a faded, misshapen T-shirt with dried mango juice all down the front, no bra or makeup, and my hair is pulled back into a ponytail that makes me look like an abused Barbie doll.

In other words, I hope whoever this is is either a female officer or blind.

I open the door.

"Hey, Ginger. Howya doin'?"

Wrong on both counts.

Seven

The only good thing about this, I ponder over my jitter-bugging stomach, is that maybe my present appearance will scare him off. Except then he gives me one of those deadly grins and I inwardly swear.

"You're looking good, Ginger."

"And you've obviously been hitting the sauce," I reply, which dims his smile somewhat.

It's those eyes, damn him, that throw me. That classic heavy-lidded gaze, simultaneously blatant and inscrutable, the blue so clear it seems almost translucent. And the five o'clock shadow. Which, come to think of it, he always seems to have. Of course, for all I know maybe electric razors come with some sort of stubble attachment, giving a guy the option of the chic bad-boy look all day long. And why, pray tell, do so many women—present company included—find that such a turn-on? Like who needs beard burn on their tits?

And don't ask me why my thoughts are going down that path, because I'm not even the slightest bit turned on. Because this is Nick and I'm too hot. *Hot* hot, not horny hot. And then I think, huh—if the man's this sexy when he *isn't* trying to come on to a woman, can you imagine what he's like when he *is?*

It boggles the mind.

Anyway, I eventually tear my gaze away from the eyes and the stubble and…the…mouth…to notice he's lugging an enormous, already open bag of some hotsy-totsy dog food in one arm and a large brown paper bag in the other, from which emanates the aromas of ginger and brown sauce. Geoff has decided this is worth dragging his lazy little butt over to investigate.

I have a bad feeling about this.

I tilt my head. "You brought the dog Chinese food?"

"And I had one helluva time deciding whether he'd like pepper steak or Szechuan beef better," Nick says, deadpan. "So I got both."

With that, he saunters past me into the apartment, where he sets the Chinese food on the counter, the dog food on the floor in front of it. Leaving Geoff to paw and whine at the dog food bag, Nick continues into the kitchen, starts opening cupboards.

"Why do women keep so much crap in their kitchens?" he asks, I'm assuming rhetorically. He's on the fourth cupboard by now and I can tell his patience is wearing thin. "Where the hell are the dishes?"

Of course, I'm still standing in the doorway, my jaw sagging open. Yes, yes, I know he did me a favor, bringing over the food, but that doesn't stop the kick-to-the-gut reaction to having my precious, private space invaded. Sure, I have people over all the time, but...

What Nick just did? Barging in like this? Well, that's precisely the reason I opted for somebody like Greg in the first place. I don't much like being around people who throw me off balance. And if it was one thing I could say about Greg, he wasn't prone to throwing curve balls. Well, with the notable exception of that little number he pulled a couple of weeks ago. But still. Greg never encroached on my space, either physically or mentally—or I, his—except by mutual consent. I was comfortable with that.

I am not comfortable with...this.

Now what? I suppose I could simply thank Nick for personally bringing over Geoff's food, and then politely, but firmly, send him and his Chinese food packing. Or I could grit my teeth and go with the flow, which would be my growling stomach's first choice. Since Nick's already set my table with two stoneware plates and napkins and is now rummaging through my drawers—kitchen, not personal— for serving utensils, I figure Option Number Two is probably the most logical choice. Even if it is making me break out in a cold sweat.

"Why?" I ask.

Nick looks up, shrugs, opens the first carton. He fishes out a piece of something—beef, I guess—and tosses it to the dog, who gulps it down without chewing. "Because I was gettin' off work anyway and figured it was just as easy for me to go look for the dog's food as to assign somebody else to do it. And because it was gettin' close to dinnertime and I figured you might be hungry, too. And since you wouldn't go get a cup of coffee with me, when this opportunity popped up, I said to myself, Hey, why not take advantage of it?"

Against my will, I think about an opportunity that popped up ten years ago which we both took advantage of.

Speaking of invading spaces.

But that was ten years ago. And I will readily admit I encouraged whatever happened between us. I'm not encouraging *anything* now. Besides, I know I'm not the same person I was then. I somehow doubt Nick is, either.

"Does..." I ransack my brain for the name. "Does Amy know?"

"Yeah, Amy knows. I called her and told her what I was doing. We're supposed to get together later tonight, when she gets off her shift at the hospital." His brow knots. "Let me guess. You don't like surprises."

"Not much, no."

"Huh." He jabs a pair of chopsticks at the table, then grins. "Tough. So sit. Eat. You know you want to."

Yeah, I do. But I don't, too.

I inch closer to the table. "You sure it's okay for you to be fraternizing with a possible suspect?"

Shaking his head, Nick sits, begins dishing out rice onto his plate. "You're not a suspect. Your alibi checks out. You got any soda or tea or something?"

I drift to the fridge, frowning. "But I said I was alone. Here, in the apartment, getting ready for work. Nobody saw me. Cherry Coke okay?"

He grimaces, but says, "Fine." I hand him the soda; he pops off the top, then jabs another spoon into the next carton, rooting around in it for a second before dumping whatever it is over the rice. Then he looks up at me, again with that deadpan expression. "Y'know, if you're gonna walk around naked in here, you might want to consider closing your blinds. One of these days, you're gonna give the poor old guy who lives in the apartment across the street from yours a coronary."

When I recover from this tidbit of news, I manage, "Gee, you guys are thorough."

"Your tax dollars at work, ma'am. You like cashew chicken?"

Wow. It's a little surreal, this being-friends-with-a-man concept, but I think I'm beginning to get the hang of it. No, I really do. Hey, Nick's been here for two hours, and my nipples haven't perked up once. Well, not after the first fifteen minutes, anyway. I mean, now that I've actually had a chance to talk to the man, it's so obvious that there is no way in hell anything serious could ever develop between us—Greg or no Greg—I don't even know what I thought I was afraid of. Now, when I look at his shadowed jaw, all I can think of is, sheesh—go shave, already.

But the evening sure hasn't suffered from lack of conversation. I found myself going on about my crazy, disjointed childhood, and in turn, he told me about how gun-shy he was for a long time after his wife left. Of course, I did do the male-female time-continuum conversion, fully realizing that a man's definition of "a long time" rarely coincides with a woman's use of the term. But he really did sound sincere when he said he'd see Paula and his brother Frank with their kids and how much he wants to have something like that, too, before he's too old to enjoy it. The thing is, though, he loves his work (just as I'd suspected, even though why somebody would love to make himself a target is beyond me) and isn't about to give it up, but where's he gonna find someone with the balls—his words—to marry a cop, have a family with him? And I have to admit I thought, beats me, buddy. I sure as hell wouldn't want to.

In any case, he said he thinks maybe Amy is the one,

because she works in the ER, so she's got guts enough to withstand the stress. Maybe.

If you want my take on it, my guess is he's not in love as much as he's simply gotten tired of looking. How do I know this? Well, his eyes don't light up when he talks about her, for one thing. Bet he doesn't know that. What he also doesn't know is that his career is the least of any prospective Mrs. Wojowodski's worries. The Italian side of that family—the side I know and avoid as much as possible—is nuts enough. From what I saw of the Wojowodski clan at Paula's wedding, they're no paragons of sanity, either.

However, it's been interesting, to say the least, getting a male perspective on relationships. I've heard it rumored that men take rejection even harder than women, but until tonight I'd figured that to be just another ploy to get a first date into bed. Fifteen years of dating in this city tends to make a girl a bit cynical. But underneath Nick's tough-cop exterior, when he talked about his wife leaving him, I could hear the hurt.

Not that we're talking a man in touch with his sensitive side, don't get me wrong. I had to strain at times to hear the subtext humming underneath his words. But I did hear it. Or more accurately, felt it.

Anyway, since we spent the last fifteen minutes discussing Gloria, the ex, now I'm talking about Greg, and my own ambivalence. When Nick stiffens, starting in again about how badly Greg had treated me, I can only say, "But what if there's some reasonable explanation for the way he acted? What if his bolting is really a cry for help or something?"

That gets a snort, which only confirms my earlier conviction that this is a pretty typical male sitting across from me.

"Okay, so maybe that's pushing it. But I mean, he didn't actually come right out and say to cut my losses."

"That's called hedging his bets, Ginger."

"Maybe. I'm not saying I'm walking around with my heart on my sleeve. For one thing, too much has happened since then for me to ruminate about that one aspect of my life. But that doesn't mean I can't keep things simmering on the back burner for a little while. Just until I'm absolutely sure."

One side of his mouth hitches up. "Like keeping the stew warm in case somebody shows up for dinner?"

"Something like that, yeah."

He stares at me for a long moment, then says, "I just don't see you as the doormat type, you know?"

My shoulders square. "There's a difference between leaving the door open for forgiveness and being a doormat, Nick." I lean forward, suddenly understanding myself what it is I feel, what it was Phyllis was trying to make me understand. "Greg and I *fit* each other. We wanted the same things out of life, had similar goals, similar outlooks, similar ideals. Yes, I'm confused and angry and hurt about what he did, but that was so out of character for him—"

"In other words, Munson was everything your childhood wasn't."

I start, then nod. "Yes. I suppose he was. Is." I angle my head. "You think that's a bad thing?"

Nick chomps the end off an egg roll, shakes his head, frowning. "I think maybe it's easier for you to stick with what you know than try something new."

One brow lifts. "Says the man who just admitted he was leery of getting involved again after his wife left him."

"I got over it," he says with a grin, then frowns. "Besides, that didn't mean I thought about getting *her* back. What would have been the point?"

I lean back, poking at a piece of limp onion on my plate. "Do you have any idea how few sane, normal men there are out there?"

He chuckles. "You're askin' this of a cop?"

"Then you should understand why it's not that easy for me to just let go."

After a moment he says, "I understand that you're *scared* to let go, yeah."

Okay, time to change the subject. "So. Any clues yet as to who might have killed Brice?"

He studies me for a second. Adjusting to the gear switch, I imagine. Then he shakes his head. "You know I can't talk about that, Ginger."

My brows lift. He sighs.

"All I can say is, we're working on it."

"And the longer it takes, the less likely the case is to be solved."

From across the table, his gaze rams into mine.

"I read that somewhere," I say.

He shovels in one last bite of eggroll, leans back in his chair, his brow crumpled. "It's a funny thing. I started out working in the East Bronx. Back then, murder wasn't exactly a rare occurrence, but we usually had a pretty good idea who to look for. Doesn't mean the cases were easy to wrap up, not with the judicial system the way it is, but at least I could do my part, y'know? We're not talking perps with acutely developed minds. Here, I can count on one hand the number of homicides the precinct handles each year. But I'm dealing with a different breed of killer now, somebody who knows how to cover his or her tracks."

"Are you saying you might not find Brice's murderer?"

His smile was half-assed. "If I thought that, I'd turn in my badge tomorrow. No, I'm not saying that. I'm just saying these cases are more of a challenge. Since I've never been one to do anything the easy way…'' He finishes his sentence with a hitch of his shoulders.

The food goes cold; the conversation eventually winds down. It's not quite eight-thirty when he gets up to leave. As I walk him to my door, I am acutely aware that he's making no move to touch me, not even an innocent graze of my arm. I try to palm off leftover Chinese food—the man brought enough for six people—but he refuses to take it. I open the door; he squats to scratch Geoff's ears, then says, ''You didn't say everything you were thinkin', did you? When I was talking about Amy?''

I give a nervous, startled laugh. ''What makes you say that?''

Nick stands, his jacket draped over one forearm, his hands crammed into his pockets. I'm wondering what he's done with his gun and holster. His eyes bore into mine, not threatening so much as…demanding, in some way I can't quite define. Razor-edged awareness once again shimmers between us, but on a level even more elemental than sex, if that's possible.

''I'm a cop, Ginger. I'm real good at reading body language. And you're pathetically bad at keeping a straight face. So when I was goin' on about Amy, how come you didn't just say what was on your mind?''

Okay, so maybe he's a tad more intuitive than I'd given him credit for.

''I…don't know. Maybe because most men aren't really interested in listening to a woman's opinion?''

One brow lifts, but he doesn't comment. Although I get the feeling it's because he decides not to, rather than because he's got nothing to say.

'''Night,'' he says instead, then turns, his steps sure but tired as he walks slowly down the hall. I watch until he's on the elevator, then turn to the dog, who's standing—if you can call what a corgi does *standing*—in the doorway.

"Did you notice he didn't even suggest we get together again?"

Geoff yawns, completely disinterested.

Which is what I should be, if I was smart.

It's now been a week since I lost both my job and my apartment. My eyesight has gone down the tubes from reading so many classified ads and my cell phone has become permanently attached to my ear. I swear I hear the damn thing ringing in my sleep.

What little sleep I get.

I officially reached panic level two days ago, which is when Max, Brice's accountant, e-mailed me with the joyful news that, despite his having gone over Fanning's books several times, it seems Brice had dipped into a couple of accounts he shouldn't have—probably fully intending to redeposit the money before payroll was due—but the upshot was, he got bumped off before he could do that and basically, there's no money. Not at the moment. Max assured me—as did Brice's lawyer when he called yesterday—that as soon as the assets were liquidated and the creditors paid, the staff would get what was coming to them, but there wasn't anything anyone could do right now. Especially as the police hadn't yet released the property.

This news, on top of everything else, has made me just a hair on the testy side, which is why the creep currently sidling up to me on the midtown subway platform should really think twice before doing whatever it is he thinks he's going to do. I mean, come *on,* do I look like a tourist, what?

My feet are killing me from running twenty blocks in heels in the sweltering heat between job interviews with two different design firms, both of which were impressed with my portfolio but not hiring (which led me to wonder why the hell they made the appointments to begin with), and now I'm on my way to see yet another apartment that, if it's anything like the last six I've seen, will undoubtedly make me puke. And I've missed lunch.

I can sense, more than actually see, that the guy is taller than I am, slender. The platform isn't crowded at this time of day, but it isn't empty, either. And I'm standing within sight of the ticket booth, too far from the edge for some loony to push me onto the tracks. So if this creep is out to mug me, he's got *cojones* the size of basketballs.

I glance over, notice the size Huge skateboard shoes, black and red, new, closer than they were ten seconds ago. My heart rate kicks up just enough to keep me alert as my right hand fists around my purse strap, straddling my torso as usual. But I'm also carrying my portfolio case today, which dangles from my left hand. My grip tightens around that, too.

The guy closes the gap between us; I decide I do not want to play this game. So I turn, startling the kid, for that's all he is, by looking him dead in the eye, then head back for the turnstile.

A second later, I feel a hand land on my butt.

A second after that the kid is sprawled on his back on the platform, grabbing his arm where my portfolio made unerring contact.

"Bitch!" the kid bellows, too late realizing the attendant in the booth is watching with great interest.

I smile at the applause that follows me back through the turnstile and up the stairs. No matter how bad things get, it's moments like this that make me realize why I love this city.

Unfortunately, my euphoria doesn't last. The apartment was, as Terrie would have so succinctly put it, a shithole.

And Annie's going to be back in less than a week now. Six days, actually.

I plop me and my accoutrements on a park bench somewhere in Washington Heights, too tired and dejected to move. I check my watch: six-thirty. There's actually something resembling a breeze stirring, although it's still hot enough to roast a hot dog. Gee. My wedding would have been—I frown, counting—sixteen days ago. Greg and I would have been back from our honeymoon and ensconced in our little—okay, so not so little—Scarsdale love nest for more than a week already. I try not to dwell on the fact that I could have been serving a lovely dinner al fresco right about now. Or getting boffed in an air-conditioned bedroom—

A droopy-drawered teenager ambles by, rap music pulsing from a boom box.

—to Mozart.

I sigh.

To add to my good humor, a funeral cortege crawls by. My first thought is to wonder if the apartment's available.

Well, this will never do. I haul myself off the bench, trying to remember where the subway stop is. Like a dog, I lift my face, decide it's that way (at this point, I don't know from east, west, or whatever). So off I hobble, feeling much like whatever that was that Geoff barfed all over my rug this morning.

After limping along aimlessly for several minutes, I finally run across an old, peanut-size Jewish man out walking his even older cocker spaniel. His yarmulke bobby-pinned to his three remaining strands of white hair, the old man is kind enough to tell me, in heavily Yiddishized English, where the subway stop is. I catch him sneaking a longing look at my legs as I walk away.

I turn the corner at the appointed intersection. The street

stretching before me is almost unbearably clean, as if a batallion of elves pour out of the light-bricked, Art deco-era buildings every morning to sweep. And it's incredibly quiet.

Windowsills bloom with bright flowers in planters. Somebody's had a baby: a bright banner yells It's A Girl! from a first-floor window. On the corner, a pair of middle-aged women, their heads wrapped in scarves, exchange gossip. I hear an excited *"Mazeltov!"* as I pass. One of them gives me a tentative smile. An Asian couple, the woman protectively cradling a tiny baby with a shock of black hair against her chest, laughingly argues on how to set up a recalcitrant collapsible stroller.

I'm charmed.

So when a fifty-ish Hispanic man pops out of one of the buildings, I hear myself asking if he knows, by any chance, whether there are any apartments available.

He studies me, caution simmering his dark eyes—hey, I'd be cautious of me too, the way I look—then nods.

"A one-bedroom on the fourth floor. I'm the super, I can show it to you if you want."

My heart leaps.

"What's the rent, do you know?"

He shrugs. "Twelve, maybe fifteen hundred a month, I'm not sure. Plus utilities. It's a nice apartment. Lots of light. Good closets."

I swear I hear a choir of angels burst into song. I grin.

"Can I see it right now?"

He shrugs again. "Sure, why not?"

"You sure there's nothing wrong with the place?"

Two days later, Randall is sitting on my sofa, sorting through a pile of CDs I decided this morning I no longer want, while, a few feet away, I am piling endless books into one of a dozen cartons I begged off the Kinko's around the corner. A chore that is a true delight, even in the sweltering apartment. Yeah, I thought I'd loved this place—and I did, I really did—but my new apartment...

A rush of pure joy zips through me.

"Rand, it's incredible. The living room is huge, and it faces south so it's light all day long, and there's a whole bedroom with a huge walk-in closet, and a separate kitchen...and all for twelve hundred bucks a month!"

"I don't get it." He holds up a stack of CDs. "I'll take these, if that's okay."

"Sure, whatever."

"There's gotta be something wrong with it. For that price?"

"Well, there sure wasn't anything that I could see. It was just painted, and the refrigerator is relatively new. The stove's on the elderly side and the wood floors are a bit scratched up, but I can deal with that. I can even see the river if I lean out of the living room window far enough."

Randall rolls his eyes. "And it just happened to be available why?"

"That's the remarkable thing. The previous tenant had just moved out a couple days before, broke his lease or something, I didn't get the whole story. Anyway, they'd just gotten it fixed up but hadn't listed it with a broker yet. And that's not all my good news. I got a job, too."

"No shit? Where?"

I name one of the city's largest department stores.

"They had an opening?"

"They did. I start on Monday. Of course, it will take a while to get my commissions perking again, but I'm going to call some of my clients as soon as I get this move done, tell them I'm back in business."

Of course, to tell you the truth, I'm not as thrilled with

this turn of events as I sound. For one thing, I vowed never to work in a department store, catering to little old ladies who just want new miniblinds for their kitchen. But the store's furniture buyer seems on the ball, and one can always special order. *And* if I can get back my clients, it'll be okay. Besides, a job is a job.

Or so I tell myself.

I get up to yank another box out of the pile teetering by the front door, nearly tripping over the dog. I frown. Despite the resolution of the food issue, Geoff is still not a happy camper. I don't think he's sick or anything, but he's not exactly brimming over with joie de vivre, either.

"I think he misses Brice," I say. "Hard to believe, considering the way the jerk treated the humans in his life, but I guess he was nice enough to his dog."

"Some people are like that." Randall gets up, looms over the dog, who rolls his eyes up at him. "You ask me, I think he's just pissed. You know, because his life has been turned upside down."

"Just what I need. A dog with issues. Hey," I say to the dog, gently nudging his rump with my bare toes. He grudgingly lifts his head, blinks at me. "If I can cope with all the upheaval in my life, you can too. You never heard of adaptability, survival of the fittest and all that crap?"

With a soulful sigh, Geoff lets his head fall back to the floor.

"This could spell the extinction of your breed, you know."

Randall tilts his head to one side, surveying Geoff's posterior. "Honey, I hate to tell you this, but this mutt's propagation days are history."

"I know that. It's the principle of the thing. Besides, I hate to see him so unhappy. I can't help but think it's my fault, somehow."

Randall looks at me. "You know, I'm not sure which one of you needs therapy more. Him or you."

"Well, since I can't afford it for either one of us, looks like we're both just gonna have to tough it out." I bend down, scratching Geoff's chest. He seems to struggle with his conscience for a moment or two, then laconically lifts one paw to afford me better access. "I just can't help thinking, though, he's not going to be a whole lot happier with whatshisname."

Turns out the only thing Brice left to anybody was the dog, to some young honey I remembered seeing flitting around the place a few years ago. I mean, after living across from Randall and Ted, who have women making futile plays for them all the time, this guy was a shock. Nice enough guy, I suppose, if a bit rough on the nervous system. I have no idea why he and Brice broke up, let alone why Brice left him the dog. Which is all in theory, at the moment, since the lawyer hasn't been able to get in touch with this Curtiss person, anyway.

I can't quite tell whether I'm going to be happy or not about giving Geoff up. On the one hand, this animal is as demanding as a whiny three-year-old. On the other, he is a good listener. There's something to be said for having someone who doesn't care if you bitch to them first thing when you walk in the door. And he doesn't torment me with well-meaning advice.

Of course, I don't think Geoff really cares. Yes, he listens, but his heart's not really in it, I can tell.

So why the hell am I becoming so attached to him?

"So," Randall says. "You tell your mother yet you're moving?"

I get up, move back to my box, surveying the piles of my life teetering all over the apartment. I had virtually

nothing when I moved in. Now look at all this crap. Ted's
right. I am a packrat. "Are you nuts?"

"She's gonna figure out something's up when she comes
over and you're not here."

"I didn't say I wasn't ever going to tell my mother I'm
moving. Although the idea is tempting. Once I'm in, *then*
I'll tell her. No way am I going to give her a chance to try
to convince me to move back in with her."

"You know, that might not have been such a bad idea.
Until you get back on your feet financially, I mean."

I look up, shoving a hunk of hair out of my face. "Would
you move back in with yours?"

He actually pales. "Not in this lifetime."

"Then I'll consider moving back in with my mother just
as soon as you tell yours you're gay."

Randall glowers, giving me a glimpse of the little boy
he used to be.

"Speaking of which," I say because I'm sick to death
of talking about me, "when's your brother coming to stay
with you?"

"Friday night."

"And just how have we decided to handle…things?"

"The old-fashioned way. By lying through our teeth."

I straighten up, my hands on my hips. "And if that's not
the stupidest idea I've ever heard, I don't know what is."

"Well, nobody asked you, did they, missy?" he says. I
snort. "Look, Ginge, it's just for a week. Al's going to go
stay with her mom. Ted's going to sleep in her room, I'll
stay in ours, Davis will sleep on the sofa bed in the living
room. He'll think we're roommates."

"Like hell he will. Ran, Al's room definitely looks like
the domain of a twelve-year-old girl. Which will not give
the impression you're looking for if you want to pull the

wool over your brother's eyes. Which I think is a dumb idea, anyway.''

"You already said that.''

"Well, it's worth repeating.''

Randall sighs. "We're not stupid, Ginge. We'll put all the girl stuff away.''

"Ran—her walls are *pink*.''

"So we'll keep the damn door closed. It's not like he has any reason to go into Ted's room anyway, right?''

"Did I mention I think this is a dumb idea? However,'' I say over his groan, figuring this is as good a chance as any to spring this on him, "not only is it really none of my business—''

"Thank you.''

"—but since your brother's going to be here anyway, he can help the two of you help me move.''

A frown smushes down Randall's brows. "Say what?''

"I've got it all worked out. I'm renting a U-Haul, see, and I figure if you and Ted can move the big stuff, Terrie and Shelby and I can do the boxes and what-all. I mean, how long can it take to empty a studio apartment? And if your brother's here, it'll go that much faster.'' I smile winningly. "One of you drives, right?''

"Uh, yeah, sure, but…''

"Great. I'll provide all the food and drink you can consume, you help me move. It'll be fun.''

"You know,'' Randall says after a moment, "ten minutes ago, I was thinking how much I was going to miss you.'' He opens the door, steps out into the hall. "I take it back.''

I stretch up to peck him on the cheek. He just rolls his pretty black eyes.

Saturday arrives. And with it, the first rain in a month. I haven't been listening to the news lately, so I totally missed that we were in line to get clobbered by what was left of Hurricane Betsy or Becky or whatever the hell the thing's name is. Damn storm churned right up the coast, stalling out over Long Island.

Today.

And Terrie called at 6:00 a.m., which was not a problem because I'd been up all night packing anyway, to say she had to go into work this morning, to give her a call when we were leaving and she'd meet us at the other end to help unload.

Somehow, she didn't sound all that broken up. And I know how much she hates having to go into work on Saturdays.

Then there's this neurotic dog, who's been cowering in a corner behind the sofa and whimpering for the past three days. Maybe he thinks I'm going to pack *him* up, I have no idea. Poor guy. I've tried several times to explain to him what's going on, but I guess he just can't get past his adaptability hang-up.

Now, having never moved anywhere but within Manhattan, I really have no idea what it's like anywhere else. I assume the chore is not a pleasant one, even in the best of conditions, like sunny weather and being able to back the moving van right up to the door. Here, however, one has to deal with several obstacles not encountered in suburbia, the most crucial one today being that the closest Ted could park the van was down the block. A long, crosstown block. So we decide Shelby—who for some unaccountable reason thought it would be fun to bring Corey and Hayley, her two kids—can stand guard while we move everything down to the lobby, which fortunately is a good four times the size of my apartment. Once my worldly possessions are amassed, *then* we can cart everything to the van, like a line of ants. With any luck, the rain will have let up by then and/or a parking space closer to the building will open up. Not that I'm holding my breath, but where there's life, there's hope.

But first, we have to get all the stuff down to the lobby, which brings us to Obstacle Number Two: the elevator. Which a) holds four people comfortably, six in a pinch, and b) moves at the speed of a ninety-year-old woman with a walker.

For some reason, other tenants don't take kindly to having to wait while some idiots on the eighth floor load a million boxes onto the elevator, especially when they discover there's no room for them when it gets to their floor. People who before either ignored you or mumbled greetings to you in passing are now out for blood. You realize once you leave, you will never be able to return.

But the best part of all this is the discovery that my sofa bed, which weighs seven million pounds, will not *fit* in the elevator, even on its end. So the guys—including Davis (who is one serious hottie, by the way)—have to carry it down the stairs.

All eight flights of them.

I mentally calculate just how much pizza and beer it's gonna take to make amends. I doubt there's that much beer in all of Manhattan.

Panting, sweating and occasionally swearing, they've made it to the fifth floor. We're all wearing T-shirts and shorts in varying degrees of disrepute, humidity and sweat having long since plastered fabric to bodies. In this weather, my hair is doing a Medusa number around my head, bobbing annoyingly as I follow the guys down the stairs, directing them around the two landings between each floor. I know it's just a sofa, but it's mine and I love it. Besides, I can't afford another one.

"Watch out!" I shriek for probably the tenth time as the sofa back comes perilously close to impalement on a metal newel post. My voice, not the most dulcet at the best of times, reverberates in the stairwell like a kid banging pots with a spoon.

All three men glare at me.

"Hey," I say cheerfully, "look at it this way. It's the last thing out of the apartment. Well, except for the dog, and he can walk."

"Hey," Randall shoots back, inching backward down the stairs, his hands full of lead-weight cranberry velveteen, "am I mistaken—careful, Dave, damn!—or do we get to reverse this process when we get to the other end?"

"Well, yeah—oh! Watch out for that corner! But that's only four flights, not eight."

"Four flights *up*," Ted squeezes out past the corded muscles in his neck.

Well, there was that.

Maybe I could feed them all next Saturday, too.

We finally reach the lobby, sofa and male tempers all reasonably intact. Shelby is ineffectually nagging the kids to quit climbing the stacked boxes. A woman I've never seen before comes through the door, her umbrella streaming. She pauses, peering with some interest at my wing chair, then points to it, addressing whoever will answer her.

"How much you want for the chair?"

"I'm not selling it! I'm moving it!" I snap, which sends her scurrying off to the now-free elevator.

I convince myself it's not raining as hard as it was, even as I unwrap the first of several plastic drop cloths I purchased from the hardware store the minute it opened this morning. While the men discuss strategy—they're all being really good sports, I have to say—I shroud the sofa in two of the sheets, securing the plastic with twine. I survey my handiwork, inordinately pleased with myself. Hey, if this new job doesn't pan out, maybe I could start my own moving business—

"Ginger? What the hell is going on?"

I whip around to meet my mother's stymied expression.

Eight

"**B**us*ted*," Randall mutters behind my back.

"Nedra! What on earth— W-why are you here?"

The entire bottom tier of her long denim skirt is soaked. "You weren't answering either of your phones," she says, folding up her Totes umbrella. "I got worried." Her gaze flicks over the lobby, then back to me. "Now I know why. You're moving?"

I nod, feeling, oh, about six?

"Were you planning on telling me?"

"Of course I was."

"While I was still alive?"

All eyes, including the doorman's, are zipping back and forth between us.

"It was kind of a last-minute thing," I say, then explain what has brought us to this moment. More or less.

Nedra looks hurt. ''I don't understand. Did you think I would disapprove or something?''

I link my arms over my damp rib cage, purse my lips. Decide to tell the truth. ''No. I thought you would nag me about moving back in with you. I just couldn't handle that.''

Her brows lift. ''Which? That I might nag you, or living with me?''

''Either. Both.''

''Holy crap!'' Ted suddenly yells, digging in his shorts pocket for the keys. ''Two people just moved their cars from in front of the building at the same time! Go, go, *go!*''

Like crazed lemmings, we all rush outside. It's still pouring, but we don't care. Ted dashes up the block to get the van while the rest of us literally stand in the blessed double space, yelling at anyone fool enough to try to park there. Shelby's kids are jumping up and down underneath the awning in front of the building, laughing. My mother turns to me. Rain is streaming down her face like tears.

''Can I help, or will that crowd you too much?''

We see the van gliding up the block, cutting through the drenching rain like a red-and-silver whale.

Lightning flashes; the kids scream. Thunder rolls across the city, shuddering the ground. ''You really want to?'' I yell as the rain comes down even harder. We're all now soaked through.

''No,'' my mother says sarcastically. A minivan tries to nudge us out of the parking spot; she bangs on the hood.

''Don't even think about it!'' she yells, and the flummoxed man behind the wheel jerks the steering wheel in his split to pull away. Nedra whips off the soaked scarf, starts to laugh. ''It was like this on the day your father and I got married, did you know that?''

We step up onto the sidewalk so Ted can park the van.

"No," I say, backing underneath the awning. Rain sluices off it in a solid sheet, the noise obliterating further conversation. I realize how little I really know about my mother, how I've avoided letting her get close enough to share her life with me.

I shiver, only partly from the rain.

She nudges my arm. I look over. "You should change out of those clothes."

"What's the point?" I yell back, and she nods in agreement. We all go inside; the men decide to load the big items first, work the smaller ones around them. Ted and Randall argue good-naturedly, like an old married couple. I wonder if they've caught Davis's curious expression as he watches them.

Busted, I think to myself with a smile.

Many hours later Davis wanders into my new kitchen, Bud in hand, squatting down to pet the dog, who has refused to let me out of his sight since his supposedly harrowing trip between Ted and Randall in the van. (I have tried to explain to him that he wouldn't have much cared for sharing a taxi with two overexcited children, but to no avail.)

"Hey," he says, standing to lean against the counter, watching me teeter precariously on a step stool as I stuff rarely used kitchen tchotchkes on an uppermost shelf. "Need some help?"

"Uh, sure. Hand me that cappuccino-maker, would you? No, not that. Yeah, that." He hoists the thing up to me, grinning.

"Women sure do collect a lot of shit."

"Well, hell—gotta fill up all these cupboards with *something.* How's the party holding up?"

"Since it's been a good half hour since anybody's said

anything worth remembering, I think it's just about petered out.''

I really like this guy. He's charming, without trying to be, if you know what I mean. I chuckle, rearranging everything I'd just put on the shelf to accommodate the newest arrival. Gee, no more having to deal with all of Annie's stuff in my cupboards. And I haven't seen a single roach. Hallelujah.

It took nearly forty-five minutes to get up here in the horrible weather, then another two and a half hours to get everything off the van and into the new apartment, even with two extra sets of hands. And wouldn't you know, the rain stopped at the precise moment the very last box had been hauled inside. The good news is, however, that it's drastically cooler. I've got all the windows open, letting in a sweet-smelling breeze.

My mother and Shelby et al left in a shared taxi some time ago, leaving me with Terrie, Davis, Ted and Randall, all of whom I think are just too tired to move. I can relate. I'm about to topple over myself. But I'm determined to get my kitchen in at least reasonable order before I go to bed.

I smile down at Randall's brother. "Hey. I can't thank you guys enough for all your help."

Oh, man—breath-stealing smile alert. He's got the same dimples as Randall, the same long, curly black lashes. But he's got hair.

"My pleasure," he says, his voice deep and laced with humor. "So tell me," he says, lowering his voice. "Is it my imagination, or are my brother and Ted more than just roommates?"

I freeze. Damn. "What makes you think that?"

"Not being born yesterday?"

I heave a great sigh. "I told them they'd never get away with this."

"Especially as I found out Ran was gay years ago."

I nearly fall off the ladder. "You're kidding?"

"Nope. But I figured, if he didn't want to talk to me about it, that was his business."

"He's afraid if your mother finds out, it'll kill her."

"Wha—? Oh, for God's sake—who the hell do you think told *me?*"

I clamp my hand over my mouth to stifle my laugh. Then I lower it and say, "And how *is* she taking it?"

Davis shrugs. "Disappointed, I guess, that he won't be giving her grandchildren. But more disappointed that he doesn't feel he can tell her."

"She won't confront him about it?"

"No way. Says it's up to him."

A burst of laughter floats in from the living room. Davis smiles.

"They seem well suited for each other." There's an almost wistful quality to his voice that makes me look at him. He smiles, shakes his head. "No, I'm not gay. Just lonely."

"Randall said you were divorced?"

He takes another swig of his beer. "For nearly five years. It doesn't get any easier."

I think of Nick. Of Terrie. Of myself, although I'm not quite in the same league. You let yourself hope, then trust, then believe…and then it all crumbles out from under you, leaving you afraid to hope and trust and believe, ever again.

"Ted and Randall have been together for about six years," I say quietly. "Ted's got a daughter, Alyssa. She lives with them, usually."

One side of Davis's full mouth tilts. "Which I'm assuming accounts for the pink bedroom?"

"And the Barbie collection and the 'NSYNC posters."

"They must've hidden those," he says, giving me this

smile, and I think, duh, lonely man, new in town, is flirting with recently jilted single woman. Only that thought no sooner shuffles past when he says, "Your friend Terrie..." He rubs the back of his neck. "She seeing anybody?"

Oh, of course. Double duh. Even as busy as I've been all afternoon, I did catch Davis's attention drifting to Terrie off and on. But then, *every* man's—every straight man's, anyway—attention drifts to Terrie eventually. Especially when she's wearing a tank top that keeps slipping off one shoulder and shorts that are probably banned in some countries.

"Not that I know of," I say casually. I descend the ladder, start unwrapping dishes, beginning to hallucinate about being in bed. Which is another thing. I now have a bedroom, but no bed to put in it. I glance over at Davis. "Why don't you ask her?"

"I don't want to come on too strong."

"A word of advice. Terrie doesn't do subtle very well." Davis grins.

"And another word of advice." I pad over to the door, check to make sure she's out of earshot, then look back at Randall's brother. "She's divorced, too. Twice."

Davis sighs, then nods. "Move with caution, in other words."

"Yeah. Which is tricky to do while not being subtle."

"I think I can handle it," he says, then strolls out of the kitchen.

An hour later in The Night That Will Not End. The guys have finally left; Terrie hasn't. I can tell she wants to talk. Since I've dumped on everybody else a million times the past few days, I don't have the heart to kick her out, even though my brain shut down at least two hours ago.

She's sprawled on my sofa, one foot on the floor, a half-empty wine cooler balanced on her bare stomach. She—or somebody—has stacked all the pizza cartons on the coffee table; I drag in a black garbage bag, dump them inside, collapse onto the wing chair that weird woman tried to buy out from under me.

Geoff trots over to the door and yips.

"Sure, *you're* wide awake and raring to go," I say, my eyes already closed. "What have you done all day besides nap and poop?"

He yips again. I open one eye, peer at him. He looks as though he'd cross his legs, if they were long enough to cross. With a weary sigh, I drag myself back upright, poking among the hundreds of boxes until I find his leash and a cotton sweater which I shrug into.

"I gotta take the dog out," I say to Terrie. "Wanna come?"

"No."

I lean over and grab Terrie's hand, heaving her up off the sofa. "Sure you do. The fresh air'll do you good."

She groans and mutters a few choice obscenities under her breath, but she shuffles into her sandals, grabs her sweatshirt off the arm of the sofa, and follows me. The elevator is waiting for us, as if it's stopped at this floor so many times today it's been reprogrammed to roost here. We get in, slump simultaneously against the back wall. It's a hideous thing, recently enough painted in burgundy enamel that, with all the humidity, is still a little tacky.

"What did you tell Davis about me?" Terrie asks.

Not that I didn't expect this. "Not much. That you were divorced."

"As in, available?"

"That you were divorced," I repeat. "That's a fact. The other's a judgment call. And I don't do those if I can help it."

Between the third and second floor, the elevator shudders ominously. Neither of us flinches. "And that was it?"

"Okay, he asked if you were seeing anyone. I said I didn't think so."

"And that's not telling him I'm available?"

"Not in my book. Now, if I'd said, 'Heck, yeah, that Terrie, she's ripe for the pickin', boy...' now *that* would be telling him you're available."

I can feel her gaze on the side of my face, can tell, that if she weren't exhausted, she'd be angry.

"How's about next time you just stay outta my business, okay?"

"Telling the guy you're not seeing anyone is hardly getting in your business, Ter. Jeez, lighten up already."

The elevator reaches the ground floor; the doors part and we emerge, our sandals slapping against the marble floor as we cross the lobby. The dog is yanking me toward the doors, making me lurch behind him.

"Okay, then, new ground rules," Terrie says as we burst out into the damp, chilled air. Geoff continues to drag me until he can jump off the curb, where he pees for like five minutes. The cold startles me, but not unpleasantly. "I am not interested in meeting a man or going out with a man or dealing with a man and/or his shit, got it?"

"Ever?"

"You got it."

"Davis seems like a really nice guy, Ter."

"Uh-huh. They all do, at the beginning. Then they rot."

"Not all of them."

She gives me a look. "Says the woman who just got dumped by Mr. Wonderful."

I am far too tired to go down that road.

"Besides," Terrie continues, "didn't somebody say Davis was divorced? So right there, what does that tell you?"

"That he was in a relationship that didn't work out? How does that automatically make him a bad person?"

"Doesn't exactly give him high marks."

"Hey. *You've* been divorced. Twice. That make *you* a bad person?"

She opens her mouth. Shuts it again.

"Now," I say because I'm on a roll and I can't remember the last time I've been able to render Terrie Latoya speechless, "if he'd expressed an interest and he was still married, *that* would make him a bad person."

Terrie humphs.

Geoff finally puts down his leg, sighs, then hops back up onto the sidewalk, tugging me down the block. New neighborhood, new smells. Oh, joy. I start walking, Terrie lolling beside me, her hands stuffed into the pockets of her unzipped sweatshirt. An occasional car passes, wicking moisture off rain-sheened streets.

"You know what?" she says, still sounding ticked, but not at me. Not as much, anyway.

"What?"

"The problem is, a man might act all perfect in order to *get* a woman, but once he's sure she's so damn much in love with him she can't see straight, one by one, he lets his flaws outta the closet. And what happens is, the woman just ends up feeling gypped. If not trapped." She shakes her head, her breath leaving her lungs in a rush. "Things'd be a helluva lot easier if they'd just let us see their flaws to begin with, let us decide whether or not it was worth our time and effort to put up with them just the way they are."

"Oh, right." I laugh, which is probably not the smartest thing to do, but I can't help it. "Can you honestly say, if you'd seen the *real* Jarrod and Boyd before you started dating them, things would have gotten as far as they did?"

"Hell, no. And just think of all that heartache I could have avoided. Not to mention the cost of two divorces."

"Okay, so maybe that wasn't the best example I could have used. But…well, how many women have the balls to let a man see the real *her,* either, right off the bat? I mean, I sure as hell don't. Do you?"

Terrie apparently thinks about this for a bit, finally shakes her head. "I see your point."

"Besides, who among us isn't screwed up in some way? I know I am. I'm too controlling, for one thing. And manipulative. And I'm sure I've got other imperfections I can't even see. But I'd like to think I've got some appealing traits, too, you know? *Some* redeeming qualities that would enable another human being to put up with me for the long haul."

Terrie quirks her mouth up at that, which makes me curious, but not enough to get sidetracked. I'm having enough trouble speaking in generalities. But then she says, "I hear what you're saying, but…"

"But what?"

She sighs. "Hell, I don't even know anymore."

We walk some more, I think some more, vaguely amazed to discover a stash of unused brain cells I had not heretofore known existed.

"Try this," I say. "What if there were some sort of full-disclosure clause that came with every new guy you met? You know, like the thingy Realtors have to fill out when they're selling a house? I mean, if you were looking for a house, would you consider one that needs some repairs because it's otherwise in a good school district with a big yard and the price is right? And if so, what kinds of things could you deal with, or overlook, and which ones would you consider a turn-off?"

Terrie swipes her braids back behind one shoulder, her brow knotted. Then she shakes her head. "Nothing."

"Nothing?"

"Nope. I'm strictly an apartment girl. Don't want any old house that's gonna fall down around my ears, or turn out to have termites, or that's gonna require constant babying in order for it to be happy. Now an apartment, something goes wrong, you just call the super and he fixes it for you—"

"Clearly you have lived in better places than I have."

She ignores me. "But you don't have to make a commitment. No commitment, no broken heart."

"What about sex?"

One eyebrow lifts. "Don't have to live in a house to have sex, sugar."

"Very funny. I mean, as in long-term, committed kind of sex."

Laughter erupts from her throat. "Don't need commitment to have sex, either."

"Yeah. But is it as good without it?"

Terrie looks down at her feet as we walk.

"You don't get a pretty backyard with an apartment, either," she says, "but that's a sacrifice you make for peace of mind."

I link my arm through hers, steer both her and the dog around to head back toward my building. "So. Does this mean you're not going to go out with Davis?"

"It does."

"Terrie, going out with the man isn't the same as marrying him."

She laughs, the sound hollow. "I know that look in a man's eyes. It's a hungry look. And not just for sex. That, I could deal with. It's a look that says mortgages and minivans and babies."

"There are worse things in the world."

"Lord, now you sound like Shelby." She turns to me. "Life's not a romance novel. Things don't turn out all right just because you want them to."

"I don't hear Shel complaining."

Now her laugh is harsh.

"What's that supposed to mean?"

"You really think Shelby's happy?"

"Well, yeah. Don't you?"

Terrie purses her lips, looks away.

I have just enough energy left to bristle. "What the hell is this? Jealousy?" Terrie's gaze whips to mine. I don't let the reciprocal anger in it derail me. "You know, this is getting real old, the way you keep letting your own bitterness color your perceptions about other people's lives."

"I am not jealous of Shelby. Or anybody else." But I see her eyes glitter before she turns away. "Yeah, okay, so maybe my past colors my perceptions a bit. But this has nothing to do with me, I swear. I just know what I see."

"And what is that? Hey, if Shel's not happy, she sure talks a good talk."

"Bingo."

I halt, right in the middle of the sidewalk. "You really think that's all a front?"

"Honey, I know it is. People who are genuinely content don't have to talk about it all the time, or feel so damn compelled to make a case for it. All that stuff she said the other night? You really think that was for your benefit? Or even mine? Uh-uh…that was about a woman trying to convince herself she'd made the right choices."

"That's nuts, Terrie."

Terrie shrugs. "Believe what you want to. No skin off my nose. But betcha five bucks I'm right."

We walk in silence for a minute or so, but my head is

spinning. Even if what Terrie's said is true, how would I have missed it? Of course, I have been a little preoccupied of late, between the preparations for the wedding and then the assorted catastrophes that have befallen me since. Still…

"But she hasn't said a word."

Terrie laughs. "You think she's gonna come right out and admit her life is going down the tubes? But did you notice how quiet she was tonight? Looked to me like Little Miss Bubbly done gone and lost all her fizz."

"She's never done well in the heat, you know that. And the kids were totally wired today…" I shake my head. "I figured she was just tired."

"Tired is right. Tired of that life she wants everybody to believe is so damn enchanted."

"You sound angry."

"Well, I suppose that's better than *jealous*. In any case, I'm pissed *for* her. Not *at* her. It's just…shit, I've been expecting something like this for a long time, since we were still kids."

"You have? Why?"

We've arrived back at my building. A pair of low brick walls flank the front step; Terrie lays her palm on top of one of them to check for wetness, then sits down. I follow suit.

"What has that girl ever had to fight for, Ginge? Everything's always been handed to her, everything's always gone her way. I don't mean she didn't work for her grades or her career, because I know she did. But even those weren't the struggle it is for some of us, you hear what I'm saying? Same thing happens when she falls in love. What other boyfriends did she have before she met Mark? I mean, serious ones?"

I think back, then shake my head. "I can't remember."

"That's because there weren't any. She meets Mark, they fall in love, they get engaged, they have the hitchless, tasteful wedding, that apartment lands in Mark's lap, they have two kids, a boy and a girl, no complications, no hassles."

She pauses. "Everything's always fallen right into place her whole life. How could she not expect things to just continue that way? She's conditioned to believe in happily-ever-after, simply because she's never known anything else. She doesn't have the coping mechanism for disaster that I have." With a grim smile, she faces me. "That you have, too. Now."

I think over everything she's said, although I know I am too wiped to absorb most of it. "Naïveté isn't a crime, Terrie."

"No. But it is a liability."

I yawn, shake my head. A shiver raises goose bumps down my arms. I skim my palm along the erect hairs on one arm, trying to order my thoughts.

"You think Shelby's changed?"

"I think life is forcing her to," Terrie says. "Like it forces us all to, at some point."

I frown.

I pass out within seconds of falling into bed a little after one, not even giving a damn that the dog has crawled up beside me. Only I wake up, heart pounding and sweaty, less than an hour later.

This is *so* not fair. I'm exhausted to the point where breathing is a chore. Yet here I lie, listening to Geoff *whup-whupping* beside me in a dream, hyper-aware of every little noise in the apartment. I tell myself it's just the new apartment heebie-jeebies, combined with being overtired. What else could it be?

Maybe I don't want to know the answer to that.

Cursing, I get out of bed, stumble through a forest of unpacked boxes over to the window, where I fold my arms across my sleep T and stare out at the street below. It's begun to rain again, softly.

An odd ache for I know not what takes root in the center of my chest, spreads up and out until my throat clogs, my eyes burn.

This is nuts. I found a great apartment in less than two weeks, I'm no longer unemployed, I'm even over the hurdle about my mother's finding out I've moved. Okay, yeah, there are still some major issues to be resolved, but basically I've yanked back my life from those fickle gods, shown them who's da man. Hell, by all accounts I should feel unbearably smug right about now. Not like, well, whatever it is I am feeling.

Geoff hops off the bed when I pad into the kitchen for a bottle of water. For him, life can be boiled down to one simple equation: kitchen=food. He snuffles at the seam of a closed bottom cupboard, then looks up at me and whines.

"Your food's not in there, doofus. Besides, there's still some in your dish if you're desperate."

He paws at the cupboard. Exasperated, I open it and show him.

"Look. *No food.* Nothing but pots and pans. Happy now?"

I can tell he's not, but he takes his stubby little body off to collapse on the floor nearby with a heavy sigh. I get my water, return to the living room to continue my ruminations. The weird, icky feeling goes right with me.

I feel…disoriented. Off balance. Okay, so I figure part of it's because of what Terrie said about Shelby—even though I'm not taking her at her word, not until I've had a chance to feel Shelby out for myself—but it's more than that. It's Terrie, too, letting a never-before-seen vulnerability leak through. It's Greg not being who I thought he was and Brice getting bumped off and my mother making normal, friendly overtures and my unsettled feelings for Nick (oh, don't look at me like that—you actually *believed* all that crap about my not being attracted to him?) and the fact that—big sigh here—I'm really, really dreading starting that job on Monday.

God. I feel like an earthquake or hurricane survivor or something. Here I've been so busy getting my life back in order, like a beaver single-mindedly rebuilding its broken dam (and yes, I know I'm mixing metaphors, but what the hell do you want from my life? It's freaking three o'clock in the morning), I totally missed the fact that my entire landscape has changed. Now that I've finally stopped to catch my breath, I have no idea where I am. The landmarks are still there, but they no longer seem familiar.

Tears I have not allowed myself since the day after the wedding slide down my cheeks, tears of confusion and frustration more than actual self-pity. I have never been an indecisive person. For most of my life, I thought I knew what I wanted. For most of my adult life, I've managed to get it. Keeping order is what I do. Who I am. Or at least, who I thought I was until about ten minutes ago. How did I manage to miss that my whole world—or at least, the one I thought existed—has changed, that everyone around me is changing, and the coping mechanisms that have stood me in good stead for so many years are no longer working?

Sweet Jesus. What do I do now?

Nine

The following Friday evening, 5:16 p.m. Shelby and Mark and the kids are coming for dinner. They're late, which isn't surprising since I imagine the traffic's pretty weird on the Henry Hudson Parkway right about now. And which is good, because I'm scurrying around the apartment playing Martha Stewart. Okay, my version of Martha Stewart, which is to make sure there's no crud stuck to the silverware, the rug is vacuumed and Geoff hasn't left a barf pile somewhere. It's gotten hot again, not as bad as it was but enough to make my hair bug the life out of me. However, I'm feeling very hostessy in this rayon slip dress I found in a little hole-in-the-wall shop on 181st Street and I even took time to give myself a pedicure, so my toenails are this bitchin' fuchsia color. So you see, I'm trying for upbeat, I really am. But...

Big sigh here.

Okay, this is the thing. You know how I said I was dreading this job? That I had a real bad feeling about it? Well, honey, chalk up one for premonition.

I mean, Brice may have been a rotten, weasely sonuva-bitch, but at least he knew what he was doing. These people have their heads so far up their asses they can see out their navels. A conclusion I've reached after less than a week.

First off, the so-called "designers" are nothing more than glorified salespeople. Which I knew going in, but still. I didn't spend four years in design school and seven years at one of the top firms in the city to follow Suzy and Joe Schmoe back and forth across the furniture floor for two hours while they dither about whether to go with the leather sectional or the English chintz trad sofa and matching love seat. See, I'm not about giving people *choices*. I'm about listening to what they want, taking notes, then saying, "This would be perfect," and they go, "Are you sure?" and I say, "Absolutely" and they take it. And love it. Badda-bing, badda-boom, done, done, done. It's nigh unto impossible to railroad somebody when they're standing in the midst of a sea of a thousand sofas. I hate it, hate it, hate it.

And all for a lousy ten percent, too.

I figure I took in this week, after taxes, all of three hundred dollars. Now, tell me, how far do you think that's going to go in New York? Hell, that wouldn't even cut it in Des Moines. The head of the design studio assured me I'd be able to pull in my goal figures, no problem, even though it would take a couple months before the special orders came in and the cash flow started seriously gushing.

Uh-huh. Um, excuse me, but customers aren't exactly knocking each other down in their split to get there.

You can imagine how wonderful it made me feel when

I told some of the other "designers" where I'd worked before and they all said, in unison, "So what are you doing *here?*"

You can also imagine how wonderful it made me feel when I called up my former clients from Fannings to say, Hey, guess what, I'm in business again, when could we make an appointment? And every single one of them—with profuse apologies, of course—informed me they'd already taken their projects elsewhere.

So much for loyalty.

There's no way I'm going to survive at that place. No *way*—

My buzzer buzzes. I call down, buzz Shelby and the gang in.

And why, you may ask, am I having my cousin and her family to dinner less than a week after moving in?

Why the hell do you think?

Well, actually, there are two reasons. The first is, I still haven't quite let go of that self-fulfilling prophecy theory thing, that people who act as though everything's hunky-dory can make it happen for them. That whole who-am-I-where-am-I-and-where-do-I-fit-in business just gives me the willies. I don't want to think about any of that now, I *can't* think about any of that now, and I figure surrounding myself with people whose situation is potentially more screwed up than mine is a damn fine avoidance maneuver.

Which leads me to the second reason for inviting Shelby and company tonight, which is that, despite my best intentions, my conversation with Terrie has been rattling around in my head like a marble in a tin can since that night we talked. So I've decided to see for myself if Shelby's okay. Hey, I've known my cousin all my life. If there's really something wrong, I'll spot it, sure thing. And tonight, I'm not going to let anything distract me. I've got it all planned, how I'm going to surreptitiously find out what's up.

Of course, if it turns out Terrie's right, I may want to kill myself. Yeah, Shelby might be a little over the top, optimistically speaking, but her marriage to Mark has been my benchmark for Getting it Right for the past six years. I do not want this to be on the rocks, believe me.

But I do want to *know*.

We do lots of hugs-and-cheek kisses when they spill into the apartment, the kids making an immediate beeline for the hapless dog. Who, fortunately, seems to be cool with it. You never know with Geoff. Not that he's ever snippy or anything. He's got far too much class for that. He can, however, be rather cool when the mood strikes. Aloof.

We do the "Do you want something to drink?" routine, I slip into the kitchen to get Shelby a glass of ginger ale, Mark a Scotch on the rocks, all the while watching their interaction. Which seems the same as it's always been, as if the two of them are encased in a sparkling, iridescent bubble of affection. Bound together by invisible threads. Something. Actually, sometimes their cootchie-cooiness drives me up the wall, but tonight I find it reassuring. Shelby seems relaxed enough, giving Mark a smile when he hands her her drink.

I have always thought these complemented each other perfectly, like when, after months of searching, you finally find exactly the right sweater to go with that marked down skirt you bought on impulse, and then the two together become your favorite outfit? Mark's the kind of guy you look at and the first word that comes to mind is "comfortable". Nothing remarkable, lookswise—sandy-blond hair, thinning on top, wire-rimmed glasses over hazel eyes, the beginnings of a paunch—but pleasant enough. A gentle man whose brow crinkles in concentration when you're talking to him, as if straining not to miss a single word. Which I suppose is a good thing for a pediatrician. I'm struck tonight by how much he and Shelby look like brother and sister, since her coloring's very similar.

"What are we having?" Shelby asks. She's wearing a loose, tan cotton jumper over a white T-shirt, expensive leather sandals. A velvet headband holds her hair off her roundish face, making her look ten years younger than she is. "I'm starving!"

Okay, now that's weird. Shelby's no anorectic, but I've never in my life heard her admit to actually being hungry.

"Lasagne and salad."

Hey, I can do lasagne. Especially when it's a pan of Nonna's that she gave me, oh, three months ago? All I had to do was defrost that puppy, then stick it in the oven for thirty minutes, which I do now. My kind of cooking, boy.

The salad is done, the table is set, the kids are occupied… I go back out into the living room, settle into the wing chair. We talk about nothing for a few minutes, warming up the way people do who haven't been together for a while. Also, as nice a guy as Mark is, when the conversation veers down decidedly female paths, he's the type to stand up and say, "Oh, well, I suppose I'll leave you ladies to it," after which he'll kiss Shelby on the top of her head, then wander off to his office or something. Unfortunately, that tactic only works if we're having dinner at their place. Since he's here, he's stuck. And since neither of us want to watch the man go glassy-eyed, we stick to safe subjects.

"So," Shelby says, "how's the new job?"

"You know how first weeks are," I say with a shrug. "Settling in and all."

Her eyes narrow, just a hair, at my skirting the question. Now Terrie would have no qualms about dragging the truth out of me, kicking and screaming, but Shelby knows if something's wrong, I'll come out with it soon enough, whether anybody wants me to or not. Why hasten the inevitable?

The kids get into a tussle about something inconsequential. I get up, give them drawing pads and colored pencils, send them to the bedroom where we can keep an ear out but still play grown-up.

Shelby then volunteers that Mark's been invited to join a consortium of physicians on Park Avenue. She's beaming. Mark makes "It's nothing" noises, but I can tell he's very pleased.

"That's wonderful!" I say.

"Might mean longer hours to start, though," he says, just as Shelby jumps and says, "Oh, my God! What was that?"

I shut my eyes. Just for a moment.

Yes, boys and girls, there is a reason why my apartment was so cheap. Actually, several reasons, the least of which is the family upstairs. I can't quite figure out how many of them there are, or how they're all managing to live in a one-bedroom apartment, but my guess is their previous residence was a bit more rural than this one.

"A rooster," I say.

"A rooster?" Shelby and Mark say together.

"What on earth—oh, dear God!" Shelby says when the thing goes off a second time. "What on earth are they doing with a rooster in a New York apartment?"

"I've decided I don't want to know," I say wearily, getting up to check on the lasagne.

Of course, the rooster isn't the half of it. For some reason these people seem to have difficulty with the concept that, when you turn the water on in the bathtub, it's generally a good idea to keep an eye on it. Three times, it's overflowed in the last week, streaming down my walls and straight into the apartment downstairs (which I gathered from the irateness of the little old lady who charged up here and banged on my door until I thought she'd break it down). The last time, the water came through the light fixture, exploding the lightbulb. While I was sitting on the john. Took me an hour to pick all the glass out of my hair.

"But it's against health regulations to keep farm animals inside city limits," Mark says. I see him look up at the ceiling, which is now shuddering. "And why is it crowing now?"

"Ask the rooster," I say, then add, probably a bit too loudly, "Oh, shoot! I completely forgot to pick up the bread for tonight!"

"That's okay, honey," Shelby says, but I divert her by directly delivering the next line in my script to Mark.

"Would you mind terribly running down the to bakery at the end of the block and picking up a couple of loaves?" I'm already to my purse, digging out my wallet to give him a ten. "Maybe take the kids with you, get them éclairs or something for after dinner?"

"Sure, no problem," Mark says, walking right into my trap. "Where is it again?"

"Just turn right when you get outside, then right again and keep walking. It's about a half block down, you can't miss it."

He calls the kids, refuses my money, disappears.

"Gee. That was subtle."

I turn and look at Shelby, just managing not to blink innocently. "What?"

She pushes a stream of air through her lips. "Yeah, right, you *forgot* the bread."

Okay, so subterfuge isn't my strong suit. But neither do I buckle easily under pressure, which circumstances have given me more than ample opportunity to prove this past little while.

"I did," I say with conviction. "Really. I mean, with everything on my mind, I'm doing well to remember my name." I flounce back into the living room, sink back into the chair, realizing if I say or do a single thing to steer the conversation in the direction I want it to go, she'll *know* I'm lying. Fortunately, I don't have to dangle the bait in front of her, because she just reaches right down in the bucket and grabs it herself.

"Isn't that great, about Mark's new job?"

"Sounds pretty good to me. I mean, it's just what he's wanted, right?"

"Absolutely. And as I told him, since I'm home anyway with the kids, he doesn't have to worry about his hours." Bright smile. "We'll be fine."

I wait. She fidgets with the arm of the sofa, then says, not looking at me, "You want to hear something crazy? The magazine called, offered me a job."

"What's crazy about that?"

She laughs. "I have two children under the age of five, that's what. As if I could go back to work now. As if I'd *want* to. Anyway, with this new opportunity for Mark, it would disrupt the kids far too much if both of us were away—"

And wouldn't you know it, just when things are getting good, Mark and the kids return, laden with bags. Methinks there's more there than a few loaves of crusty bread and a couple of éclairs.

"You know what they had?" Mark says to Shelby as both kids climb up onto the sofa with Mama, chattering like magpies. "Fresh-baked pumpernickel!"

Shelby seems to perk up. "Really?"

"Yep. Weren't you just complaining the other day how

you hadn't had any good pumpernickel in ages? Here.. take a whiff of this.'' He takes the round, uncut loaf from the bag, carries it over to her.

''Oh, God...that smells so good!''

''Didn't I tell you? Huh?''

Shelby giggles, gently swats him on the stomach, then loops her arms around Hayley's waist to return the tiny girl's effusive hug. ''Honestly, you're as crazy as the kids.''

Geoff joins me in the kitchen to help me slice the bread, spread the garlic butter inside. Only he starts in again with his cupboard-clawing routine, which he goes through at least three or four times a day. And each time, as I do now, I open it, show him there's nothing for him inside, then show him his food. Do you have any idea how long it takes a corgi to work his way through a forty-pound bag of dog food?

Shelby wanders in about this time, stares at the bag.

''Criminy. That's the biggest bag of dog food I've ever seen.''

''I know. I'm wondering if the dog will live long enough to eat it all.''

Geoff whimpers.

''Sorry. Just a casual observation.''

''If I may ask a dumb question...why'd you buy such a big bag to begin with?''

''I didn't. Brice did. It was in the apartment after...you know.''

She nods. ''What's happening on that front, anyway?''

I shrug, open the oven door, take out the lasagne, slip in the bread, let the door bang shut. ''You know as much as I do. Probably more, since I haven't seen or heard any news in a week.''

Which topic naturally conjures up an image of Nick, an

image I immediately, with paltry success, attempt to delete from my brain.

"Hey, honey," Mark calls from the living room. "Come see this."

Shelby leaves; I grab Geoff's empty dish from the floor, scoop out a bowlful of food and set it back on the floor, then stand there watching the dog scarf food as though he hasn't eaten since Clinton's first term in office.

The melancholia suddenly hooks one claw around my ankle, threatening to drag me under. I grab a pair of pot holders, carry the lasagne out to the table just in time to see Mark standing behind Shelby with his arms wrapped around her waist, both of them laughing at something the older kid apparently just said. I search my cousin's face, but see no sign that the laughter, or the contentment radiating from her eyes, is false.

Sorry, Terrie, I think, breathing an inward sigh of relief that this one landmark in my life, at least, has remained constant. Except, right on the heels of my relief comes another feeling, not exactly resentful, but sharp-edged enough to be uncomfortable:

That Shelby has what I thought I was going to get, even though I didn't know I wanted it. That her life is basically all mapped out, defined, settled, while here I am, past thirty and suddenly unsure of what I want to be when I grow up.

Or who I want to be.

I plaster a smile to my face. "Hey, guys—let's eat!"

The following Monday, I get home from work, grab Geoff's leash and whisk him outside before he bursts, then come back inside to find three messages on my machine. One is from the caterers, asking—politely—if I'd sent them the rest of their money. One is from the florist, asking—not quite so politely—if I'd sent them the rest of their money. Now, if the universe had gotten its rear back in gear, the next call would have been from Greg saying, "Hi Ginge, just wanted to let you know I've paid all the bills," but, since the universe clearly wasn't interested in being the least bit orderly, the third message was instead from Curtiss James, who had finally answered the messages the lawyer had left about Brice leaving him Geoff.

"Hi, Ginger, we'll be up somewhere around seven-thirty to pick up the dog, but listen, don't get too bent out of shape if we're a tad late, since we're coming all the way from Forest Hills."

Hmm. Does that make him the Queen of Queens?

I glance at my kitchen clock: 7:14. I look at Geoff, who's lolling crookedly on one hip, panting away, his stubby little back paws facing north while the rest of him faces east. My heart cramps. He looks so happy. I've tried to prepare him for what's about to happen, but we haven't quite worked out the language barrier problems. I squat down beside him, stroking those wonderful, ridiculous ears. He snaps shut his mouth, clearly aware that something's not right.

"He's a nice person, I'm sure," I say. "Brice wouldn't have left you to him, otherwise, would he? No, of course he wouldn't." Mindless of my dress and panty hose, I slide my butt down onto the floor beside him, leaning up against the cabinets. Geoff plants the front half of his body on my lap, which isn't a particularly pleasant experience with those bony elbows of his. Especially when a thin ribbon of drool puddles on my right thigh. But I don't care. After tonight, there won't be any ribbons of drool to avoid, thin or otherwise, a thought that depresses the hell out of me.

Speaking of depressing. I have no idea why, maybe because I'm bored out of my ever-loving little noggin at work, but Greg's been on my mind an awful lot the past couple of days. For the most part, that whole episode of my life had congealed into a dull little ache in the center of my chest, but something—maybe watching Shelby and Mark?—has nudged it into life again. I've been so busy just trying to stay afloat that I hadn't fully realized just how much I'd missed him.

Not that I think things will ever go back the way they were. Not now. Intuition tells me too much time has passed, that if Greg were going to repent, he would have done it by now. I keep thinking I should give Phyllis a call, just to check if he's surfaced, but that would sound pathetic. And God knows, I don't want to sound pathetic.

I suppose I could sell the ring to pay the bills?

The doorbell buzzes. Geoff looks up at me expectantly. I give him a gentle hug around the neck, then clumsily get to my feet.

"Hi," says the brightly smiling vision in the hall when I open the door. The vision sticks out a much bejeweled hand. "Curtiss James. You must be Ginger."

Dear God, it's a walking bordello. Skin-tight red leather pants, sheer purple shirt (heavily beaded), flowing print scarf, red cowboy boots. Spiked, bleached-blond hair, but with fashionably dark roots. Many earrings.

I smile, trying not to squint from the glare. "Unfortunately, yes."

"Now, now, Ginger's a great name. After all," Curtiss says, sweeping—and I do mean sweeping—into the apartment, "it certainly did well by Ginger Rogers. Christ, what a fabulous apartment! I've heard great things about some of the places up here, but this is the first one I've actually been in. Ohmigod, is this *Geoffrey?*" Curtiss turns to me, hand on chest. A pinky ring with a rock as big as Central Park winks back at me. "This *can't* be Geoffrey—he was

just this big—'' he spreads his hands six inches apart
''—when I last saw him.''

The dog and I look at each other. Geoff's expression
says, ''You're kidding, right?''

''So…you've already met?''

''Oh, God, yes, although Brice and I were already having
problems by then. I was the one who thought a baby might
help save the relationship. But you know how that goes.''
He squats down, pats the floor in front of him. ''C'mon,
Geoffrey. C'mon, baby…yeah, that's a good boy…''

Geoff has not only gone to Curtiss, but flopped onto his
back to get his belly rubbed. The dog twists his head around
to look at me, upside down.

Traitor.

Still, some of the tension inside me eases at how much
Curtiss actually likes the dog. I mean, if I have to give him
up, I just want to be sure he's going to be loved as much
as I…

Damn.

''I'm sorry it took so long for the lawyer to find me,''
Curtiss now says. ''My honey had a photo shoot in Aruba,
so we decided to make it a working vacation. And God,
did we ever need one!''

A two-parent home is good, right?

''So how come Brice got the dog when you two, um,
split up?''

By this time, Curtiss is sitting cross-legged on the floor
(although how he's managed that in those pants is beyond
me) dragging a set of manicured nails repeatedly across
Geoff's chest. The dog is doing everything but groan.

''I decided Brice needed him more than I did.'' He
glances up at me, his smile a little sad. ''He was a lonely
sonuvabitch.''

''He was horri—'' I catch myself. This man had been

Brice's lover, after all. But Curtiss gives me a surprisingly charming smile.

"Yes, he was. Although with his background, it's not surprising his people skills were a little lacking."

He says this as if I should know what he's talking about. I don't. Nor do I particularly want to know. Because then, knowing me, I'd end up feeling sorry for the man. And *poof!* Years of perfectly justified antipathy would go right down the tubes.

Curtiss gets to his feet, rearranging himself in the pants, then says, "Well, I hate to dash, but Liam's circling the block in the car. So, if you could just give me Geoffrey's things…"

"Oh. Of course."

I've already filled a plastic bag with his bowls and toys and stuff. I get it from the kitchen, digging a pink rubber ball out of the bag. Geoff yips and wags his rump. "Not this time, sweetie," I say over a tight throat, then to Curtiss, "This is his favorite. If I can't get him out much, I toss this for him for a half hour every night. Otherwise, the way he eats, he'd look like a torpedo. Which reminds me…"

I return to the kitchen, lug out the half-full bag of food. It's probably down to twenty-five pounds, but I still feel as though I'm dragging around a dead body. "This is the only dog food he'll eat."

Curtiss eyes the bag curiously. "Guess I won't have to buy any for a while."

"There's a…yogurt container already in it." *I will not cry, I will not cry.* "He gets two scoops a day."

"Got it. Well, honey," he says to the dog, snapping his leash to his collar. "Let's go meet your other daddy!"

I stand at the door, watching them walk down the hall, the bag of food hefted onto Curtiss's nonexistent hip. They reach the elevator. Curtiss shifts the food to his other hip, pushes the button, calls out, "Thanks for taking care of him!"

"No problem."

The elevator grinds into place; the door opens. And just as I'm thinking Geoff doesn't even have the courtesy to say goodbye, the dog swings his head around and looks at me, yips once, then trots onto the elevator.

The apartment seems almost unbearably empty. And quiet. Which is odd considering that, a)I've lived alone for ten years, I *like* living alone, and pre-Geoff, I'd never even had a parakeet to take care of, and b)the people upstairs must be getting ready to sacrifice that rooster, if the vibrations coming through the ceiling are any indication. But like most New Yorkers, I'm pretty good at tuning out noise not directly related to me, wild rumpuses included.

Hunger propels me into the kitchen, where I contemplate dinner. Gotta keep up my strength and all that. Let's see...I root amongst all the few mystery packages shivering in the fridge, my butt hanging out to Jersey....

Well, there's some deli stuff in the drawer that will soon need carbon dating in order to tell how old it is, about three bites of pasta salad, something in foil I no longer recognize, which I rewrap and stick back in. And some lasagne left over from the other night, although after three days, I'm getting pretty sick of it. But—and this is the bright note to the evening—I bought another loaf of that fine French bread, and thus can make some more garlic bread.

So. Pop a serving of lasagne into the nuker, slice up the bread, spread the garlic goop on it, turn on the oven...

What on earth is that strange...pinging sound? Yes...it's definitely coming from the oven. Curious, I open the door—

Something flies out and bounces off my chest. I scream,

throwing myself backward over the step stool, just catching sight of a gray streak zipping across my kitchen floor to vanish underneath the molding at the base of my sink.

It takes me a minute. Then I scream again, jumping up and down and forking my fingers through my hair whilst violently shuddering, vaguely aware of my current resemblance to my upstairs neighbors. After my hysteria runs its course, I drop onto the top of the step stool, listening to my thudding heart as I look over at the cabinet that Geoff had kept pawing at all the time.

And what were the odds Hunka Munka and all the little Muncateers were snickering behind their little furry paws? Or maybe not. Maybe their sentinel's close brush with broilerdom has sobered them somewhat.

I tell myself I'm only imagining the scent of seared mouse fur.

I give up on the garlic bread idea—wouldn't you?—eat the lasagne, the three bites of pasta salad, and half a thing of Godiva chocolate ice cream, then get into my jammies and click on the tube, where I sit, zombie-like (except for the occasional jerking to be sure I wasn't seeing rodents zipping past), until I apparently pass out in the wee hours without bothering to turn off the TV or pull out the sofa bed. At least, such is the state in which I find myself when, at some ungodly, still-dark hour, somebody decides it would be fun to repeatedly ram a four-by-four into my door.

"Jesus!" I yell. "What the f—"

"Get out!" a deep male voice booms on the other side. "The apartment above you's on fire!"

Ten

Talk about your motivational speeches. Now gagging on the smell of smoke, I grab my robe, shove my feet into the first shoes I find, which happen to be the Lucite-bottomed mules, yank my purse off the kitchen counter and my tote bag with my laptop and cell phone off the wing chair and book it out of there. The hallway is riddled with cussing and yelling and about a million people all bumping into each other, the children excited and babbling, the old people wandering in dazed circles like rundown wind-up toys.

Trying to tie my sash around my waist while hanging on to all my crap and stay balanced on these stupid shoes, I take two or three seconds to wake up, get my bearings. Figuring the firefighters—there are two of them, scary as grizzly bears in their full attire, lumbering and jangling as they try to direct the tide toward the stairs—have better things to do, like, oh, put out the fire in the *APARTMENT RIGHT ABOVE MINE,* I take over herding the more confused and frightened of the older people down the hall and toward stairs I doubt any of them have used since 1966. Yeah, I'm scared shitless, too, but at least I have a clue as to what's going on.

"There's nothing to worry about, I'm sure getting everyone out's just a precaution," I say, smiling for one poor old gal, her scalp pink and fragile-looking underneath thin white hair held hostage in a row of pin curls. In a crisp, new housecoat splashed with tropical flowers, her feet encased in plastic slippers, she clamps on to my arm, her grip surprisingly strong. She smells faintly of mothballs and old perfume. "I'm sure everyone's apartment will be fine," I say.

She's staring at the stairs with wide eyes. "You'll help me down?"

"You betcha. Hang on...there you go..."

We take one tentative step toward the stairs, the rest of the tenants swirling around us. The noise is deafening.

"What's your name?" she asks.

"Ginger."

She glances over at me at that, then says, "I'm Esther. Esther Moskovitz."

"Nice to meet you, Mrs. Moskovitz."

That gets a smile. "How nice, a young person who uses my last name. Nowadays, nobody uses your last name," she says, shuffling at about the speed of a glacier along the tiled floor. "Everybody wants to be your buddy, thinks it's okay to use a person's given name, like it's their right or something."

Despite the load I'm already carrying, I find myself wondering if I can pick her up, carry her down the damn steps. It occurs to me at this rate, by the time I get her outside, either the fire will be out or the building will have burned down.

"You're that new girl who just moved in, aren't you?"

"Uh-huh." Okay, three more feet before we begin what I know is going to be a torturous descent.

She takes another cautious step, then squints up at me. "You're Jewish?"

"Only half. Okay, now just lower your foot to the next step…"

"*Damn,*" she says on a grunt as her knee cracks like a gun. "What's the other half?"

"Italian."

She sighs, clearly disappointed. "Too bad. My grandson just got divorced, so he's back in the market. But no Italians. His last wife was Italian," she says, as if that explains everything.

I hear clanking and stomping and swishing coming up the stairs. A chocolate-eyed firefighter appears on the landing below, sizes up the situation immediately.

"Come on, sweetheart," he says to the old lady. His grin is huge and heart-stopping, and I just know this man has a pregnant wife and three other kiddies at home. He holds out his arms. "Want a ride?"

And before Mrs. Moskovitz has a chance to think about it, he gently picks her up and carts her down the stairs. Over his shoulder, I see her startled, shocked expression slowly give way to childlike glee.

I clomp along behind and, finally, out into the muggy night. The firefighter once again consigns Mrs. Moskovitz to my care, directing us to where the rest of the evacuated tenants are standing, staring up in mute fascination. I turn, gasping at the sight of actual honest-to-God flames leaping out the windows, licking at the night.

"Oh, dear," Mrs. Moskovitz says. "That's your apartment right underneath, isn't it, honey?"

My throat closes. All I can do is nod.

"Hope you have renter's insurance, because the water and smoke damage is going to be a bitch."

I swallow, then ask if she'll be all right, I just need to step over...here to make a phone call. Nedra answers on the second ring, her voice heavy with sleep.

I burst into tears.

"Ginger?" she says, tentatively. Then, "Oh, my God, Ginger! What's happened, baby? Are you all right?"

"I need you," was all I could say.

"I'll be right there," Nedra said. "Just hang tight, sweetie, okay? I'll be right there."

Twenty minutes later a taxi pulls up and Nedra flies out of it.

I fall into her arms, sobbing like a twit. I can feel her look up. "Wait...that's the fifth floor, right?"

"The apartment right over mine." We watch as a fireman, cantilevered over the street in one of those cherry picker things on the back of the biggest truck, aims the hose at one of the windows. Eerily illuminated by the undulating flames, the hose jolts to life, water rocketing into the apartment. Gallons and gallons and gallons of water, all merrily finding its way down into my apartment, drenching my furniture, my rug, my books...my *stuff*. *My* stuff, dammit.

Not letting go of me, my mother twists us both around to look into the crowd. "You know who lives up there?"

I've stopped blubbering long enough to follow her gaze. "The m-man in the white sleeveless T-shirt, I think. The one with the heavy moustache."

My mother gives me a squeeze, wipes my cheeks with

the palm of her hand, then leaves me to go talk to the man in all probability responsible for ruining what scraps of my life were left to ruin. A minute later she returns. I notice she's wearing a sweater over a cotton nightgown.

"Grease fire in the kitchen. They were frying something, I didn't quite catch all of it, he was speaking a Spanish dialect I didn't know—"

"Chicken," I say, my voice dead.

"What?"

"Were they frying chicken?"

She looks at me as if I've lost it. "I have no idea. Anyway, I just wanted to make sure they had someplace to stay tonight."

My turn at incredulity. "You have got to be kidding me."

"Noo-oo, why would I be kidding you?"

"You would actually offer the people responsible for destroying your own daughter's apartment a place to stay?"

Her brows dip, the expression in her dark eyes more stunned than angry. "No, I hadn't planned on bringing them home with us. But I know places where they could have stayed, gotten help. As it happens, they've got relatives in the Bronx, they'll go there for a while, the man said. But honestly, Ginger..." She huffs out a sigh. "Those people have probably lost everything they owned. For all intents and purposes, they're homeless. You're not."

She reaches over, takes my tote from me and starts toward the cab. I click along behind, hugging my purse—and my thoughts—to my chest. As I pass the upstairs family, I see the man my mother talked to, cuddling a toddler to his chest. A woman I assume is his wife clings to his arm, looking up at the apartment, her eyes huge with worry.

Three or four older children huddle at her side, one little girl with her thumb in her mouth.

And, safe in its cage at the man's feet, the rooster cocks its head at me.

"I'm sorry," I say sometime later in the taxi.

I sense my mother stir in the darkness at the other end of the seat. "For what?"

"For being such a shithead."

She chuckles. "You've been through a lot this past month. You've every right to be a shithead."

I find that comforting, in a bizarre sort of way.

At four in the morning, the streets are nearly deserted. The cabbie hits all the green lights; we're home in what seems like only a couple minutes.

Home.

I suck in my breath, shocked at how easily I slip right back into thinking of my mother's abode as mine. But it's only temporary, I tell myself as Nonna, in a sleazy nightgown through which one can easily see her udderlike breasts, greets us at the door, takes my purse. I can't stay here, after all. Not for a second longer than absolutely necessary. Just as soon as...

Just as soon as what? Nonna ushers me to my old room, my freshly made double bed turned back, welcoming me. I have no money, probably no furniture, and a job that pays diddly. I swallow down the panic that threatens to overwhelm me, reminding myself it could be worse, I could have been killed.

Those people upstairs might have been killed. Their children...

"We talk in the morning, *sì?*" my grandmother says, pulling the covers up over my shoulders as though I'm still a little girl. Her heavy accent—the legacy of a woman who didn't even speak English until her marriage to an American GI during the war—washes over me like a gentle breeze. "In the morning, we plan. We start to fix." She leans over, places cool, soft lips on my cheek, her long white braid slipping over her shoulder and tickling my neck. "You are safe, *cara*," she whispers, then tiptoes out of my room.

A new round of tears slip from my eyes, stain my pillow. I hate feeling sorry for myself, but my resistance is shot to hell. So might as well enjoy my pity party, right? Even if I am the only one here to appreciate it.

Oh, dear God. That which I have most feared has come upon me.

Safe? Yes, I suppose I am. Physically, at least. But what do I have left, besides a ring I don't know if I can bring myself to sell? And a Vera Wang wedding dress that's still, as far as I know, in Ted and Randall's apartment somewhere. Everything, *everything*, has been taken from me. The man I loved, my apartment, my job…even my dog. Okay, so Geoff never was my dog, but you know what I mean. The point is, here I am at thirty-one, starting over from scratch.

This is the last straw. I'm exhausted. Defeated. And worst of all, no better off than one of those vagrants I used to resent my parents taking pity on, all those years ago.

The fire department let us into the apartment the next afternoon. And, yes, it's every bit as awful as Mrs. Moskovitz assured me it would be. There's no fire damage per se, but it smells like the Devil's barbecue. And the water damage…

I look at my lovely, drenched, sooty Pottery Barn sofa and begin to weep.

"Come on," my mother says softly. "Let's see what's salvageable."

There are places that specialize in cleaning fire-damaged

stuff, she's saying as I pick through the soggy debris. (And here I was complaining about the upstairs neighbors' bathtub overflowing.) There doesn't appear to be any damage to the bedroom, other than that awful smoke smell, so maybe my clothes will be okay, she says. My papers and bills and stuff are all in a metal file cabinet, so all of that is fine, as are maybe half of my books if I can air them out enough. The other half, those in the bookcases closest to the kitchen, are ruined, as is all my furniture, my printer, my entire entertainment system, such as it was.

Silently, I carry over a box I brought, dump the files from the cabinet into them.

"Your insurance should cover most of this, you know," Nedra says.

Yes, I do have renter's insurance. At least that. But that won't pay for replacing all my stuff plus the upfront costs for renting another apartment. Which depresses me just to think about, going through *that* again.

I call the insurance company that afternoon to file a claim. Very sweet, very sympathetic lady with a Southern accent on the other end of the line says to hold on while she brings up my account.

I hear computer keys clicking, soft music in the background. Then an, "Oh, dear."

I shut my eyes. "Anything wrong?" I say, although of course there's something wrong, every goddamn thing I touch these days goes wrong so why should this be any exception?

"Well, um, according to our records, we never received your last premium payment."

"Oh, no, there must be some mistake. I sent that check in…" I grab my checkbook out of my purse, frantically flip through the register.

I laugh nervously. "Okay, hold on a sec, I'm a little upset and not focusing clearly, here—"

"That's certainly understandable," Miss Sweet and Reasonable says soothingly. "You just take your time, honey."

But two more frantic flips does not reveal a check made out to my insurance company. Okay, I'm screwed.

"W-when was that due again?"

"May 25th."

Which means the thirty day grace period ended... yesterday.

I thank the nice lady and hang up, contemplate doing the same to myself, except I know I don't have the *cojones*. And I'd never be able to live with myself if I gave Nonna a heart attack.

I've never, ever forgotten to pay a bill. Never. But I sure as shootin' missed this one.

I look up at the heavens and say, *"Why?"*

There being no answer forthcoming, I do what any sane woman would do in my situation: I take to my bed.

Four, five mornings later, who the hell knows, I sense my mother looming over my bed. I don't have to see her to know her hands are planted on her hips.

"Okay, grieving's over. Get the hell up."

"Get the hell *out*," I mumble and pull the covers over my head.

"Hey. This is your mother you're talking to."

"I know that."

The covers are yanked back. Damn, it's bright. "You're worrying Nonna."

The one argument for moving my carcass out of this bed I might actually consider. Which Nedra knows.

"And Shelby called, wanting to know why she couldn't get through on your cell."

"You told her, I suppose?"

"It's not exactly a secret."

I roll partway over, clutching the sheet like a baby its security blanket. "Which means she probably called Terrie, right?"

"Honey, if I know Shelby, she's probably taken an ad out in the *Post*. Jesus, Ginger, your breath stinks. Now get up and function, for God's sake. I'm going into school for a meeting, I'll be back at lunchtime. The cleaner's said your clothes would be ready by this afternoon."

I stare down at the pajamas I was wearing the night of the fire, which have probably fused to my skin by now. "And what, pray tell, am I supposed to wear in the meantime?"

"Check the drawers and the back of the closet. There's stuff there from when you still lived here."

My eyes widen. "You saved my old clothes?"

"Not exactly. I just never got around to throwing them out."

Yeah, that sounds like Nedra, who would save newspapers until they decomposed if it weren't for Nonna's pitching them on the sly.

I struggle to sit up, hugging my knees. "I hate to tell you this, but I have exactly two hundred sixty-four dollars in my checking account. Until something comes in, I can't get those clothes out of hock."

"Don't worry about it—"

I jump up when my mother goes pale, sinks into the chair in front of the desk in my room.

"Nedra! Are you okay?"

She plants an unsteady hand on her chest. "Nothing that digesting your grandmother's stuffed peppers won't cure."

"Look," I say, finally untangling myself from the sheets and getting out of the bed. "This is nothing to joke around

about. It could be serious. Nausea and dizziness is ofte
the first sign of a heart attack in a woman, you know.''

Nedra rolls her eyes at me, then gets to her feet, tuggin;
down her blouse over her skirt. "I'm not having a hear
attack, Ginger. I'm having agita. A couple of Tums, I'll bo
fine. Now, go clean yourself up, for God's sake. I'll bo
back soon.''

Actually, now that I'm vertical, it's not so bad. If a little
weird, since for some reason, I expected my room to look
exactly the same as it had when I left some twelve years
ago. Instead, a good half of it's crammed with file cabinets
and bookcases, my bed, dresser and old desk huddled
against the wall like bullied children. All my posters, my
dolls, the books I deemed too juvenile to cart off with me
when I moved out, are gone. Or at least, out of sight. Like
my clothes, I'm sure they're lurking in a drawer or closet,
banished but not annihilated.

I paw through the dresser for undies, shorts, a T-shirt.
Did I really used to wear shorts that short? Jeez. What a
hussy. Twenty minutes later, bathed and dressed, I plod out
to the kitchen to find Nonna, as ever, surrounded by bowls
and rolling pins and other cooking paraphernalia, humming
to herself as she goes about fulfilling her mission to feed
people. Dressed in one of those murky-colored sacks they
must sell by the boatload in some dumpy little store on
Delaney Street, she beams when she sees me, her arms
flying open. I step into her embrace, having to bend over
to give her a hug. She is short, but solid, like a tree stump,
and she always smells faintly of onions and garlic and tal-
cum powder.

"Sit, sit. I fix you breakfast. You feel better today?''

"Marginally. What are you making?''

"I think maybe stuffed ziti. How does that sound?''

"Like heaven." She gives me another broad smile, and *marginally* cranks up another notch. To *passable,* maybe.

I let her feed me—pancakes, sausage, scrambled eggs, coffee—after which I feel reasonably ready to face the world. Or what's left of mine, in any case. I turn on my cell phone, call everyone I can think of who might need to know where I am, including the store to tell them I still need a few days off. Elise Suderman, the head of the design studio, isn't happy but there's not a whole lot she can say. I mean, please. What's the worst they can do? Fire me? Oooooh, I'm shaking in my boots.

Then I call the caterer, still on the cell's speed dial. I have no idea what I'm going to say, or how I plan on paying the still overdue bill, but I figure the least I can do is keep the lines of communication open.

"But we got a check for that on Monday, hon," the gravel-voiced bookkeeper says, clearly a little surprised.

My hand grips the phone. "Mr. Munson paid the bill?"

"Sure did. Even included ten percent extra to cover the inconvenience, he said."

My head buzzing, I call the florist, get the same story.

The hotel? Yep. All paid up.

Whoa. I mean...

Okay, this is good news, right? One less thing to worry about, one problem solved. Yet...I don't know. Something's...bugging me about this, but I'm too stunned to figure out what it is.

Over Nonna's vociferous protests, I wash up my breakfast dishes. And it's when I'm wiping my hands on the country kitsch terry cloth dish towel that the significance of Greg's paying off the bills hits me.

Now it's over.

All three places said the checks were dated well before the fire, which means he could've gotten in touch with me, if he'd wanted to. That he hadn't could only mean one thing, which was that he wasn't going to change his mind. Or even give me the courtesy of a face-to-face explanation.

The past month, I realize, I've been like a person sitting by a deathbed, praying for a miracle, unwilling to let go as long as there was even a shred of hope. Well, honey, the body done been carted off and buried now, and there ain't nuthin' left to hang on *to*.

My grandmother looks up from her work, frowns. "Are you all right?"

I shake off those last shreds of false hope and smile for her. In a way, I feel relieved. Free, even. Depressed as hell, but free.

"Yeah. Yeah, I'm fine," I say, then head back to my room, for the first time since my return taking the time to reabsorb the place I'd had no choice but to call "home" for the first two-thirds of my life to date.

The apartment is one of those grand old dames common to so many prewar buildings north of 96th Street, the rooms spacious and high-ceilinged, the wood floors wood slightly slanted, the hundred-times-painted over walls and ceilings trimmed with cornices and molding. The windows were replaced seven or eight years ago, but as a child, I remember my father joking that you could practically gauge the wind velocity by how far the curtains would blow out from the sills.

I don't suppose I should be surprised that being here makes me think of my father. But now, as I regard a collection of photos hanging crookedly on the wall outside the kitchen, my eyes burn at a picture of the three of us on what I think is my fifth birthday, right after we moved here from the tiny three-room apartment on 114th Street.

Next to my father, Nedra looks almost petite. Leo—short for Basilio—Petrocelli was six-three or four, with thick, curly black hair and a full beard and moustache. Gee, if he'd lived long enough for his hair to turn white, he would have made the perfect Santa Claus, complete with the booming laugh. Dressed in almost identical fisherman's sweaters and jeans, we're all smiling like goons in the picture, my father possessively hugging my mother to his side, his cheek nestled in her hair. I'm standing between them, one of their hands in each of mine.

I certainly look happy enough in the photo, don't I?

I turn away, shaking my head at the living room, which is one of two rooms Nonna gave up on trying to bully into order years ago. "Less is more" is not a concept with which my mother is familiar. Piles of books and papers and magazines, like a drunken city skyline, take up most of whatever space isn't occupied by furniture that was comfortably worn when I was little, but is now simply pathetic and threadbare. Because she's still giving her salary away, I wonder? Or because she simply can't be bothered calling her daughter to help her go look for something less disreputable?

Nedra's bedroom, the old dining room, is right next to the living room. Through the slightly open French doors I catch glimpses of discarded clothes and more piles of books, competing with the magazines and papers scattered across her unmade bed.

I have to smile. Yep, that's my mother, a woman too busy *being* to be bothered with cleaning up after herself.

And then there's my grandmother, I think as I stop in front of a room that would put a Marine recruit to shame. Or a nun. Underneath a crucifix (a large, gaudy, gruesome thing I found totally fascinating as a kid) stands a single twin bed, tightly made, keeping company with an armless upholstered rocking chair she brought with her from Italy more than fifty years ago. The dark wood dresser is bare except for a statue of the Madonna centered on a tatted lace doily; there is not a speck of dust on the damn thing.

How on earth have these two women managed to live together this long without driving each other nuts?

And how odd that I am like neither of them.

Once back in "my" room, I turn on the fan on the dresser, then crawl back onto the bed—which I haven't yet made—and sit cross-legged, elbows on knees, chin in hands, and take stock of how I feel. I decide not bad, but not good, either. This is when, logically and true to my nature, I should be recouping, planning, figuring out where I go from here. For some reason, it's not happening. Although whether it's because I'm feeling rebellious or because I'm simply worn out, I can't quite tell.

I should call a Bitchfest.

Then again, maybe not. The way I feel right now, Terrie's cynicism would push me over the edge.

Not to mention Shelby's serene little smile.

On a sigh, I haul my butt off the bed, decide—because it's not as if I have a pressing schedule or anything—to see just how much of my past my mother has managed to hang on to. The cedar-lined closet is a fairly big one, with lots of shelves and crevices. When I was little, I used to torment my mother by hiding inside, refusing to answer when she called me...until the tone of her voice warned me she was no longer amused. But it was nice, even if just for a few minutes, pretending that no one could find me, or bother me, or disturb my thoughts. By ten or eleven, though, I'd outgrown the practice, which was sad because then I really had no place to be by myself.

I pull the cord to turn on the overhead light. Criminy. Here are my teenage years, tucked away for all eternity— the clothes, those posters, all rolled up inside each other in a corner, boxes of books.

And on the top shelf, a splotched, banged-up wooden case that still smells of linseed oil and turpentine.

Something stirs in my blood, something I'd thought long since dead and forgotten. I yank down the box, nearly beaning myself in the process, then carry it to my bare desktop to open it. My heart rate speeds up, my fingers tingle, like a lover disrobing her beloved after too many years apart.

The bent, squashed tubes huddle together, deformed and smeared. I pick one up, gently squeeze it to find it still pliant. Most of the other kids in my art classes preferred acrylics, with their brighter colors and faster drying time. Not me. I loved the way oils smelled, the subtle depth of the colors, their patience with a neophyte's experimentation with blending and shading, even the different textures and feels of the different pigments. A pathetic romantic then, I even loved the sense of connection with artists from centuries before.

I'd turned to painting about the time I'd outgrown the closet.

I'd let myself wander around for hours in the world I'd create with my brushes, oblivious to the comings and goings in the apartment. My parents encouraged my explorations, never hesitating to buy me whatever supplies I needed, no matter how expensive a tube of Alizaron Crimson or a pure sable Number 10 round brush happened to be.

Even during those weeks when all we ate was macaroni and cheese.

Gee. That wouldn't be guilt pricking my conscience, would it?

Further rooting around in the back of the closet turns up a stack of canvases, some half finished, some only primed. And my old easel, too...

I find myself wandering into the third, now-empty bedroom, the one Nedra had said I could use as an office. Or something.

It's the one room that faces north, due to a funny jog in the building. A battered chest of drawers, a couple of chairs are all that break the monotony of bare floor, unadorned walls. The old roller shade snaps up when I pull it; clear, bright light floods the room.

"Found your paints, huh?"

Despite its softness, my mother's voice makes me jump, crashing out of my dream. God—what was I thinking? That I'd start painting again? As if the reason I'd given it up to begin with has changed?

"You should have ditched all that crap years ago," I say, my voice shrill, hollow, in the empty room.

"Wasn't my crap to ditch." A floorboard creaks as she comes into the room, her arms crossed. She crosses to the window, struggles with it for a minute before coercing it open. A hot, airless breeze drifts into the room, spiked with sounds of traffic, voices, a child crying somewhere in the building. "This would make a great studio, wouldn't it?"

I glance around, shrug. "I suppose."

Nedra drops into one of the chairs, an old Mission-style thing I'd always hated. "You were good, Ginger. I never did understand why you gave it up."

Her words provoke simultaneous pride and annoyance. Nedra's not one for empty praise. Neither is she much for seeing something from someone else's vantage point.

"You know damn well why I quit."

"Because you'd rather take the easy way out."

"Because I'm not the starving artist type. Which you know."

"Not all artists are starving."

"No, only most of them. Come on—how many of those friends of yours ever made it even past the bottom rung of the ladder, let alone to the top? You know damn well what the odds are against becoming a success. Or even simply making enough to live on. I'd've had to have a screw loose to even think about pursuing a career as a painter."

"So you were afraid to even try."

"I didn't *want* to try. That's not the same as being afraid to."

"Isn't it?"

"Jesus, Nedra!"

"Sorry."

I let out a bark of laughter.

"All right, I'm not sorry. Because it kills me that you'd rather spend your life decorating other people's houses, executing somebody else's vision, than expressing your own."

"And has it ever once occurred to you that maybe, just maybe, I *like* what I'm doing?"

"I think you've convinced yourself you do."

My arms fly up in defeat before I spin around, tromp back to my room. Seconds later, the guard chain rattles against the door as my mother leaves again.

Why do I argue with her? There's a better chance of settling differences between the Palestinians and the Israelis than between my mother and me, yet I keep falling for the bait, over and over again.

My throat inexplicably clogged, I cram all the stuff back into the closet. When things settle down a bit, I'll see about chucking it completely—

"Is everything all right, *cara?*"

Nonna stands in the doorway, her hands loosely clasped in front of her stomach, her still-dark brows tightly drawn. I sigh.

"Nedra and I had a fight."

"That much I could tell," she says with a slight smile.

"The apartment, she isa not that big. She wants you to take up your painting again, *sì?*

"As if I could."

"Why not?"

"Because that's simply not what I do anymore, Nonna. Or who I am."

She comes into my room, perches on the end of my bed, reaches up to pull me down beside her. "You think your talent, she is no more?"

I wasn't ready to think about that too hard, so all I said was, "Painting was a part of my life at a time when I needed an outlet for everything I was going through after Papa died. I don't need it anymore. That's all."

I've outgrown that closet, too.

Her hand feels weightless and soft in mine. But when she squeezes it, she passes to me what feels like the concentrated strength of every generation of womanhood that has come before her. Her eyes, dark and far too assessing, find mine.

"Your mama, she is not—*Come sei dice?*—diplomatic, no? But I think maybe she speaks more truth than you are willing to hear." She pulls me over to place a whisper of a kiss on my forehead. "Your painting, she comes froma your soul. I also do not think it is a good thing to deny your soul what it needs to say."

You know, all I ask of life right now is a single ally.

"Nonna, I—"

My cell phone rings, hidden somewhere in the room like a phantom cricket. While we both search for the damn thing—Nonna finally unearths it from underneath the bedclothes—I try to compose myself. Only to have that tenuous composure shot to hell the minute I say hello.

"Christ, it's about damn time you answered your cell!

And what's this I hear about you gettin' smoked out of your new apartment?''

Now I know what it feels like to be in direct line for an asteroid hit.

Nonna has shuffled out of the room, taking a thousand years of woman strength with her. "Please don't yell at me, Nick," I say softly. "I'm not in the mood."

I hear an expelled breath on the other end. "Hell, Ginger, I'm sorry, I didn't mean to come on so strong. But Jesus H. Christ—I try callin' your regular phone and get nothin'. So I try the cell, still get nothin'. So I get worried, thinkin'…" Another sigh. "I don't mean to sound negative, but it's like every time I turn around, somethin' else has happened to you."

"Tell me about it." Then I say, because it's taken this long to work through, "You were worried about me? Why?"

"Because, like I said, it's like you got a sign on your back or something that says Kick Me. So I figure it wouldn't hurt to check up on you. And Paula's been on my case, big-time, wanting to know how you're doin'."

"So how come Paula didn't call?"

"If I couldn't get through, how could she?"

Good point. "So…how'd you find out about the fire?"

"I finally went over to your old apartment this morning, hoping maybe one of your neighbors might know something. One of the guys who lives across the hall from you—the black dude?—said you'd just called them, that you were back with your mother?"

"Oh. Yeah."

"I take it this calls for condolences?"

"Hey. You've met my mother."

"That was for two minutes, maybe, more than ten years ago."

"And I bet you remember, with crystal clarity, every second of that meeting, don't you?"

He chuckles. "Now that you mention it, yeah. I do. But people change."

"People, maybe. Nedra, no." I flop back on my bed, the back of my hand draped dramatically over my eyes. You know, I have no idea why he called. And you know what else? I really don't care. Sure, the man's pushy and borderline obnoxious, but at the moment he's all I've got. It occurs to me, if I let the tears come right now, he wouldn't consider it a sign of feminine weakness. I might, but he wouldn't. So I let them come.

"I've had it, Nick," I say, my voice all wobbly. "Up until a month ago, things were going great, you know? Then bam, bam, bam—no wedding, no job, no home, no home—again—no dog…"

"The dog? What happened to the dog?"

I explained about Curtiss and the will. I wasn't sobbing or anything, just occasionally sniffling. Just enough to apparently make the big old tough cop on the other end of the line go all gentle and stuff. Which was fine by me.

"Hey," he says. "How's about you come out here for the Fourth?"

Tissue pressed to my nose, I say, "Out…where?"

"Here. Brooklyn. My place. Well, Paula's and Frank's, actually. I mean, somehow I got the night off, and they're doin' this whole cookout number, and you wouldn't believe how well you can see the Macy's fireworks from the roof. So come on. It'll be fun."

God. Where had June gone? But the Fourth was only five days away. I give this shaky sigh. "Gee, I don't know…"

"Ginger, if there was ever anybody who sounded like

she needed a change, a break—somethin'—it's you, okay?''

I roll onto my side, propping myself up on one arm. "I…can't."

"Because?"

"Because…because I just…can't."

"Because you haven't had three months to think about it and decide whether or not this fits in with your plans for your life, what?"

I almost laugh. "I'm not *that* anal."

"Then what? Oh, hey, if you're hesitating because of Amy—"

"No, of course not," I lie.

"—that's over."

"Oh?" I sit up. "Oh, crap, Nick…I'm so sorry."

"Don't be. I knew it was comin'. I just didn't want to admit it."

He's trying to do that male stoic number and failing miserably. "What happened?"

"One word. Kids. As in, she doesn't want 'em. I mean, to be fair, she'd been up-front about that all along, I guess I just thought…I dunno. That maybe, if things got goin' good between us, she'd change her mind." He sighs. "I guess she figured it was better to end it now. Well, actually, she's been tryin' to end it for some time. We didn't date. We argued. Finally broke up that night after I was at your place. You know, when I brought over the Chinese food?"

As if I needed a memory jog. Of course, paranoia immediately kicks in. "And…that's why you invited me to come out there? Because you're suddenly at loose ends?"

"No. No, I swear. I mean, okay, I can understand why you might think that, but in fact, I hadn't even thought about inviting you, since I figured your reaction would pretty much be what it was. But after we got to talking and

I heard how upset you were, I thought, What the hell, right? It was worth a shot."

I go silent.

So Nick says, "Hey, I like you, okay? I like being around you, being around someone who's different from all the other women I know. But honest to God, there's nothing more to it than that. Of course, if the feeling's not mutual, if you don't like being with me..."

I'm still absorbing what I'm pretty sure is a compliment when I realize I've almost missed my cue. "Oh, no, Nick! It's nothing like that. I like you, too." Probably more than I should. "It's just...oh, crud, I don't know. I'd be really lousy company."

"Then that makes two of us. So whaddya say?"

Oh, God. I'm weakening, I can feel it. I stare at my toenails, contemplating what they'd look like purple. Or maybe blue. "As long as it's not a date or anything."

"There you go again with the date business," he says wearily. "Look, you can call it anything you want, Ginger, okay? I really don't care. Hell, you can hang out with Paula and the kids all night if you want to. I mean, I'll just go off and quietly hang myself, but I'll understand."

A giggle bubbles out of my throat.

"This is for you, Ginger," he says softly. "Okay? Just come."

I hesitate. Really, there is no earthly reason I shouldn't do this. Greg is now firmly In The Past. Which doesn't mean I'm up for anything, I don't mean that, it's just...

It's just a cookout, for heaven's sake. An invitation to watch the fireworks, which I really haven't seen since Macy's used to set them off at this end of the city when I was little. And I really do need to get outside of myself, even if just for one evening.

"O...kay."

''Don't knock me over with your enthusiasm, now.''

''No, I mean it. Okay. I'll come.''

''You sure?''

''Not at all. But I'm coming, anyway. Just tell me which trains to take.''

''Forget it. I get off at four, I'll swing by and pick you up—''

''You don't have to—''

''Were you born this stubborn, or is this something you've fine-tuned over the years? I'm not gonna kidnap you, for crissake.''

''I know that. It's just…''

''I took an oath to protect, Ginger,'' he says softly. ''An oath I take very seriously. I'm not gonna do anything to you, or with you, you don't want me to. Unless you don't stop being such a pain in the ass. Then all bets are off.''

I nod, then realize he can't see me. ''Sorry. I'm just…''

''I know,'' he says. ''I've been there. Hell, I *am* there. Now tell me where you live. And for God's sake, keep me informed if you move again, okay?''

I smile, give him my mother's address. After I hang up, I once again remind myself I have nothing to worry about. Nothing whatsoever.

If you don't count the gut-deep premonition of doom, that is.

Eleven

I'm not going to burden you with all the details of the past five days, but suffice it to say not a whole lot has happened to improve my mood by the time Nick comes to pick me up. The cleaners could only save/restore about half of my clothes, and the management company for the building not only gave me grief about breaking the lease, but then had the nerve to try to keep the damage deposit, as if the fire were *my* fault! And I just used up what was left on my Visa to pay the salvage company to come cart away what was left in the apartment.

As for work…trust me. You don't want to know.

I clumsily juggle me, my purse, and a pasta salad large enough to feed Bulgaria to get in Nick's vintage Impala, after which I yank shut the door and ram the seat belt home. Nick frowns at me, but with amused overtones.

"Let me guess. Things aren't looking up."

"Good call."

His gaze wanders over my left leg, bare from the thigh down. Which, if I'd managed to get in the car with any grace, wouldn't be showing. But I'm wearing this long, red jersey sundress that buttons all the way down the front so one can leave it unbuttoned as far up one's legs as one dares, which in this one's case is mid-thigh. And the damn car seat is covered with this burgundy-colored plush…stuff that grabbed the fabric before I could sit down. Not to mention clashes horribly with the red.

"Nice…dress," he says as we pull away from the curb.

The temperature rises a good eight, ten degrees inside the car. We've only gone two or three blocks. It's still not too late to get out.

Okay, we're only down to 110th Street, all I have to do is say I've changed my mind…

"You know," Nick says, "if I didn't know better, I'd say you were scared of me."

I jump. "I'm not—"

He chuckles. I fidget in the seat, then sigh.

"Am I that transparent?"

"Like glass."

I sneak my own peek. Nick's ditched his suit jacket and tie, unbuttoned his white shirt at the collar, rolled up his sleeves. His scent fills the un-air-conditioned car, setting my frayed nerves to doing things I don't want to think about too hard.

He glances over at my leg again.

"I really wish you wouldn't do that," I say.

He effortlessly merges into Broadway traffic. "You don't want somebody looking at your legs, you should wear pants. Which would be a shame, because you've got really,

really great legs. Not too skinny, not too muscular. Just right."

For what? I immediately wonder, but manage to keep my mouth shut. I spare them a glance myself. "Yeah?"

"Yeah."

My gaze drifts up to his face. His mouth is pulled up into something resembling a smile, but tension has etched lines around that mouth, corded the muscles in the forearm stretched to the wheel. There's a faint scar along his temple I hadn't noticed before.

"How's the case going?" I ask.

One shoulder hitches. "Okay."

"Uh-huh."

He smirks, checks his rearview mirror, switches lanes. "Off the record? It blows." His gaze darts to mine, back to the street. "Plenty of clues, none of them seem to fit together. I mean, I'm a patient man, but…" He shakes his head, then says to me, "But tonight isn't about me. It's about you. So. For the next two minutes, you can bitch about whatever's going on in your life. Then you're not allowed to do anything except enjoy yourself for the rest of the evening."

"Gee. Two whole minutes?"

"Take it or leave it. And the clock's ticking."

I consider telling him about Greg, about work, about my mother. It's not as if I don't have plenty of topics from which to choose. Then I change my mind. "Much as I appreciate your generous offer, I'm going to turn it down. I've whined about stuff so much the past month, I can't stand my own company anymore."

I catch his shrug out of the corner of my eye. "Suit yourself. But if you change your mind, I'm here for you."

After a good three seconds, I say, "I'll keep that in mind."

* * *

"Uncle Nick!" Paula's little girl hurtles her tiny body into Nick's arms the minute the door swings open.

"Hey, baby!" He swings her up, grinning when she plants a noisy kiss on his cheek, then tickles her bare midriff. "You miss me?"

"Uh-huh—"

"Oh, my God, look at *you!*"

I tear my eyes away from the sight of this great big man cradling the munchkin in his arms to Paula. Who is pregnant again. Which I didn't know.

A rugrat hanging on to one leg beneath the hem of her maternity shorts, she holds out skinny arms adorned with lots of jangly gold bracelets. From the neck up, it's Prom Night 1985. From the neck down, it's the softer side of Sears.

I set the covered salad bowl down on a table in the hall seconds before I'm engulfed. For a skinny woman, Paula's got a hug like a brown bear.

"Jesus, you look *great!* Doesn't she look great, Frank?"

She holds me at arm's length, grinning, her dark brown hair fluffed and gelled within an inch of its life. Hovering and grinning just as widely behind her, Frank Wojowodski is a couple inches shorter than Nick, a little softer, a little balder. And completely at ease with grape jelly smeared all over his Knicks T-shirt. He waggles his eyebrows. "Yeah, she looks great."

Paula smacks him without even looking.

"But not as great as you, babe." He slips an arm around her waist, resting his palm on her belly as he nuzzles her neck. "The bigger you get, the more I want you."

"Jesus, Frank, the kids!" Paula whispers through an immobile mouth, even as she leans, beaming, into her husband's embrace. I notice her eyelashes are nearly as long

as her bangs. Then she swats Frank's hand. "Get outta here
and go get them glasses of tea. And Nick, take the salad
to the kitchen, put it on the counter. We'll take it out back
later." Her eyes flash to mine. "Or would you rather have
a wine cooler? Frank, did we get coolers the last time we
went to the store?"

Already halfway down the hall, he says, "Yeah, I think
so, baby, let me check—"

"No, no…tea's fine," I say, trying not to panic when
Nick, who's set the little girl down, slips my purse from
my shoulder and carts it off somewhere, effectively trapping me.

"You sure?" Paula says, genuine concern shining from
her big brown eyes. "What is it, Tiffany?" she says to the
blond twerp now tugging at the hem of her shorts. The kid
says something unintelligible. "So, go, already. It's not like
you don't know where it is. And take your brother with
you—" she pries the dark-haired little boy from her thigh,
places his hand in his sister's "—it's been three hours since
he went. Yes, you have to go potty, Dominic, quit whining.
Because, really," she says, not missing a beat as the two
little ones wander off, hand in hand, "it's no trouble for
Frank to check…"

"Paula, chill," Nick says. Slipping an arm around *my*
waist. "You'll scare the poor woman off."

Paula's eyes zing to that hand-on-the-waist move, then
to her brother-in-law's face.

"For the love of God, Nick—whatshername's been out
of the picture, what? Like two minutes? Quit pawing the
poor woman," she says, then grabs my hand and pulls me
away from her brother-in-law. I know I should be taking a
more active part in this scene, but it's like trying to hop a
ride on a merry-go-round that's already going.

She drags me into the shrine to Country Kitsch that is

er living room, teeming with hearts and cutsie tole paint-
ng. I jump when Paula's hand cups my jaw, then go very
till so as to minimize the risk of permanent scarring from
hose long red nails.

"Nicky told us about…everything. God, it's just been
one thing after the other for you, hasn't it? You okay?"
She mercifully drops her hand to her hip. "Jesus, listen to
ne. Of course you're not okay. Your life's gone to hell in
a handbasket, how could you be okay?"

Nick moves in behind me. Close. Doesn't matter that
he's not actually touching me, I can tell by the way I'm
starting to salivate that he wants to.

That I want him to.

Told you I shouldn't have come.

"Hey, Paula," he says, "don't you have to go gestate
or something?"

Her hands go up. "What? What's wrong with asking the
woman how she's doin'? For your information, Mr. Nick,
I think that's called bein' polite. You know, showin' concern for my guest? Who just happens to be my cousin, even
if I haven't seen her in…what is it now? Five years? Six?
Frank!" she yells back to the kitchen. "How long since
Ginger and I have seen each other?"

Frank strolls back into the living room, a glass of tea in
one hand, a wine cooler in the other. He hands me the
cooler, Nick the tea.

"Beats me. When Justin was born, maybe?"

"Yeah, that's right. And he's gonna be seven come October. Jesus. So, sit," she says to me. "We're gonna have
dinner out back, but until then, we'll talk, I can show you
pictures of the kids. Frank and Nick get to do all the cooking today. And take the kids with you!" she shouts as the
men leave. Reluctantly. At least, I'm going to read Nick's
odd expression as reluctance.

From the glass-topped brass coffee table—an aberration from the country motif—Paula drags over a ten-pound photo album smothered in blue moire and white eyelet.

"I'm so glad Nick got you to come," she says, then cackles with laughter. "Or maybe that part happens later, huh?"

My cheeks burn. Suddenly, feigning interest in nine years of baby pictures doesn't sound so bad. "We're just friends, Paula."

"Whatever," Paula says with a shrug, grunting a little when Tiffany crawls into her lap. A feeling almost like hunger claws at me as I watch her cuddle her little girl, automatically smooth down a strand of flyaway hair. "But I'm here to tell you, honey, if he's *anything* like his brother—" one side of her mouth lifts "—you won't know what hit you!"

"I know Paula's your cousin and all," Nick says, much later, his gaze directed at my cousin and her family buzzing around the picnic table at the far end of the tiny backyard, "but damn, she gets gabbier with each pregnancy." He's changed into jeans and a plain gray T-shirt, worn loose. A river-scented breeze ruffles his short hair as he stretches out on a wood-framed outdoor lounge chair taking up most of the decklet stretching across the back of the house. He takes a healthy swallow of tea. "If she has too many more kids, I may have to put her down."

I sputter with laughter. Except I've never seen a man crazier about kids. At least, his brother's kids. Little Tiffany, especially, to date Paula's only girl. I've also noticed the wistfulness in his expression when he looks at them, when he thinks nobody's watching.

"You're going to make a great daddy someday," I say.

Surprise flickers across his features. "Where'd that come from?"

I perch on a matching Adirondack chair a few feet away. "Watching you with the kids. Intuition." Fingering the cooler bottle, I look away. "It must've killed you when Amy said she didn't want children."

After a long moment he says, "I'll get over it."

I rub my hand on my leg, then nod toward a half-finished wooden play fort wedged between the picnic table and the side fence. "That's going to be nice."

"If I ever get it finished."

My gaze snaps to his. "*You're* building it?"

"Slowly but surely. I'm aimin' for Justin's birthday. So. You get enough to eat?"

"God, yes. Did I really put away three hamburgers?"

"I wouldn't've believed it if I hadn't seen it with my own eyes. Do you always eat like that?"

"Hey. Don't knock my life's work."

He chuckles. "By the way, your salad was pretty good, too. Even if I didn't recognize half the stuff that was in it."

"Confession time." I take a swig of my warm wine cooler. "My grandmother made it, not me."

"You don't cook?"

"Not enough to count. Left to my own devices, I would've brought deli macaroni salad or something."

While he seems to be mulling that over, I nod toward his tea. "I wouldn't've expected that. The tea, I mean."

After a moment's hesitation he says, "Five years ago, you would've been right."

I lower the cooler bottle that's just about to meet my lips. "Meaning?"

"I'm a recovering alcoholic." He looks at me, challenge simmering in his eyes. "That bother you?"

"No. Why should it?"

He studies me for a long moment, then said, "Since I never, *never* drank on duty, I didn't think it was out of control, y'know? Until I woke up once with my car on its side in a ditch. Scared the shit out of me."

"Oh, God. Were you all right?"

"More or less. Car was totaled, though."

"But Paula never said…"

"We don't talk about it much. I mean, Frank and Paula are supportive and all. We just don't make a big issue of it, you know what I mean?"

I nod, then say, "Was that…was that the real reason your wife left?"

He shakes his head. "No. If anything, I used her leaving as an excuse to drink more." His arms crossed, his attention drifts to Frank, arbitrating some fracas or other between two of the kids. "My old man was a drunk. So was my grandfather. But I dunno, back then, nobody thought much about it, I guess. Not unless somebody was missin' work or beatin' up on his wife or something, you know? It certainly never occurred to anybody it was a disease."

Nick pulls himself upright, straddling the lounge.

"It apparently skipped Frank, but hit me like a ton of bricks. Frank didn't say much up until that night, but…" He sighs. "Pop died when Frank and me were still kids. I guess Frank wasn't too hot on watching the same thing happen to me. So he threatened to tell my captain if I didn't get help. The thought of maybe losing my spot on the force…that woke me up, boy."

"But the accident…weren't the police called?"

"That was part of the deal between Frank and me. He brought his wrecker, pulled me out. It was 3:00 a.m., nobody around. I didn't even bother with the insurance. I just wanted to pretend like it never happened. Which was okay with Frank, as long as I got help."

I start to take another swig of the cooler, but stop. Nick notices my hesitation. "Hey, don't worry. I decided five years ago that I was stronger than the booze. That it's got no power to drag me down again."

"And?"

He smiles. "And…it's a constant struggle. But then I think what I might've lost if I hadn't stopped drinking, and that pretty much ends the discussion."

Dusk has taken the edge off the heat, some of the spunk out of the younger kids. There are four of them, the three boys all clones of Paula with their dark hair and eyes. I've been watching her all evening, the way she juggles her attention from one to the other and her husband and Nick and me with seemingly no effort. Her only career is being a mother to these children, a wife to the man she obviously adores. And she's clearly content with that, as Shelby is with her decision to take time off from her career to raise her kids, as my mother is with all her causes. All these women who know who they are, what they want from life.

Up until a month ago I would have counted myself among them.

I look back at Nick, who I catch watching me intently, his expression serious. That he doesn't avert his eyes unsettles me in ways I understand all too well. So I'm the one who turns away. "Did you always know you wanted to be a cop?"

His brows hitch, but he says, "Yeah, pretty much. At least I did by the time I hit high school."

"And you've never had any doubts? I mean, not even when cases don't go the way you want them to?"

That gets a laugh. "Hell, yeah, I have doubts. On a regular basis. But then I think, So what's the alternative? Selling insurance?" He shudders, making me smile. "I do what

I do because it fits who I am, I guess. Which is about as philosophical as I get, so don't push it.''

I laugh along with him, but way deep inside, that strange emptiness begins to spread through me again, that something's missing, something's off-kilter. I feel as though I've lost my footing somewhere along the way, that I'm about to fall, need to grab onto something, anything, to regain my balance…

Despite the warm evening, goose bumps crop up along my arms, making me shudder.

"You okay?"

I look at Nick, at the kindness in his expression, as much a part of him as the blue of his eyes. But it's not the kindness that strikes me so much at the moment as the simplicity and conviction behind his earlier statement. What must it be like, to know who you are?

And am I the only person I know who doesn't?

And maybe I should get over myself already. I mean, really—sitting around and worrying about my identity? Who the hell does that? Well, other than some underfed, neurotic TV character with far too much time on her hands.

I watch Frank and Paula, throwing bits of hot dog buns at each other while their kids scream with laughter. For them, it's clearly all about sex and kids and food and having a good time. The basics. Which isn't such a bad deal, if you think about it.

It's nearly dark. A soft "boom" floats in from the river.

"Hey, they've started!" Paula yells, as excited as the kids. "Oh, crap, we haven't done the ice cream sundaes yet!" She scurries around the table, dragging cartons of ice cream out of the cooler. "Come on, come on, everybody, so we can get up onto the roof before they get goin' good. Nick! Did you set up those chairs like I asked you to?''

"This morning," he says, then to me, "You got room for ice cream?"

"Always."

He grins, then swings one leg over the lounge to stand, holding out his hand to help me up. I hesitate, he says, "God Almighty, you are a case and a half," then reaches down, grabs my hand, and yanks me to my feet hard enough to send me itty-bitty titties smack into his hubba-hubba chest.

"You did that on purpose."

"You got a suspicious mind, you know that?" But his grin has widened.

And it occurs to me that I understand men less than I understand myself. Which, as we've just ascertained, isn't a whole lot. Take the one now gently shoving me toward the feeding trough, his hand at the small of my back sending all these *bzzt-bzzt-bzzt* dealies all up and down my body. Yeah, yeah, yeah, he wants to be my friend. And maybe he does. But my guess is, right now, he's probably thinking about sex. I mean, I am, so why wouldn't he be, right?

Or maybe I'm just delusional...

Uh, mmm...I just spilled some ice cream on my hand and he just lifted it to his mouth and licked it off.

Okay, so I'm not delusional. Any other time, I might have figured that was a good thing, but now...

Oh, man, that *tongue*—

"Jesus, Nicky," Paula says. "We do have napkins, you know."

He drops my hand, reaches behind him for a napkin, all the while doing this whole devilish-glint-in-the-eye number. Kids are crying and shrieking and jumping all around us and my hormones are crying and shrieking and jumping around inside me, and Paula is giving us dirty looks and I can't breathe properly because I have basically turned into one huge erogenous zone. And I should be annoyed, if not downright angry, except I can't take my eyes off his mouth.

"For God's sake, you two!"

Paula, again.

"You gonna make me get the hose or what?"

Nick does this slow, oh-sweet-Jesus grin and my knees begin to buckle. Then he takes me by the just-licked hand and leads me back into the house, where I hiss, "You got me here under false pretenses."

Blue, blue eyes fasten to mine. "I believe what I said was, I'm not gonna do anything to you, or with you, you don't want me to. That still holds."

Then everybody troops back inside and up to the roof, leaving me thinking *Ishouldn'thavecomeIshouldn'thave-comeIshouldn'thavecome….*

Our feet sink into the roof's surface, softened from the heat. I'm relieved to see there's a wide lip, maybe three feet high, so kidlets can't fall off. The house sits on a higher level than the rest of Greenpoint, offering an unimpeded view of the East River and the fireworks barges. Despite being an old, jaded woman, a thrill shivers along my spine, momentarily making me forget that I'm confused and shaky and pathetically horny.

Nick snaps open a webbed folding chair, plunks it down behind me. I sit, staring at the skyline silhouetted against the last traces of sunset. Amazing how different things look from a new perspective.

We've missed the first few rounds; now, we all sit, breathless, as explosion after sparkling explosion ripples through the night. I glance over at the kids, who are all staring at the show, totally spellbound, while their mother punctuates every burst of color with a childlike, "Oooh!"

I laugh, feeling good. Then I feel Nick's gaze on the side of my face and feel something else. Good, but not. Scared...but not.

Nick reaches over, links our hands.

Never in my life have I felt so much at peace and so antsy at the same time.

Never in my life have I felt so turned on when I know I have no business being even interested.

Never in my life have I been so sure I was about to make a fool of myself.

Or looked forward to it more.

The littlest Wojowodski has passed out by the time the fireworks are done; with the efficiency of a pair of army sergeants, Paula and Frank marshal the remaining troops and herd them downstairs and to bed. Nick picks up one of his nephews to aid the exodus, silently commanding me to stay put.

As if I have a choice. I am totally and completely drained, physically and emotionally. Can't move, can't think, don't want to do either. A breeze dances across my skin, laced with the faint tang of gunpowder, enough to make my eyes sting a little. I can hear murmurings from other nearby roofs, people scraping chairs, laughing, setting off a *verboten* firecracker. I lift to my lips what's left of the same cooler I've been nursing all night, grimacing at its sourness.

Nick's footsteps behind me send a shiver up my spine. I sense his walking around my chair, watch as he leans back against the low wall, his hands braced on either side of his hips. I suck in a sharp breath—just seeing him sitting on the edge like that makes my heart start hammering, my mouth go dry. And no, that's not desire, that's vertigo.

"What's wrong?" he says.

"You. The roof. Images of things that go splat on the sidewalk."

There's only a half moon, barely enough to see his silhouette, his smile flash in the darkness. The neighbors have all gone inside; silence blankets the neighborhood.

"It's perfectly safe," he says. "Come here."

I shake my head. He laughs.

"Chicken," he says softly, and somehow I don't think we're talking about the roof anymore.

"Damn straight."

"Come here," he says again. Challenging. Daring.

I know, if I go to him, what will happen. I know I'm in control, that it's my choice what happens—or doesn't.

What do I know about this man, really? Or he about me, for that matter. We're barely more than acquaintances, although I think we could be friends, in a weird sort of way. I do like him. I think I even trust him. Except the part about his wanting to be *friends*. Don't think I buy that anymore. I'm even less sure that would work for me. Not the way I'm feeling right now, like I could eat the man alive.

And go back for seconds.

What is it with me and Nicky Wojowodski, that he should keep happening into my life when I'm most vulnerable and in need of major ego-stroking, that I should be so willing to let him stroke it? Hell, to stroke anything that catches his fancy.

You know, what we should do is talk. Like we did the other night, when he brought over Chinese food (was that only a couple weeks ago?). I mean, I suppose there's the off chance that the heated gaze I can barely see in the sucky moonlight is due to something else entirely. What, I have no idea, since every time *I've* seen that look in a man's eyes, it's meant, *You. Naked. Now.*

He holds out his hand. "Last chance."

Yes, I know it's stupid and pointless and selfish. But God Almighty, I've never felt this kind of physical ache before for anyone, not even Greg, this need to connect with someone—some*thing*—as solid and strong as he is. I think the word I'm looking for is ravenous. Although brainless would work, too.

Because the thing is, see, I know what this is. It's just the body trying to seek some sort of release from all the tension I've been dealing with lately. Has nothing to· do with the brain. And it doesn't help that Nick is kind and good and sexy as hell and I find fireworks amazingly erotic—

"Hey," he whispers, his hand lifting my hair away from the side of my face. Which is when I realize I've closed the distance between us. "You're thinking too much again."

Then one knuckle trails along my temple, down my cheek, along my jawbone.

Oh, gee, thanks, Nick. My nipples are now hard enough to punch tin.

I start to cry.

He pulls me into his arms, rests his chin on top of my head. His heartbeat *whomp-whomps* in my ear.

"C-can I have my two minutes now?"

He fingers a corkscrew of hair that's worked loose. "Sure, why not?"

So, blubbering softly, I tell him about finding out that Greg paid off the wedding bills and how I know now it's over. Really over. And how I know I shouldn't be feeling empty like this, but I do, because all my plans really have gone *pffft* and I have absolutely no idea what to do next.

We listen as, three stories below, footsteps scrape along the sidewalk, fade into the darkness. Nick places a gentle kiss on my forehead, then sets me just far enough away to skim his hands down my bare arms, linking his fingers with mine.

"What would you say if I said I'd really like to kiss you right now?"

My heart stops. "Why?"

"Well, this may be a long shot, but because I think maybe we'd both enjoy it? And because your mouth drives me crazy."

So what do I do? I lick my lips. Oh, yeah, like that's a bright move.

"What happened to wanting to just be friends?"

He seems to consider this for a moment, then says, "What? Friends can't kiss?"

I open my mouth to protest, then think, oh, what the hell. What's it gonna hurt, letting him kiss me just once? Besides, it's not as if I remember much from ten years ago. If there's too much tongue or something, well, then, that'll neatly kill off whatever this is and I'll be home free, right?

"Okay, sure. Go ahead."

Nick laughs, shaking his head, then swoops in for the kill.

What am I, nuts? I mean, after the ice-cream licking episode, I should have known he'd know *exactly* what to do with his tongue.

Oh, mmm, he just pulled me closer…and closer still…and any closer and we're both going over the parapet, here…

I brace my hands on his chest. Carefully. Since the last thing I need to add to my list is the trauma of pushing somebody off a roof. As if being an inch away from having casual sex isn't enough to deal with. Which, come to think of it, I've only done once before, and that was with Nick, too.

I scrunch up my nose. "This isn't a date, right?"

Now don't ask me how he takes this as an invitation to start unbuttoning my dress, but he does. And I let him.

"Nah. Not a date. C'mere, you're too far away…" He starts to nuzzle my neck, his breath tickling my already-heated skin as his mouth finds its way to the top of my lace bra, where that tongue flicks out to skim right along the edge.

I nearly scream. Nick chuckles, his hand poised at the front clasp of my bra. "May I?"

My hands fly up. "Oh, what the hell? Just don't expect them to tumble free or anything. They just sort of sit there."

"Glad to hear it," Nick says, struggling a second or two with the clasp. "I wouldn't want things to get—"

Oh, *thank* you Lord, for giving me nipples!

"—out of hand."

So then we settle in for a nice long kissing and petting session until we're both breathing pretty hard and every nerve cell I have is screaming, "Hallelujah, sister," and I'm thinking, hmm, I'm having an awful lot of fun here for somebody who was in love with another man not all that long ago and just what does that say about my character? Well, I'll have to get back to you on that, because right now, all I can think is that I can't get enough of him…and wait a minute—how did we get turned around so I'm the one sitting on the wall—

"Holy cow, Nick!" What sounds like a shout in my head comes out more like a tortured wheeze. I clamp my arms around his neck so hard I'm surprised I'm not choking the man. "I'm going to fall off!"

"No, you won't," he whispers against my neck. "I've got you."

Oh, yeah, he's got me, all right. And he can have me. All of me. Preferably very soon.

I force my grip to loosen on one shoulder just long enough to grab his hair and yank his head up to look into my eyes. "This is serious rebound stuff, you realize," I say. "I mean, on both our parts."

Speaking of parts. The things he's doing to some of mine...

"I do," he says.

"I'm...oy...just using you."

"What are friends for?"

Okay, I can't argue with that one. But then I toss out, "I've never just, um, had sex to, well, have sex."

"Ginger, for God's sake!" Tortured look here. "If you don't want to do this, if you've changed your mind, tell me. Now. Because in about thirty seconds, it's either fuck you or throw myself off this roof."

Oh, my God. Talk about a turn-on.

"I didn't say I didn't want to do this. I just wanted you to know I don't *usually* do this."

A wry smile stretches across his face. "Except with me."

"You noticed that too, huh?"

His hand slips underneath my dress, my panties, to make unerring contact with the Spot That Knows No Reason. I moan. Wriggle a little.

"Is that a yes?"

All I can do is nod.

Still clutching me to him, he lifts my hips and removes my panties, leaving nothing between me and the rough brick wall save the back of my dress, nothing between me and sanity except...well, nothing. I hear a zipper being undone, realize he's about to take me—

"*Here?*" Yes, that's panic in my voice, since that's a lot of air behind me.

"You on the Pill?"

I nod.

"Then here's as good a place as any, sweetheart."

My heartbeat is pounding nearly as loudly in my head as it is in…other areas. "But what if Paula or Frank or somebody comes up here?"

Apparently this either doesn't concern him or it adds to his ardor, I'm not sure which, because he's positioning my legs around his waist and murmuring assurances that he will *not* let me go, and then he's inside me—hard and high and full—and I don't care. About anything. About my screwed-up life, about the fact that I'm having sex on the roof with a man I barely know, because this feels good, it feels *wonderful,* and I've never been so terrified or awestruck or excited in my entire life.

Except then I remember all that air behind me and, well, let's just say we lose the moment.

"So maybe the roof wasn't such a good idea," he says, breathing hard into my hair, and I mumble something about the idea of falling three stories to my untimely death being kind of inhibiting.

Next thing I know his pants are up and mine are God-knows-where, and I'm being yanked by the hand down the stairs, through his apartment—exposed brick walls, overstuffed furniture, lots of neutral colors, tidy—into his bedroom. A light clicks on: I see a king-size bed with navy-blue sheets. What's left of my clothes (note to self: retrieve drawers from roof before leaving) swooshes to the floor. A scant breeze from an open window licks at my damp skin as he skims his hands along my rib cage, kissing me, almost frantically exploring with his hands, his tongue…surprising me. Tormenting the bejesus out of me.

Suddenly my face is cupped in his hands, his eyes dark and intense. His thumbs skim my cheekbones, gentle and rough at the same time. His breath is coming in hard, short bursts. "If it kills me, after tonight, you'll forget all about the broom closet. Got that?" he says, and I say, "Okay, sure," and the next thing I know his clothes are off and I'm on the bed.

Which smells of fresh, clean-just-in-case sheets. I crush a pillow to my nose, throw it at him. "You *planned* this."

He deftly catches the pillow, even more deftly pins me to the bed. Oh, my. His eyes go dark. Serious. I swallow. Hard. "Hoped, maybe. Not planned. Especially not the roof part."

I have to admit, mentioning the roof does interesting things to me. Of course, the way we're lying here is doing some pretty interesting things to me, too. But I'm barely working up to thinking about this when Nick starts over again with the kissing and the nuzzling and the stroking, and I keep gasping because I realize I can't second-guess what he's going to do next, not that I care, but this is a guy who doesn't approach sex with a battle plan, but rather makes love as the spirit moves him.

Very nice.

And now he's inside me again, and I'm feeling very sexy and wanton and a whole lot of other very un-me things. My eyes drift closed to better savor the moment.

"No," Nick whispers. "Look at me."

"Can't. Eyes might pop out of my head."

His laughter is warm on my face. "Do it anyway."

I drag one eye open, then the other. Now, no man has ever looked me dead in the eye during sex before. I'm tempted to feel a little weird for, oh, about two seconds, until I realize I'm about to have one hell of an orgasm.

And a one…and a two…and…

"Ohgodohgodohgod…oh…oh…my…Ga…Ga…Ga…GAAAAOOOOD!"

Told ya.

Seconds pass.

"Damn," Nick mutters in my ear.

After another few seconds I manage to raise my head enough to look at him, except I'm breathing so hard I can hardly talk. "Damn?"

He lifts himself up on his forearms so he doesn't squish me. "Only once, huh?"

Takes me a minute. Then I let out a flummoxed, "You have got to be kidding."

He does the male equivalent of a pout. You know, that thing they do when they find out you really *do* have a headache? "I just thought...you know."

My head flops back on the pillow. "What is it with men and their ridiculous competitive streak? It's not about giving me a double orgasm, okay? It's not even about giving me one—"

"You want me to take that one back?"

I'd smack him, but the blood hasn't reached that far yet.

"It's about," I say, ignoring him, "being close. Caring."

Which is when I make my fatal mistake, apparently, because now he's braced himself over me again and we're doing that eye-connecting thing, and I think, *Uh-oh.* Because, yup, there they are. Kids and minivans and a house in Brooklyn.

"I can do close," he says.

And there's not a single shred of a glint in his eye.

I'll say one thing about me: when remorse hits, it doesn't pussyfoot around. I shove Nick off me and bound off the bed, scouring the room for my clothes. I hear Nick call out as I shoot into the bathroom, lock the door behind me. God, my hands are shaking so hard, I can barely turn the water on in the sink. I should take a shower, I know that, but somehow that seems too intimate, too comfortable. Would take too long. And I have to go find my underpants.

Jeans on, Nick's in the kitchen when I come out. "Here."

My panties come sailing across the room. I fumble for them, not sure whether or not to excuse myself to put them on. And how dumb is that?

"Thanks," I mutter.

"I'll take you home," he says, his voice low, strained. But he's not looking at me.

"No," I say, slipping on the panties as quickly and discreetly as possible. "I'll take the train—"

"Like hell, Ginger! No way am I letting you ride the subway at this hour."

"Get over yourself, Nick. I've been riding the subway alone since I was thirteen. At night since I was seventeen. I know how to take care of myself."

"Yeah, you sure do, don't you?"

The ice in his voice stops me. "What's that supposed to mean?"

"Forget it."

"No. No, I want to know what you meant by that."

"No, you don't. You don't want to know what anybody thinks. Not unless it happens to coincide with whatever you've already decided, the way you've already mapped out your life. Jesus, Ginger—why do you fight everything so much?"

"I don't—"

"Yeah, you do. You got a real problem with just letting go and enjoying the moment, don't you? Have you ever been able to just see where things lead without trying to force them to go the way you *think* they should go?"

You know, this would be so much easier if the sex had been bad. Or even forgettable. But noooo, it had to be Grade AAA Superior, didn't it? God, I'm still tingling. I can still, with very little effort, feel him inside me. And

God help me, I want him there again. But not like this. Not like…

"Nick, please—this is so not fair to you. We both just broke up with people, we're not ready for…anything. I don't know what planet I was on, letting myself do this. I mean…"

Great. Can't even finish my damn sentence.

Nick gives me one of those stoic looks men are so good at, then goes over to his sink, rinses out some glass that had been sitting there. This should be my cue to leave, but when I open my mouth to say as much, his voice fills the void between us.

"You know, I remember my mother tellin' me something that's always stuck with me. That sometimes, while we're so busy knockin' ourselves out tryin' to get something we think we want, we end up missing out on something better. And that whenever it seems like what we wanted so badly slips outta our grasp, maybe it's because somebody's tryin' to tell us something. And that's the problem with what just happened, isn't it? What just happened tonight didn't fit in with your plans."

"Don't be ridiculous, Nick. I wouldn't have gone to bed with you if I hadn't wanted to."

"Then why are you runnin' scared, Ginger? Have I said anything to make you think I've changed the game plan?"

"N-no."

"That's right. I haven't. I haven't done or said a goddamn thing to threaten you or make you feel backed into a corner." He crosses his arms over his chest. His voice is calm, his posture casual, but tension and anger radiate from him in hot, brutal waves. "What? The sex didn't live up to your expectations?"

"Oh, God, Nick, no…the sex was great—"

"Then what's the problem, dammit?"

I remember the look in his eyes, hug myself. "It's... complicated."

He lets out a harsh sigh. "Yeah, I'll just bet it is. Jesus. If I live to be a hundred and forty, I'll never understand why women have to make things so damn *complicated* all the time."

Confusion makes me lash back. "At least that's better than a kill or score mentality that makes men think all of life's problems can be solved with either sports, violence or sex!"

He almost smiles. "This from the woman on the other end of that I'll-use-you-if-you-use-me conversation. Or is my memory playin' tricks on me?"

Tears bite at my eyes. "No, Nick. Your memory's not playing tricks."

"Well, that's a load off my mind. So tell me, Ginger, why is everything suddenly so complicated?"

God, I feel like a dork. A stupid, brainless, selfish dork. "I can't explain it. Okay? I'm sorry, I can't. Dammit, Nick—stop looking at me like that!"

"Like what? Like maybe I give a shit and that's messing with your head too much?"

Inside my chest, my heart feels as though it's going to explode.

"I can't do this," I say, and practically fly from the apartment.

And right now you're probably thinking, is this woman nuts or what? I mean, you must be, because God knows I am. Yeah, I suppose I could just go ahead and have an affair with him, isn't that what the hip single woman does these days? Sex for sex's sake? Well, I can't. I mean, I could, but I can't. Not with Nick. He wants more, I know that, but...Nick and me would never work.

He scares me, okay? Not because I think he'd ever hurt me, it's not that, it's…it's not just that Nick Wojowodski views life in an uncomplicated way, it's that *he's* uncomplicated. Everything's right there on the surface, solid and predictable and readable. Me? *Pfuh.* Thirty-one years old, and basically little more than an amorphous mass of estrogen-riddled protoplasm.

I've reached this cheerful conclusion just about the time I get back to my mother's apartment. It's nearly 1:00 a.m. I let myself in with the set of keys I still have, slipping off my sandals, then avoiding the creaky floorboards as I tiptoe down the hall to the kitchen to get a drink of water after the long train ride. As I pass the living room, however, I feel…a presence. As if someone or something's watching me.

My heart leaps into my throat, effectively trapping the scream roaring up right behind it. I turn, willing myself to distinguish between the shadows in the living room, but there's so much crap piled in the room I can't.

Then I hear it. A rustling sound, so faint I almost miss it.

Oh, God. I *so* do not need this right now.

It's finally happened. After twenty-five years of my mother's staunch refusal to install a gate over the fire escape window in the living room, somebody's broken in and is now lurking in the shadows, waiting to bludgeon me to death for having come upon him. Or her. But maybe if I can just…sidle over to the light switch, right…there…

After a few fumbles, my hand finds the switch on the wall behind me. This is totally insane, what I'm about to do. But it's him or me, and maybe my life is worth squat right now, but it's the only one I've got and I can't bear the thought of leaving it in this much of a mess.

I flip the switch and shriek my brains out.

Twelve

My mother comes flying out of her room in a T-shirt and underpants, feet pounding, bosoms bouncing. My grandmother, bless her, sleeps like the dead.

"Ginger! For God's sake, what on earth—"

I turn on my mother, hardly able to get the words past my gritted teeth. "What…the…*hell*…is…*that* doing *here?*"

My arm swings out toward the rooster locked in his wire cage. The bird jerks his head to one side, impaling me with his beady little gaze, before letting out an ugly, offended squawk.

"The Ortizes couldn't keep it where they were," my mother calmly says. "They remembered I'd said to call me if they needed help, so they called." She ends her sentence with a shrug, as if that's all the explanation necessary.

All I can do is stare at her. "And somehow that translates to giving sanctuary to a chicken?"

"Only for a few days. Until they find another place, maybe with another relative."

"And they didn't think to call Animal Control? No, wait, *you* didn't think of calling Animal Control?"

"I couldn't do that! They would have destroyed Rocky."

"Rocky?"

"*Chicken Run* is their little boy's favorite movie."

"Nedra. Listen to me. It's against the law to keep livestock in Manhattan. Has been for probably, oh, for a hundred years, give or take."

"Honestly, Ginger." She crosses her arms, indignant. "You're acting as though I brought home a cow or something."

Now do you see what I've had to put up with all these years?

"Jesus, Nedra—what are the neighbors going to say?"

"They won't know—will they?—unless somebody with a big mouth tells them."

"The *rooster* will tell them, for God's sake!"

Presumably because my turning on the light has thoroughly disrupted his biorhythms, Rocky picks that precise moment to demonstrate his crowing technique, stretching up *en pointe* and beating his wings against the sides of the cage. A feather flies out, drifts to the carpet. I don't even want to think about the various…things that might live in that feather.

"Look at that," Nedra says. "You're upsetting him."

"I'm upsetting *him*—?"

"And for someone who just had sex, you're sure cranky."

If my mouth hadn't already been open, it would have dropped to my chest. Since I'm a rotten liar, there's little point in denying it, although God knows how she knows. Some kind of latent motherly radar or something, I suppose. In any case, the best I can do is shoot back, ''Yeah, well, at least one of us did,'' before turning smartly on my bare heel and tromping off to my room.

''Don't be so sure about that,'' she says behind me. But by the time I recover enough to turn back around, she's gone.

The rooster, unfortunately, is not.

If there'd been any way of avoiding the kitchen the next morning, believe me, I would have. But after less than five hours' sleep—rudely interrupted by enthusiastic crowing—setting foot outside the apartment without a major caffeine injection would have been foolhardy, if not downright dangerous to the general public. So here I am in the kitchen—feeling reasonably pulled together in a crisp white sleeveless blouse and a long, straight black skirt with a slit up the front—trying to ignore the rooster perched on the back of *my* chair, Nonna chattering in what I can only surmise is Italian baby talk to the rooster perched on the back of *my* chair, and my mother sitting at the table next to the rooster perched on the back of *my* chair, nonchalantly sipping coffee and reading the *Times*.

Criminy. The woman is downright *glowing*. Which I might be, too, if I weren't so screwed up.

No. *No.* I am not going to think about me. Nick. Us.

So I'll think about my mother. Which isn't actually making me any more comfortable. To be perfectly honest, the idea of my mother getting it on is almost weirder than having a rooster perched on the back of my chair.

I grab a piece of toast, ignoring Nonna's entreaties to sit down (like I'm going to let this thing peck at my hair) eat a real breakfast, I'm too skinny, and contemplate the fifty-year-old woman sitting in front of me. There she sits, in a shapeless, sleeveless patterned dress, her hair boisterously free around her shoulders, her brows pinched in concentration, and I'm thinking, God, she's beautiful. And it's not as if I'm repulsed by the idea of her having sex, don't get me wrong. More power to her. Frankly, I think she should have been hitting the sheets years ago, if you ask me. It's just…she hasn't. Not once since Dad died that I know of. And of course, part of me wants to grill her: is this an ongoing thing? Do I know the man? Is this serious?

Is she really as happy as she looks?

I sneak another peek at her face through the rooster's tail to check.

Hell, my guess is that she's delirious.

And this is bothering me because…?

My cell rings. I sprint down the hall to my bedroom to discover Nonna has already made my bed. When did she do that? I pick up the phone before it hits me. Oh, God, what if this is Nick? What am I supposed to say?

What am I, thirteen?

"Hello?" I say cautiously, hoping to distract myself by trying to figure out where the hell Nonna put my black T-straps.

"Ginger? Hi, it's Curtiss James. Geoffrey's new daddy?"

"Oh—" Aha. There they are. In the closet, of all places. "Hi," I say, relieved and not at the same time. That it's not Nick, I mean. Figure that one out. Anyway, so here I am, trying to hang on to the phone and hook the strap on my right shoe with one hand. "How are you?"

"Well, I'm fine. But…we have a problem. It seem Liam's allergic to dog hair, which we didn't know until I brought Geoff home. I mean, we thought it was something else at first—we really wanted it to be something else, be-

cause Liam absolutely *adores* this dog—and then he had
to go away for a few days on a shoot, but then when he
came back, boom! His eyes are so red, he looks like a child
of the devil. Not even antihistamines work, before you
ask—''

I wasn't going to.

"—so the long and the short of it is, we can't keep the
dog. So we were wondering—hoping, actually—that we
could return him to you?''

I momentarily freeze. Then a little shudder of joy ripples
right down my spine. After all these weeks of things being
taken away from me, you mean I'm actually going to get
something *back*?

"Of course you can! Oh, God...I mean, I'm really sorry
it didn't work out for you, but I'd love to have him! When
can you bring him? Oh, wait—I'm not where I was—long
story—and I had to move back in with my mother, so let
me give you that address.''

"Hold on...Liam, honey? Can you toss me that pen?
Thanks, you're a doll.'' Then to me, "God. You're back
with your *mother*?''

"And you don't even know her.''

"I know mine, and that's bad enough. Okay, shoot.''

I give him the address, he says he'll bring the dog by
around seven, and we hang up. Only then do I realize I
didn't even bother asking my mother if it was okay for me
to bring back the dog.

Excuse me? There's a rooster strutting down the hall—
I can hear it's little chicken toenails scraping the bare floor,
yech—and I'm worried about bringing in a *dog*?

Oh, crap. What if the dog eats the rooster?

Then again, what if the dog eats the rooster?

Oh, well. Them's the breaks.

* * *

The kitchen, later that evening. Geoff has wedged himself in backward between the refrigerator and the cabinet, alternately whimpering and snapping at the rooster, who, with much wing-flapping and ballyhoo, is doing the poultry equivalent of break dancing in the middle of the kitchen floor. While my mother and I argue over the best way to catch the stupid bird and get him back in his cage, Nonna, armed with a broom and emitting a constant stream of frantic Italian, is trying to keep the bird from pecking the dog's eyes out.

Now, I'm not a total idiot. I'd told my mother about Geoff, she was cool with it—what else?—so we'd put the rooster in his cage when Curtiss dropped off the dog and all his stuff, including the never-ending bag of dog food (which actually, is finally down to about a third). Anyway, we were in the midst of giving Geoff the grand tour of his new home when, in a blur of feathers and agitated clucking, Rocky burst into the kitchen and attacked the poor dog. Who knew the damn thing knew how to undo the latch to the cage?

"Wait!" I say, blinded by a flash of sudden inspiration. "My laundry basket!"

I dash to my room, dumping my dirty clothes in a trail along the floor as I sprint back to the kitchen. By now, Rocky is strutting back and forth in front of the dog, apparently satisfied just to torment him with his presence. Geoff seems more pissed than anything else, curling back his lip and issuing the occasional growl, although he keeps shooting me "Would you *please* get this damn thing outta here" looks. My grandmother sees the laundry basket, which I'm now holding upside down in preparation for the Big Pounce, tosses the bird what looks like a crouton. (Seems a waste of a perfectly good crouton to me, but desperate times call for desperate measures.) Anyway, the chicken goes for the crouton, I go for the chicken. The basket neatly dropped down over it, I then yell to anybody who'll listen to get the cage.

The bird now securely ensconced in his cage, which has been removed to my mother's room—"You brought him here, you can keep him with you," I said, and she didn't argue—the poor dog allows Nonna to entice him from his hidey-hole with scraps of the roast beef we had for dinner.

"Hey. He's only supposed to eat his own food," I say, pointing to the rolled-up bag lolling against the leg of the kitchen table. Nonna eyes it, hands Geoff another piece of beef. As much as she seemed taken with the rooster, I can tell fur wins over feathers, no contest. Especially as the furred thing has a *brain*.

"Why such a big bag? Is too much food for such a small dog, no?"

"Don't ask me, ask Brice." I wince. "Well, you could have asked Brice if he were, you know, alive."

Her duty done, Nonna says, *"Basta"* to the dog, then turns and glowers at the bag. "Open bag, is no good. Things will crawl in. You go out, find something with a lid to put it in."

Forty-five minutes later Nedra and I are trooping back up Broadway at eight o'clock on a balmy summer night, lugging home a miniature garbage pail, complete with lid. I have no idea why she decided to come along, but she keeps giving me these looks, as if she wants to talk but doesn't quite know how to go about it. Since we're not prone to having cozy little mother-daughter heart-to-hearts, I can understand why. I'm also not going to make it easier for her.

Never mind that my brain is about to explode with curiosity.

Dusk has purpled most of the sky, save for the brilliant rim of orange along the horizon, just visible at the crosstown streets through the trees along Riverside Drive. The atmosphere is relaxed—for New York, anyway—the scene almost carnival-like. The sidewalks are clogged with people and laughter, strollers and the creaking, wheeled shopping carts unbiquitous to the city. Bodies swarm around the open-air fruit and vegetable stands, filling the air with a dozen languages; dogs tied to parking meters stare fixedly through a thousand passing legs at store entrances, dodging passersbys' attempts to get their attention, only to explode into dance when their owners finally emerge.

Morningside Heights has changed a great deal since I was a kid, as have most Manhattan neighborhoods, I suppose. Many of the family-owned businesses that gave each area of the city its unique flavor have gone the way of the ten-cent pay phone in favor of franchises that threaten to make New York no different from Houston or Des Moines. But New York is all about attitude, I decide as we sidestep a pair of Hispanic teenage girls giggling so hard about something they can barely walk. Attitude, and energy, and survival. And each neighborhood has its own slant on that, something that can't be completely annihilated by the Great Franchise Invasion.

"Oh, look," Nedra says, nudging me as we pass West Side Market. "They've got cherries on sale."

We both grab plastic bags, assume our positions on either side of the trio of slanted bins stretching across the front of the store. The can shoved underneath the bleacher-like space formed by the raised bins, I begin plucking the best cherries from my side, along with about a hundred other people. I catch my mother watching me, but she averts her eyes when I look up.

Something pings off my head.

I look across the bins at my mother, who is frowning in concentration at the cherries. I think, *hmm,* and resume picking.

Two seconds later, *thunk,* a cherry bounces off my shoulder and back into the bin. My gaze shoots across to my mother, who looks up. "What?" she says.

But her eyes are sparkling like jet.

I wait for my opportunity, then lob a cherry at her. Only a little old Spanish lady gets in the way and the missile bounces off her forehead. The poor woman looks around, puzzled, then starts gesticulating to her companion, going on in rapid-fire Spanish about what just happened.

My mother and I don't dare look at each other.

We hold it in until the cherries are paid for—we each get about three pounds, which is way more cherries than we'll be able to eat before they rot—and stowed inside the garbage pail for the six block trek back to her building. Giggling, we each grab a handle and start up the block, exploding into howling laughter before we hit 111th Street. People are looking at us. Some smile. Some frown. I do not care.

I can't remember laughing with my mother like this since I was little.

Hell, I can't remember laughing like this with *anyone,* not in a very long time, at least.

As we cross 112th Street, we both automatically glance east toward Amsterdam Avenue. At the end of the long, narrow block, The Cathedral of St. John the Divine looms in quiet majesty over the neighborhood. Nedra says, "Do you remember my taking you to the park over there when you were little?"

Do I? Oh, yeah. We went there often, no matter what the season. She'd sit on the grass or one of the park benches

nd gab with other mothers, while I'd play tag with children
f a dozen different colors....

"You remember that time one of the peacocks suddenly
ppeared in front of you with his tail fanned out?" Nedra
ays, laughing. "I thought you'd wet your pants."

My own laughter blends with hers. "I did." I throw her
 glance, a smile tugging at my lips. "Maybe my aversion
o fowl can be traced to that initial childhood trauma."

"Oh, stop," she says, but she's smiling, too. "Okay, so
naybe the rooster was a bad idea."

"You think?" I say, and she shrugs, jostling the can
etween us.

We walk in silence for another block before she says,
"So. You're over Greg?"

"She said hopefully."

"She said hopefully." She flicks a glance in my direc-
ion. "Well?"

Now it's my turn to shrug. "I don't know. Yeah, I sup-
ose. But...the other night has nothing to do with that."

"Oh?"

"No."

"Oh," she says. Another few yards, then, "This is Nick
ve're talking about, right?"

I glance over, but it's gotten too dark to see well. "You
emember Nick?"

She smiles. "Oh, yeah."

"Okay, fine. It was Nick. Your turn."

Her laugh is low. "Nice try."

"God. You are so evil."

Another laugh. "I am, huh?"

My assumption is this means I do know the man. Great.
Now I'm going to be obsessed with trying to figure
ut who it is. Like that gal who has to guess Rumpelstilt-
kin's name.

"Okay," she says, "before you burst something in your brain, ask yourself—does it really matter? Who it is, I mean?"

"Is that guilt I hear in your voice?"

"Hardly. Just…a need to keep some things private. At least until I figure a few things out for myself first."

I nearly come to a dead halt right in the middle of the sidewalk. Nedra, insecure? Nedra, who doesn't have a dubious bone in her ample body?

"So…this isn't just one of those I've-met-someone-and-I'm-hearing-wedding-bells kinds of things?"

Her laugh booms from her chest. "God, no. This is more like I've-met-someone-and-the-sex-is-great-but-this-is-nuts kinds of things."

Now I'm really intrigued. Enough to not even flinch at the weirdness of talking about sex with my own mother.

Now *she* comes to a stop, nearly yanking my arm off. I spin around. Her mouth is drawn into a tight line. "When it comes to men, I'm clueless, you know?" She looks away, swipes her hair out of her face with her free hand and holds it to her temple, then looks back at me. "I don't know the rules. Hell, I don't even know if there *are* any rules. God. I was barely eighteen when I met your father. I fell in love, had you, got married, never looked back. Leo was the only man I ever slept with, believe it or not. And when he died…"

Again, she hesitates, then lets out her breath in an abrupt sigh. "I was only thirty-two," she says, almost as if she can't quite believe it herself. "And yet I figured, Hey, it's over for me. I had my great love, I have a great kid, I have my work…who needs sex to muck things up? Now don't ask me why I had to wait until menopause to figure out what I'd been missing for eighteen years, but better now than not at all, I suppose."

I need a minute to sift through all that, so I tug at the can, get us started again. "So…what you're saying is, I shouldn't expect a stepfather out of this?"

"No."

"Oh, my God—he's not married, is he?"

Horror streaks across her features. "Honestly, Ginger—give me some credit!"

"Sorry." Then I ask, because I've got to know, "Are you happy?"

"I'm…content with things the way they are, I suppose. In some ways." She sighs. "God. If this is what you younger types go through, I sure don't envy you. All this angst, this indecision, this wondering if I'm doing the right thing…how the hell do you stand it?"

"That's easy. Häagen-Dazs."

"The weird thing is," she continues, "that when I'm with him, nothing else seems to matter. It's when we're apart I get very confused."

"And this isn't driving you nuts?"

"Sure it is. But what's the alternative?"

"Maybe finding someone who doesn't make you confused?"

After a moment she says, "You mean, like what you did with Greg?"

"Well…yes, actually. I mean, the whole reason I was attracted to him was because being with him *didn't* put me through a million changes." Unlike some other people I could name. "I never felt confused when I was with him. I felt safe. I felt *sane*."

"Well, hell—where's the fun in that?"

"I'm not like you, Nedra. I don't like living on the edge."

I can feel her scrutiny on the side of my face. "You think following your heart is living on the edge?"

"If it makes you feel off balance, yes."

The conversation is making my stomach knot, but just when I start to say I think we should change the subject, Nedra says thoughtfully, "I suppose I felt safe with your father, come to think of it. Because I knew we were supposed to be together, I suppose, which is its own kind of security. Still, being with Leo also always made me feel…I don't know…more alive, somehow?" She laughs. "The man always kept me on my toes. Always challenged me, made me look at things in a different light. He always inspired me to be…*more.*"

"But this…whatever it is, it's different from that?"

She gives me the first on-equal-footing look I think we've ever shared. "Right now, it's all about the sex. About having a good time together. This man makes me feel good about myself and my body. May not be a lot, but I'll take it."

Something like envy zips through me. Yeah, maybe Nedra says she's conflicted, but that's not stopping her, is it? Hell, no. *She* didn't storm out of her lover's apartment like some neurotic doofus. *She* isn't letting a little thing like stark terror keep her from enjoying the moment.

But that's the difference between us, I guess. She likes danger. I don't. What she calls "alive," I call "petrifying."

And I don't much like being petrified.

We begin the uphill climb from Broadway toward her building. "You ever regret the choices you made over the years? About how you've chosen to live your life?"

My question clearly startles her for a moment, but then she says, "No. Not about the big stuff." She glances at me, then away. "For the most part, I like who I am. What I do. I know I tick a lot of people off—including you—but I wouldn't be happy trying to be somebody else, would I?"

After a moment I say, "No, I guess not."

"But I do have two regrets in my life, I suppose, even if one of them isn't something I could have controlled anyway."

"And what's that?"

"That I never had another kid. Leo and I would have liked that."

This is news to me. I'd always assumed I was an only child by my parents' choice. "And the other thing?"

I catch her smile out of the corner of my eye. "I'm sorry I told you to call me by my first name when you were little."

"You're kidding?"

"Weird, isn't it?" She laughs softly, then says, "I was so young when I had you, I guess I couldn't quite grasp the idea of being somebody's mother. But now...now I wish I'd heard you call me Mommy."

I cock my head at her, then shake it. "You're not a mommy, Nedra. Sorry."

"Yeah. I know."

We get to the door of my mother's apartment building. José, the night doorman, raises one eyebrow at our loot, but only shakes his head.

"How'd you get the rooster in, anyway?" I ask when we're safely out of earshot.

"I walked quickly and pretended it was a parrot."

My cell is ringing when we get inside the apartment. Nonna hands the phone to me, taking the can from us and carting it down the hall, but not before I notice the woman whom I've never seen wearing anything but housedresses in murky prints—which is what she had on when we left forty-five minutes ago—is now sporting a black T-shirt of mine that declares It's All About Me.

Cue "Twilight Zone" music.

I go into my room to answer the phone. It's Terrie, who

barely lets me get out "Hello?" before she says, "Okay, so Davis calls me, right? And we end up spending like two hours on the phone, and I'm thinking, this is really weird, because I cannot remember the last time I heard a man able to focus for two hours on anything that didn't involve uniforms and a ball of some kind. So then he asks me out, and I hear myself accepting, because what else was I gonna do? Turn the man down after we just talked our butts off for two hours?"

Takes a second before I realize there's a pause, which is the first chance I have to say, "How'd he get your number?"

Another pause. Then, "Okay, so I gave it to him. I mean, it wasn't like I expected him to actually *call.*"

I decide against pointing out that if she hadn't actually hoped he'd call, she wouldn't have given him her number. But then, this is Terrie we're talking about.

"Anyway," she says, "so what was I supposed to say? 'Thanks for the nice conversation and by the way, have a nice life'? I mean, that would have been—"

"Rude?" I suggest. Not because I agree with her, although I'm beginning to feel eerily as though I've been down this path myself. Very recently.

"If not downright mean. I mean, that's what I keep telling myself, you know? So, anyway, we go out—he gets tickets to the ballet, *and* he not only doesn't fall asleep, he knows more about the dancers than I do—and then we go to some fine club downtown with some fabulous jazz until like, I don't know, one in the morning or something, and then we come back here to my place and we talk some more and not once does he pull out some sorry business about why his wife left him. A-and then somehow we start kissing—okay, so I came on to him because those pretty lips of his were just making me crazy—but that's all that happened because he says he doesn't want to rush me into anything, he wants to take this nice and slow, and then he leaves me feeling like a truck just ran me over and god-damn it to hell, Ginger, *why* do I keep doing this to my-self?''

She's in tears by this point. Hysterical, actually, which scares me because Terrie never cries. At least, she never has in my presence. And I'm sitting here on the edge of my bed thinking, Oh, uh-huh, like I'm really the one to help you sort out your love life.

''When did all this happen?'' I ask, stalling.

I hear nose-blowing, then a shuddering breath. ''T-two nights ago.''

''And you're just calling me now?''

''Well, see, Davis took me out to the Hamptons for the day yesterday.'' The last syllable ends on something like a wail.

''And…I'm guessing you had a great time?''

''Yes, dammit! Oh, God, Ginger—this is so *stupid!* You know as well as I do exactly what's going to happen. He'll be all perfect and understanding until I fall in love with him—which at the rate things are going, should take about another ten minutes—and then he's gonna do the same thing they all do. I mean, *Je*sus, it's like the gods are sitting up there, snickering behind their hands while they look down at my sorry ass and say, *Suckah.* And I've got nobody to blame but myself. I didn't have to stay on the phone with the man, or go out with him, or go spend a perfect day with him. But I did. And now I'm gonna pay the price.''

Oh, yeah. Know how that goes, boy. Still, some perverse optimistic streak in me—and God knows where this is com-ing from, since recent personal experience certainly doesn't bear this out—prompts me to say, "And maybe this is the one time it takes."

That gets a snort on the other end of the line.

"No, Terrie. I'm serious."

"Yeah," she says on a sigh. "I know you are. And you know what really bites? After everything I've been through, everything I know about me and men, I want to believe you. That, after all's said and done, I still want a man in my life. Not to take care of me or provide for me, but just to be there for me. For *me*." I hear a thump, as though she's just smacked her own chest. "I still want to believe there's a good man out there whose smile is gonna make me grateful for every breath I take. And how dumb is that? I know what the reality is. I *know*. And yet here's this damn…hope in the center of my chest that will not die. No matter how often it's been ripped to shreds, it just keeps on regenerating, taking inordinate pleasure in making my life a living hell."

Yep, that damn hope thing screws us every time. But then, I suppose that's what keeps our heads out of the ovens, too.

I pull one foot up onto the edge of the bed, contemplate repolishing my toenails. Something frosted and pale this time, I think. "You could break it off with Davis," I say.

"I know."

"So…?"

I hear a long, soul-shuddering sigh.

"Well," I say again, sounding all together and knowledgeable, because that's what she needs me to be at the moment, "then I guess you have to ask yourself which you want more—to avoid the pain, or take the risk on the hope."

I ignore the little twinge of pain in my own gut.

"You know," Terrie says, "I really hate it when you get all logical on me."

Then she hangs up. This is getting to be a bad habit with her.

I lie back on the bed, willing my mind to go blank. This works for maybe five, six seconds, until, from down the hall, I hear what sounds like a small avalanche as Nonna apparently dumps the rest of the dog food into the just-purchased plastic can. Then:

"*Per Dio!* Ginger! Nedra! *Venite! Subito!*"

I jump off the bed and take off down the hall, nearly colliding with my mother halfway there as images of rats or worse (whatever that might be) scurry through my brain. My grandmother is standing over the garbage can/food bin, her hands clamped to her jowls. At our entrance, she turns, her eyes as wide as her favorite pasta dishes, then jabs one finger at the bin.

"*Guardate!*"

We peer inside. There, nestled in a sea of kibble, sits a large size Ziplock bag stuffed with what I'm guessing are a helluva lot of hundred dollar bills.

"I do not think is good, no?" she whispers.

And here I thought our butts were in a sling with the rooster.

I'm sitting at my kitchen table, looking up at Nick, who is wearing worn jeans, a formfitting navy-blue knit shirt, and a scowl.

"Look," I say, scowling back, "all I know is what we all already told you. Nonna upended the bag and there was the money. How it got there, I have no idea." I look down, concentrating on stroking Geoff's furry rump with my bare toes. The dog is lying at my feet, torn between protecting me from the grumpy, snarling man and guarding his food a few feet away, in which everybody and their cousin has suddenly developed a profound interest. Although he occasionally swings a furtive glance in the direction of my mother's bedroom, just to make sure The Thing isn't about to burst forth and flap him to death. In the living room, another officer is questioning my grandmother, while a third leans against the counter, listening to Nick questioning me.

And my mother is standing in the doorway between the two rooms with a very smug expression on her face.

Damn.

The only reason I called my old precinct substation is because I thought this might have something to do with Brice's murder, although I hardly expected Nick himself to show up. Except, as he pointed out—irritably—it's his case.

God, I hate the way he's not looking at me. You know, wearing that tough-guys-don't-sulk expression that just rips your heart out? Not that I blame him, but…crap. Now I can hate myself on top of everything else. I mean, yeah, I don't have a problem with watching out for my own butt, but I don't get off on steam-rolling over other people's feelings, either.

Especially not people like Nick. He deserves better than that.

"So. Any of you handle the evidence?" he asks, all business.

"No. Well, I know my mother and I didn't. And Nonna says she just upended the bag and dumped everything into the bin. I guess I can't swear that Curtiss or his partner didn't, but why would they?"

"For all you know, they might have put the money in there to begin with."

My eyes go wide. "Then bring me back the dog in order to hide it here? Why on earth would they do that?"

"Because people sometimes do very strange things, Ginger," he says, pinning me with that icy-blue gaze. "Crazy things. Illogical things."

Okay, okay…I get the point. Sheesh.

Nick then hooks his thumbs in his front pockets, which isn't the smartest move he could have made, considering how that stretches the denim right across an area smack at my eye level. Then he shrugs. "Besides, you said you don't really know these people."

"Well, no, but…that just doesn't make sense. The bag was getting pretty low. We would have found the money anyway in a couple of days, maybe a week at the most."

"But you did say this Curtiss James was an old lover of Fanning's."

"Yeah, maybe three years ago—"

My grandmother is hustling the young cop who questioned her—a dark-haired, black-eyed looker from the old neighborhood—back to the kitchen. I think she's trying to push freshly made tortellini off on him. I look back at Nick, who immediately lowers his eyes to his notebook. The second officer drifts away, sucked in by my grandmother's tortellini-pushing. *Sì, sì,* she has plenty. *Sì,* it reheats in microwave, two minutes, no problem…

"Hey," I say in a low voice, "the bag came from Brice's apartment originally. Well, not *originally,* but you know what I mean. And hey, again, he's the one who's dead. And we know he was pilfering funds from the accounts."

Nick's eyes dart to mine. "You know that?"

"Yeah, the accountant told me. That's why I haven't been paid. And won't," I add, just because, "until you guys release the building so it can be sold."

Nick ignores that. "So…you're saying at least five people that you know of have come in contact with this bag since Fanning's death?"

"Six. Counting you."

His gaze snaps to mine, horror blooming in his eyes just as the old bell goes *ding* in my brain. Okay, so if this can be construed as Nick having removed evidence from a possible crime scene...

Oops.

Behind us, one of the cops laughs at something my mother says; the radio attached to Nick's belt spits out garbled noises; Geoff lifts his head, growling low in his throat, his snout pointed directly toward my mother's room. Nick opens his mouth to say something, only to swerve his head in the same direction as Geoff's.

"What was that?"

My mother and I exchange a split-second glance.

"Damn dog growls at everything," I say. "Probably just the people upstairs..."

"No, listen...there!" Nick looks at me. "Did you hear that? Sounds just like...crowing?"

Naturally, Geoff gets up and trots over to the door between the kitchen and my mother's room, where he sniffs at the crack in the door, then looks back at me as if to say, "Remember the mouse?"

And naturally, the rooster answers. The sound is muffled, to be sure, but to the trained ear, there's no mistaking it for, say, a hamster wheel.

You know, right now I'm thinking chicken stew sounds very good. I mean, for crying out loud—the stupid thing is in my mother's room, in a cage with a blanket over it, and it's nearly nine o'clock at night. *Why the hell is he crowing?*

"Must be something outside," my mother says, but Nick is already at the door. Geoff gives Nick an if-you-open-this-door-I'll-be-your-best-friend grin, except, naturally, the minute Nick does, Geoff hightails it for parts south.

And Rocky outdoes himself, boy. They should've named this bird Pavarotti.

Nick turns to me. I cannot accurately describe his expression right now, but for the moment, let's just go with *stunned*.

I point to my mother. I may have wilted the man's...ego, I may be an inadvertent accessory to a crime, but no *way* am I taking the rap for this one.

Nick looks at my mother, who obviously can't decide whether to look cute and sheepish—which isn't working, anyway—or defiant. "Mrs. Petrocelli," he says wearily, "I'm sure you know it's against the law to keep a rooster in a Manhattan apartment."

"Told ya," I mutter.

"It's just for a couple of days," Nedra says, hands on hips. Going for defiant, looks like. "Until the owners find some place to live out of the city. It's a pet."

Nick looks at my mother, his expression almost sympathetic. "I doubt that," he says quietly. "More likely, it's being raised to fight. Which means it's probably going to die a very nasty, cruel death."

My mother gasps—well, I do, too, just not as loudly—only to quickly recover. "No. I don't believe that. The Ortizes have children, one of them even named the rooster, they'd never do anything like that...."

I turn to the still-scowling Nick, fully intending to explain that they're the family who burned me out of my apartment, only this is the moment the dog decides to assert the *cojones* he hasn't had for some time. Apparently realizing the rooster cannot get to him, Geoff rushes into the room and right up to the cage, barking his fool head off. The doggy equivalent of *"Nyah-nyah-nyah, nyah-nyah."* Understandably, this pisses Rocky off, who in turn launches himself at the wire barrier and squawks *his* fool head off.

And over the barking/squawking melee, Nonna—who's supposed to be the deaf one in the group—yells, "Door-bell!"

Well, jeez, with all this noise, it's no wonder, I muse as I tromp down the hall. Probably one of the neighbors. Hell, probably *all* of the neighbors, standing out in the hall with bats and brooms and iron pipes, ready to rid 4-C of its demon inhabitants.

I fluff my hair, throw back my shoulders, and swing open the door to the avenging hordes.

Only it's not the avenging hordes.

It's Greg.

Thirteen

"Ginger! What on earth are you doing here?"

My brain has just dissolved into a million bits of insentient fluff. Which means, when I open my mouth, nothing comes out of it except a tiny, airless squeak. Oh, enough of the fluff coalesces for a moment or two to take in his slightly longer hair, the snappy collarless shirt tucked into a pair of equally snappy gray pleated trousers. That he smells just as good as I remember. That, behind snappy black wire-rimmed glasses, shock and anxiety shimmer in equal measure in his hazel eyes. Then I hear footsteps on the floorboards behind me.

Many, many footsteps. A vertible deluge of footsteps.

I turn, jerkily, like a just-wound doll. Nedra and Nonna have both dropped their jaws. Nick has taken scowling to new heights. The other two officers, who of course don't have a clue, are expressionless. I have no idea what the etiquette is in situations like this, so I paste a bright smile to my bloodless face and mumble, "Greg Munson, Nick Wojowodski."

No, I don't bother with explanations. Are you kidding? Besides, I was doing well to get that much out.

Oh, God. Can you feel it? Man, there's enough testosterone in here to fuel the NFL for an entire season. Have you ever noticed how a man can sense when another man is, has been, or might someday be, competition? I swear to God, I expect them to sprout antler racks and engage in a duel to the death, right here in my mother's hallway.

It occurs to me that there are far too many swaggering cocks in this apartment right now.

Nonna steps in with, "Maybe you nice boys would like some tortellini? It'sa fresh, just made it today."

I shoot my grandmother a look. She shrugs. Nick mumbles something I don't quite catch, orders the other cops to bring the dog food bag as well as the, um, stuff—although, I notice with some regret, *not* the rooster—then brushes past me and out of the apartment.

Regret slices through me. I like this guy, I realize. As a person, you know? I would have liked being friends with him. But could I leave it at that? *Nooooo*. I had to go and let sex mess everything up.

Would somebody, anybody, please explain to me why I dropped my knickers without so much as by-your-leave with Nick—twice, no less—when I didn't go to bed with Greg until we'd been dating for *months?*

Oh, right. Greg.

Who's standing three feet away with his hands stuffed in his pockets, looking lost.

I sigh.

* * *

My mother and grandmother have retreated to their rooms. Would that I could have done the same.

We've gone into my mother's travesty of a living room, but neither of us has sat down. My stomach is churning, my brain is still fluff, and I'm thinking a long, dreamless nap would be good right about now.

Greg is in the process of forking one hand through his hair, his face contorted as though he's about to lose his cookies, when the rooster does his thing on the other side of the double doors. The man tries a smile, but it's not really his best effort.

"Was that…a rooster?"

I nod, my arms folded across my stomach in a vain attempt to staunch the trembling. "Mmm-hmm. My mother's latest rescue mission."

"And…do I dare ask why three policemen just left?"

"Do you really want to know?"

He has to think about this for a second. "No." There goes another almost smile. "The crazy Petrocellis are at it again, huh?"

Which pretty much says it all, so I don't bother.

"And who's this?" he says, squatting down to call Geoff to him. The dog studies him for a minute, then apparently decides it might be worth the effort to investigate, just in case this new person has a hamburger in his pocket or something. However, once he discovers that all Greg's offering is a scratch behind the ears, Geoff's expression changes from wary eagerness to polite boredom.

"I had no idea you were here, Ginger," he says softly, almost more to the dog than me, "or I wouldn't have just shown up like this." He looks up, and I see in his eyes what I can only describe as stark terror. "I swear. Look, I can tell, this has really thrown you…do you want me to leave?"

I force myself not to look away. To respond, at least on some basic level. Damn, I'd forgotten how incredibly handsome he is. Okay, so maybe not exactly forgotten, but not exactly remembered, either. Neither do I remember those lines etched around his mouth, that deep groove between his sandy brows. Sympathy socks me like a hard right to the solar plexus.

"No, you can stay," I say. Which is not the same as my saying I don't want him to leave. And he's too smart not to catch the difference. "For a little while, anyway."

Look, I'm conflicted about this whole situation. It was only a few weeks ago that I was ready to spend the rest of my life with him, a few *days* ago that I finally decided there was no chance of our ever getting back together, which is the only reason I let myself get carried away with Nick—oh, dear God!—*last night*, and here Greg is, thoroughly scrambling my brains. I don't know what I'm thinking. Hell, I don't know what *to* think. So give me a minute, okay?

Which is what I give Greg, too.

"So why *are* you here?" I ask.

"I tried to call your old number, but it's no longer in service. So I went over to your place, discovered you didn't live there anymore. So I thought…hey, I had no idea if your mother would even talk to me, let alone tell me where you were, but I figured it wouldn't hurt to try."

Please note, my arms are tightly crossed over my ribs. "You could have called. You have my cell number."

"No, I don't. Remember? You went with a new service right before…at the end of May. I never got the new number."

Oh, right. Everything was so chaotic right before the wedding, I forgot. Of course, that's nothing compared with how chaotic things got *after* the wedding.

Not to mention how chaotic they are at the moment.

"I'm sorry I took so long to pay all the bills," he says. "But I finally got them taken care of last week. Did you know?"

"Oh. Yeah, I do. Thanks."

Silence whines between us for several seconds.

"Mother said you and Nedra came out to get your things?"

I nod. My eyes start to burn, making me blink.

"If I tried to touch you right now," Greg says, "you'd probably slug me, wouldn't you?"

"Good call. Dammit, Greg—why did it take you so long to come looking for me?"

"Because I'm an idiot? Will that do?"

"Maybe. For starters, anyway."

His smile kinda flickers, then fades. "I wish I had a better answer, because God knows you deserve one. But I don't. Not really. Not unless you count thinking, well, hell, I blew that one to kingdom come. What possible chance did I have of patching things up? Oh, Ginger…honey, you will never know how sorry I am for what I did, for what I must have put you through. I swear…I don't know what came over me. I mean, you know me… I just don't *do* things like that."

Do you hear this? He's groveling. How ironic, that three, even two weeks ago, I would have *killed* to see Greg Munson grovel. Now I just feel…embarrassed.

But not *that* embarrassed.

My arms are still crossed. Half a room and more than a month of non-communication still separates us. "What are you saying, Greg?"

There's despair in them thar eyes. "Not saying. Asking."

He takes a step toward me. Geoff growls at him. He glances at the dog, stops. But doesn't retreat, either.

"Geoff, it's okay," I say, and the dog waddles a few feet away, only to lie down in a position where he can watch every move the intruder makes. One false move and those designer-socked ankles are history, boy. Then I look at Greg, arms still crossed. "Go on."

"We were good together, Ginge. Really, really good. And I can't believe I threw that away. Or…nearly threw that away."

I feel one brow arch. Wow, I didn't know I could do that. Cool. "No, I think your first assessment is correct, Greg. You humiliated me."

"I know I did."

"Well, that hurt. It still does. Especially because I didn't expect that of you. A few words aren't going to make it all better, just like that. How can I trust you now? How will I ever be able to believe what you say?"

He nods, rubs the back of his neck. "Yeah, that's kind of what I'd figured. So let me ask you…what can I do to make it better?"

"I don't know. Hell, I don't even know if I want you to try." And you have no idea how hard it was for me to say those words. "I'm sorry, but I honestly don't see any way of this getting off the ground again. I won't be made a fool of twice."

This time, when he moves to close the space between us and the dog growls, Greg looks down at Geoff and says, very quietly, "Enough." And, basically because he's got the courage of a gnat, Geoff whimpers and lays his head between his paws.

I glower at the miserable beast. *Some guard dog you are.* But the thought no sooner forms when I feel Greg's fingers on my chin, gently turning me to face him. Dammit—why does he have to look so stricken? Why can't he just act like it was all my fault, like any other man would do?

"You loved me once," he says. "A love I admittedly didn't deserve. Or appreciate, until it was too late. I don't deserve it now. But as God is my witness, I'll do whatever it takes to win back that love. And your trust. If you'll give me that chance." He reaches into his back pocket for his wallet—only Greg Munson would have the arrogance to defy the pickpockets like that—and takes out a card. "The Scarsdale house is on the market. I'm living in town now. There's the new number if you decide I'm worth taking that second chance on. Or you can reach me on my cell, anytime. I'm leaving word at the office to put you through, whenever you call, no matter what I'm doing."

He bends over, kisses me gently on the forehead, then walks down the hall and lets himself out.

Geoff and I stare at the closed door for several seconds, until I pull myself together to go secure the chain and the two dead bolts, at which point it hits me. Whoa—somehow or other, I now have *two* men's balls in my court.

Unfortunately, I'm not sure I want to play with either set.

Amazingly enough, nearly two weeks have passed without a single earth-shattering event. If the money hidden in the dog food was significant to the murder case in any way, it didn't make it to the news, at least, because I've been keeping an ear out. The rooster is still here, unfortunately, but Nedra and her magic quilt have somehow trained him not to crow before 8:00 a.m. It finally dawned on me that, since it's summer, I think a lot of the tenants—mostly Columbia staff—are gone, and the summer students subletting their apartments aren't about to bring attention to their own activities by blowing the whistle on a rooster.

Which is not to say that Rocky is going to be our permanent roommate, either. Actually, I think Nedra's looking into finding another home for him, although she hasn't exactly said that. But if I know my mother, even the possibility of his being sent back to an abusive home is keeping her up at night.

And on the Nedra vs. Ginger front, things actually aren't as bad as I thought they would be. Which is a good thing since it doesn't appear I'm getting out of here anytime soon (big sigh here—my checking account is running on fumes, folks). Oh, Nedra and I still lock horns about something or other at least once every twenty-four hours, but get this: the other day, we were sitting and watching TV in her room, some political talk show on cable, and this moron starts spouting off at the mouth about women's rights and before we knew it, we were both yelling at the TV and telling the moron in no uncertain terms where he could stuff his whacked ideas. Of course, two minutes later, some other moron came on, only Nedra agreed with *that* moron while I didn't, and we ended up yelling at each other, as usual. But, oh, well.

She still refuses to tell me much about her Secret Lover, which is driving me crazy. But it is her life, after all. And what—or who—she does has no bearing on mine. So I'm keeping my mouth shut.

Although my ears and eyes are wide open, believe me.

As for the Nick-and-Greg saga…well, there isn't anything to tell, really. I haven't seen or heard from either of them since the night of the Great Dog Food Caper, for which I'm profoundly grateful. Not that that doesn't keep me from thinking about both of them. Or talking about them, which I've been doing for the past half hour or so to Terrie and Shelby, who've met me for lunch at some little Greek eatery around the corner from the store. Which—the

store, I mean—is a whole 'nother story that I do not feel
like getting into right now.

"Girl," Terrie says, waving a forkful of spinach pie at
me, "I cannot believe you actually have two men drooling
over you. Although, frankly, I'd've been tempted to castrate
one of them. And I don't mean Nick."

"You've never even met Nick," I point out.

"True. But I have met Greg."

We've already been updated on the Davis Crisis, which,
after two more dates and one heavy petting session, is still
Status Unresolved. I have to say, however, that Terrie
seems to be enjoying her misery an awful lot.

My situation, of course, is more of a dilemma than a
crisis, although instinct is telling me it would just be easier
to wipe the slate clean and start over than try to figure out
any of this mess.

"So let me see if I have this straight," Terrie says.
"You're hot for Nick, who you don't really know, although
you think you might like him, even though you don't think
there's any real possibility there."

I think about this, stuff a stuffed grape leaf into my
mouth, and nod, noticing that Shelby, who's been unchar-
acteristically quiet through the entire meal, has barely
touched her moussaka. Then I add, "You forgot the 'he
scares me' part."

"Uh-huh. But you're also saying you're not sure you're
as out of love with Greg as you thought you were?"

I sigh. "I don't honestly know what I am. I mean, it
didn't make sense to stay in love with him if it was really
over. And I know, I know, I should want to see his spleen
nailed to the wall. But God, Ter—you should have seen his
face. I mean, if he'd been the least bit arrogant or anything
like that, I would've shown his sorry butt the door, I
swear." Yum…a Greek olive hiding under the lettuce.

"Anyway, if *I* screwed up, I'd sure want someone to give me a second chance. I mean, we do have a history."

She gives me a look. "Girl, I'll take *hot* over *history* any day. Besides, I somehow can't see you walking out on somebody the way he did."

I give her a look back. "I walked out on Nick."

"Not on your wedding day."

"Well, okay, that's true. But I still hurt him. Or at least, ticked him off."

"And you don't think this man who, by your own reckoning, has probably boinked dozens of women, hasn't ticked off one or two of them?"

"Don't confuse the issue," I say, although at this point, I'm not sure what the issue even is anymore. "Anyway, as I was trying to say, I'm not overlooking the fact that Greg screwed up. I haven't changed my mind about that, just because he's giving me those sad, puppy dog eyes. It's just…"

"Oh, for God's sake, would the two of you just *shut up!*"

Terrie and I—along with patrons at the tables on either side of us—turn and gawk as Shelby, whose face has gone very red.

She looks from Terrie to me, then back again, her fists clenched by her plate. "Do either of you ever really listen to yourselves? *God!* I mean, between the two of you, you've got three really fabulous men after you! And you can't make up your minds what to *do* with them? Don't you get it? You can do whatever the hell you like! You're free as birds, every option in the world open to you, men eating out of your hands, treating you like gold, and…and…"

Shelby jumps up; Terrie and I both clamp onto the table so it doesn't tip over. She grabs her purse, slams down her napkin, says, "You two are the most self-absorbed, fucking *stupid* women I've ever known in my life!" and storms out of the restaurant.

"I'll pay," Terrie says, fumbling for her wallet. "You go after her."

I tear out of the restaurant, then stand in the middle of the sidewalk, hoping Shelby didn't get into a taxi. Of course, the sidewalk is jammed with people and I have no idea which direction she went, but somehow, I catch a glimpse of blue Laura Ashley flowers a half block to my right. Not even three-inch heels keeps me from racing through the crowd to reach her, grabbing her just as she's about to step off the curb without looking.

With a startled gasp, Shelby whips around. Her face is streaked with tears.

"Let me go!" she shrieks, trying to jerk away from me.

"Forget it, Shel. Jesus, honey—what's wrong?"

"None of your business!" She yanks her arm from my grasp and takes off across the street, still against the light. Tires screech; horns blare; Shelby plows ahead.

"Dammit, Shelby!" I dodge three bikes and a Checker cab to reach her again. She speeds up, her little Pappagallo flats giving her a decided advantage. Who knew she could make tracks like this? Still, my legs are twice as long as hers; I close in, vising her wrist so she can't get away. People looking at us probably think we're having a lover's spat. Like I care.

Panting, Terrie—who's wearing shorts and Adidas, the jerk—catches up to us, grabs Shelby's other wrist. "Okay," she says, "you gonna tell us what's going on, or do we have to beat it out of you? And trust me, I can take you without even breaking a nail."

But Shelby isn't smiling. In fact, her face is crumpling

even as we speak. "Why should I even try telling you two anything? You just wouldn't get it, anyway."

"Listen, you little twerp," Terrie says, "*you're* the one who's gonna get it if you don't cut out this shit and tell us what the hell's going on."

"Yeah," I say.

She looks from one to the other of us, then spits out, "I'm pregnant again."

Judging by her ravaged expression, my guess is this is not a happy event. So I doubt she'd understand the nasty little "Not fair—how come she gets three when I don't have any?" stab of envy that just shot through me.

But, hello? This isn't about me?

"But…" I say, knowing I'm treading dangerous waters, "I thought Mark had a vasectomy?"

Shelby just looks at me.

"He didn't?"

"It didn't take," she says, thoroughly disgusted. "So much for giving your med school buddies your business."

She turns and starts walking down the street, but not fast enough to be construed as an escape attempt. Terrie and I shrug at each other and follow. Shelby stops at another restaurant, this one with outdoor tables.

"Oh, *God,* I need cheesecake," she says, eyeing a waiter's serving tray as it zips past. "Come on. My treat."

"Whoa." Terrie peers at both of us over her sunglasses. "Do you realize what this moment signifies?"

Shelby and I look at each other, then Terrie. Her mouth twisted, Shelby says, "What? That I said the 'f' word?"

"Well, yeah. That, too. But do you realize that this is the very first time *you've* called a Bitch Session?"

"This isn't—"

"Sure it is. Come on."

Shelby throws me a wide-eyed glance as Terrie takes her

arm and steers her inside the barrier that separates the restaurant from the street, plunking her butt down at a sidewalk table the size of a bottle cap.

I sit down directly across from Shelby so I can't stare at
her still-flat tummy and ponder the tiny life beginning to
form inside.

Amazing. For all our determination to rise above biol-
ogy, in the end, it always wins, doesn't it? No matter how
good we get at ignoring our wombs, eventually we can't
even hear ourselves think over the chant of our rapidly
aging eggs going, "Where's the sperm? Where's the
sperm?"

Survival sucks.

Anyway, as I said, this isn't about me. Or Terrie, either,
whose expression probably pretty much matches mine.
Guess her eggs are shrieking their little hearts out, too. But
Shelby's cheesecake is a good two-thirds demolished before she finally says, "Sorry, guys, for going off on you
like that."

We both make appropriate demurring noises.

A little smile plays over Shelby's light pink lips, then
she shrugs. "Damn hormones."

"And…?" I say.

Her eyes lift to mine.

"I've seen you through two other pregnancies, Shel.
What happened back there was a lot more than hormones."

Another bite of cheesecake disappears, but not before I
see her eyes go all glittery. "There are times when I envy
the two of you so much I can't stand it."

Terrie and I exchange startled glances, then say,
"Why?" at the same time.

"Why? Because you're *free*. Because you can go and do
whatever you want without having to answer to anybody
else, that's why. Because you don't have two little kids

sucking you dry every day. Soon to be *three* little kids. Oh, God—'' She presses a trembling hand to her chest. ''That sounds so *horrible.*''

''But, honey,'' I say, ''you wanted kids.''

''I know, I know. And I suppose, at some point, I'll want this one. I know this makes no sense. You know how much I love my kids. And Mark. And I'm not saying that just to try to convince myself I do. But I wish…'' A sigh spills out. ''I wish I'd stopped to think things through a little more, that I'd taken more time for myself before I started having children. That I'd maybe explored a few more options.''

My brows lift. ''As in…?''

Another sigh, then a tiny laugh. ''Who knows? *Something.* Criminy, I never even lived on my own, did I? I mean, I thought I knew who I was, what I wanted before I got married, but…'' She waves her hands. ''But that's water under the bridge. What's bugging me now is that, oh, months ago, I realized how much I miss my work. How much I miss *going* to work and talking to other adults about something besides potty training and ear infections. I know this sounds so petty, since I have so much to be grateful for, but…I was so sure that being a mommy would give me this incredible sense of fulfillment as a woman. And God knows, there are times it does….''

Watery gray eyes bounce from Terrie to me. ''But it's not enough. And now there's another one coming, which means that part of my life's been put on hold for another five freaking years, and I don't want to resent my family for needing me, but I do. And it's making me sick.''

Terrie and I both reach out, take her hands. It doesn't matter that I don't completely get why this is upsetting her so much. This is my cousin and my friend, and she's confused and hurting. Thus, I hurt for her, as I have since we were little.

"Have you talked to Mark about how you feel?" I ask.

She gives a little "hmph" that's supposed to pass for a laugh. "Oh, right. Like he's going to understand. He gets to go out to work every day, have his life, come home to clean kids, gourmet dinners, sex three times a week…hey, for him, life is perfect. How could he possibly understand how I feel?"

A single tear tracks down her cheek. Terrie hands her a napkin to blow her nose. "Let me guess. You haven't told Mark about the baby yet, have you?"

Shelby shakes her head.

"Why not?"

She wipes at her eyes, looking like a helpless, scared little girl in her cute flowered frock. "Because I'd only do this. And if it's one thing I'm not anymore, it…it's a c-crybaby. Oh, *God*, all this talk about women having choices…it's all bull…s-shit. Yeah, you can choose whether or not to have children, but once you have them, that really narrows those choices down. At least it does for me."

"So…why don't you see about putting the oldest two in day care?" I say. "It's not as if you and Mark can't afford it."

But she shakes her head, a stubborn little knot forming between her brows. "They're my babies. I didn't have them to let someone else raise them."

"Now, see, that's what's bullshit," Terrie says, just as I'm beginning to see the light myself. "For crying out loud, sugar, giving your kids an opportunity to explore their world without Mama hovering over them isn't relinquishing your responsibility for their care. Do you have any idea how many women would *kill* to be able to give their babies that kind of opportunity?''

Then I see it, in Shelby's eyes. That sense of being trapped. By circumstances, by her own fears, by the impossibly high standards she's set for herself. And I realize that nothing either Terrie or I can say will make one shred of difference. Because, no matter what choice Shelby makes, she's going to beat herself up about it.

And I think, well, he*llo,* that's what women do. We're all neurotic twits, scared shitless of making the wrong decision. Look at Terrie, afraid to continue seeing Davis, unable to stop seeing Davis, doomed to feeling like crap no matter what choice she makes.

And then there's little old me. Go for it with Nick? Yeah, well, intriguing possibility, but not a practical one. Reestablish ties with Greg, who, whether I like it or not, still tugs at something inside me I can't even completely define? Mmm…not sure. Forget about both of them, which as I said before, would probably be the wisest choice? Nope. Don't much care for that one, either.

Nick is right. We do make things complicated.

Twenty minutes later Terrie and I put a slightly calmer Shelby in a taxi, then stand with our arms crossed over our middles, watching the cab blend in with a hundred others streaking north. Then she slugs me and puts out her hand.

''Told you she was unhappy. Now fork over five bucks, honeychile.''

I'm still pondering all this when I get back to the apartment that evening after work. I don't think I totally agree with Shelby about the freedom thing, even though I finally understand what she's saying. Somewhat. I suppose taking care of three little kids under the age of five would scare the pants off me, too. Still, I have to admit it would be nice not to have to wonder "Where is this relationship going?" ever again. A blissful state I'd thought had been within reach mere weeks ago.

Which being unmarried and childless is not, despite Shelby's conviction that I'm completely free to do whatever I want. Oh, yeah, I really chose to spend my days watching my brain slowly rot in this dead-end job, to move back in with my mother. I haven't *chosen* to feel this… unsettled, as though my life's been put on hold just as much as Shelby feels hers has because of the kids.

God. Listen to me. I mean, things could be worse, right? A lot worse. Okay, so I'm in limbo, both physically and emotionally. But, as Terrie would say, ain't nuthin' gonna happen for the better with a negative attitude.

So…is it kosher to say I'm *positive* I'm thoroughly confused?

I drop my keys on the hall table, kick off my heels. Nobody greets me, although I can hear Nonna banging stuff around in the kitchen. I presume Geoff is in there, keeping an eye on things. Where the rooster is, I do not know and do not care.

I stop in my room long enough to change into a pair of shorts and a tank top, then pad barefoot to the kitchen. The day hasn't cooled off any, so the fans are still going in the living room and kitchen windows. My grandmother is wearing a loose white T-shirt—mine—over a pair of hot pink capris—also mine. Which probably accounts for the fact that, instead of hitting her three inches below the knee, they hit her three inches above the ankle. The black orthopedic shoes add an interesting twist to the look.

She glances over from the stove—where else?—and gives me a sheepish smile. "I wear these while clothes are in laundry. You do not mind?"

I shake my head, going for the dog's leash hanging on

a hook in one of the cupboards. "Color looks good on you."

"You think so? Oh, you don' have to take out the dog, your mama, she took him out before she left."

Geoff throws her a chagrined look, as though gypped out of the doggy equivalent of going back into his fave online chatroom, as I say "Left?"

I pour myself a glass of tea, then lean over to scratch the dog's head. Back on food watch, he barely acknowledges my presence, apparently afraid if he lets my grandmother out of his sight, she'll disappear.

"*Sì*, she's out. Again. With *that man*."

Hey. You don't suppose…?

"What man?"

"The one she does not tell anyone about."

So much for that. Then it occurs to me… "Does it bother you, that she's dating somebody other than Dad?"

Nonna halts her mission—which, judging from the mass quantities of food she is setting out on the table, is to feed the entire Upper West Side—to give me a weird look.

"Since your father has been in the grave for eighteen years, no. Come, sit. Eat while itsa hot."

A three-second scan reveals roast pork and manicotti and spaghetti with marinara sauce and foccacia bread and salad…and God alone knows what's for dessert.

"Nonna, honest to God—who on earth do you expect to eat all this?"

She shrugs. "I'ma never sure what you might be in mood for, no? So I figure, I cover all bases."

I sit, pile a little of everything on my plate. "So tell me…is this the way you cooked for my grandfather?"

"Oh, *sì*. It was what was expected of women then, you know?"

"Seems like a helluva lot of work."

She smiles at that.

"What?" I say.

"A woman who pleases her husband in the kitchen can count on him pleasing her later in the bedroom."

And she's not even blushing.

"So," she says, tucking into her own dinner, "you make a decision about Gregory?"

I shake my head.

"*Grazie a Dio.* I think I like this Nick better, anyway."

"What makes you think—"

She gives me a look, cutting me off. "*Cara.* You think is a secret, the heat between you two?"

I do, however, blush. Nonna laughs.

"That's just…" Oh, hell. "Sex."

"And this is a bad thing?"

I give her my best grown-up, woman-of-the-world look. "It wouldn't work, Nonna."

Only she gives one back that sends mine whimpering into the corner. "And you think it would with this Greg?"

"Well, I did once before, obviously."

She mutters something in Italian. I let it go. Then I say, "Were you happy with Poppa?"

Her eyes dart to mine. "What is this question?"

"Were you? I mean, did you ever regret marrying him?"

"It was arranged marriage. I had no choice in the matter."

My brows rise. "I thought you were a war bride?"

"Was a quick arrangement." She smiles.

I say, "Oh."

Then she laughs. "That does not mean I was not content. My parents, they chose well, this handsome soldier going back to States in two days. And Carlo was a good man. Good provider, good in bed…" She lets out a heavy sigh, shakes her head, then returns to earth. "But, *sì*, maybe I do have one regret."

"Which is?"

"That I sleep with only one man. Women today, they can—*come sei diçe?*—comparison shop, yes? Not that I can complain, *capice?* Your grandfather, he understood what makes a woman happy. What to do to make her welcome him into her arms night after night. Still, I think it would have been nice, to see what sex is like with another man. Only now, is too late." Her shoulders lift, drop. "Who would want me?"

I laugh, and that should have ended the discussion. But something else is nagging me. "How have you and Nedra managed to get along so well all these years? The two of you are so different."

Nonna gets up to get more sauce for her manicotti. "I think it is *because* we are different that we can live together." She grins at me over her shoulder. "We do not fight over who cooks, for one thing, no?"

"Well, that's certainly true." Cooking has never been my mother's forte.

Nonna returns to the table. "But I admire your mother. Even if I do fear for her immortal soul."

You'd have to know my grandmother to understand the depth of the love behind those words. Steeped in old school Catholic tradition, Nonna really *does* worry about my Jewish mother's soul. Enough that, after more than thirty years, she still harbors hope that Nedra will see the light. Of course, there's a better chance of a member of the Gambino family being canonized, but you know how it is. "You admire her?"

Twin black brows lift. "Do not sound so surprised, *cara.* There is much good in your mother. For one thing, I never see my Leo so happy as when he is with Nedra. For another, she is woman who knows who she is, who follows her heart—''

Hmm. There's that phrase again.

''What is not to admire in that?''

''But the way she always picks losing battles...'' I shake my head. ''Why does she always have to do things the hard way?''

Nonna tilts her head at me. ''And is bad for a woman to fight for those who cannot? Who has the courage to be one of the drops of water that will eventually wear away the rock?''

Okay, I have to think about this one. But in the end, I say, ''No, of course it's not *bad*...but what's the point?''

''The point is, *cara,* that more women should have her balls.''

I burst out laughing, but from across the table, Nonna is frowning at me.

''What?'' I say.

''You are very like her, I think.''

''*What?*''

''*Verissimo.* Is why you two fight so much.''

''Nonna, no disrespect, but that's crazy. We're nothing alike. In fact, we fight so much *because* we have nothing in common.''

''No, no...you fight because you and your mother, you are both strong women. Stubborn women. Your mother, she isa stubborn for to fight for what she believes in, *sì?* But you, you are stubborn for to fight *against* who you really are.''

''What on earth makes you say that?''

''Alla years I know your mama, even after your papa dies, she is happy. She is content. She does not sit in corner like mouse and wait for life to find her, she goes out looking for it. I think she feels good about who she is. But you?'' She blows a puff of air through her lips. ''You keepa yourself busy, *sì,* with your work and your friends, but I do not see the happiness in you. You do not look for life. You run from it.''

I must be too shocked to be angry. Still, I say, *''Run* from it? After everything I've done the past few weeks to overcome all the crap that's happened to me? I haven't exactly been sitting in a corner, either.''

Her dark eyes seem to sear straight through me. ''Only because life keeps throwing you back into center of room. But instead of stretching your arms, feeling your freedom, you only try to get back in corner, back by walls you know, where you feel safe.'' Her mouth droops. ''And now I make you angry.''

''No,'' I say, although I notice that my hand is knotted by my plate.

''Ginger, *cara*…'' Nonna leans forward, grabs my fisted hand, gently strokes it open. ''I have watched you for many years. I see how you try to be not like your mother, ever since you were little girl. But you try too hard, you see? It is like you, um, decide who it is you should be, instead of finding out who you really are.''

She lets go of my hand, sitting back in her chair to continue her meal. ''When you bring home this Greg, I think, isa not man for you. He is nice, yes, but not enough for you. And I am right, *sì?* To run away from wedding—*pah!* I do not know what he wants now, why he comes back, but isa not good. Trust me.'' She slaps her hands on her thighs, rises from the table. ''You wanna cannelloni?''

Man. This is the most my grandmother has said to me at one time since I can remember. Besides her hearing problems, English is hard for her, so she's not given to lengthy dissertations. For her to have forced herself to say as much as she just did shows just how strongly she feels about the subject. Which is why I'm sitting here right now waiting to get my breath back.

On top of everything else I've been through, having my grandmother tell me I'm just like my mother is the last thing I need. I mean, have you ever heard anything more preposterous? Yes, maybe I have deliberately chosen a path as divergent from my mother's as possible. There's a reason for that. But every decision I've made, about my career, my lifestyle, even about Greg, stemmed from what I genuinely wanted to do. I've never done anything on impulse, for heaven's sake. Unlike Nedra who *does* first and *thinks* later.

And no, I'm not counting the Nick episode, so you can't, either.

Of course, I can't discount Nonna's observation about my being unhappy. Although that's probably too strong a word for whatever it is I'm feeling. Have felt. I just don't think my malaise has anything to do with…what was that she said? My resistance to being like my mother? What is that supposed to mean, anyway? That I'm suppressing latent Socialist tendencies? That I'll find peace and a sense of purpose on a picket line somewhere, carrying a placard and shouting obscenities at gray-haired men in Brooks Brothers' suits?

I don't *think* so.

A freshly made cannelloni lands in front of me. I mutter "thanks" and begin to shovel it in, letting the whipped cream squish between my tongue and the roof of my mouth. When I feel Nonna's hand on my hair, I look up. "Your mother, she loves you very much. And she worries about you. *Sì*, she does, so do not make face. You look in her eyes, you will see."

After dinner, I threaten my grandmother with bodily harm if she doesn't let me clean up. She and the dog go into her room to watch TV; I put a dozen plastic containers in the fridge, wash the dishes, then head for my own room to read or something.

Nedra has removed the file cabinets into the empty room beside mine, so I have some space back. Of course, I filled it up with new bookcases and what's left of my books after the fire, but it still doesn't feel right. Not like home.

Whatever that is.

For reasons totally beyond me, I dig the Tiffany box with the ring in it out from underneath my new underwear, snap it open. Just as I crawl onto the bed, Geoff comes wandering in. He lays his snout on the edge of the bed and whuffs at me; I haul him up onto the bed and show him the ring. He seems mildly interested. Until he discovers he can't eat it. So he lies down and pants on my knee.

"I could sell this, you know," I say to him. I'd had it appraised for insurance purposes. I wouldn't get quite that much, I don't imagine, but enough to maybe get me out of here. "But somehow, that doesn't seem right." Geoff groans. "I know. I guess I should give it back to Greg, don't you think?"

But that doesn't seem right, either.

I hear several of the locks being undone. A few minutes later my mother, dressed in a black-and-red print kaftan I think she wore to my high school graduation, stops at my door.

"You're home early," I say.

She smiled. "It was just dinner. And no, I'm not going to slip and fill in any more blanks."

Damn. "Just answer me one thing—do I know him?"

"Not going to answer that."

"Oh, come *on*, Nedra—"

"Ginger? This is my business. Not yours."

Guess I can't argue with that.

I surprise myself by patting the space beside me on the bed. Nedra surprises me by taking me up on the invitation. Geoff doesn't seem to care one way or the other.

The bedsprings groan under her weight as she sits. I catch a whiff of expensive perfume. I wonder if *he* gave it to her, since I can't ever remember Nedra wearing perfume before.

She nods toward the boxed ring, still in my hand. "You're not thinking of putting that hideous thing back on, I hope."

I have to laugh. "Hey. I increased my left biceps by a full inch from wearing this." My laughter fades as I stare at it. It really is pretty, in an ostentatious kind of way. "But no. Although I suppose I should think of *something* to do with it."

Nedra crosses her arms. "I know a women's shelter that could use a good-size donation."

"Hell, so could your daughter. But…" I snap shut the box, lean over to set it on my nightstand. "'Tis not mine to sell."

"I think technically, it is."

"Well, Miss Manners, I wouldn't feel right about it. In fact, I'm thinking about taking it over to Greg's, handing it back to him. Speaking of giving back…what's doing with His Most High Featheredness in the other room? Have you heard from the Ortizes lately?"

Nedra busies herself with smoothing her dress over her knees.

Oh, hell.

"Okay, look, I did call them, but the phone number Manny Ortiz gave me is out of service, so what am I supposed to do? I don't even know where he is, now. I…I don't think they're coming back."

Other people get kittens dumped on their doorsteps. Or babies. We get chickens.

I just stare at her. She sighs.

"I promise, I'll see about finding him a nice place in the country or something. Where he can live out the rest of his natural life."

I nearly jump when my mother's hand slips around mine, which is when I notice the circles underneath my mother's eyes…and the worry lurking in them. Oh, Lord, Nonna's right.

"I know how much it must be killing you not to have your own place," she says. "If I'd had to move back in with my mother at your age, I think I would have killed myself."

Yes, I can imagine she would. If you think Nedra's something else, you should see Grandma Bernice, who now lives in Phoenix, of all places. I remember, when my grandparents still lived in the neighborhood, going to this little butcher shop over on Amsterdam Avenue she used to like. There was one time we went, I was maybe seven or eight, that she nearly had the butcher in tears, making him drag out every single chicken from behind the glass so she could inspect it. So maybe I don't have it so bad, huh?

I smile for my mother. "I'm fine, Nedra. Really."

"Of course you are. You're my daughter." She leans over, kisses me on the forehead, then seems to force herself to her feet. "Jesus, I'm more tired than I thought." On a huge yawn, she adds, "Guess I'll go on to bed, since I'm about to pass out anyway. 'Night, sweetheart."

"'Night."

After she leaves, I find myself staring up at my paints on the closet shelf. Then bringing them down. Then opening them.

My fingers tingle.

So what could it hurt, playing around with them once in a while? You know, as a hobby? I mean, it's not as if I'd think about doing this for money or anything. And I do have a lot of time on my hands, especially since I doubt I'll ever date again.

And while this depressing thought is worming its way into my brain, my cell rings. I freeze. Is it Nick? Greg? Terrie?

Am I going to stand here and wonder all night or check the Caller ID?

It's Paula.

"Hey, you," she says, "what's the big idea rushing off like that on the Fourth without bothering to say goodbye?"

"I'm sorry, Paula. It's just…"

"It's just that you and Nick are both idiots, that's what. Y'know, I'd knock both of your heads together, if I could get you close enough."

I shut my eyes. "How much do you know?"

"Well, let's see. The party ends, you and Nick never come down off the roof—at least, not down here—and then, oh, an hour and a half later you go running off without even taking back your salad bowl. Which is all washed and waiting for you, by the way. So Frank and I figure you two had sex and somebody got scared. And my guess the somebody was you."

I hesitate, then say, "It was a mistake, Paula. A rebound thing, you know."

"Hey, don't knock rebounds. Frank was a rebound."

"He was?"

"Sure. Don't you remember? Oh, you probably don't, we weren't that close then."

Not that we're close now.

"Anyway," she says, "I was going with this turkey named Joe Simeone, and we were like an inch from getting engaged. So we were at some party at his friend's house and I had to go pee, which meant I had to go down the hall to get to the bathroom, only when I passed by one of the bedroom doors, I hear this very familiar male grunting sound coming out from the other side of the closed door, a sound I had, in fact heard in my ear only the night before, if you get my drift. So I thought about bustin' in on Joe and whoever it was, only I'm a lady, you know? So I waited out in the hall until this little slut Cindy Montefiore came out, her hair this rat's nest like you wouldn't believe. And let me tell you, she looked like she was gonna mess her pants for sure. Anyway, I wasn't interested in her—where was the challenge?—so I barged in on Joe the Schmuck, who still didn't even have his pants pulled all the way up—"

Nice image.

"—only after I punched Joe's lights out, I got to crying so hard I thought I was gonna throw up. And Frank came to the rescue and took me away, and a month later I got pregnant and we got married and it's been happily ever after. Now why did I get started on that, huh? That's not why I called. I'm calling because Grandpa Sal has decided he wants a big birthday bash for his ninetieth in a couple weeks, and guess who's been elected to give it?"

And guess who sounds secretly pleased to be so honored? Sal is Nonna's brother-in-law, my grandfather's brother. One of two surviving siblings of eight, he's apparently determined to invite everyone he's ever known who's still breathing to this party of his. Which would include my grandmother.

"So you'll bring her?" Paula is saying, adding when I've apparently held my breath too long, "And I doubt Nick will be anywhere around, if that's what's worrying you. This isn't his family. Besides, it's on a Saturday afternoon.

I think he's on duty that day. And no, this isn't a trick. Trust me, I've got no energy for matchmaking.''

A less charitable person might think that's because she expends it all talking.

Against my better judgment, I say yes, after which I go next door to my grandmother's room to find her sitting up in her overstuffed chair, dozing in front of some cop show. She jerks awake when I turn off the TV, then frowns.

"Damn. I never see end of anything anymore.''

Her mood improves, however, when I tell her about the party. In fact, her whole face lights up. Funny thing is, Nedra tries to get her out at least once a week, to go out for lunch if nothing else, or do a little shopping, but she almost always declines. From her expression, however, you'd think the poor woman had been imprisoned for years and this was her first reprieve.

"A party? For Salvatore, you say?''

"Uh-huh.''

Her mouth gets all flat as she frowns again.

"What's the matter?''

"I just remember. Salvatore Petrocelli isa pain in the butt.''

I sit on the edge of the bed, hopeful. "This mean you don't want to go?''

Surprise flickers in her black eyes. "Why would you think that? Of course, I want to go. He thinks I'ma pain in the butt, too.'' Then she does this…thing with her shoulders that I've never seen her do before. Almost as if she's…preening? "But only ifa you take me shopping for something new to wear? I want to look—'' her eyes drift to mine, full of the devil "*—più caldo.*''

Fourteen

Hot, huh?

Sure. *You* try to find clothes for a four-foot-ten, hundred-thirty-pound, hunched-over, eighty-year-old woman whose boobs are intimately acquainted with her navel. But it's been three hours since we started this shopping trip, and every time I try to steer her toward anything that looks even remotely as though it will *fit*, let alone not make me want to vomit, she bellows something in Italian and hits me with her pocketbook.

Remind me later to ask Nedra what on earth I did as a child to warrant this level of punishment.

"I have closet full of old lady clothes," Nonna says, pouting. "Now I want to looka like Britney Spears!"

I'm not making this up, I swear.

I point out, as diplomatically as I can with a throbbing

head, swollen feet and splintered nerves, that most females Britney Spears's age can't look like Brittney Spears. And that few *over* her age would want to.

She smacks me again and drags me into the next junior department, pawing at some sleazy...thing with spangles and chains. I glance over, notice the chickipoo a few feet away holding up a dress the size of a Kleenex to her non-existent breasts. Two other chickipoos in hip-hugger mini-skirts, midriff-baring tank tops and way too much makeup—whose combined ages would still make them younger than me—are giggling and snapping gum beside her. My grandmother looks over at their hideous platform shoes.

"Can I get something like that?"

"You have something like that," I say, pointing to her orthopedic Oxfords.

She glances down. Nods. Continues mauling the sleeze. And I don't know why it's taken me this long, but I suddenly get what this is all about. She knows she can't wear any of this stuff. And I'll bet my butt when we walk out of here, she'll let me take her to the right department, get her something that won't make people gag. Or mistake her for a hooker who didn't know when to quit. But Nonna never had the chance to be a chickipoo. Raised in a tiny town in Italy by strict, God-fearing parents, even if stuff like this had existed then, she wouldn't have been allowed to even look at it, let alone wear it.

She's just playing, is all. And fighting me the way she never got to fight her own mother. Not my idea of fun, but hey, she's eighty. Who am I to say?

Nonna holds up a glittery tank top like the chickipoos are wearing. "What do you think of this?"

"You can't wear a bra with that, Nonna."

"So?"

"So your nipples would hang out at the bottom."

She glowers at her reflection in the mirror for several seconds. Then, with a sigh, she hangs up the top, looks at me. "Ima being a pain in the ass, *sì?*"

"You betcha. Come on. Let's go up to the third floor."

As I suspected, she meekly follows—it's about damn time the old girl runs out of steam, sheesh—and within fifteen minutes, we pick out a lovely two-piece rayon challis dress in a bright, tropical print. One with which she can wear that marvel of engineering she calls a bra.

She grins at me in the dressing room mirror. "I looka hot, no?"

"Nonna, you're gonna knock 'em dead."

"Per Dio—!" She crosses herself, her eyes wide. "You watcha you mouth. Mosta people at this party, they already gotta one foot ina grave."

On the way out of the department, she snags my arm, then nods in the direction of the store's beauty salon. "I think I shoulda get my hair trimmed a little, maybe."

I nearly gasp. Nonna's hair falls to her waist, and always has. To my knowledge, no one's ever taken scissors to it. "I can do that for you, you know."

But she shakes her head. "I have never been inna beauty salon," she says wistfully, and again, I get it. Only this time, I catch the urgency in a way I hadn't before. That she *is* eighty years old. That whatever she hasn't done and wants to, she better damn sight do now.

"We'll see if they have any openings," I say. "And what the heck, maybe I'll have them take a couple inches off this rat's nest, too, while we're at it."

Sometime later, we're standing at the front of the only coffee shop in a ten-block radius from the store Nonna would deign to set foot in, waiting to be seated. "Let me see your mirror again," Nonna says, her eyes bright.

With a smile, I dig in my purse for my hand mirror. Instead of having them take a couple inches off her hair, she ended up with only a couple inches *left*. And she looks absolutely adorable. Like an Italian elf. Ears and all. Who knew she'd been hiding such wonker ears under all that hair? But really, she doesn't look a day over seventy-five. And the lady in the salon insisted on plucking her brows a little, dusting her cheeks with a pale blusher. The transformation is truly amazing.

"I look almost asa sexy as you," she says.

Oh, yeah. I had them take all my hair off, too. I still look like a poodle, but a shorn one. With this really great neck.

"Right this way," an overly eyelashed hostess says, and we're led back to a dimly lit booth. And not a moment too soon. I slide into the booth with a huge sigh, letting my eyes drift closed as my legs slowly register that they're not carting me around anymore. God. I've had orgasms that didn't make me feel this good.

My hand bumps something; I open one eye, see a folded up *Post* someone left on the seat. With mild interest, I pick it up, scan the article in front of me.

"So," Nonna says, handing me back my mirror. "What are you going to wear to this party?"

"I have no idea," I say, distracted, then I let out a gasp. "Oh, my God..." I look up. "The police caught Brice's murderer."

I'm reading the newspaper article out loud to Nonna while she slowly chews her turkey club, unmindful of the blob of mayonnaise stuck to her chin. I have to shout over the restaurant din so Nana can hear me, but even so, I'm not sure how much she's actually caught.

"Your boss, he was dealing drugs?"

"Apparently so."

So, after all that, it wasn't a former lover, or Carole, the disgruntled senior designer (just between you and me, I kinda suspected her). Or even an architect. Just some hit man with very bad karma.

I'm not sure I understand all the details, nor do I want to. What gets me, though, as I'm reading this, is the sense of satisfaction I feel for Nick. And pride. He's even quoted somewhere in here, something about thanking the community for their cooperation. You think maybe that includes me?

After that fades, however, I realize I can let the guilt go. For not feeling worse about what happened to Brice, I mean. Not that I think he deserved to die, exactly. But I'm not sure he deserved to live, either. Sorry, but drugs creep me out. And people who use them—or sell them—creep me out even more. Which is probably why I don't get asked to a lot of parties.

Except for ones where the average age of the guests is eighty-five, that is.

"You should call him," Nonna is saying, even as she tries to work a piece of something out of her bridgework with her tongue.

"Who?"

"Nick. To congratulate him. *Per Dio—!*" She reaches inside her mouth, pokes around for a minute until she dislodges a piece of turkey large enough to make a whole new sandwich. She waves the mangled piece of turkey at me for a second, saying, "It would be nice, *sì?*"

No way am I going there.

The flowers are waiting for me when I get home. Red roses. Three dozen of them. Which I should find tacky, if ot clichéd. Instead, my breath leaves my lungs in a long, 'Ooooh...''

My mother plucks the card from the box, shoves it at ne. "Maybe you should see who they're from before you wet yourself—ohmigod! Where's your hair?"

"Somewhere around 34th and Broadway."

"And where's your grandmother? And I hope to hell you don't give me the same answer."

I'm still ogling the roses, nestled so sweetly in their little issue-paper lined coffin. "Talking to the doorman. She'll be up later."

"You left her on her *own?*" Nedra flies to the door, opens it, peers out into the hall.

"For God's sake," I say, opening the card, "she can find her way to the elevator by herself."

My mother tromps back to me, gives me a disgusted ook, presumably because I'm not.

"I take it from your expression," I say, "that you already know who they're from."

"So? I put back the card, didn't I?"

Of course, they're from Greg—you didn't really think his was Nick's style, did you?—but there's no note or anything. Which is strange, but also intriguing, in a bizarre kind of way.

"So the man can pull out a credit card and order a bunch of roses," Nedra says. "Big hairy deal."

I say nothing as I gather them up to go find a vase. Noticing I'm headed for the kitchen, Geoff trots along beside me, ever hopeful.

"You're not thinking of resurrecting that relationship, I hope."

I pretend I can't hear her because of the water running. 'm not thinking of anything, really, except that these are very pretty roses and I had no idea I was such a sucker for clichéd romantic gestures. From down the hall, I hear my grandmother's return, followed by, "Ohmigod! What happened to *your* hair?"

My purse, lying innocently on the kitchen table, suddenly rings. Geoff, who apparently has mistaken me for Nonna, barks at me until I answer the phone.

"Ms. Petrocelli? This is Dana Alsworth from Alsworth Interiors, you interviewed with us a couple weeks ago?"

You have got to hear this Southern accent to believe it. Dallas-born and bred, Dana Alsworth married a Northerner probably thirty years ago, hauled the accent up north along with the matched Gucci luggage. I swallow down the impulse to drawl, "Yes, ma'am?" into the phone, instead opting for a simple, "Yes?"

"Well…" An airy, slightly nervous laugh flickers through the phone. "I believe you were working with Annabelle Souter before…when you were with Fanning's?"

"Yes, I was. She was one of my best—" as in, spent her husband's money like there was no tomorrow "—clients."

"Well, honey, she brought her project to us a couple weeks ago and since then, she's chewed up and spit out all my top designers. Now she's saying she only wants to work with *you*."

This little hum of excitement begins to purr in my veins. "Oh, gee. I'm really flattered, but…I'm working somewhere else."

"Where?" comes the duck-on-June-bug reply. I tell her, she gives a dismissive snort, then says, "Name your price."

I like the way this woman thinks.

"Annabelle can be a tad…particular," I say, which gets a shrill, panicked laugh on the other end.

"Oh, Lord, sugar, if you're as talented as you are diplomatic, you're worth your weight in twenty-four-karat gold. So I repeat—you tell me what you want, and you've got it. And by the way, Miz Petrocelli—if you can handle this woman, I've got a midtown hotel remodel comin' up that might be right up your alley."

"Which one?"

She tells me. I start to salivate. I also know how big the Souter project is. Four-thousand-square-foot home out on the Island. Annabelle likes to "freshen up" the place every three years or so. And we're not talking a couple new throw pillows on the couch.

"I'll need my own office. And an assistant."

"You got it."

"And we discuss partnership in a year."

"Well, my, my…you certainly have brass ones, don't you?"

"All the better to handle the Annabelle Souters of the world, Ms. Alsworth."

That gets a throaty laugh. "Honey, you get this she-devil off my back, you'll be partner in six months."

"Then you've got yourself a new designer."

Dana's relief was palpable, right through the phone. "I'll call her right away. If you've worked with Mrs. Souter before…"

"Three times, including her husband's law offices and her daughter's Riverside Drive co-op."

"And you still sound sane."

My mother and Nonna wander into the kitchen. "Believe me, I've had lots of experience dealing with crazy women."

They both glare at me.

"So…can I say Monday?"

Gee…today is Thursday. Is three days notice enough to give the store that I'm quitting? The store where, if a customer does manage to find her way back to the dreary little design studio, a half dozen designers pounce like roaches on a bread crumb. I mull this over for, oh, maybe three seconds, then say, "That will be fine."

"Bless you, darlin'. Just be sure to come in a little early so we can fill out that boring paperwork."

My phone is making weird sounds, a precursor to cutting off because it needs to be recharged. So I plug the little dear in, then grab my mother and dance around the kitchen with her, Geoff barking at our heels. I'm finally getting my life back! I'm going to have money again! My own apartment again! My own bathroom! A fowl-free environment!

Except, after I'm done babbling all this for several minutes, I catch the expressions on my mother's and grandmother's faces. The "I'm trying to be happy for you because this is what you want but…" look. You know, the one guaranteed to make you feel about two inches tall?

But you know what's really weird?

I don't think I'm as happy about this as I should be, either.

I had to call Greg to thank him for the roses. Yes, I did, don't look at me like that. Not that it was easy. By the time I finally got up the nerve to make the call, my stomach was in a thousand knots. A fact not helped by his abrupt, "'Lo?"

"Oh! Uh…Greg? Um, hi, it's me."

Stunning example of grace under pressure, don't you think?

"Ginger?" A pause. "I'm sorry, honey, I didn't recognize the number on my Caller ID, and I've been getting so damn many solicitors recently…"

"What? Oh, right. It's the home phone. My mother's home phone, I mean, since I don't have one. I had to recharge my cell, so I had to use this one, so that's why the number's not right—''

Jeez. Sound like an idiot, why don't you?

"Anyway. I called to thank you for the flowers. They're really gorgeous."

I swear, I do not know how this happened, but…well, within half a minute, we fall right back into the easy camaraderie we used to enjoy, filling each other in on our lives—well, my filling him in on mine, anyway—which in turn leads to my telling him about my new job, which somehow leads to his offering to take me to dinner to celebrate.

And I'm sitting here on my bed, dog head in lap, rooster making very strange noises down the hall, thinking, mmm, no, I really shouldn't. A nice phone conversation is one thing. But an actual date?

"Oh, I don't know, Greg…"

"It's just dinner, honey."

"I know, I know, but…" I sigh. "I don't want you to think this means…anything, okay? I mean, I was going to call you before the flowers came, because…I really need to give you back the ring."

Then I wince, waiting.

"You don't have to do that," he says, his voice a little tight around the edges.

"Yes, I do."

"No, I don't mean that the way it sounds. It's just, um…" He clears his throat. "Look…even if…things should work out that we get back together—I'm not pushing, I swear, just saying *if*, okay?—under the circumstances, I don't think we'd want to use the same ring, would we? So what I'm saying is—"

Notice how he just zipped right through before I had a chance to say anything?

"—I don't expect you to wear that ring again, in any case. But I sure as hell don't want it back. Do whatever you want with it. Sell it. Bury it. Leave it to charity, I don't care."

I think I just lost my voice.

"Look, Ginge—I know you spent a lot of money on the wedding, too. Maybe this will make up for it?"

Damn, he's making it hard to remain objective.

"Wow. I'm not sure what to say."

"That you'll go out to dinner with me?"

After a moment I say, "You play dirty, Munson."

He chuckles. "So I've been told." Then, more seriously, "I know I've got a lot of making up to do. And that, in the end, you might still tell me to go to hell. I'd certainly deserve it, God knows. But, on the other hand, how can I prove you can trust me if we don't spend some time together?"

Okay, conflict time. On the one hand, I'm thinking, oh, why not? Especially since he's the only person who seems to understand why I'm thrilled about this job. And it's just dinner, for crying out loud.

But am I ready for this? To take a second chance on somebody who shredded my heart? I want to believe him. I really do. But now I'm gun-shy and I'm not sure I can.

But, oh dear God, I want to.

Jeez. Now I know how Terrie feels.

In Greg's and my case, however, there's all this past stuff I can't just summarily dismiss. I mean, Greg's and my relationship was a no-brainer. At least, it was before. Look, you know how, when you're with most guys, you end up exhausted by the end of the evening, just trying to figure out where you stand, what they want, what they're thinking? That if you accidentally brush up against them when you're walking, they'll take it as a come-on? Or…or if you suggest doing something that could even remotely be construed as In The Future, they get this look on their face like somebody just told them their genitals were going to self-destruct within the next twenty seconds? But, somehow, it was never like that with Greg.

Being with Greg was easy. Comfortable. I knew, almost from the first time we met, that I could count on him to be, well, just Greg. I never had the feeling he was trying on different personae, the way most men do, trying to be what he thought he should be, or what he thought I wanted him to be…and God, that was nice. And maybe that doesn't sound like much, but to me, it was heaven. Greg understood me, understood what I needed.

Who I needed to be.

Unlike being with somebody like, say, Nick, who keeps me on edge all the time. Demanding things of me I can't even identify, let alone *do*.

Demand*ed*, I should say. Past tense.

"You're thinking too hard," Greg says, a smile in his voice.

And he's right. I am.

It's just dinner.

"Monday after work?" I say, and I can hear his exhaled breath on the other end of the line.

Do you know how long it takes to ride the subway from 116th Street and Broadway all the way to Brooklyn?

"So," Nonna bellows, "you're really going to go out with that Greg again?"

Does that answer the question?

We're standing on the platform at 14th Street, waiting for the L train. Last leg of the journey. I'm very aware that the air, such as it is, is teeming with billions and billions of sloughed-off dead skin cells. "You know, you look absolutely adorable in this,'' I say, plucking at the sleeve of her new dress.

''Don' change the subject. Why you do this? Why you setta yourself up for heartbreak again, eh?''

I lean down, trying to direct my whisper right into her ear, taking care not to hook my lip on a rhinestone clip-on earring the size of a hubcap. ''I'm not setting myself up for anything. Except dinner.''

Her mouth twists, disgusted. A garbled message blasts through the station. Years of practice enable me to decipher it.

''Damn. Ten minutes before the next train comes. Come on—let's go sit down.''

I hustle her over to a nearby bench; we just manage to squeeze our butts into the last two spaces, hugging our purses to our stomachs.

''*Sei pazza!*'' she mutters.

I sigh. Yes, I probably am crazy. I also know this isn't going to go away simply because I don't want to talk about it, so, despite an audience of roughly a thousand people, I decide to explain what Greg and I had—maybe still have— ending with, ''He made me feel safe, Nonna. What's so bad about that?''

''Safe? *Pah.* You want safe, get a Saint Bernard.'' She squints at me. ''You wanna man who will excite you, getta you juices going.''

I blush. ''Not to worry. Greg gets my juices going just fine.''

She bats the air between us. ''I notta talk about *that.*'' She leans over, then whispers, only not, ''Anything witha hand and mouth can get *those* juices going. Summa day, maybe I tell you about me and Graziella Zambini, righta before the war.''

Along with at least a dozen other people, I stare at my

grandmother for several seconds, then shake my head and say, "I'm not looking for exciting, okay? *Exciting* wears me out. Hey, what are you doing?"

She's grabbed my shoulder bag, digging around in it for the romance novel she knows is inside. She yanks it out, lifts a brow at the cover, then wags it in my face. "You don' want exciting? Then why you read this a stuff?"

"For escape, Nonna." I pluck the well-thumbed book from her hands, stuff it back inside my bag. "Besides, that's fantasy. Not reality."

She shrugs. "You show me a woman who doesn't wanna be swept off her feet, I show you a dead woman."

I can feel the African-American lady beside me shaking with silent laughter.

Mercifully, the train comes screeching into the station.

I swear, Paula looks twice as pregnant as she did the last time I saw her, which was, what, a couple weeks ago?

The house reeks of tomato sauce and garlic, booze and cigars, Paula's perfume. "It's twins," she says with a laugh, following my eyes to her middle. "Boys, no less. Aiyiyi, am I gonna have my hands full or what? And oh, my, don't you look pretty as a picture, Aunt Renata? Come here and let me give you a hug, sweetie!"

Okay, if somebody tells me *this* woman is just putting up a front, that she's not as happy as she genuinely seems, I'm going to shoot myself.

"Your mother didn't come?" my cousin asks me, her plucked brows dipped.

"Said she wasn't feeling well. Upset tummy or something."

"Oh, dear…nothing serious, I hope?"

I shake my head, although this is the second time my never-sick mother hasn't been well in less than a month. If she's not all right when we get back, I swear, I'm going to get her to go for a checkup if I have to dump her into the grocery cart and wheel her there.

The house is positively abuzz with voices and laughter and Frank Sinatra. A caravan of dark-haired kids streaks past, shrieking and giggling. I peek into the kitchen as Paula leads us back to the family room where the main party is, see a half-dozen loud, bosomy women I only vaguely recognize doing whatever it is domesticated women do in kitchens. Chopping and stirring and whatnot.

"Okay, ladies, you're on your own," Paula says, still smiling. "Food's in the dining room, just introduce yourselves."

Paula's Colonial Revival family room has been invaded by a tribe of Italian gnomes, several of whom look a little stoned, frankly, although the affliction is more likely rampant deafness. My great-uncle Sal, however, apparently had a double dose of uppers with his All-Bran this morning.

"Renata!" His grin is eerily reminiscent of Kermit the Frog's. But with teeth. Lots and lots of teeth. Which I suppose compensate somewhat for the five strands of gray hair stretching across his bald pate. His arms look too long for his frail-looking, shapeless body; if it weren't for his suspenders, no way would he be able to keep up those rust-and-vomit green-plaid polyester pants. "Comma here and give your brother-in-law a bigga hug."

They kind of lurch toward each other across beige sculpted wall-to-wall, arms precariously spread, Sal's white patent-leather loafers glittering in the sunlight slanting through the patio doors leading out to the backyard. Two feet before they actually dock, Nonna says, "You toucha my butt, you loosa you teeth."

Sal does this asthmatic braying sound that passes for

laughter, "Heh…heh…heh. I loosa them already, t'irty-t'ree years ago. So too late."

They embrace carefully, so bones won't shatter. Although they still manage to knock both their glasses askew. They part just as gingerly, fussing at each other.

Wow. It's been ten years, at least, since these two have seen each other. Paula's wedding. That Nonna hasn't given any indication that she's missed her old neighborhood, not in all the time I've known her, seems odd. Then I look at her eyes as they sweep the crowd, the way they light up as this one or that grasps her hands or hugs her, and I realize, ohmigod, she *has* missed them.

So why didn't she ever say anything? Nedra or I would have been happy to bring her out for visits once in a while—

"Paula definitely gives a wild party, doesn't she?"

I swing around so hard, I nearly knock myself over. Nick's hand shoots out, catching me by the elbow. My nipples immediately tingle.

Damn.

He looks at my head. Nods. "Looks good."

"Thanks." Then I frown. "I thought you were supposed to be at work."

He shrugs, leans against the doorframe, arms crossed over his knit shirt. Black this time, tucked into soft, black jeans. "Decided to take a few days off. After the case was solved, you know?"

"Congratulations on that, by the way. Saw it in the paper."

His eyes are positively hooked to mine. "Thanks."

"I, uh, take it there was no problem with, um, the dog food?"

His expression doesn't change. "It never came up."

I nod.

"So," he says, "how's it goin'?"

"Oh. Good, actually. Got a new job, one I think I'll actually like."

"Hey, that's great. And…whatshisname?"

"Greg?"

"Yeah. Greg. You kick him out on his ass?"

I could lie. I should, probably. "Not exactly."

Nick doesn't seem surprised. In fact, he doesn't seem much of anything. "So you gonna get back together with him."

"How do you go from 'not exactly kicking him out' to 'getting back together'?"

He looks away, shaking his head, his mouth pulled up in a half smile. One of those man looks, you know? Then he leans close, whispers in my ear, "You jump outta my bed like you found fleas in it, then I see this guy in your apartment, looking like his dog just died. Then I see how you look, and believe me, it doesn't take a genius to put the pieces together."

I lick my lips, trying to ignore my pounding heart. See, this is just what I was talking about, the way guys like Nick always put you on the defensive, somehow. You can't just *be* with them, you're always having to justify yourself.

"We went together for nearly a year, Nick." Now I look away, watching my grandmother toddle around the room, having the time of her life. I look back at Nick. "I have to give it a chance. Give *him* a chance. That's just me."

"You love this guy?"

"I did."

His brows lift. *"Did?"*

"Hey, he hurt me. I'm not denying that. And frankly, I'm not sure what I feel for him. About him. But I just can't…walk away, okay?"

Those cool blue eyes keep mine snagged for several more seconds, then he does exactly that.

Damn.

These old people sure know how to party, boy. Two hours later they're still going strong, boogeying their skinny little butts off to Big Band music and stuffing their faces with a whole bunch of things they probably shouldn't, and laughing. Oh, my, the laughter. Oh, yeah, there are the occasional spats to break up—somebody remembering some infraction or other that happened forty years ago, stuff like that—but for the most part, they're having a blast.

And so am I, amazingly enough. I've danced some myself—you haven't lived until an eighty-year-old man who barely comes up to your boobs has taught you how to swing dance—and generally tried to forget about all penis-enhanced lifeforms under the age of forty.

But eventually, the old guys wear me out, causing me to seek sanctuary in Paula's living room, where she's lounging on the sofa, her sandaled feet up on the coffee table. The youngest-to-date is asleep beside her, his head in what's left of her lap. His cheeks are flushed pink, his curls tousled, his mouth open just enough to emit soft snoring sounds. Paula is barely fingering his curls, a serene smile on her face.

I flop onto the recliner across from her. She looks up, her smile broadening into a grin. "I can only hope I've got that much energy left when I'm that old."

"I somehow think you will," I say, and she laughs. I take a swig of the diet Coke I've been hauling around for the last hour, nod at her belly. "So. You think this will be it for you and Frank?"

"Yeah," she says on a sigh. "High time we do what every other fertile Catholic couple does and ignore the pope. Six should just about do it.'' Her head lounges against the back of the sofa. ''But the kids are so excited about the new babies. The oldest two helped me get out the baby clothes yesterday.'' Another laugh. ''Not that they stayed packed for very long!''

''You don't mind, having so many kids?''

She lifts up her head, her brow furrowed. ''Mind? Why would I mind?''

''They don't leave much time for anything else.''

''Anything else…? Oooh, I get it. Look, Ginger, I'm not like you, you know? I was never really good at much in school, never really wanted a career. This was all I ever wanted, to be a mommy, to be a wife. What more could I want, huh?'' She looks down at the baby again, stroking his cheek. ''Maybe my choice isn't exactly politically correct or whatever you wanna call it, but it's *my* choice. I'm happy with it, and frankly, I don't give a damn what anybody else thinks.''

After a moment I say, ''So how does it feel to be the only unconflicted woman on the planet?''

She hoots. ''Pretty damn good, if you wanna know the truth.'' Then she frowns. ''Nick told me you were gettin' back together with your boyfriend?''

I sigh. ''I didn't say that and Nick knows it. What I *said* was that I have to give it a chance.''

Her eyes narrow. ''Meaning what, exactly?''

''Meaning, we're having dinner on Monday.''

Her mouth screws up, as if she wants to say something but is figuring it's better not to. And no way am I going to encourage her. Then she does say, ''As long as you do what you want to do, Ginge. You know what I'm sayin'?''

A phone rings from within the pile of purses by the sofa.

''Gotta be yours,'' Paula says as the little boy stirs beside her. ''Nobody else has a cell.''

I think about not answering—who on earth could it be?—except curiosity won't let me ignore it. So I get up, pawing through a mountain of fake leather handbags with gaudy clasps until I find my trusty Coach bag and the obnoxious, demanding phone that therein resides.

"Is this Ginger Petrocelli?" a man's voice, tinged with Pakistani or Indian overtones, asks.

"Yes?"

"This is Dr. Pahlavi, calling from St. Luke's hospital. Your mother is here, in the emergency room."

My heart wedges into my throat. "Ohmigod—what's wrong? Is she okay? What—?"

"Please do not trouble yourself, Miss Petrocelli. Your mother is stable for now. Resting. We are running some tests—"

"Tests? For what?"

I feel Paula's hand grasp mine.

"To find out what the problem is, to rule out the obvious. I would prefer not to discuss it over the phone, but Mrs. Petrocelli has asked for you—"

"Yes, yes, of course..." *Shit!* "But I'm in Brooklyn, it may take a while. Is she okay, though? I mean..."

The doctor chuckles. "I doubt her condition is life-threatening. Just some precautionary measures, you understand. Again, please do not worry. We are taking very good care of her. Whenever you get here will be okay."

I turn to find myself surrounded by the gnome tribe, my grandmother's worried eyes the first ones I see.

"Nedra's in St. Luke's, they won't tell me what the matter is...we have to leave, get there..."

A strong, firm hand grabs my elbow. I look up into determined blue eyes.

"I'll drive you," Nick says.

* * *

I am in no condition to argue. Hell, I'm in no condition to do anything. If I'd had to get us back to Manhattan on the subway, no telling where we would have ended up. In the back seat, Nonna is muttering her way through the rosary with enough fervor to raise the dead.

"I don't get it. Nedra's just never sick. Never."

"It's okay, honey," Nick is saying, his voice low, calm. The voice a cop uses to keep people from jumping off ledges. And I know he knows he probably shouldn't be calling me "honey," but right now, I really don't care. "The doctor said it wasn't an emergency, right?"

"Then w-why did she go to the emergency r-room?"

"Ginger. Breathe. No, not gulp…*breathe.*"

"Dammit! What are all these *cars* doing on the road?" I flap frantically. "Why can't you put the red light dealie on the car roof, do your siren, you know, *get the freakin' lead out?*"

That elicits a gasped, *"Per Dio!"* behind me, followed by a marked increase in rosary recitation speed.

"Because," Nick says calmly, stopping for a red light, "that would be abusing my position."

I fold my arms across my chest and glower.

A scant half hour later, I burst into St. Luke's ER like a crazed woman, Nonna tottering along behind me, Nick bringing up the rear.

"I'm looking for Nedra Petrocelli!" I practically yell at the poor nurse or aide or whatever the hell she is at the desk.

She doesn't even look up. "Down the hall, second exam room to your right."

I shoot down the hall and into said room to find my mother on her feet, clothed, and looking slightly…stunned.

"Nedra! What happened? Are you okay? They called and said they were doing some tests…"

Her hand goes to her heart. "Christ, Ginger—how did you get here so fast?"

"Nick was there, at the party. He brought us back to Manhattan."

We're in each other's arms now, she's stroking my hair and trying to shush me out of my anxiety attack. "It's okay, *bubelah*, it's okay…"

Whoa. I don't think I've ever heard her call me that.

I pull back, look her in the eyes. "What's…wrong?"

A funny smile plays across her mouth. "You know how I said my stomach was bothering me? Well, then I got dizzy and I thought, okay, this is dumb, but what could it hurt to come over here, see what's going on? I mean, just to be on the safe side, right?"

She pauses. I freak.

"Ohmigod, it's your heart, isn't it? Do you need surgery? What—?"

"No, honey, it's not my heart."

Relief rushes through me, only to be immediately followed by an even more sickening dread. "Oh, *shit!* Is it…is it…?"

"Ginger, stop. I'm perfectly healthy. In fact, a helluva lot healthier than I thought I was."

What *is* with that weird expression on her face?

"Okay. I'm lost."

My mother hands me something. A photo…of…

Of…?

My eyes shoot to hers. She gives me a wobbly smile.

"Congratulations, *bubelah*. You're going to be a big sister."

Fifteen

What the hell is this, an epidemic?

"You're *pregnant?*" This last word is screeched.

"Seems so."

My knees give way. I sink into a molded plastic chair nearby. "But...but...you said you hadn't had a period in more than six months."

Nedra shrugs.

God, I so don't want to hear this. Be living through this.

"How...how far along?"

"Six weeks, maybe? Eight at the most." She goes over to a mirror in the exam room, pulls a comb from her purse, runs it through her hair. Her hand is shaking, as is her voice. "For thirteen years, Leo and I tried to have another kid, and nothing. And now..." She sighs. "God, life is weird, isn't it?"

To say the least. "Is it…this whoever it is you've been seeing, is he the father?"

Her eyes meet mine in the mirror, a wry smile twisting her mouth. "You think I'm sleeping with more than one man?"

I cross my arms. "Think maybe it's time to tell me who he is? Maybe even introduce him to Nonna and me?"

She turns, twin wrinkles marring the space between her heavy brows. Then, shaking her head, she lets out a short laugh.

"What?"

"To say my getting pregnant wasn't part of the plan is a gross understatement. To be honest, I haven't gotten that far in my thinking. So all I can say is…I'll keep you posted."

"Are you going to tell…the father?"

"Eventually. Not yet. Not until…"

But she doesn't get to finish whatever it was she was going to say because a short, chocolate-skinned doctor with a white turban comes into the room, just as cheery as he can be.

"Ah," he says, extending a delicate-looking hand. "You must be Mrs. Petrocelli's daughter." At my expression, the smile vanishes. "Oh, dear." He looks from me to my mother and back again. "She has told you her news?"

I nod.

"Ah." He links his hands together over his crotch. "I suppose finding out one's fifty-year-old mother is pregnant would come as a bit of a surprise."

You could say that. Which is more than I can, because, right now, I can't say anything. So I slip into a nice catatonic trance while the doctor chats with my mother for a few more minutes.

"Ginger?" I look up at my mother, realize we're alone again. "I can go now."

I try to get to my feet, but my legs aren't sure they want to support me.

"Hey," Nedra says. "*I'm* the one who just found out she's pregnant. Not you."

"I know, but—"

"Would you rather it *had* been a heart attack?"

"No, of course not. It's just…God. What are you going to do?"

"Start shopping for baby clothes?"

"That's not funny. Jesus, Nedra—how can you even think of having a baby at your age?"

Her expression turns to stone. "How can I think of embarrassing you, you mean."

"This isn't about me—"

"You're right. It's not." She grabs her purse, slings it over her shoulder. "I'm sure they need the room. We'll talk about this later."

My head spinning, I follow her out of the exam room. When she spots my grandmother and Nick in the waiting room, she says, "Not a word to anyone. Not until I've decided how to handle this. Understood?"

I nod, even though, right at the moment, I don't understand *anything*.

Nick insists on driving us back the few blocks to the apartment, my mother in front, Nonna and me in the back seat. Once Nedra assures my grandmother that she's fine, she's sorry she called us away from the party, a silence thick as smoke settles inside the car. I can practically hear the gears grinding inside Nick's head.

Nick pulls up in front of the building; my mother and grandmother get out first, head inside. But I stay behind for a moment, leaning on the open window to say thanks. Nick startles me by reaching for my hand.

"Look, I just want you to know...you need someone to talk to, about anything, whatever, I'm here."

I smirk. "Believe me, you don't want to get mixed up with this crazy family."

He shrugs, does that crooked grinning thing again that makes me nuts. "What family isn't?"

I look at our layered hands, slip mine out from underneath his to fold my arms across my stomach. "Why are you being so nice to me?"

On a half chuckle, he straightens up behind the wheel, gazing out the windshield. "Damned if I know," he says, then pulls away from the curb.

I go straight to the freezer when I get inside, chomping down into the Häagen-Dazs bar before the paper's even all the way off. Since I've sworn off booze and it doesn't look good for sex within the next twenty minutes, fat-laden empty calories will have to suffice.

Except they don't. Because—I finally realize as I stamp back to my room, Geoff trotting at my heels—this frustration isn't going to be eased by putting something *in* my body, but by letting something *out*.

But what? How?

And what is it I'm so frustrated about, anyway?

Nonna and my mother are in her room, arguing. I only catch snatches, like wisps of smoke coming down the hall. Then, silence, followed seconds later by a low, shocked, *"Per Dio!"*

Then it hits me: my mother is pregnant, and probably needs me.

My eighty-year-old grandmother has just found out my mother is pregnant. She probably needs me, too.

And maybe they could both use a Häagen-Dazs bar.

I go back to the freezer, pull out two bars, then continue on to my mother's room. Geoff opts to stay outside the door, since the rooster, though securely caged, is giving him the evil eye.

"Here," I say, handing each of them an ice cream. "Won't solve anything, but it beats the alternatives."

My mother is sitting on the edge of her unmade bed, Nonna on a stool at its foot. There being no other uncluttered surface on which to plant my tush, I sink cross-legged onto the floor, glowering at the rooster. We sit in silence for some moments, licking our ice cream bars and thinking our thoughts, until Nedra says, "I've never been more scared in my entire life."

We both look at her. And my mother, who's yelled at politicians and policemen, who's spent more than one night in jail, who's never been afraid to confront anybody about anything, is crying.

Holy shit.

I'm instantly beside her on the bed, hugging her to me. My grandmother sits on the other side, stroking her hand.

"It's gonna be okay," I say, but she shakes her head.

"I'm fifty freaking years old. I know how high the odds are that something could be wrong, could go wrong."

Wow. "You really want this baby, don't you?"

She nods, wipes at a tear. "It's crazy, I know, but I really do."

I reach up, sweep her hair out of her face. "Well, then. Odds are higher that everything will be fine, you know."

"I know, but…" She stares at the licked clean Häagen-Dazs wooden paddle in her hand, then lets out a long sigh. "But what if they aren't? What if…?"

I exchange glances with my grandmother, who looks as

though she's ready to cry, too, and I think, no, Nick. Women don't *make* things complicated. Life just *is*.

The next day, I popped—okay, dragged—myself out of bed with Big Plans, the most immediate of which was to take my grandmother to mass, something I hadn't done in, gee, years.

When I was around six or so, long before Nonna came to live with us, she apparently decided she could no longer tolerate what she labeled my parents' spiritual neglect of their only child, so she hauled her then-bony little butt all the way up from Brooklyn to in turn haul my bony little butt to my first mass. Not to be outdone, the instant my maternal grandmother got wind of this, *she* decided it was high time I began to appreciate my Jewish roots, as well, never mind that up until then my heathen upbringing hadn't seemed to bother her one way or the other. Hence, the following Saturday I set foot in a synagogue for the first time.

My parents, devout agnostics both, didn't seem to care one way or the other as long as it was understood that this was simply for exposure purposes and not a sign-on-the-dotted line kind of thing. Since I got to spend precious alone time with each of my adored grandmothers, I shrugged and went with the flow for several years. Then adolescence reared its doubting, secular head, and I discovered I'd rather spend my weekend mornings with my friends than God, it never occurring to me at the time that the two weren't mutually exclusive.

In any case, neither grandmother—or dogma—"won." Oh, I believe in God, even if I do think He has a perverse sense of humor at times. I've just never declared any party loyalty. I have no qualms about putting up a Christmas tree *and* attending Shelby's elaborate Seders every year. Some years I go to Easter mass, then the following fall observe the High Holidays. I'm cool with all of it...from a careful distance. I haven't yet decided what to do if I have kids, but I suppose I'll figure it out. After all, I turned out okay, didn't I?

Don't answer that.

Anyway, it occurred to me that Nonna probably hadn't been to church in a while, a suspicion proved true by the way her eyes lit up when I asked her if she'd like to go. My chest ached at that—attending daily mass had been part of this woman's life for so many years; not going at all must've been killing her. Yet I knew my mother would have taken her, at least occasionally, if she'd asked. Except that would be putting someone out, a far worse sin in Nonna's book than missing mass. Which got me to thinking again about how much my grandmother gave up, coming to live with us. And wondering why she stayed on after my father died.

So I ask her, sitting across from her after church at the Hungarian Pastry Shop at Amsterdam and 111th Street, one of our favorite haunts when I was little. She looks at me, clearly startled at my question, then sets down her teacup, folds her hands in her lap. She's wearing her new dress; I've taken the curling iron to her silver hair to make it wave softly around her face. I see the cute, headstrong young woman she must have been.

"Your mother, she needed me," she says with a shrug. "That is why I stay."

Now it's my turn to be startled. "Nedra doesn't need anybody."

"She isa good actress, yes?"

"But you yourself said how strong she is—"

"Ah..." One bent, knobby finger comes up in a point.

"But that strength, it would crumble without other people around her."

I sit back in my chair, my arms folded over my floral sundress. Well, duh, Ginger. I'd said it myself, that Nedra derives her energy from the people around her, just as I need my solitude.

"But that still doesn't explain why you thought you had to stay. After all, she was almost never alone in those days. I was still there, for one thing."

"But I was the one who was *always* there. Inna spirit as well as body. Like your father. You were there, yes, but you don' wanna be, and your mama knows that." She carefully cuts a corner off her Napoleon; the whipped cream squishes out from between layers of flaky phyllo pastry. "When you go, she miss you more than she can say." Her eyes float to mine. "But she won' say anything, because is what children are supposed to do, leave the nest, go out onna their own. So I stay, be her strength." Her mouth pulls up into a wide grin. "She cannot suck Renata Petrocelli dry, eh?"

I laugh, poke at my own pastry with the tip of my fork, then ask, "But did you stay because you felt you had to, or because you wanted to?"

She looks at me. "I don' understand."

I look back. "I saw your face at that party yesterday, Nonna. How happy you were. Like…like you were home."

She quickly lowers her gaze back to her half-eaten pastry. "It wasa nice, seeing everybody again. Thatsa all."

I reach over, take her soft hand in mine. "If you could do whatever you wanted, would you move back there?"

She snatches her hand from mine. "Why you ask me these questions?" she says, her words trembling around the edges. "Did you hear Sonya ask me to move in with her? Is that what this is all about?"

Sonya, my grandfather's younger sister. Now widowed herself, she and my grandmother had been very close before Nonna moved from Brooklyn, more like sisters than sisters-in-law.

Behind Nonna's glasses, tears shimmer in her eyes. "How can I do that, with your mother having a baby?"

"Nonna, for God's sake—you're eighty years old! Nobody, least of all Nedra, would expect you to help raise another baby at this point in your life! Hey, you want to go live with Sonya, you go live with Sonya, okay?"

"And who will be there for your mother?"

I cross my arms, my mouth thinning. "The one who should have been there all along. Me."

"But you will get married someday, move out again—"

"Hey, not your problem, okay? My mother, my responsibility."

Nonna lifts a napkin to her nose, honks into it, then nods. "Your mama, she isa very lucky."

"Damn straight. Now let's go pick out a few of these to take home, okay?"

Unable to decide what Nedra might like, we get a half dozen different goodies so she can choose. I suggest a taxi—it's only five short blocks north, but the two long crosstown blocks are killers—but Nonna insists she'd rather walk. So we do, Nonna completely hidden from me by the beige umbrella she's carrying to shield her from the sun. Which suddenly shifts to one side so she can squint up at me through her glasses.

"In church, I light a candle for your mama, pray to the Virgin Mother. I hear the Holy Mother whisper your mama will be fine. Baby will be fine. You will see." She squints at me. "Is a gift, this child. Like Sarah's Isaac, in the Bible."

I shift the *Times* I bought earlier to my other hip, realizing I'm doomed to get newsprint ink all over my dress. "Except wasn't Sarah like ninety-something when she had Isaac?" I squint in the harsh sunlight at my grandmother. "How would you like to have a baby in ten years, Nonna?"

A horrified look crosses her face. "How you say, *inna you dreams?*"

I laugh, feeling a little better. Because, see, the reason I was taking my mother's bombshell so personally is because, quite simply, I'm jealous as hell.

I'm the one who's supposed to be pregnant. Not my mother. And now I've just assured my grandmother that I'll be the one who'll stick around and see my mother through this pregnancy. An offer I didn't make just to hear myself talk, or give Nonna an out. Seriously. This new twist on things might have thrown me for a loop, but I really do want to help…even though that just effectively screws up any chance I thought I had of reclaiming my *own* life. How am I going to have my own babies if I'm busy helping my mother raise my thirty-plus-years-younger-than-me sibling?

Not that babies of my own seem to be in the offing.

Okay, I'm just making myself depressed, here, so I'm going to stop.

Geoff greets us at the apartment door, looking…well, relieved is the only word I can come up with. I frown at the dog for a moment, puzzled. Nonna goes to her room to change, I slog down the hall with the goodies to find my mother sitting at her computer in her office, glasses perched on handsome nose, trolling the Net. I come up behind her, place the fragrant white box beside her, squinting at the screen.

Your Baby and You, it says.

And so it starts.

Nedra's opened the box, given a gasp of delight. "All

morning I've been having these weird cravings—quick, hand me a napkin or something!—but I couldn't figure out for what. Now I know!''

The nearest thing is a tissue, which I hand her, but the first pastry is already half devoured. Nedra has whipped cream on her chin, which I reach over and wipe off with another tissue.

''I better get as much of this stuff now as I can, because you know what my doctor's going to say as soon as I go in for my first appointment.'' She puts down her fork, horror streaking across her features.

''What is it?'' I say.

''I have to buy *maternity* clothes!''

She sounds both horrified and delighted. I smile, then take a deep breath and tell her about Nonna. And Sonya's offer.

Nedra wipes her mouth, looks at me. ''Are you sure?''

''I had to drag it out of her, but yeah. She just told me.''

''Oh, for crying out loud...'' Nedra shakes her head, her mouth twisted in annoyance. ''Why the hell didn't she just come out and tell me?''

''Sonya just asked her yesterday, at the party. She didn't have a chance.''

''No, I mean before this. That she was unhappy here.''

''Because she wasn't unhappy. In fact, I don't think she fully realized how much she wanted to go back to the old neighborhood until she got out there yesterday, saw all those people.''

''Still, I wonder why she stayed with me all these years?''

''Because...I think she convinced herself you needed her.''

My mother blinks at me. ''*I* needed *her?* Are you serious?''

I nod. Nedra laughs a little, stares into the box as if contemplating a second pastry. I push the box toward her.

"Live. The baby will thank you for it."

She takes a second pastry, this one with almond paste and chocolate icing, and I hear myself say, "I think I've just about got her convinced that she doesn't have to worry about you if she goes, because I said I'll be here for you."

Nedra chokes. I jump up, run into the bathroom for some water. When I get back, she's staring at me, her hand on her chest, her eyes watery from the choking. She grabs the cup of water from me, chugs down several swallows, then says, "Now you listen to me, and you can relay this to your grandmother, too. I don't expect anyone to mold their life around me, or to give up anything for me—"

"Oh, shut up, Nedra," I say, and she does, even though her mouth is still very much open. "I just realized I've spent far too much of my life being a self-absorbed brat. Now, you gonna give me the chance to atone for my sins or not?"

"No," she says without missing a beat.

"What?"

She huffs a sigh, then brushes pastry crumbs off her bosom. "You heard me. Hell, Ginger, I don't even *want* you around. I love you, baby, you know that, but you drive me totally nuts."

"Then what was all that crap about trying to get me to move back here after Greg's no-show?"

"This is still your home. I'm still your mother. It's written in the contract that you have to be willing to take your kids back if they need a place to recoup, no matter what."

"Well," I say, rising, "it's written in *my* contract to be there for my mother when she gets herself knocked up. So deal with it."

I toss my head, then stomp from the room and down the

hall, feeling pretty damn smug, if I say so myself. It's not until I go into the living room, which, as you may recall, looks directly into Nedra's bedroom, that I notice something's missing.

The rooster.

I stand in shock, staring at the space in the corner of Nedra's room where the cage used to reside, then turn and stomp back to her office.

"Where's Rocky?"

She looks up from her computer, frowning. "The Ortizes came and got him. Why?"

"And you let them take him?"

"Well, yes. Since he's their rooster."

"But you heard what Nick said, what they're probably going to do with him!"

She lowers her reading glasses to peer at me over them. "And this bothers you why?"

"Jesus, Nedra! Just because I didn't wish to share living space with the thing doesn't mean I want him to get pecked to death!"

She resets her glasses, goes back to clicking away on the keyboard. "They assured me that wasn't going to happen."

"And you *believed* them?"

The glasses get whipped off, her dark eyes bore into mine. "What choice did I have? Gladys downstairs told me this morning that the guy who just moved in next to her heard Rocky in the airshaft, said he was calling Animal Control tomorrow morning. It was either get the bird out of here immediately or wait for them to come take him away. While I was trying to figure out what to do, Manny Ortiz called me, said they were living with his cousin out in Weehawken now and he wanted to come get the bird. And he's got a new job, driving for his cousin. He was so tickled, he insisted on giving me a business card...now where did I put it—?'' She riffles through a million notes and papers on her desk, hands me a plain white card with black lettering. I scan it, look up.

"His cousin owns a funeral home?''

Nedra shrugs. "In his business, everybody's a potential customer, I guess. Anyway, he's gainfully employed, Rocky will have a yard to strut around in. You should be happy.''

She's right. I should. But I'm not. Which leads me to believe I'm in a lot more trouble than I'd thought.

It also means I have to go back to setting my alarm clock.

Well. On to the next item on my list, which is to trot on down to the Jewelry District and see what I can get for the ring. Yes, I've finally decided to sell it. I did the honorable thing by offering to return it to Greg, right? So I figure I'll take the money, invest it or something. Since it doesn't look as if I'm going to be moving out anytime too soon. A thought which seems a lot less scary than it might have a few weeks ago.

I'm on my way back to my room when I hear my phone ring. Takes me a while, but I finally find it in the bathroom.

"Hi, there, sexy lady!''

It's Ted. I grin, settle onto my bed cross-legged. "Hi, yourself. What's up?''

"Well…got a favor to ask.''

I of course agree without even asking what it is, because these guys have been there for me something like a million times over the past five years, including, but not limited to, nearly killing themselves getting that sofa bed down eight flights of stairs. Anyway, it turns out Randall won this trip for two to someplace very exotic from his company and they'd had it all arranged that Alyssa would spend the week with her mother, who then got an emergency call from *her* company and has to leave tonight for Europe for a week, so could Al please come stay with me?

"Ohmigod, I'd love it!" I say. "We can do all kinds of dumb girl things."

Ted breathes a huge sigh of relief. "That beats her going out to stay with her grandmother all to hell." So we make all the when-I-should-pick—her-up arrangements and then I get off the phone to tell my mother, who's standing at my doorway and is delighted—yes! a refugee!—and my grandmother, who's equally delighted—yes! another mouth to feed!—and Geoff, who doesn't really seem to give a damn. And then I remember I'm supposed to go out with Greg tomorrow night.

Unfortunately, I say this out loud, which apparently causes my mother no small distress.

"I didn't know you were going out with him again."

"Sure you do. I told you."

She looks at me. "No, you didn't."

I think. "Okay, so maybe I didn't. But what's it to you?"

Her hand rakes through her hair, holding it back from her face. "I…just don't want to see you getting hurt again. I don't trust that man."

"You never did."

"With good reason, it turns out."

I sigh. Gee, I do a lot of that these days. "Look, it's just dinner, okay? If nothing else, I'd like to hear his side of things."

"Are we talking closure, here?"

"Well…"

"Yeah, that's what I thought. Jesus, honey, why on earth would you want to go there again?"

"Jesus, Nedra, why don't we remember we're supposed to be living our own lives here?"

Her mouth seems tighter than usual. "What can I tell you? I worry."

"Hey." I plant my hands on my hips. "You can't tell me you want me to live my own life, then throw a hissy fit when I try to. You want this baby, I want to figure out what I'm supposed to be doing here. That includes deciding *on my own* what to do about a man I was ready to spend the rest of my life with. To quote somebody else in this room, this has nothing to do with you."

She gives me an odd look, but says nothing.

I change into gray capri pants and a matching tunic—serviceable, but chic—slip on a pair of backless sandals, stuff the ring box into my purse, then go searching for the Yellow Pages, which I finally find in my mother's office. Ten minutes and a half dozen phone calls later, I get the name of someone to ask for at the Diamond Exchange down on 47th Street, which I scribble on the back of a business card on my mother's desk, which also gets stuffed into my purse. A half hour later, I'm there; twenty minutes after that, I've got a big, fat check in my purse...and that business card. Which, yep, you guessed it, is the one Manny Ortiz had given to my mother.

I stand there on Fifth Avenue, staring at the card...

No, I can't do this. I mean, I didn't even like the stupid bird. What do I care what happens to him?

I pivot north, march smartly past Rockefeller Center, cross the street and cruise Saks for a half hour or so, then head back across Fiftieth Street to the uptown IRT station. Only, when I get to Seventh Avenue, I cross the street to the *downtown* station.

I do not believe I'm doing this.

My heart is thundering in my chest as I refill my Metrocard. I mean, even if I manage to find these people once I get to Weehawken, what the hell do I think I'm going to do? A single woman commando raid to rescue a chicken? Then what?

I stand at the turnstile, my card hovering over the slot. I can still change my mind. Turn around, go back up the stairs, cross the street, go home.

In the distance, I hear the roar of the oncoming train.

I ram the card through the slot and hurtle myself through the turnstile.

Sixteen

By the time I catch the bus at Port Authority that will take me to Weehawken, I am a woman obsessed. Or maybe possessed. I ask the driver if he perchance knows which stop is closest to the address on the card; he doesn't, but the thick-waisted little Cuban lady who just got on ahead of me does.

Feeling cheered that I at least won't be riding the bus aimlessly around Weehawken for the next two hours, I sit, resisting the temptation to gnaw on a hangnail. Shortly thereafter, the bus spits me out on Kennedy Boulevard. Behind me, across the river, looms midtown Manhattan. In front of me, stupidity does.

Having no earthly idea where I'm going, I head west, praying for guidance. Or at least somebody who speaks English. Finally, I get directions to the funeral parlor, which turns out to be only a fortuitous few blocks away. The parking lot is virtually empty, which means—thank God—I'm not interrupting anything.

The front door is open. I go in, following the sound of voices to an office down the hall. Two heads snap up at my sudden appearance, a man and a woman's, both middle-aged, dark-haired. Startled.

"I'm looking for Manny Ortiz," I say before either of them can hit me with a sales schpiel. Not that talking about my own death particularly bothers me—exactly—it's just that it's highly unlikely I'd choose to be interred in Weehawken.

"He's off today," the man says. "Can I help you?"

"It's…personal. I don't suppose you could tell me where he lives? We, uh, used to be neighbors. In Washington Heights."

I guess I don't look terribly threatening, because the man nods, then gives me directions to the Ortiz house. Which turns out to be his, as well. Ah, the cousin.

Central Weehawken—the emphasis being on the "wee"—is filled with shady streets lined with a mishmash of housing styles in varying degrees of upkeep. The Ortizes live on a worn-around-the-edges street that was probably, at one time, almost elegant. The house itself is a brown clapboard two-story with a porch, circa early twentieth century. A dog barks as I approach; cooking smells emanate through the screen door when I get to the top of the porch steps.

I realize I have no idea how much, if any, English these people speak. And my Spanish is from hunger.

Mrs. Manny comes to the door, the youngest one on her hip. Her hair is piled atop her head; one bra strap, red, has escaped from under her black tank top to strangle the top of her arm.

"Mrs. Ortiz? My name is Ginger Petrocelli. I was looking for your husband?"

She squints at me, then grins, revealing a missing tooth. "You are woman from old place!" she says, standing back to let me in. That I've shown up out of the blue doesn't seem to either surprise or worry her. She shifts the baby higher on her hip to shake my hand, tells me her name is Benita. "Come in, please. House is mess, but with so many children...?" She shrugs. "We hope to get our own place soon. You would like a Coke, maybe?"

"No, no thank you." Relieved at least about the language thing, I scan the living room, filled with bulky Mediterranean-style furniture on carpeting the color of root beer slush. The room is clean, the "mess" strictly kid effluvium—toys and crayons and stuff. "I can't stay. I just...came to see about the rooster. Rocky."

She turns to me, her smile fading. "The rooster?"

"Yes. My mother was taking care of it? Your husband came to get it this morning?"

"*Sí, sí, comprendo.*" She lets the toddler down, then smooths her hair off her pleated brow. "He is in the back, with the others." She licks her lips. "My husband is not here. I do not think he would want you to see..."

But I'm already halfway through the house, storming through the immaculate kitchen to the walled backyard, which has been divided into a number of small pens. Each one contains a rooster.

No hens, just roosters.

I turn to Benita, who is regarding me with worried eyes, even though, in theory, there's nothing I can do to make trouble. After all, I have no proof the cocks are being kept to fight.

"Is not my idea," she says quietly, her arms folded across her doughy stomach. "*Hombres estúpidos.*"

There are four of the creatures, majestic things in their own chickenish way. I can't save them all. Nor can I stop the *"hombres estúpidos"* from continuing the practice, not today, not by myself. Calling the authorities would be useless. But suddenly, I understand what drives my mother, and others like her, to fight what might seem like losing battles: because, as Nonna said, somebody has to speak up for those who have no voice.

Okay, so it's only a chicken, but it's a start.

"How much is he…worth?"

Benita understands what I'm asking. She shrugs, tells me. I think of the check in my purse, many times larger than the amount she just quoted. I get out my checkbook, add a hundred dollars to her figure, then hand it to the stunned woman. "I'll take him with me," I say, realizing, with that one sentence, I have just officially slipped over the edge.

As I trudge back to the bus stop, a rooster-filled cage in tow, I realize my zeal has faded along with my options. Assuming I even manage to find transportation that will allow livestock, just where do I think I'm going to *take* said livestock once I get on whatever it is?

So much for my foray into impulsive behavior.

Oh, yeah—behold the fun-filled antics of the hip young urbanite, I'm thinking as I switch the heavy cage from one hand, now gone numb, to the other. Gee—I could be standing in line in some coffeehouse right now, schmoozing with other hip young urbanites, not a care in the world beyond which trendy restaurant I'm going to sample next. Instead, I'm schlepping a rooster down the street, the cage banging the hell out of my thigh, hoping against hope that tying the damn thing to my back and swimming the Hudson isn't the only way I'm ever going to escape New Jersey.

For at least the first half hour, things aren't looking too good. When a bus finally comes chugging along, the driver laughs in my face, shuts the doors, and drives off, leaving Rocky and me to choke on exhaust. Nor is there a taxi in sight. By now, I'm working up to having to pee, I'm sunburned, and I'm this close to tears. And no closer to a solution. Just when I'm beginning to envision being interred in Weehawken after all, a large, black vehicle approaches from the north, eventually stopping in front of me.

A hearse. And you get one guess who's behind the wheel.

My blood runs cold (never thought I'd ever have the opportunity to actually use that phrase) as I entertain unpleasant thoughts concerning enraged rooster owners and dumb *gringas*.

The dark window on my side lowers. Cautiously, I bend at the waist, peer inside.

"You need a ride?"

Right. God knows what he's going to do to me.

Except then Manny Ortiz grins. A nice grin, not a your-neck-is-thin-enough-to-snap-with-one-squeeze grin. Then I notice one of the kids, a little boy, tucked into a car seat by his side. "My wife, she tells me what you do, that you buy the rooster. The bird means a lot to you, *sí?*"

"Yes," I lie.

He chuckles. "You want a rooster, I could have told you where to get one much cheaper."

"I didn't—" Oh, hell. Like I can explain this.

"Is very generous, what you do. The money, it will help us get a place of our own sooner. *Gracias.*"

I nod. *"De nada,"* I say, which is as far as my Spanish goes. Then I add, because I have absolutely nothing to lose at this point, "And the other birds?"

His brows shoot up. "You want to buy them, too?"

"No, no. But…"

I lose my nerve. Manny sighs, skims a hand across his thick hair. "You women, too soft-hearted." He slants me a look. "I think about it. In meantime, I will take you wherever you need to go, okay? Your mother and you have both been very good to my family. A ride is the least I can do to repay you."

I hesitate.

"There is no one in back, if that is what is bothering you."

Well, hell, I hadn't even thought about that. "No, it's just I'm not sure where to tell you to take…me…"

Oh, God. Dumb and dumber strikes again. "Can you take me to Brooklyn? To Greenpoint?"

"No problem. Put the bird in the back and hop in. Benita, she'll be just as happy to have the little one out of her hair for a while, *sí?*"

I deposit the cage in back then climb in beside the little boy, who gives me a shy, sweet smile.

"Jesus, give me a heart attack, why don't you?" Paula is standing in her doorway, her hand on her chest. "Was that a *hearse?*"

I wave to Manny and little Benito as they drive off, then turn back to my ashen-faced cousin. "It's a long story, and I really, really have to pee—"

Her eyes have gone to the cage. And its occupant.

"I'm afraid to ask," she says, "but why do you have a rooster?"

"Paula? I'm going to piddle all over your stoop."

"Oh, Jesus, come in. No, wait, leave the rooster…well, shit, I don't know where to leave the rooster! Frank! Come see this thing!"

I scurry down the hall to the bathroom, making it there

by the skin of my…teeth. When I come out, Rocky's cage is surrounded by a veritable herd of Wojowodskis in varying sizes. Now that my bladder is empty, I quickly run through the entire series of events that lead up to this moment, at which point Nick comes down the stairs from his apartment, his eyes widening when he sees me. Then he spots Rocky and his eyes narrow.

"Gee. That rooster looks awfully familiar."

Rocky cocks his head at Nick and kind of…gurgles at him.

"You were right, they were raising him to fight," I say in a rush. "My mother gave him back to the Ortizes but I couldn't stand it, so I went and, um, liberated him."

I think that's what you'd call bemusement in Nick's eyes. "And brought him…here."

My gaze bounces from Nick to Paula to Frank and back to Nick. "It's just until I find someplace else for him, I swear."

"Ma, he's like, so cool," Frank Jr., the oldest boy, says. "It's like we're living on a farm."

"Which we don't," Paula says, then turns to me. "Honey, swear to God, I'd do anything for you, but I can't keep a rooster."

My eyes are burning. I feel stupid as hell. And desperate. How come my mother can pull these things off with dignity and I just look like an idiot? "It's just for a few days," I repeat. "I promise, I'll find someplace to take him. By the end of the week," I declare, even though, again, I have no idea what I'm promising.

"Ginger—"

"I'll take care of him," Nick says quietly to his sister-in-law, although his eyes are pinned to mine. "And I'll find a new home for him, too. I've got connections," he says when my brows lift.

"Mom, look!" Frank Jr. says. "It's like he knows we're talkin' about him!"

"It's a chicken, for cryin' out loud!" Paula says. "They're like the stupidest creatures on God's green earth!"

At that, Rocky turns his beady little eyes on Paula, stretches up on tiptoe, and crows his heart out.

"Jesus," she says. "I'm sorry."

"I owe you guys," I say, heading for the door before Nick can get to me, even though if I'll admit it, he already has. But I'm not admitting anything. "Anytime you need a baby-sitter, just holler, I'll be here."

Then I hug Paula and get the hell out of there, fully aware as I hot-foot it down the street toward the subway station that Nick has come out on the stoop and is watching my retreat.

Dinner's long since over by the time I get home, although Nonna insists on heating up some leftover eggplant parmigiana for me. Gee, when she goes back to Brooklyn, either my mother or I will have to learn how to cook. Bummer. I tell them both about my afternoon's adventures; they both stare at me, speechless.

"And Nick said he'd take care of it, find it a home?" my mother says.

"Uh-huh."

Nonna grunts. "An' alla this Greg did was send you roses."

After dinner, I find my mother in her room, hand her a check. After deducting what I paid for the rooster, it's what I just got for the ring. I've left the Pay To The Order Of part blank.

She looks at the figure, blinks. Looks up at me.

"For that shelter you were talking about," I say, then

go to my room, rip off my clothes and fall into bed, and thence into the first decent night's sleep I've had all summer.

In the midst of the weekend's events, I'd nearly forgotten I was supposed to start a new job today. Or that I was supposed to be there at nine, which was twenty minutes ago and I'm just now getting off the bus at Fifth and 86th to begin my sprint over to Lexington Avenue, where Dana Alsworth has her gallery and offices. I'm a veritable vision in Mushroom-and-Creme, right down to my classic, but up-to-the-minute, matching slingbacks. The weather is even being decent—relatively blue sky, relatively oxygenated air, relatively cool crosstown breeze. So, all of this having put me in a good mood (even if I am running late, my mother is pregnant, I spent several hours yesterday rescuing a rooster and I have a date tonight with a man I have no idea what to do with) I skim across the sidewalk at a brisk enough pace to put some color in my cheeks, but not enough to leave me panting when I arrive.

I stop at the showroom's front door, both to catch my breath and ease myself back into what I like to think of as "my" world. As I stand there, I feel an actual transformation take place. The crazed, impulsive woman of yesterday is fading…fading…yielding to the secure, confident, sane creature I used to be.

God, I'd missed her.

Alsworth's is twice as large as Fanning's, with designers and assistants scurrying around like the critters in Disney's *Cinderella*. Dana herself emerges from the back within seconds of the sleek, black receptionist's announcing my arrival, *whisks* me back to her office. I get the feeling things get *whisked* a lot around here.

I sit (elegantly, legs crossed but close together, hands on

knees, chin up), we chat, I fill out forms, I'm shown my office (nice view, not spectacular but plenty of light), then am given a brief tour of the rest of the facility (three conference rooms, huge sample room, accessories showroom, other offices, bathrooms, everything in muted pewters and taupes). By this time, Mrs. Souter, aka Devil Lady, has arrived. With a smile, I *whisk* the diminutive hellcat into my new office, mentally making a note to ditch the tired wing chair in the corner for something much more *au courant,* then buzz Liandra at the front desk for coffee, making a mental note to ask her where she got those fabu earrings.

Then I sit behind my desk, lean back, and wait for Contentment to surge through my veins, since, after all, this is exactly what I'd worked for my entire adult life.

It almost happens, but not quite.

Guess I'm just out of practice.

At twelve-thirty my intercom buzzes.

"There's a gentleman out front to see you," Liandra purrs.

"Did he give his name?"

"I asked, but he's not telling. Says he's here to surprise you."

My heart bolts into my throat.

"Blond or dark-haired?"

"Oooh…we have a choice?" She laughs. "Dark."

Greg? What the hell—?

Many winged creatures take flight in my stomach. Which is a good sign, yes? Tell me it is, I need to hear it. I get up, take a few seconds to tweak and twitch and fluff, then sweep out into the reception area.

Greg's eyes widen—oh, right, he hasn't yet seen my new short 'do—then he gives me a very appreciative grin, which begets more fluttering. "Very nice," he says, I say,

"Thanks," then he says, "I've come to spirit you away for lunch."

Suddenly, something seems…off. "But aren't we having dinner tonight?"

Hands in pockets of charcoal pin-striped Armani, smile in place, he shrugs, "What can I say? I couldn't wait."

Behind me, Liandra is going, "Mmm-mmm," under her breath. Dana just happens to emerge from her office at that moment, sucks in an audible breath. As does the young man following her.

"Gee, I don't know, Greg…I've got a ton of work to do…"

Everybody in the room stares at me.

Well, he's thrown me, dammit. I now realize the fluttering isn't from glee, it's from apprehension. I need advance warning for this, which I thought I had. Since when does Greg Munson ambush people, do things on the spur of the moment? He's supposed to be predictable, dammit. It says so right on the box.

"Well, if you're too busy…" he says, looking—I sigh—crestfallen.

"Oh, now, Ginger," Dana drawls, "there's nothin' that couldn't wait another hour. Or two." She spears me with an if-you-don't-take-him-I-will look. "Is there?"

Another sigh. "No, I suppose not." So, I do the introduction routine, stall as long as I can by going potty, putting on more lipstick, getting my handbag, finally telling myself I'm being perverse and childish.

The minute we're outside, Greg apologizes.

"I didn't mean to throw you, Ginge, honestly. I just thought…" His chest rises on an inhaled breath. "I just don't want you to feel I take you for granted."

Where the hell did that come from? I adjust my bag higher on my shoulder, shake my head. "I never felt that from you,'' I say, which is the God's honest truth. ''Why should I now?''

''Just something Dad said, that's all. That women like to be showered with attention.''

''I'm not a poodle, Greg. I don't expect you to give me treats.''

He laughs, then steers me around the corner to a cute little French restaurant I'd already pegged as someplace I wanted to try. The place is minuscule—just seven tables in a storefront that used to be a bakery or something—the prices outrageous. The kind of eatery we used to frequent when we were dating. Okay, yeah, this is nice. *Very* nice.

I begin to relax.

We order, then sit and chat over Perrier (me) and a single Scotch on the rocks (him). A couple comes in, sits on the other side of the restaurant, which is maybe all of twelve feet away. She's older, maybe mid-forties or so, very well dressed. He's twenty-five at the most, casual to the point of bumminess.

Greg leans over. ''An affair,'' he whispers.

I grin in spite of the residual nervousness that hasn't quite let go. We used to do this all the time, make up stories about other couples, give them lives of our own devising. I lean over, as well. I can smell his cologne. Armani, as well. To my surprise, sexual awareness wallops me right in the gut. ''She's married.''

''Oh, God, yes. Fifteen years. One kid, a daughter, in prep school upstate.''

''No, abroad.''

Greg glances over, nods. ''You're right. Definitely abroad.''

''He's…a musician.''

''What instrument?''

I slant a glance in his direction. ''Violin.''

"She's keeping him."

I laugh. "His patron?"

"Her boy toy."

Of course, not five minutes later, we hear the guy groan, "Jesus, Mom!" and that ends that. We laugh, dig into our salads. I tell him about my weekend's adventures, leaving out the part about my mother's pregnancy, for obvious reasons.

"You mean to tell me," Greg says, chuckling, "you went all the way out to Jersey to rescue a chicken? *You?*"

I hadn't realized until this moment that my telling him was a test, of sorts. That I was holding my breath about what his reaction might be. And how relieved I am—not to mention nonplussed—that he's not horrified.

"Unbelievable, isn't it?"

He grins. "I can just see you hauling that thing around. So where'd you end up taking it, anyway?"

Nick's blue eyes flash into my thought. Oops.

I look down at my salad, thinking, *Just keep sniffing that Armani, honey.*

"My cousin Paula's. In Brooklyn. For the time being, anyway."

"Paula, Paula…oh, right—she's the one who married the Polish guy, right? Has all the kids?"

"Yeah. You never met her, though."

Behind his glasses, his eyes crinkle. "Maybe now I will."

It's now clear to me just how much he means to win me back. I should be flattered. I *am* flattered. I'm also not entirely sure what to do with…any of this. But damn, he's being attentive. And funny. And charming. And when we leave the restaurant and he takes my hand, something warm and familiar washes over me. Another definite surge of sexual interest.

But it's too soon, and I tell him so, just as we reach Alsworth's door.

"I know that," he says softly, then slips his hand to the back of my neck, lowers his mouth to mine.

Holy crap, I'd forgotten how well this guy can kiss. And now I remember the way he could make my entire body sing with his touch, how he always knew exactly what to do, how to not only get me hot, but to keep me begging for hours.

When he breaks the kiss, I frown. "Why did you stand me up, Greg?"

His lips curve into a gentle smile. "You're a formidable woman, Ginger, in case you don't know. And I thought, how could I possibly ever be enough for her?"

I chew on that for a minute, then say, "And now?"

Instead of replying, he kisses me again, winks, then walks away.

And I thought this man was *safe?*

I snag a taxi after work, swing by to pick up Alyssa. I'd called first, so she's waiting outside, chattering to Arnold, the night doorman. An old pro, she tosses her duffel bag in the front with the cabbie, then scrambles into the back beside me. We do the huggy-squealy number—it's been too long since I've seen this kid, smelled her shiny, child-verging-on-woman scent.

"God! You cut your hair!" she says, bug-eyed.

"You like it?"

"It's totally awesome." She grabs a hunk of her own silky tresses, frowns at it. "Think I'd look good like that?"

"Cut your hair and die," I say mildly, and she giggles.

Traffic's heavy. After five minutes of inching up Third Avenue, I bang on the Plexiglas, suggest maybe going through the park at 96th? The driver nods, cuts across two lanes of traffic to get to the west side of the street.

Alyssa starts talking about boys. There are two in her life at the moment, both of them in the summer music program she's been attending (she plays piano). One likes her, but he's a dork. The other's, like, so totally cool, but he doesn't even know she's alive.

I sigh. "Sounds familiar. I think I was a senior in high school before it actually worked out that I liked a boy the same time he liked me."

Horror streaks across her features. "You mean, I have to wait *that* long?"

"Trust me," I say, thinking about my own situation. "That's when the problems start."

But then she's onto a new topic: how her father absolutely refuses to let her wear anything that shows even part of her stomach, not even a *sliver,* when all her friends are and nobody's else's parents are being so anal about it and when is he going to realize she's not a *child?*

I was just about her age when my father died, I suddenly realize. Pain clamps around my heart for a moment before I grab her hand. "He probably never will, honey."

She makes a face. I laugh, only to sober at the thought of actually having to tell one of these of my own, one day, that she's not showing off her midriff at twelve, either. Except God alone knows what twelve-year-old girls will be showing off by then.

We pass the rest of the ride in quiet, relatively peaceful conversation, which, had I known the chaos awaiting me, I would have appreciated more. Because the instant I open the door to the apartment, Geoff bursts into the hall, circles us three times, then zooms over to the just closed elevator door, where he plops his butt on the hall tile and gives me this, "Well?" look. I see my mother—who just this morn-

ing remarked about not having any morning sickness—
stumble out into the hall from the bathroom, clearly having
puked her guts out; and my grandmother informs me that
Shelby called a half hour earlier, desperate because Mark
surprised her with tickets to something or other for her
birthday but the baby-sitter backed out on them and is there
any way I could take the kids—Nonna says she said it was
no problem, to bring them on over—and, by the way, Terrie
is in the living room, waiting for me.

Did you get all that?

I hand Alyssa her duffel bag, tell her to take it down the
hall into my room, then say, "Nonna, I have a date tonight,
remember?"

Nonna does the sour grapefruit thing with her lips, which
leads me to think she does indeed remember but had hoped
I'd forgotten. But then she squares her shoulders and says,
"Is notta problem. Alyssa and I take care of the bambinos.
You go, get ready, go on your...*date*."

Right.

Alyssa, who's done as I asked and is now standing behind Nonna (and who is, I'm noticing, a good six inches
taller than my grandmother) chimes in with, "It's okay,
Ginger, really. I baby-sit for the Jorgensens downstairs all
the time. I can handle it."

But they can't handle my sick mother. Or Terrie.

Jeez, I wonder what's up with *her?*

I finally manage to wedge my way into the apartment,
where I drag my phone and Day-Timer from my purse.

"Forget it," I say to my grandmother as I punch in
Greg's cell number. "He took me to lunch today, anyway.
I can cancel, he'll understand...."

No answer.

I call his condo.

Voice messaging. Wow, progress.

"Hi, it's me," I say to the voice messaging fairies, "I hate to be so last minute, but something's come up—" okay, so poor word choice "—and I have to back out for tonight. I'll call you."

Okay…who first? My mother or Terrie?

Geoff yarps and immediately moves to the head of the line, because let me tell you, a corgi's sharp little bark in an empty, high-ceilinged, tile-floored public hallway cuts straight through the skull. "Has he been out yet?"

Nonna hands me his leash. The humans in my life will have to wait because clearly Geoff can't. He yanks me down the stairs—forget the elevator, life is too short—then we pop out past the doorman, at which point I head toward the curb, the dog toward the park. We both yelp, but I win. Barely. There's a lot of power in those stubby little legs.

"Sorry, bud. Not tonight."

You should see the look he just gave me. However, it's not as if he has a whole lotta choice, so he pees, he poops, I scoop, he mopes, we zip back up to the apartment.

Alyssa's in the kitchen with Nonna already, doing something with pans and bowls. I zip into the living room long enough to hug Terrie and ascertain that she looks deranged.

"Hang tight," I say, one finger raised. "I'll be right back."

I poke my head into my mother's room. She's pulled the shades, but I can make out that she's lying on her side on the bed.

"How do you feel?" I whisper.

"Like hell."

I feel helpless. And worried. And somehow guilty, though God knows why. *I* didn't get her pregnant, after all. "You need anything?"

"A coma would be nice."

I make a mental note to surreptitiously ask around, see

who knows anything about home remedies for pregnancy nausea. I close the doors behind me, see Terrie standing up, gathering her purse.

"I should go, this obviously isn't a good time—"

"Sit," I command just as the intercom crackles in the kitchen.

"Just let them in," I say to Nonna. "It's just Mark or Shelby, bringing the kids over. It's okay, I swear, I'll be right back," I say to Terrie, then jog down the hall to swing open the door.

Okay, so I'm obviously really bad at this guess-who's-at-the-door game.

It's Greg—of course—who not only clearly didn't get my message, but is early.

I check my watch.

Okay, not that early.

Well, it would seem we're dressing down tonight, since he's in Dockers and a maroon polo shirt, open at the collar, loafers with no socks. Some of us, however, are doing the straight-from-work crumpled look.

"Ready?" he says, and I want to say, "Are you blind?" except the elevator doors open again, spitting out Mark, a pair of small, unruly children, and a Big Brown Bag full of God-knows-what.

"God, thank you so much for doing this at the last minute like this," Mark says, leaning way out to hand me the bag in order to keep one hand on the elevator door so it won't close. He's so intent on dumping kids and getting out of there he's totally missed that there's somebody else standing in the hallway. Let alone who the somebody else is. "Everything you could possibly need is in that bag," he says, stepping back inside and punching the button five or six times. "We should be back to pick them up by eleven at—"

We don't hear that last bit because the elevator has swallowed him alive.

Both children begin to sob. Huge, drooling, heartbreaking sobs, punctuated by off-sync "Daaaadddeeeees" every half second or so. So here I stand, a wailing two-year-old in my arms, whiny four-year-old at my knees, and a clueless ex-fiancé in front of me.

I hike Hayley up higher on my hip, trying not to wince as her high-pitched screams drill straight through my brain. "Plans have changed," I shout.

"So we'll take them with us."

This from a man who has obviously never spent any length of time in a restaurant with two children under the age of four. I almost laugh, but he really means it.

"That's very brave of you," I shout over the din, "but I've also got a twelve-year-old camping out, a sick mother—" no need to go into details on that one "—a depressed friend who I haven't even talked to yet, since I got home maybe ten minutes ago, and a grandmother who's definitely not up to handling two young children."

Greg shrugs, then bends down to Corey, who clutches my skirt even more tightly. Have to give the guy credit, he doesn't even flinch at the amount of snot glistening on the kid's upper lip. "Hey, guy. My name's Greg. What's yours?"

He looks up at me. "It's okay, honey," I say. "He's a…friend."

"Corey."

"You like Chinese food, Corey?"

"Y-yeah, I g-guess. Egg rolls."

"So," Greg says, straightening up, "Who's good for delivery around here?"

"Greg, really, you don't have to do this—"

"Yeah. I do," he says, then herds us all inside.

Seventeen

'Twas a night to do Fellini proud.

Once my little cousins realized that a) the histrionics were pointless since Mommy and Daddy weren't around to hear it, b) Auntie Ginger had a *dog,* the noise level diminished considerably. For, oh, five minutes or so. Because then, see, they discovered that tearing up and down Auntie Ginger's forty-foot-long hallway would make Geoff chase them. And what, pray tell, could be more fun than that?

Of course, this made me a nervous wreck, because of my mother and all, and consequently I kept doing that trying-not-to-yell tense thing with my voice to get them to stop. Which worked about as well as ordering a fish to get out of the water. Eventually, my mother stuck her head out of her bedroom door to tell me I was making five times more noise than the kids, for God's sake, at which time she caught a glimpse of Greg, turned an even worse shade of green than she had been, and ducked back inside her room, slamming shut the doors behind her.

In fact, everyone in the apartment over the age of thirteen—except me—was giving Greg a wide berth, which was really beginning to annoy me because not only was he trying his damnedest to be nice, but he was about to spend a fortune buying all of us dinner. Which I pointed out to Terrie when she followed me down the hall to my room to change Hayley's fragrant diaper. Everyone else would just have to cope for five minutes without my running interference.

Man, this apartment hadn't seen this much activity since 1982.

We duck into my room, I plop the baby on my bed, rummaging around in the shopping bag for Huggies and wipes.

"What the hell is Greg doing here?" Terrie says.

"Watch your language and we had a date." I smile for the baby, who giggles and tries her damnedest to knock out my teeth with her feet. Aren't kids supposed to be potty trained by two?

"You're nuts, girl, you know that?"

I decide to ignore that. I finish up with Hayley, then wrap up the stinky diaper, stuff it in a little plastic poopoo bag. The baby flips over onto her tummy, shimmies backward off my bed and takes off, yelling, "Doggy! Doggy!" as she pounds down the hall. "And you're here why?" I say to Terrie, replacing everything in the shopping bag.

She silently fiddles with one of the six rings on her right hand, looking stricken.

I gasp, leaping to a conclusion with a single bound. "Ohmigod, Terrie—are you *pregnant?*"

"What? Christ, Ginger! Of course not! Why would I be pregnant?"

"Sorry. It just seems to be the crisis of choice these days."

"Well, it's not mine." She perches on the end of my bed. She's wearing tight hip-hugger bell bottoms, one of those little tops like Nonna was looking at. On her, it works. And damn well. And she's ditched the braids, her hair now framing her head and shoulders like a glistening chocolate cloud.

Since we've quickly eliminated my first choice, I grab for the second one. "You still going out with Davis?"

Her chin begins to wobble.

I figure while I'm in here, I might as well change, so I yank open a dresser drawer, pull out a T-shirt and a pair of baggy shorts. Clean, neat, totally unsexy. "Okay," I say, shrugging off my wrinkled dress and tossing it... somewhere, "let me guess. You've been seeing Davis every day, sleeping with him for a week—which is, like, *the* most incredible sex you've ever had—" off go panty hose and slip, on go shorts "—you think you're in love with him but you're so scared, you can't sleep, can't eat, and your work has gone straight to hell."

"Damn, you're good," I hear as I wriggle into the T-shirt.

Well, gee, it's not as if we haven't had the conversation once or twice in the past fifteen years.

"So what should I do?"

Now what you've got to remember is, this is the woman who saved Shelby's and my butts on a daily basis when we were kids, who aced all her classes in school, who handles other people's money for a living—extremely well—and who I've watched singlehandedly talk down a gang of, shall we say, miscreants when we took the wrong bus one night when we were fifteen and ended up in a part of town we shouldn't have. But when it comes to her love life, she's a total and complete wuss.

And under normal circumstances, I'd let her talk it out, weep on my shoulder, indulge her insecurities. But right now, I've got a sick, preggo mama in one room, three kids to take care of in another, and an ex-fiancé in the kitchen who's simultaneously creeping me out and turning me on. And the doorbell just rang, which means the Chinese food is here and it's nearly eight o'clock and there's a container of shrimp in garlic sauce with my name on it out there. So we really need to fast forward this scenario a bit.

"I can't tell you what to do. Hell, I can't figure out what to do with my own love life, such as it is, let alone figure out anyone else's. But you know something? I really think you need to get over this fear you have about getting involved with someone because, well, golly gee, he might be *flawed*."

I can't tell from her expression whether she's stunned or pissed. I decide I don't care.

"I mean, honestly, Terrie, so you decide to go for broke with the guy? What's the worst that can happen?"

"Hey, that's easy." Her arms cross over her ribs. "I'll get screwed again."

"Or maybe not. But think about this for a minute—could you live with yourself if you let this go just because there's no guarantee? What if Davis is *It,* but you're just too damn scared to take that chance?"

She stares at me for a long moment, then gets up, goes to the bedroom door, only to turn when she gets there. My guess is that she hasn't exactly derived a lot of comfort from my words.

"I just got one question."

"Which is?"

"Who are you and where did you put my girlfriend?"

* * *

It's ten o'clock. Terrie left pretty much right after our conversation. Both the little Bernsteins have conked out and been tucked into my bed, Nonna and Alyssa are watching TV in my grandmother's room, and my mother is feeling well enough that she's come out of her room several times to glare at Greg.

Who is lying on the living room floor on his stomach, actually looking as if he's having a good time playing tug-of-war with Geoff, whose eyes are bugged out with the effort to hang on to the knotted rope toy Greg brought him.

Is this man kissing up or what?

And I'm sitting on the old, lumpy couch, my feet tucked under me, my fist propping up my cheek, not sure what to think about any of this. Correction: not what to think about this New and Improved Greg Munson. Not that I hadn't liked the old version just fine, but...

But...

But I don't know.

He rolls onto his back; the dog flops by his side, smacking him in the face with the chew toy. With a laugh, he looks up at me. "You look pretty tired."

"It's been a day and a half."

He sits up, laughing again when the dog's head becomes a blur in his zeal to break the toy's neck. "Kill it, boy! That's it! Kill it!"

Geoff drops the toy, his tongue lolling out the side of his grinning mouth. Greg pats his lap and the dog trots over to flop onto his back to get his tummy rubbed.

"Wish it were this easy to win over your mother," he says.

"I don't think she's much for having her belly rubbed."

Then again, what do I know?

"She really hates me for what I did to you, doesn't she?"

"Greg, I hate to break this to you, but she didn't much like you *before*."

"But why?"

"Well, this might be a reach, but my guess is it has something to do with the fact that your family represents everything she's spent the past thirty years working against."

He glances over at me, adjusts his glasses on his nose. He's let his hair grow out a little, just enough to affect that endearing tousled look. "In other words, she's never going to call me 'son'?"

"Greg, I—"

"Sorry. That was presumptuous."

"Yes, it was."

After a moment Greg says, "Your life used to be like this a lot, didn't it? When you were a kid?"

"Yeah, I guess so." Only now it doesn't seem to bother me so much.

Huh.

Greg watches me for a couple of seconds, then gracefully gets to his feet. "I should go, let you get to sleep before you pass out."

I'm much too tired to point out that sleep is not in my immediate future, at least not until somebody comes and removes the two tiny humans from my bed. And I have to run Geoff out for his final whiz of the night. But I force myself upright, following Greg down the hall.

I open the door, lean against the door frame. He seems reluctant to leave, which, if I'd been more awake, I might have found more flattering. Or frightening. I wonder if he's going to kiss me.

I wonder if I want him to.

I smile, thinking how long it's been since I've stood

outside this apartment door, wondering if I was going to get as lucky as I ever got as a teenager, prolonging the inevitable moment when I had to finally go into the apartment. The number of times a neighbor's sudden appearance would interrupt the course of lips zeroing in on mine.

Now I'm the kind of woman who has sex on rooftops.

Or who can at least list it on her résumé.

Greg touches my jaw, almost tentatively. I mean, after this afternoon's liplock, why the reticence? And the anticipation that he might kiss me again is not wholly unpleasant, it's not that. I wasn't making up that stuff about how good he was—is?—in bed.

You know, for someone who didn't let a boy even touch her breast until she was seventeen, I've turned into a major slut.

"I think we need to get you out of here," he says.

I blink away the mental fog. "Huh?"

"This can't be good for you, living here again."

I laugh. "Tonight was exceptional, even for this family."

"But remember what we had, how you used to say how comfortable, how sane things felt when we were together?"

There is no urgency in his voice, his touch. Just a mesmerizing, calming levelness. Then I remember how Greg used to coax me into bed, seducing me with a subtlety that was frankly refreshing after some of the guys I'd known.

"Did I?"

"Mmm-hmm. This craziness…this isn't you."

I feel the muscles in my forehead pull tight, that something isn't fitting together, but I can't figure out what. "You didn't have to offer to stay, you know. And I could have sworn you seemed to be enjoying yourself."

"Oh, I did." He laughs, skimming his hands down my arms, just the way he used to, with a gentle pressure guaranteed to arouse. "Your little cousins are adorable. And I think maybe I began to win over your grandmother, at least, don't you think?''

I think he's a bit optimistic about that, but I say, ''Sure'' because I don't feel like going into this just now.

''But I know you, honey. You can't deal with that kind of chaos on a steady basis. You told me so yourself.''

''No, but…'' Why am I feeling defensive? And what am I feeling defensive about? ''Hey, these people are my family. My friends. They don't pick when they need me, you know?''

''And I understand that. In fact, that's one of the things I most admire about you, that you're always 'there' for the people you're close to.''

Am I? Well, shoot, I guess I am at that.

''But…?''

''But admit it. You're fried. Right?''

''Okay, so I'm a little beat—''

''And when I leave, you still have all that to face by yourself.''

''Well, yes, I suppose—''

''Then all I'm saying is, remember what it was like before, when we were together. What it could be again. Just the two of us, going to dinner, going for walks, reading the *Times* together in bed on Sunday mornings…among other things,'' he adds with a soft smile. ''I didn't realize how much I missed that, that simple, uncomplicated existence that was 'us,' until I didn't have it anymore.''

No comments from the peanut gallery.

But I have to say, at the moment, the whole idea of refuge from…everything is a very seductive one. I mean, it really does seem that the more I try to get my life squared away, the more it seems to go bonkers on me.

I open my mouth to say something, although I have no idea what; Greg silences me with a finger to my lips. ''You don't have to say anything. Not yet. I won't pressure you, I promise. Except…I certainly wouldn't mind another date?''

Would another date up the ante? Do I even *want* the ante upped? Do I *not* want the ante upped? Do I have a single reasoning brain cell left?

''Okay,'' I say. ''Dinner? Seven o'clock, Friday night?''

He presses the button for the elevator, then turns back to kiss me lightly on the lips. Not enough to get anything boiling, but enough to generate a sigh.

''Dress up,'' he says. Then, with a wink, he disappears inside the elevator.

I slink back inside the apartment, leaning heavily on the wall to keep from falling over. However, as I have a bed to yet make up for a certain young lady, I must keep going. I must, I must.

There's a futon in the unused bedroom; I struggle with the stupid thing for several minutes, yelping when it suddenly splays apart as if shot. Alyssa wanders in—my grandmother has nodded off—and asks if she can help. I say sure. Being a smart little cookie, she notices my befuddled state.

''Are you mad because I'm staying over?''

Startled, I look up from tucking in sheets. ''No! I'm thrilled to have you, you know that.''

Her mouth hints at a smile. ''Really?''

''Really. Hey—you wanna come into work with me tomorrow?''

''I've got camp.''

''Oh, right. What time you have to be there?''

''Nine.''

I nod, we continue making the bed. Except Alyssa gets bored and wanders over to poke inside the closet. She spots some of the canvases, pulls one out before I realize what she's doing.

"Wow. Who painted this?"

I look over, wiping sweat off my forehead. It's one I somehow missed during my own explorations, an early one of my father. He's bent over his desk grading papers, the stark light from the desk lamp sharply delineating his strong, carved features. "I did. About a million years ago." I walk over, hold it up to the light from the floor lamp, which isn't wonderful. But good enough to see I was a lot better then than I give myself credit for. I've never been a realistic painter—more van Gogh than Rembrandt—but I caught something in that painting I hadn't even realized at the time: my father's essence. His calm strength, his gentleness, even, somehow, his sense of humor.

And I think of the times he took me to Tom's on 112th Street and Broadway, all by myself, to get one of their incredible chocolate shakes. Or how he'd read the same book over and over to me without ever complaining or trying to skip pages, how he always made time to listen to whatever I had to say, no matter how silly.

How could I have ever thought myself neglected?

"It's my father." I gently stand it up on the edge of the futon, back away from it. "He died when I was thirteen."

"You painted this when you were like, my age?"

"No, later. From memory."

"How do you do that? I mean, without something to look at?"

"I don't know. I never did. I just…feel whatever I'm painting, somehow. And it just comes out of my fingertips onto the canvas."

I fully expected her to say that was creepy or weird or something, but all she says is, "How come you don't paint anymore?"

"Just got interested in other things, I guess."

She looks up at me, her eyes bright. "Could you paint one of me? For my dad? His birthday's in November."

My heart knots inside my chest. "Oh, gee…it's been so long…"

"Pleeeease? I really think he'd like it. An' I can pay for the paints and stuff out of my allowance—"

Laughing, I slip my arm around her shoulders, hug her to me. "You don't have to pay me, for heaven's sake," I say, realizing what I've just agreed to.

"But I want to. It would be a—what do you call it? A commission?"

I look at this beautiful, bright, giving child, and something, a process, begins to bloom inside me, as the tangible, human Alyssa takes on another, more visceral form in my brain.

I would love to paint her.

I *have* to paint her.

I have to paint, period.

The revelation slams into me, taking my breath, infusing me with newfound energy.

"Ginger! Are you okay? Why are you crying?"

I wasn't even aware that I was. I shake my head, laughing. "One day, I'll explain it to you. But right now, let's see if I've got a blank canvas to start sketching on."

I've got the portrait—a full figure, dressed in jeans and a midriff-skimming top—nearly sketched in by the time Shelby and Mark arrive to pick up the kids.

"We've got a taxi waiting," Mark whispers, gently picking up Corey, tucking the limp form against his chest like a sack of potatoes. Shelby goes to get Hayley, but I stop her, picking her up myself instead.

"You're pregnant, remember?" I say in a hushed voice.

She hesitates long enough for Mark to leave the room, then turns to me, very toothy. "I just want you to know I'm okay."

Brow lift time. "Meaning?"

"Meaning I realized I needed to get over myself. That maybe, yes, this baby is a curveball, but maybe it's also a blessing." A shrug. "Apparently this is what I'm supposed to be doing now. I can always go back to work later."

The woman is lying through her orthodontically enhanced teeth. But what can I say?

"Oh, and I felt the baby move for the first time today!"

Feeling...weird, I tell her to grab Geoff's leash, figuring I might as well drain him at the same time I see her downstairs. When we get to the first floor, I say, "So...you're really cool with this?"

"Well, of course, I am sweetie."

Only she's not looking at me. She's looking at Mark, who's putting the kids in the taxi, that staunch little jaw of hers poked out to kingdom come.

I watch their taxi pull away, totally incapable of deciding how I feel about what just happened.

"People are very strange creatures," I tell Geoff as we walk inside. My voice reverberates in the vast, marbled lobby, which manages to stay cool no matter what the temperature is outside.

When we get into the elevator Geoff slouches on one hip in the corner, panting, demanding sympathy for his rough life.

"My heart bleeds," I say.

He slurps his tongue back inside his mouth and gives me an offended look.

I'm still trying to get the last lock undone to the apartment when I hear my phone faintly bleating on the other side of the door. Who on earth is calling me at this hour?

I fall inside, lunge for the phone on the hall table.

"Hey, you just get in?" Nick says.

I will my heart to stop pounding so loudly. "I was out with the dog—"

"So how'd it go?"

This is getting downright surreal.

"How'd what go?"

"Paula told me you had a date with whathisname tonight."

I tiptoe past bedrooms where everyone is now sleeping and go to the kitchen. I need a Häagen-Dazs bar. Now.

"And this is your business how?"

"I'm nosy."

I viciously rip the paper off the bar. "Then it went fine," I mumble around that first, glorious bite. "Satisfied?"

"You don't sound exactly happy about it."

"What I'm not happy about is having one man bug me about my date with another one."

"This is not bugging, trust me. You have no idea what I'm like when I put the screws into someone."

I roll my eyes, take another bite of the ice cream bar. *Dulce de leche.* Yum.

"Anyway," Nick says, "I bet you'd give one of your girlfriends all the juicy details, wouldn't you?"

I swallow, then lower my voice. "Yeah, well, I'm not sleeping with them."

"Glad to hear it…waitaminnit—slee*ping?*"

"Whatever—*Jesus,* you're confusing me. Are you always this irritating, or are you just having a bad day?"

"What can I say? I get a kick out of yanking your chain."

"So I noticed."

"Is it as good for you as it is for me?"

"Screw you."

"Is that a promise?"

"God, you are being *so* junior high tonight."

He chuckles, then says, totally throwing me off balance, "I found Rocky a good home."

"What?" I lean against the counter, plucking the jagged pieces of chocolate off the rapidly softening ice cream and cramming them into my mouth before they fall into Geoff's. "You did? Where?"

"What are you eating?"

"Eyesch cream."

"What flavor?"

"*Dulce de leche.* Wan' some?"

"I only eat flavors I can pronounce. Anyway, one of the guys at the precinct, his brother has a small farm upstate, said he needs a new cock since his old one died a couple weeks ago."

No way am I touching that one.

"So…I'm off on Saturday. Wanna drive up with me and see the bird's new home for yourself?"

Surrealer and surrealer.

I suck the last of the ice cream from the stick, then say, "Gee, I don't know. I think I might have to work."

Silence.

"Well, okay, just thought I'd ask. But I'm leavin' here around ten, since it takes a good two hours to get up there. So if you change your mind…"

I can feel the pull, right through the phone. But it's a pull toward…what? A game of hormonal Ping-Pong? The odds of my surviving an entire day with Nick Wojowodski with my sanity intact are slim to none.

"Nick…I'm seeing Greg again Friday night."

Silence. Then, "Got it. Look, Paula says hi, okay?"

He hangs up before I get a chance to say anything else.

Shit, shit, shit.

Eighteen

It rained most of Tuesday and Wednesday, leaving behind clean streets, collective improved humor and a promise of fall. As much as I detest New York summers, I adore the falls—gold and crimson leaves vibrating against a clear blue sky, the first inclination to go Christmas shopping, the first opportunity to finally wear that sweater I couldn't resist buying the instant it showed up at Bloomie's in July. I know, I know, September's still weeks away, so I'm rushing things, but at least being able to see the end of this crazy summer, that my life is finally beginning to settle down—somewhat—is making me almost giddy with relief.

Of course, there's still my mother and her little "situation," both the logistics involved and the fact that we won't know if everything's okay until her amnio next month. And I find myself thinking about Nick a lot, even though I'm so busy at work, I barely have time to pee, let alone think much about anything unrelated to fabric swatches and furniture vendors. Still, I keep feeling as though I should call him, or something, even though I have no idea what I would say once I did that. We didn't really have anything going—and I'm sure he'd be the first person to admit that—but…

And I've been ruminating about this far too long, apparently, since my cell's ringing has just jolted me out of a stupor I've apparently been in for—hmm—a good twenty minutes.

It's Greg, calling from work. Like me, he's probably sitting at his desk with a half-eaten sandwich in front of him, in imminent danger of being crushed under a mound of paperwork. He was recently handed a plum case involving defending some huge company, something about anti-trust violations, I can't really explain it, but I can tell it's got his adrenaline really pumping. We've talked twice a day since Monday, pleasant enough conversations that always end with his alluding to how much he's looking forward to Friday—tomorrow—night.

And I am, too, I suppose. He's promised to take me to this new place in the West 80s that's been getting rave reviews. I know the spot. By which I mean, I know the chunk of real estate which this hotsy-totsy restaurant occupies, since I've eaten at no less than six different permutations of same over the past ten years.

"Hi," I say brightly, flipping through yet another Scalamandre fabric swatch book in the pursuit of exactly the right shade of velvet for Annabelle Souter's *Moulin Rouge*-inspired dining room chairs. "What's up?"

"That's what I'd like to know."

I stop flipping. "Greg? Is something wrong?"

"Just tell me one thing…how long have you been communicating with my brother?"

The swatch book flaps closed. "Your brother? Why would I be talking to your brother?"

"You tell me."

"Greg, I'm sorry, but I have no earthly idea what you're talking about."

"Okay, since you seem to need a memory jog, try this on for size. I bumped into Bill downtown, we decided to have lunch since we haven't seen each other in a while—"

"You had lunch with your brother?"

"I don't hate Bill, Ginger. I just don't understand why he delights in tormenting our father. But that's not the point. The point is, we both got calls on our cells during lunch, both put our phones down on the table, then apparently picked up each other's instead of our own. A fact I didn't notice until I checked my call listings and saw your mother's apartment number listed…from this morning."

"But…I haven't even called you today…"

"Exactly."

A blinding flash sears through my brain.

"Oh, dear, God…"

"So. You admit you're calling my brother?"

I take a second before I reply. Damn. I am so not good at this. "I swear to you, I haven't seen or talked to your brother since the day we went out to get my clothes from the Scarsdale house. But even if I had, I don't appreciate the jealous act. I can, and do, talk to other men occasionally. And will continue to do so. And third…"

Uh-oh.

"And third…? I mean, come on, Ginger—if *you* didn't call Bill this morning, who the hell did?"

"Look, I'm breaking up," I say, scraping my fingernails across the phone. "I'll talk to you later."

Right after I talk to my mother.

"How long?" I say.

I've closed the door to my office, turned on some music to further muffle the conversation, should somebody have nothing better to do than to listen in to my private conversations. Yes, this should wait until I get home, but I know that Greg is sitting and stewing, which means the sooner this gets sorted out, the better.

My mother's already admitted to both making the call and to her affair with Greg's brother. After a moment she says, "Since we went up to get your things."

"Is he...?"

"Yes," she says on a long, weary-sounding sigh. "Now do you understand why I didn't want to tell you yet?"

I shut my eyes, trying to come to grips with the revelation that my mother is pregnant by a man only three years older than I am. After the first shudder subsides, I say, "Does Bill know yet?"

"I told him a couple of days ago."

"And...?"

"And...we haven't decided what we want to do. What *to* do. I mean, he's actually kind of excited about the baby, but..." Another sigh. "We're not in love, Ginger. I'd never marry him, and that has nothing to do with our ages. Or even because of his family—"

"Never mind that Bill's family was enough to put you off accepting Bill's brother as a potential son-in-law."

"Another issue entirely. And now we're talking about Bill and me. Who I like a lot. In small doses. If I'm with him for longer than a couple hours, I want to smack him upside the head. I mean, he's incredible in the sack, and he's funny, and good to me, but he can be such a child at times. Oh, God…this was just supposed to be a *fling,* Ginger. I—both of us—had fully expected this to run its course and we'd part amicably and that would be that. The last thing either of us expected was to be figuring out joint custody arrangements.''

"So, you do plan on splitting the responsibility for raising the baby?''

"I don't know. I suppose. Please, Ginger—could we just get through the amnio first?''

I hear the apprehension in her voice, take a moment to collect myself. Then I say, ''What I don't get is how you expected to keep this a secret.''

"I don't suppose I did.''

"Good. Because I've got to tell Greg. Today. Before he blows a gasket.''

"I really wish you wouldn't.''

"I'm sure you don't. But things are only going to get worse the longer this is kept under wraps. Whatever comes of whatever this is, it's worthless unless it's built on a foundation of trust and honesty.''

"Oh, right. Which means, I suppose, you're going to fill Greg in about your little thing with Nick?''

She would bring that up.

"Probably,'' I say. ''At some point. But it's not the same thing.''

"No, it isn't. And what exactly do you think is going to happen when Greg finds out his brother got your mother pregnant? You think the Munsons are going to embrace this child with open arms, accept you into their family now?''

Okay, I can see where this could be a problem. ''I don't expect them to be exactly thrilled with the news, no. But they've always been very good to me. No, really,'' I say when she snorts. ''Here's a news flash, Nedra—the Munsons don't eat their young. And it's only fair that we get the truth out in the open as soon as possible, for everyone's sake. You're carrying their son's baby, for crying out loud. Their first *grandchild*. Phyllis isn't going to be able to resist getting involved.''

''Oh, now there's something to look forward to,'' Nedra says dryly.

''Look, I know these people. They're perfectly reasonable human beings. They're bound to come 'round eventually.''

Her pause is too long, too…significant. ''Then I think you're being very naive.''

''What's that supposed to mean?''

Another pause, then, ''Doesn't it strike you even a tiny bit odd how Greg's trying so hard to win you back?''

''Not really, considering how badly he screwed up.''

''See, that's why I didn't want to say anything, because you've already made up your mind what you're going to do, what you're going to think—''

''Dammit, Nedra, how many times do I have to tell everybody, I haven't made up my mind about *anything!* I know you don't believe that, but it's true. And it's not exactly insignificant that the man paid all the wedding expenses and then some. He's apologized, he's tried to explain as best he can why he bolted—what else do you expect him to do?''

''And you've never once asked yourself why?''

My eyes burn. ''Well, Ma, this might be a long shot, but maybe it's because the man *loves* me! Or is that too impossible a concept to wrap your brain around?''

After two or three beats have passed, she says, very quietly, ''And has he ever told you that?''

Before I can think of what to say, I hear a soft click in my ear.

It takes me another several seconds before I realize that for the first time since I can remember, I called my mother by something other than her first name.

Of course, for all my blustering at my mother, once I get Greg on the phone, somehow the words "Your brother got my mother pregnant" don't exactly come trippingly off my tongue. And even worse, I lie. I open my mouth, and out comes, "They're working on some cause together, apparently, that's why she called him."

I am such a toad.

But then, he *hasn't* said he loves me, has he? I don't mean now, I mean…ever. And how did that happen, that I accepted a marriage proposal from a man who never told me he loved me?

Won't happen a second time, I can tell you that.

By the time Greg arrives at the apartment to pick me up, I've decided to sound him out on a few things, even if I haven't exactly outlined the whens and hows yet. My mother's condition is high on the list, obviously, although I think I'll leave the "by whom" part for later. Then my painting. And somewhere in there, I'm thinking I might come right out and ask him exactly what his feelings are. Which might not be fair, really, since I don't really know what mine are, either. But still. He is, after all, the pursuer while I'm just the pursuee. I'm allowed to be ambivalent.

The thirty-block taxi ride won't really be long enough to hit all the topics, but I figure I can at least make some serious inroads.

"Hey," he says after he's given the driver the address, "what's with your hands?"

Okay, I guess the painting's just gone to the top of the agenda. After my mother assured me the oil paint smell wouldn't bother her queasy stomach, I'd started on Alyssa's portrait a couple nights before. It's not ideal, not being able to paint in real daylight, but you play the hand that's dealt you. Anyway, my pretty fingernails are history, polish and all, and no matter how much I scrub my hands with turpentine, I can't get all the paint off my skin.

"I used to paint, when I was younger. I thought I'd take it up again."

"You're not thinking of giving up your career, are you?"

I tell myself it's only my own paranoia making me hear that hint of condescension in his voice.

I look over, smile. "Oh, no. Just a hobby. It relaxes me."

"Well, that's good, isn't it?"

That he didn't say anything about wanting to see any of my work isn't lost on me.

I fold my mottled hands tightly in my lap, staring at the purple-and-red swirling designs in my long crepe skirt. Although it's still pretty warm, the breeze coming through the open window is strong enough to raise goose bumps along my arms, right through my knit tunic.

"Greg, there's something I have to tell you."

Greg looks over, smiling benignly until he sees my expression, at which point the smile vanishes. "What?"

Okay, folks, batten down the hatches.

"My mother is pregnant."

He starts to laugh, then stops. "Christ, you're serious."

"Oh, yeah."

"But she's…isn't she too old?"

"Apparently not."

After a moment of tense silence he says, "Is this one of those artificial insemination things?"

I shake my head.

"Oh. Well. Um, is she planning on marrying the father?"

"According to her, no. It's…complicated."

"Tell me he's not married."

"No, it's not that. But the thing is, I'm telling you this, now, because you need to know I'm going to be there for her. To help, if she needs it."

He looks vaguely horrified. "You mean, as in living with her?"

"I don't know. Maybe. If that's what she needs. My grandmother's probably going to move back to Brooklyn, so I'm all my mother's got."

That begets, understandably, a moment of silence. Then he says, "She's a grown woman, Ginger. Plenty of single women live with their kids on their own."

"And maybe my mother will decide she can, too. I'm just saying, this is something I have to be prepared for. That's all."

After a moment he says quietly, "I can't believe you'd let yourself be coerced into doing something like this. Ever since I've known you, you've always been about making your own choices—"

"Hey." I reach over, lay my hand on his arm. "This *is* my choice. Nobody's coercing me into doing anything I don't want to do."

He covers my hand with his, then sighs. "Sorry. I'm just…concerned for you, that's all."

"Thanks." I take back my hand. "But nothing's been decided yet. I just thought it was only fair to let you know how things stand."

He leans back against the seat, his arms crossed, apparently mulling this over. Then he nods, slowly, and says, more to himself than to me, "Yeah, I suppose that could work…" Another second or two passes, then he looks over at me, takes my hand in his, lacing our fingers. It feels…nice. Not earth-shattering, but nice. "It's a shock, certainly, but not insurmountable. Hey, I knew going in that your mother's a bit on the…eccentric side." He laughs, although the sound isn't as substantial as I might like. "I doubt anything she could say or do would surprise me."

I manage a smile that I hope doesn't come across as *too* panicked.

We're nearly there. Greg leans over, taps on the Plexiglas window. "Right past that dry cleaner's. Yes, that's it."

We pull to a stop, Greg shoves a much larger bill than necessary into the pay slot, waves to the driver to keep the change, as usual. I find this encouraging, for some reason.

The restaurant is intimate and stark, lots of black laquer and chrome with touches of the same purple that's in my skirt. Not exactly conducive to appetite stimulation, but then, dining out in New York isn't nearly as much about eating as it is about being seen eating out. Which is why so many of these places can get away with charging forty bucks for a couple of shrimp nestled with a square of something gelatinous on a bed of bitter greens. Of course, not too many of them stay in business, either, while the cheapo *comidos chinas y criollas* dives that dot Broadway like a string of pearls just keep trucking along, year after year.

"They may be waiting for us already," I hear Greg say to the maître d', which certainly gets my attention.

"'They?'"

He gives what I'm sure he thinks is a confident smile. In reality, he looks as though he just swallowed something extremely vile.

"My parents showed up this afternoon, totally unannounced. I invited them to join us. I hope you don't mind?"

Nineteen

Of course I don't mind Greg's parents being here. Exactly. Not that I wouldn't have preferred a bit more time to deal with feelings and issues and things on a one-to-one basis with their son before turning this into a reconciliation-by-committee thing, but it's not as if I can't cope. My neck is burning, however, as we march over to the white-clothed table tucked inside a high, round, black booth that reminds me of a whirlie ride in a theme park, because I might have appreciated a little warning.

His silver hair gleaming, his navy-blue suit impeccably tailored, Bob Munson rises at our approach, giving a warm smile. I get The Handshake—one hand firmly around mine, the other gently clasping my shoulder, his sharp blue gaze radiating "sincere."

"Oh, my goodness, look what you've done with your

hair!'' Phyllis exclaims in the slightly sluggish speech of a woman with a couple of Manhattans under her belt. As always, she's expertly coiffed, her delicate frame swathed in something pale, simply cut and expensive. A large diamond pin in the shape of some sort of animal—a dragon, maybe?—hunches just under her left shoulder. She lifts her hands, my cue to lean down for a don't-really-touch hug. Her perfume nearly knocks me over. ''It looks absolutely adorable, sweetie! Doesn't it, Bob?''

Is it me, or does she seem not quite as warm as I remember?

''What? Oh, yeah.'' Greg's father scrutinizes me, slightly squinting, then turns to his son. ''Greg, a Scotch? And white wine for you, Ginger?''

Dining out with Bob Munson is always an exercise in self-assertiveness. ''Actually—'' I smile up at the waiter, a dimpled I'm-only-doing-this-to-pay-for-my acting/dancing/singing/music lessons type. ''I'd prefer designer water, please.''

After the slight pause that ensues while everyone absorbs my gall, the men's conversation settles on politics and work, while Phyllis grills me about my new job.

Fine by me. Compared with every other potentially incendiary topic that comprise Ginger's Insane Summer, at least this won't blow up in anyone's face.

We've gotten as far as the appetizers, a house special potpourri of totally unrecognizable delicacies. Feeling reckless, I pop something into my mouth and chew with abandon. Not bad, actually. Just don't ask me what it was.

''And how is your mother, dear?''

Hmm. *Step away from the land mine and nobody will get hurt.*

''Oh, she's fine,'' I say. ''Getting ready for the new

school year. Teaching an undergrad course this semester, I think, for the first time in ages.''

''Ah.'' Phyllis picks something from the platter, studies it, lowers it to her plate. ''I trust she managed to stay out of trouble this summer?''

I'm barely aware of the hitch in Greg's conversation, a foot away from me. I look up, catch Phyllis's eyes riveted to mine.

She may be a little numb from her drinks—she ordered another one after Greg's and my arrival—but she is far from drunk. And there's a hardness to her smile that cuts straight through me. That weird one-note piano piece from *Eyes Wide Shut* starts playing in my brain.

I smile back. ''She hasn't done anything to get herself arrested this year, if that's what you mean. Anyway, she pretty much confines her work outside the lecture hall to women's causes. She finds fund-raising more effective for implementing change than protesting. Although,'' I say with a little laugh, ''with my mother, you never know.''

Phyllis's smile freezes solidly in place.

Fortunately, our orders arrive, and the next few minutes are spent admiring and praising the food. Which isn't bad, actually. A little pretentious, perhaps, but at least I can find the swordfish under the sauce.

Bob Munson lifts his wineglass.

''To the kids, back together, just like they should be.''

Underneath the table, Greg squeezes my knee. When I glance at him, he winks. A wordless ''don't worry about it.''

''Now, Robert,'' Phyllis says, ''let's not jump to conclusions. I imagine you two have a lot to…work out yet, don't you?''

We all stare at Greg's mother. His father is obviously stunned that his wife actually disagreed with him, however obliquely, and I'm pretty sure Greg is right behind him. I'm not sure what to think, however. I mean, really, I should be grateful that someone else here understands that it's far too early for assumptions. But something in her tone is setting off alarms. I'm getting a real strong feeling I'm not the one she's trying to protect here.

Greg laughs, cracking the tension. "You're getting way ahead of yourself, Dad. As Mother says, nothing's been decided yet." He looks at me, a gentle smile curving his lips. "Ginger told me she needs time, and I respect that."

Okay, I feel a little better now.

"Oh, hell, women always say that." Greg's father shakes his head as he cuts into his filet mignon smothered in some sort of concoction I don't dare look at too long. "Saying they need 'time' is just their way of making sure they get exactly what they want out of the deal. Right, honey?" he says to his wife.

Strike the feeling better.

"Excuse me, Bob?" I say sweetly. "What is it, exactly you think I'm out to *get?*"

"Ginger—" Greg reaches over, takes my hand, his smile stiff. Pleading. "It's okay."

"No, I'm curious. I'd very much like to know what he means by that."

"Oh, don't be coy, honey," Bob Munson says, chewing away. "You wouldn't be sitting here unless…" He hesitates, scrutinizing me for a moment, before waving his fork in his son's direction. "This boy's got a bright future—a *very* bright future—ahead of him. No telling how far he might go, in fact. Don't tell me that fact hasn't crossed your mind."

"Dad, please. I haven't discussed any of this with Ginger yet."

"Any of what?" I say. Blink, blink.

"Politics, sweetheart, politics." Bob grins, takes a sip of his wine. "See, by the time the next senatorial election rolls around, I figure the tide will have turned sufficiently to give the incumbent a run for her money. By that time, Greg here will be ready to go up for my old House seat." Now he points the damn fork at me. "And you're just the one to help him get it."

"Excuse me?"

"Dad. Stop."

Bob falls back against the booth cushions, his bushy brows practically meeting his hairline. "Well, when the hell'd you plan on telling her, son? After you had the campaign buttons made up?"

Greg lowers his gaze to his plate. When he speaks, his voice is tightly controlled. "I haven't told her because I haven't decided anything yet."

"Oh, come on, that's a load of B.S. and you know it—"

"Dad. Please. I'd like to change the subject?"

I pick off another bite of swordfish, deciding to keep my big fat mouth shut for once in my life. Maybe it's just me, but there seems to be something missing here. I know Greg's a dynamite attorney, in his own soft-spoken, even-keeled way. But I've never gotten the feeling he was much interested in either changing the world or reclaiming it. Nor, from what I can tell, does he have the kind of ego requisite to go into public office. In short, the guy is not a born politician. His father is. Whether I agree with Bob Munson's agenda or not, I have to admit the guy's got what it takes to get votes. Greg could charm the skin off a snake, but he doesn't exactly ooze charisma, if you know what I mean.

And while I might marry a Republican, that doesn't mean I'd campaign for one.

In any case, it doesn't sound to me as if Greg's exactly salivating over this idea himself, so I decide not to worry my pretty little head about it. Besides, it's time to order dessert.

And the conversation mercifully turns to discussing the summer's movies.

After coffee, Phyllis suggests visiting the powder room. After all those Manhattans, I'm not surprised. The woman must have a bladder the size of the Gulf of Mexico.

The ladies' room is classy but minuscule. I let Phyllis use the toilet first, unsuccessfully trying to ignore her tinkling as I pull out my burgundy lipstick, attempt to repair the damage left by the swordfish and dessert. The toilet flushes, she emerges, and we slide around each other to trade. I no sooner squat when I hear, "You've got to talk your mother into aborting this baby."

I freeze, mid-pee. Finally, I get both my heart and my urine going again, finish up, then realize there's no window or anything I can crawl out of to escape.

I catch my reflection in the mirror when I emerge. Yep, no blood left in the face. "How do you know she's pregnant?"

"Bill told me." She shakes her head, her laugh an inch away from maniacal. "He was too excited to keep it a secret, he said. God, men are so stupid."

While I stand there, listening to my own breathing, she whips out her own lipstick, carefully applies it, presses her lips together. Then she looks at me in the mirror. "No comment?"

"Not at the moment, no."

"Nedra cannot have this baby, Ginger. It's too...sordid to even think about."

Well, that certainly gets the blood flooding back into my face. I yank on the water, chafe my hands under the lukewarm stream. "That's a little harsh, don't you think? Be-sides—" I shake the water off my hands, punch the button to the dryer thingy on the wall "—I don't see how my mother's having a baby has anything to do with you."

"Oh, please—it has everything to do with me. If Bill's really the father."

I'd whip around, but the room's too small. "And what makes you think he isn't? Look, this knocked me for a loop, too, but apparently they've been dating for nearly three months."

"What a quaint way of putting it. But you know as well as I do the kind of woman your mother is. You were born out of wedlock, too, if memory serves."

No way am I continuing this conversation. I turn to leave, but perfectly manicured, frosted nails snag me before I can get to the door.

"I went along with Robert, after Greg brought you home and Robert said you would be the perfect mate for our son, that your ethnic background could help him get the minor-ity vote. And I do like you, Ginger. You're attractive and intelligent and you've got guts. What I said before, about your being good for Greg, is still true, because he's going to need a strong woman behind him when he runs for of-fice. That damn mother of yours, however…I always knew she was a liability. I said so to Bob, even though I knew he wouldn't listen to me about that any more than he's ever listened to me about anything. But damned if I wasn't right on the money. If Bill *is* the father, how pathetic that she had to seduce a man nearly twenty years younger than she—"

"Okay, hold on a minute! Don't even go there, Phyllis. Your *baby* is thirty-four freakin' years old—which is not *twenty* years younger, since we're counting—which is def-initely old enough to decide who he wants to sleep with."

Angry tears glitter in her faded blue eyes. "No, *you* hold on. Damned if I'm going to let your mother screw up my life. Or what's left of it. I sacrificed everything for my husband's career, and now for my son's. I refuse to just sit by and let it all go down the tubes."

"And my mother *should?*"

She lifts her chin a notch. "Either this…situation is taken care of, or you can forget getting back with my son."

I cannot believe I'm hearing this. What, the john's become a time-travel device, zipping us back a couple of centuries or so?

"Whether Greg and I resume our relationship has nothing to do with you. Or my mother. Or her being pregnant."

She gives a short laugh through her nose. "Greg doesn't know about this yet, does he?"

"Yes, as a matter of fact he does. I told him this evening."

Her brows arch like a pair of synchronized snakes. "You told him your mother's carrying his brother's child?"

"Well…"

The corners of her mouth lift. "And if it really didn't matter, why didn't you tell him the *whole* truth?" she says, then sashays out of the rest room.

I have to admit, it was a damn good exit line.

Pity it wasn't mine.

I don't care if I am wearing three-inch heels. If I don't walk off some of this agitation, I'll bust.

Greg's parents have gone off to wherever in a taxi; Greg's insisted on seeing me home, although I imagine he would have preferred taking a taxi to hoofing it.

"I apologize for Dad," he says. "I had no idea he'd bring any of that up."

I glance over. "Is it true? That you're thinking of running for office?"

"It's…an option I'm exploring."

I sigh. "Greg, you hate politics."

He stuffs his hands into his pants' pockets, shrugs. No zealous explanation about what he feels he could accomplish, that he's gotten what amounts to a calling, nothing.

And if he's not driven about that, how committed is he, really, to us? I mean, is Phyllis right, that as long as everything's smooth sailing, he'll be there for me, but that the slightest bump in the road—like, say, his discovery that his brother's the father of my mother's baby—would change how he feels about me?

Which, since we're on the subject, is exactly what, by the way?

I mean, this is nuts. After that tête-à-tête with Ma Munson in the loo, I should just cut my losses, right? Then why don't I? Why don't I just turn to Greg, shake his hand, thank him for a memorable (!) evening, and march my little self up Broadway and out of his life?

Because I can't give up until I know, beyond a shadow of a doubt, whether this is worth any further energy expenditure on my part.

I turn, trying to read his expression in the half light coming from a shop window. "Do you love me, Greg?"

He looks a little startled, but then he says, "Of course I do."

"Then how come you never said it? I mean, I can't remember you ever once telling me you loved me, not even when you asked me to marry you."

He shrugs. I'm beginning to find that a very annoying habit. "I don't know. I'm just not very demonstrative, I guess. Besides, I thought I was doing a pretty good job of showing you how much I cared."

"Yes, I know. But…a woman likes to hear the words, you know?"

He stops, grabs my hand. "Okay, fine. I love you, Ginger. Is that better?"

I glance around; we're standing in the middle of Broadway at nine o'clock at night. The sidewalk is teeming with people, as it is almost any hour of the day or night in this town. I notice a narrow passageway between two buildings, obviously leading to an airshaft.

A very dark, very private airshaft.

A desperate craziness surges through my veins, almost blinding me. I have to give Greg one more chance to prove to me that…that he's *alive*. That he's got the guts to do something crazy. Wild. Unplanned.

"Come here," I whisper, my blood pounding in my temples. I entwine my fingers with Greg's, yank him toward the passageway.

"Ginger? What are you doing?"

Okay, so this might take a little convincing. I steer the two of us into the shadows, latching onto Greg's lapels, then kiss him, tongue and everything. He sorta kisses back. "Make love to me," I whisper into his mouth.

He backs up, a slow grin spreading across his face. "Your place or mine?" he says, even as I realize…wait—I don't want this, not really, that I'm hanging on to something I've already outgrown.

Yet the craziness makes me say, "Neither. Here. Back there, I mean."

Even in the faint light, I can see the grin die. "Christ, Ginger!" His head torques, as if he's petrified someone's heard us. "What the hell has gotten into you? I can't make love to you in public!"

Reason shrieks inside my head, to laugh it off, forget about it, tell him I'm kidding. Yet I press my breasts into his chest, rock my hips to join our crotches. Hmm, I'm not exactly being overwhelmed by what I'm finding here.

"It's totally dark back there," I whisper, frantic now. But not for sex. For the truth. "No one else will know. Well, unless you make me scream—"

"Stop it!" He jerks out of my grasp, nearly stumbling back out onto the sidewalk. And that's not mounting arousal contorting his face. I follow, far less disappointed than I should be. "God, you really are just as insane as your mother, aren't you?"

I halt in my tracks. "What?"

"Dad was *so* convinced you'd be right for me, that you'd be so good for my career, and I tried to go along with him, I really did. He was furious when I ran out on our wedding. I mean, all my life, I've busted my ass to please the Great Robert Munson, to be the kind of son he wanted, even to the point of being willing to marry someone I—"

"Didn't love?" I finished for him.

He scrubs a hand across his face, shoves his hands into his pockets. A few passersby give us mildly curious looks, but keep going. "I do care about you, Ginger, I really do. Enough that I couldn't go through with the wedding when I realized it was a lie on my part. And I thought, well, Dad will just have to get over it. Except I hated the way he looked at me, that awful disappointment in his eyes, as if I'd failed him. It was exactly the same way he looks at Bill, you know? And I'd do anything to wipe that disgust out of his eyes. Anything."

"Including pretending you wanted me back."

He glances away, then back at me, letting out "Yeah" on a brutal sigh.

Well. I suppose this is one way to take the decision out of my hands.

And then it hits me: all of Greg's charm and consideration and agreeableness had been nothing more than finely tuned technique. A lie, in layman's terms. Just like his love-making had been, I thought with a start. Press Button A, get this result, stroke Slot B, get this one. Twice, if all goes well.

What was I thinking? Greg wasn't *safe*. Hell, he wasn't even *sane*. All he was, was a weak little man unable to stand up to his own father.

I turn away, start back up the street.

"Ginger?"

I twist around, but keep walking backward.

"You don't have anything to say?"

So I stop. Think a second. Then say—and by now, I'm a good fifteen, twenty feet away, far enough to have to raise my voice, "Yeah. Two things. One, my grandmother's right. You're definitely not enough man for me. And two, I should be so lucky as to be exactly like my weird, eccentric, generous, aggravating, dynamic, ballsy mother. Who, by the way, is carrying your brother's baby."

Even in the dark, I can see him blanch.

I, however, smile all the way back to the apartment.

I find my mother in the living room, in jeans and a stretched-out T-shirt, cleaning.

Wait. My mother. Cleaning. What's wrong with this picture?

Nesting, I think they call it. I've watched Shelby go through this, twice. But usually not until her eighth month.

"What's this all about?"

Nedra straightens. I notice her face is already beginning to fill out a bit.

She unhooks the barrette holding back her hair, reclips it off her face. "Apparently, with this new hormonal shift, I get the urge to clean when I get nervous."

"What are you nervous about?"

A stack of ancient magazines slides into a black garbage bag. "How'd it go tonight?"

I laugh, then sigh. "About as well as I imagine you expected it would."

Her eyes meet mine. "It's over?"

"Dead and buried."

She shoves a pile of stuff aside to perch on the edge of the coffee table. "You okay with that?"

I think a moment, then nod. "Yeah. I am."

"What happened?"

I tell her. Some of it, anyway. I mean, she knew how the Munsons felt about her. No point going into ugly details.

"I can't believe Bill told his mother," she says.

"Just as well. Now it's out in the open."

"Yeah. I suppose."

"Then Greg said something, something Nonna had actually said to me weeks ago, only it didn't make sense until I heard it come out of his mouth."

"And that was?"

"That I'm exactly like you."

"As insane as I am, you mean?"

"Apparently so."

A smile twitches around her mouth. "That must have come as quite a shock."

"Actually, it's kind of a relief. Like having a name to attach to the symptoms." I ditch my shoes and stockings, then cross to a now-clear chair into which I flop. Geoff plods over to wash my toes, his tongue warm and soothing. About all I want in a male right now, I think. Except then I hear myself say, "Nick found a home for Rocky, did I tell you?"

"No. Where?"

"Somebody he knows. Well, this guy's brother. Upstate. He asked me if I'd like to drive up with him tomorrow."

"And you said?"

I link my hands over my stomach, grimace. "The wrong thing."

"So go call him and say the right thing."

I grimace some more.

"How do you feel about him?"

"I don't know. Except…I don't know. I mean, I keep thinking…maybe I could really go nuts over this man? Someday? When I figure out who the hell I am? Except then I think, *that's* nuts. We're totally different. I mean, Greg and I at least shared common interests, we liked the same music, the same movies…"

"And look how that turned out."

There is that.

"Better to be with someone who provokes you, surprises you, on a daily basis than someone who bores you to tears."

That, too, I guess. Although it's a little scary.

Then my mother says, "As for the figuring-out-who-you-are bit—just when do you think that's gonna happen? Besides—" Now she's actually lifting up sofa cushions. This could get interesting. "There's nothing that says you have to look for yourself alone. Might even be more fun, with the right guy. And it doesn't hurt if he makes you so hot, you can't stand it. Hey, here's a couple of tokens."

She hands them to me.

"They don't use these anymore," I say.

"Damn."

I laugh, but it's not one of my better ones.

"What if he thinks I'm an idiot?"

She shrugs. "I suppose there's only one way to find out."

* * *

I'm so nervous on the train ride out to Greenpoint the next morning, I keep fiddling with the buttons on my dress like they're worry beads. I mean, I blew the man off. He could tell me to stuff it, and he'd be well within his rights. But like I told Terrie, you can't let fear stop you, just because there aren't any guarantees.

After what seems like about twelve hours, I emerge into nearly blinding, late summer light. I can't help it; I run toward Nick's street (good thing I decided to wear my Keds) even though my stomach's churning and my legs are so wobbly I'm amazed I haven't toppled over. Finally, I turn the corner onto his block; I can see the old Impala, parked at the curb. I speed up, as does my heartrate. I wipe my sweaty palms down the front of the dress.

Eight houses away. Six houses away. Four…three…

The door opens; a very pretty blonde comes out onto the top step, clutching her shoulder bag to her stomach. Nick follows. Reflexes I didn't know I had send me ducking behind another parked car, peering over the trunk. Something cold and vicious slices through me as I watch Nick take hold of the woman's shoulders, frowning into her face. She lays a hand on his chest; he briefly covers it with his own before leaning down to—

Well, I don't see what comes after that, because I turn tail and head back to the subway like a rabbit with a starving fox on her tail.

Not that I have any reason, none at all, to be jealous. After all, I'd just been out with Greg, even tried to get him to have sex with me in a dark alley, even if I didn't really mean it or really didn't want it…

"Ginger! Wait!"

But I can't. Won't. My feet have taken on a life of their own, like winged Mercury, as I sprint past neatly kept up brownstones and brick houses, past the occasional elderly person out walking his or her dog. I hit the subway station at a run, zip down the steps with the speed and grace of someone who's been practicing that trick since she was five, the hem of my dress billowing out behind me. The train is just pulling into the station; I fumble for my metrocard in my pocket, shove it through the slot, barrel through the turnstile and jump onto the train just as the doors close. I hear Nick, right on the other side, bellowing to the engineer, spin around to see him flashing his badge toward the front of the train.

On either side of me, people spring up like spooked pigeons and surge for the adjacent cars. I, however, have just been pinned to the opposite doors by one very large, very mad, hardly out of breath cop.

Oh, my.

"I don't suppose you'd be interested in *listening?*"

"Why?" I yell over the wheels's whining against the steel rails. "You don't owe me any kind of explanation. I mean, there's nothing between us, I had a date last night, so why shouldn't you bring someone home—"

"Ginger, shut up."

So I do.

The train screeches into the next station—which is when I realize I was going in the wrong direction—and Nick pulls me off of it, his grasp tight around my wrist.

"Where are you taking me?"

"I don't know. Somewhere where I can turn you over my knee, maybe."

"I'll yell police brutality."

"Oh, baby, you'd yell, all right, but not because I was brutalizing you."

Oh.

He takes me to a little coffee shop on Manhattan Avenue, practically shoves me into a booth. "You want coffee?"

I nod. A timid little waitress brings us two heavy ceramic cups, a silver pitcher of Half-and-Half, leaves without meeting our eyes.

"First off, I didn't have anybody at my place last night, okay? Second, that wasn't somebody new. It was Amy."

I spend a long time stirring my two packets of Sweet'n Low into my coffee. "So you're back together, that's nice—"

"Dammit, Ginger—" He lets out his breath in a gusty sigh, then pins me with his gaze. "You gotta stop this jumpin'-to-conclusions business, 'cause it's really startin' to annoy me."

"Sorry."

He nods, but his brows are knotted. "Okay, it's like this. We're not back together, there was never any possibility of that happening. Are we clear on that?"

I nod. God, his eyes are going to sear straight through me.

"The thing is, see, she came over to tell me…a couple things. One is that she's leavin'. That she got a job she'd been hopin' for in Albany, in a private hospital up there—"

"Oh. Oh, I see. I'm sorry, it was just—"

"—and the second thing is that she's pregnant."

The bottom drops right out of my stomach. I look suspiciously at the glass of water set in front of me.

Nobody says anything for a very long time.

"But I thought…" I take a breath, start over. "I mean, didn't you tell me…but she's the one who doesn't want kids, right?"

His fingers plow through his short hair, and I realize, Oh, crud, he's just found out about this himself.

"She doesn't. Believe me, we weren't bein' careless. In

fact, she told me she'd only have the kid if I was willing to take it after it was born."

I suck in my breath, even as tears sting my eyes. "She doesn't even want to help raise her own child?"

He shrugs, a helpless gesture from a man who I imagine isn't used to feeling helpless.

No profound words of wisdom are springing forth from my tongue. Hell, at the moment, I'd settle for banal. Instead, all I do is sit and sip my coffee, wondering at all this. Finally, Nick breaks the silence with, "I mean, maybe I'm jumping to conclusions myself, but I take it you didn't come all the way out here to tell me you and Munson were getting married, did you?"

I shake my head. "No. That's over for good."

"What happened?"

He sounds genuinely concerned. Interested, even. But I wave my hand. "Long story. Which I'll be more than happy to explain someday when I've got a little better perspective on it. Let's just say…I woke up."

He lets out a relieved-sounding sigh, then says, "So…why *did* you come out here?"

"I'm not sure, actually."

"Mmm." He leans his head in the palm of his hand, studying me. "Just like you're not sure why you ran hell-for-leather when you thought I'd spent the night with someone else."

I make a face. He reaches across the table, covers my hand with his great big one. It feels much better than "nice." "We'd be a total mess together, Ginger."

"I know."

"And we'd fight all the time."

"I know."

With his other hand, he lifts his cup to his lips. "And I'm gonna have this baby to take care of in a few months."

"So am I, so I guess we're even on that score."

He spews coffee all over the table.

"Oh, God, I'm sorry! My mother's pregnant! Not me."

He grabs a napkin, wipes up his mess. "You sure?"

"That my mother's pregnant?"

"That you're not."

"Positive on both counts. Well, negative on mine...oh, hell, you know what I mean."

He seems to need a second or two to absorb this. "Jesus."

"Oh, it gets better. Greg's brother is the father."

At that, he lets out an enormous boom of laughter, loud enough to make heads turn. "No shit?"

"God's honest truth."

Still chuckling, he says, "Your family has got a serious screw loose, Ginger."

Then his face gets all serious. "This is really... complicated."

All I do is lift one brow. He laughs. Looks sheepish. And so...solid and sure, I can barely swallow. "So," he says, "you sayin' we should give this a try?"

I nod. After several seconds, he grins.

Then he stands, gathers the guest check, and holds out his hand. Which, after maybe a nanosecond's hesitation, I accept.

"Where are we going?" I ask when we get out on the sidewalk.

He slips one arm around my waist. "It's about this frickin' chicken we have to take upstate?"

"Oh, yeah," I say, and with that, my world makes more sense than it has in, well, forever.

Epilogue

The following May

I think it's a riot that it's taken me this long to figure out that trying to make myself into who I thought I wanted to be, rather than accepting who I am, is a colossal waste of time. And if it hadn't been for that whacko succession of disasters/crises last summer, I'd probably still be clueless. Or worse, married to the Munsons.

Pardon me while I shudder.

Of course, if anything, things are whackier now than they ever were. I've got babies coming out of my ears, for one thing, what with Paula's twin boys and Shelby's new one, and of course my baby sister, who is so incredibly perfect and beautiful, Bride-of-Frankenstein hair and all. And then there's Nick's little girl, a bald, blue-eyed cutie who's got her daddy, who's taken an extended family leave to care for her, alternately stymied and totally wrapped around her little finger. I am totally besotted with all these tiny people, and for the moment, not quite so eager to have one of my own.

Not quite.

On the career/occupation front, I'm painting my heart out and loving it. Ted was crazy for the portrait I did of Alyssa, which in turn spawned more work. I'd never intended to go into portraiture, but that's what's happened, so I'm just going with the flow. Strangely enough, however, I'm still at Alsworth's, too. Apparently there are two "mes," and one of them still wants to do interior design. So I'm one busy little bee.

Nonna moved out to Brooklyn to live with Sonya in October, only to call right before Christmas, begging to come back right before Christmas. Living with another "old bitty," as she put it, drove her *pazzo*. So we're all still together, although we've hired one of Benita Ortiz's younger sisters to help with the housework and child care when both Nedra and I have to be away.

And in other news…Terrie finally broke it off with Davis, which wasn't exactly a surprise, but I was still bummed. I'm really sorry she didn't have the guts to give it a chance. But we all have to figure out these things on our own, and I still love her.

As for Bill Munson and my mother, well, Nedra's right. They'd never make it as a couple, even though he was present at Hillary's birth, and is crazy about his daughter. But you want to hear the kicker to all this? I don't know the whole story, since Bill seemed a little vague on the details himself, but apparently Phyllis Munson finally realized she was tired of sacrificing herself for her husband and his career, so she walked out. Bill says she says *I* inspired her. I'm still reeling from that one. And last I heard, Greg's apparently dating a local newscaster, a sweet blond thing with a finely honed killer instinct. So much for ethnic diversity. It will be interesting to see whether he actually does run for office.

But of course, what you really want to know is what happened between me and Nick, right? Well…consider it a work in progress. There's been no one else for either of us since last summer, and we call each other every day, and he and Nonna and Nedra all get on like gangbusters…but he's got his hands full with his new daughter, and I've got my hands full making up for lost time in the Unearth the Real Ginger department. Gotta find my own soul first, then I'll worry about the soul mate.

Except, you know, it's like Nedra said: the right man can really help in that department. And Nick has certainly been more than ready and willing to give me a kick in the pants whenever I've been tempted to slip back into old, pointless habits. And then he just happened to mention the other day that the building next to his was on the market, and he was thinking of buying it, and that there was plenty of room for, well, everybody.

And then he did that grinning thing.

I've got to think about this. I mean, combine our families? Raise his daughter and my sister together?

Marry a cop? A *pushy* cop?

Live in *Brooklyn*?

Criminy. I'd never be by myself again.

Which, come to think of it, doesn't sound like such a bad deal, huh?

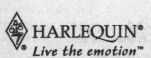

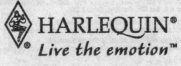